OUT OF THE
SHADOWS

ENDORSEMENTS

Out of the Shadows, the story of twenty-one-year-old Ali Lamarque's quest to support her father in his grief and to find her own healing after her mother's recent death, is a heart-pounding page-turner. As the two of them fly to the Amazon to complete her father's research project, Ali finds herself being followed. With unexplained danger at every turn, this well-written story will hold your attention to the very last word—and linger in your heart long after you've closed the cover.

—**Kathi Macias**, (www.kathimacias.com) best-selling author of more than fifty books, including her most recent release, *To the Moon and Back*.

SALLY CHAMBERS

Elk Lake
PUBLISHING, INC.
PLYMOUTH, MASSACHUSETTS

Cover Design: Cheryl L. Childers
Interior Design: Cheryl L. Childers
Editors: Cristel Phelps, Deb Haggerty

PUBLISHED BY: Elk Lake Publishing, Inc., 35 Dogwood Dr., Plymouth, MA 02360

Library Cataloging Data

Names: Chambers, Sally (Sally Chambers)
Out of the Shadows / Sally Chambers
318 p. 23cm × 15cm (9in × 6 in.)
Description: Three months ago, Ali Lamarque's mother died in an accident Ali is convinced she could have prevented, and what little faith she had is fading. Grief-stricken, her father, a renowned scientist, has sold their California ranch and buried himself in his work. He will soon leave for Brazil's Amazon Rainforest on business. Ali's relationship with her childhood best friend, Kane, is changing, and suddenly she's being followed. Insidious and relentless, it's harassment with no proof it ever happened.
Identifiers: ISBN-13: 978-1-946638-82-3 (trade) | 978-1-946638-83-0 (POD) | 978-1-946638-84-7 (e-book) Elk Lake Publishing, Inc. 2018.
Key Words: thriller, corporate espionage, women, contemporary, Brazil, orchids, faith
LCCN: 2018941379 Fiction

DEDICATION

To God: our heavenly Father

ACKNOWLEDGMENTS

Thank you to my family, friends, and readers, for your love, support, and prayers, for listening and for believing in me, especially my two sisters-in-law, Brenda Kessell and Carolyn Lott, who tirelessly read through every word of the raw manuscript.

Profound thanks to dear online friends of many years who were instrumental in the writing of this story—author, speaker, and editor, Kathi Macias, and author, Zillah Williams, of Australia.

Thanks to author and friend, Terri Tiffany, who encouraged me and reviewed and critiqued this story to get it polished and ready for submission to my publisher.

Thanks to my agent, Diana Flegal and Hartline Literary Agency, my editor, Cristel Phelps, and Deb Haggerty, Publisher and Editor-in-Chief of Elk Lake Publishing, Inc., and her staff.

A special loving thanks to my daughter, professional photographer, Deborah Sandidge, World Photography, who took the Author Portrait for *Out of the Shadows*.

Thank you to all those who have prayed for me and this story as I wrote it. I've named only a few, but named or unnamed, each of you hold a place in my heart and I thank God for you.

He brought them out of darkness and the shadow of death, and broke their chains in pieces

(Psalm 107:14 NKJV)

CHAPTER ONE

Cold Spring Arch Bridge lay ahead. The sight of the vaulted bridge iced Ali Lamarque's insides every time she crossed over. Though constructed of welded steel, the arch seemed as flimsy as a sand castle compared to the vast canyon the bridge spanned. She checked the rearview mirror. Several cars following her turned left onto Stagecoach Road leaving no one behind her but the white pickup truck. She'd noticed the pickup passing cars over the last few miles. Now the distance between them closed fast.

She maneuvered her convertible through one of California SR 154's long lazy curves. The trunk of the Mustang bulged with suitcases and boxes. If she'd stuffed one more thing in there, she'd have had to wire the trunk shut. She was headed home to Solvang—the UCSB campus, Tropicana Dorm, Santa Barbara, and her junior year lay behind her now. California's early summer sunshine toasted her arms as she let her mind drift to Kane, her best friend as well as a UCSB senior.

Other than their conversation totally avoiding the tense subject—she'd be missing on campus this fall—breakfast with Kane at their favorite little sidewalk café had been fun. He'd helped her pack a few things in the car before he'd left to take his last exam then head home early. She'd finished her last exam and left soon after two on this beautiful Friday afternoon.

Ali glanced into her rearview mirror and slowed. The white truck had nosed into the left lane, and the image in her side mirror reflected gleaming chrome bars within a grille surrounding the stylized T in the Toyota emblem. A Toyota Tundra with no front plates? Must be new or not from California.

Eyes on the road!

Plenty of room for him to pull in front of her. The few cars ahead were already on the bridge and the gap between them widened.

Go ahead … pass me.

She checked the distance between them, then for oncoming traffic. None.

Well? Come on! You're running out of road!

Surely, he would *not* wait and illegally pass her on the bridge with those two skinny lanes and nowhere to go but straight ahead or four hundred feet straight down.

She stuck her arm up and sent him a wild motion to pass. Instead, he moved back in behind her.

Really? What was his problem?

Again, he pulled into the left lane.

Still he didn't pass. Instead, he slid back behind her—this time, tight behind her.

Close. Way too close.

The Tundra's grille threatened like horizontal rows of polished silver prison bars in her rearview mirror. Her nerves chafed with agitation.

"Okay, you're bigger than me, what are you trying to prove? For heaven's sake, just go ahead and pass."

The bridge loomed ahead, coming up in seconds.

Focus!

The Mustang's front tires thumped onto the threshold of the bridge, and the edge of the ravine fell away beneath her, along with her breath. The pickup stayed behind her as if grafted to her rear bumper. She increased speed. So did the pickup.

This was a deadly game, and she didn't want to play. Suppressing panic, she gripped the wheel and idled back into the speed limit, hoping he wouldn't hit her. No impact, only the roar of the Toyota's engine.

A bulky shadow beside her. Nothing but Tundra. *No way!* The imbecile *had* crossed the double lines to pass her on this bridge. But he wasn't passing her. The pickup matched her, door-to-door, as if there were four lanes instead of two on this arch over oblivion.

She hit the brakes. So did he, but he also compressed the few feet between them into inches. The car ahead of her passed the midway mark on the bridge leaving her and the Tundra several car lengths behind. Still no oncoming traffic to force him to drop back.

Nowhere on this bridge was there room to pull over and stop or she would have. Maybe or maybe not.

Was he crazy? Targeting her? A chill scattered through her. Was he *trying* to hit her? Scare her? Push her to the edge? Or worse, flip her over the side? If he tried, would the bridge's curved metal suicide barrier save her? Or become a launch pad? Would her life end at the bottom of this canyon?

Sick to her stomach, shaking, her mind filled with replays of watching another vehicle's too-recent deadly trajectory. She didn't know this truck but maybe the driver? Ali glanced to her left. For a few unsafe seconds, she strained to see through the pickup's tinted side windows. The view was like peering through murky water. A man, blurry, but definitely a man. Big, maybe muscular. Nothing about him looked familiar. Another person in the backseat? She couldn't tell. Why did all this feel so deliberate?

Mom would have prayed.

I just wish he would stop.

The inches between their vehicles suddenly shrank. The pickup slowed. Good. He was backing off. Ali watched the passenger side doors, then half the hood, slide past. Her eyes darted between the view through her front windshield to her left side mirror. What was he …?

She watched horrified as the right front of the Tundra whipped toward her Mustang's rear fender. A hard, dull *thud* of dense composite bumper against the Mustang. She was thrown against the door, seatbelt yanked tight around her. The Mustang swerved across the highway toward the opposite side of the bridge. Toward the suicide fence. Toward …

Ali screamed, fought for control with tires squealing in a sideways slide. Time stretched from seconds into terrifying minutes. She steadied the pressure on the brake pedal until the car's braking system took hold, then jerked the convertible back into the right lane, grateful she'd slowed down. If she hadn't … She clenched her fingers around the steering wheel and willed her hands to stop trembling.

The pickup stayed a car-length back with no other traffic behind him. The few drivers now far ahead may not have seen or heard anything.

With no warning, the powerful truck jetted forward, skirted around her, and flew by. Staying in the left lane, the pickup closed the distance between the cars ahead, passed them, then dove into the right lane. Horns blared. Braked tires seared the tarmac as he barely missed a head-on collision.

Then he was gone.

Ali left the bridge and turned into the deserted Vista Point pull off. Shaky, heart pounding against her ribcage, she had to get herself together for the rest of the drive home. She nosed the Mustang into a tree-shaded spot and parked near a picnic table. Melting back against the seat, she shut her eyes, counting breaths as the storm of adrenaline and anger eased and the vividness of what had happened coursed through her mind.

There had been no rear plate on the Toyota. No plates, front—or rear. Stolen truck? No numbers to report even if she decided to. The idiot of a man probably didn't have a driver's license.

Great. All she could do was sit there, quake, think about truck plates and the man having no license?

She sucked in a breath and got out to check the damage to the car. The impact had been like a silenced gunshot smacking into drywall. The only evidence was the dented fender. If her father noticed, she'd have to tell him.

She sat on the wood picnic bench, the ground around her etched with sparks of sunshine. And if her father didn't notice? She hated the thought of upsetting him. He had enough on his mind. She'd think about telling both her father and Kane later.

There'd been no oncoming cars, no death-dive from Cold Spring Canyon Bridge. She had slowed, and he hadn't sped up to shove her completely out of control. She'd been lucky. There hadn't been a hard impact, but he'd used a maneuver on her like she'd seen on the news when police used them to end highway chases. This guy had tapped her in exactly the right spot, but there was no way to tell if he was someone in law enforcement or not.

Had she done something to make him mad? She reviewed the route she'd taken from the campus to the bridge. Traffic had been light. She hadn't cut anyone off, hadn't driven too slowly, nothing. No reason for road rage.

The situation was as if she had been stalked, targeted, unsafe with no reason why, unless the driver got his kicks from terrifying people. And if he did want to scare her, his tactics had worked.

Strange how even in the midst of her fear, she felt like she'd been protected. As if every small movement on her part had been orchestrated for her safety. But logic said they hadn't been, that she was imagining things. No, she hadn't been protected. No one, nothing, had protected her mother either. Divine protection was all a nonsensical notion—nothing but pure luck she hadn't been hurt.

She flicked a fallen pine needle from her shorts. Nearly three months since her mom's accident, and she still hadn't gotten back to her normal self. Guilt, depression, grief, doldrums—whatever nameless demon held her clamped in its talons—had to let go soon or she'd …

She'd what? Go crazy? But how could she let those feelings go when she couldn't even talk about them? Exams were over—as over as her junior year. The time she'd be away from college would only amount to taking a very late gap year. She wouldn't be here with Kane to cheer him on as he worked toward his master's degree, and she'd deal with next year's registration, next year.

Her father had been dead set against her taking time away from college until last week. She was still rattled after the hour-long Skype session with him. They'd gone head-to-head in a surreal conversation leaving her with lots to plan in a very short time—if she could keep everything straight. Between the words they'd spoken, her heart had squeezed. Her father's brokenness echoed her own. Her place was with him, yet he argued.

"There are a dozen reasons I have to go, sweetheart. And you'd be bored silly in Manaus. We'll talk about you coming to Brazil next year. But this summer, you'll be better off living with Grandma Dansk, then staying on campus your senior year."

"No, Dad. I'm coming with you. I have as many reasons why as you do." She looked into his eyes, willing him to know she would not stay home. Her tattered spirit needed to heal, she needed her daddy more than she could put into words. She blinked back tears. "No way am I staying here with you a million miles away."

And she'd won. Everything she'd brought to the dorm last year was jam-packed into the Mustang, and her things-to-do list was growing.

She flopped back into the car and leaned against the seat, drained of energy. The outcome could have been worse. She could be at the bottom of the ravine. She could be …

Forget it. The incident wasn't worth the time and effort to call the highway patrol to report. It would be nothing but her word against his. Long gone, he'd gotten off easy. The scare was over. Her father didn't need the stress of knowing about this, nor did Kane. She needed to let the whole thing go—completely—and get back on the road.

Ali drove down the tree-lined drive toward the house, the sight as welcome as a hug. Chaton whinnied from the pasture and loped along the fence line, pacing the Mustang. Tango should have been on his heels. She winced, missing the sight of her mother's mare. Her father had sold Tango in April. Too many painful memories.

She pulled the Mustang into the garage. Still at his office in Solvang, her father would be here in an hour or so. Just as well. She craved some quiet time to think of what lay ahead. A rush of dark amber eyes, fur, and wet kisses, Gabi met her at the door. Except for the tap of the big German Shepherd's nails against the tile floor as she followed Ali through the kitchen into the mud room, the house was silent.

She sat on the pine bench and traded her sandals for the boots that hugged her feet like the old friends they were. Silly, comforting thing to do.

Home—and with no more white pickup sightings—safe. She rested her back against the wall, her mind a battlefield, littered with guilt, regrets, and bits of the ugly argument with her parents in March. Her simple request to live in an apartment in town and share expenses with Stephanie during their senior year had worn the chains of "no."

She'd pushed hard, made her points, one by one, her voice even, her tone civil. They listened.

Her father remained silent as her mother stonewalled. "No. We've been over this. An apartment's not safe. You know what's been happening to girls living alone in apartments in town. No, and that's final. End of discussion."

"But …"

Wait. Her mom's line of thinking was totally unreasonable. All of it. She shut her mouth and walked away, anger scratching at her like an irritating burr. There'd be another chance to convince her mother in the morning. If the argument didn't ruin their planned ride, maybe she could change her mom's mind.

But the ride—

Gabi's cold nose touched her hand. She drew in a breath and straightened, dreading the thoughts which might follow. Would she ever stop reliving the past? That was March. This was June.

She stood and paced. Kane was as unhappy as her father about Ali not finishing her senior year on schedule. He might not be happy, but at least Sunday could stay a day full of celebration for them all. Monday, they'd planned a ride into the mountains, and Kane would probably fight her on her plans again. She expected nothing less from him. But, she could do this—had to—and she wasn't about to budge from her decision, one which could ease her father through his grief and help stop her terrifying flashbacks. Maybe. Why did everything pivot on maybes?

CHAPTER TWO

Ali left Gabi at the house Monday morning and strode to the barn to saddle Chaton. Loneliness wrapped her in a tight gray shroud, and guilt circled like a lasso. *Had* she made the right decision?

Always before, the weathered structure welcomed her with scents of wood, hay, and leather, but now she found no comfort in any welcoming reminders. Chaton followed her out of his stall, pushing at her back with his nose as if to try to break her unsettled mood. She stopped and pressed her cheek against his head.

She'd been so thrilled and proud of Kane on his graduation yesterday. The day had been exciting and memorable with his award of Highest Honors. His party at the McKenzie's had ended late.

Strange how events lined up sometimes. Coincidence? Her father's angle on everything said logic. Her mother always said such events were God's providence. And after getting home from Kane's party, her father's logic had been to sit her down and tell her he'd accepted an offer for the sale of the ranch on Friday. He'd waited to tell her, so she could stay focused on her exam, her drive home, and enjoy Kane's big day. None of them had anticipated the ranch would sell this fast.

The phone next to the barn door rang. Ali answered with one hand, Cha's reins in the other. "Hello?"

No reply. Nothing—until the seconds began to fill with the sound of someone breathing, then a click and silence. An image of the white Tundra pickup twisted a bolt of uneasiness through her. She shook her head and hung up. *Wrong number.*

The usually frisky black gelding stilled as she readied him but pranced like a yearling as she led him from the barn. She dug her vibrating cell phone out of her jeans pocket. Kane's text lined the screen. *See u in ten.*

At the gate, she nudged Chaton into a gallop and couldn't stop her smile. Her horse beneath her, the wind tugging at her hat, the early morning sunshine. A flush of exhilaration soared through her. Better than she'd thought though—not having climbed back into the saddle since the accident. Riding was exhilarating and felt right this morning.

A half-eaten apple in hand, Kane waved from the trailhead. His six-foot-two frame draped over his horse as easily as syrup over ice cream, and at her five-feet-six inches, she was just plain short when she stood next to him. He rode bareback and always had, moving as if he and Bear were one body instead of two.

Ali's heart peppered her chest with nervous beats. *Kid stuff. So why did he have to own a grin so cute it made her heart* do *that?*

No. The real question was why after all these years of being best friends was she suddenly thinking about his grin like this? Now of all times, she didn't need these feelings. She slowed Chaton into a vigorous trot.

"Hey, you! You picked one beautiful day for a ride. Are you sure you're up for this?" Kane took another bite from his apple and tossed the core into the brush.

"I am!" Ali brought Chaton alongside Kane's dusty-gold buckskin and they rode side-by-side. "I really needed this … to just get back up here and ride again. Running this guy flat out for a few minutes actually felt great."

Chaton shied and sidestepped as a chipmunk skittered across the trail in front of them.

"Easy, Cha-boy, easy." Chaton's ears flicked with the sound of Kane's soothing voice.

Ali gave Chaton's neck a reassuring rub. She'd been nine when her parents brought the lively two-year-old colt into the paddock and put the halter reins in her hand. She had been thrilled to have the small carbon copy of Black Beauty.

"Good boy, Cha." He tossed his head, his nicker soft as Ali closed her eyes, listening to the sounds of the metal and leather of his bridle. He needed this run as much as she did.

She brushed wisps of hair away from her face and urged Chaton into another fast gallop, leaving Kane behind.

The trail wove through the rolling terrain of the Santa Ynez Mountains, winding over ridges and knolls in the chaparral-covered high hills. Stands of pine, laurel, and oak trees lined the meandering track. Dressed in soft pastels, the wildflowers of early June peeked out from thick sagebrush and rocky outcroppings.

Ali stopped on a rise and breathed in the sage-scented air. The view from there made the little town of Solvang look like a miniature replica of itself. With the town's Danish roots, Solvang had cradled her mother's side of the family for three generations.

Could she stand to be away for so long?

"Anneliese Aleksia Lamarque … Ann … Mom." She whispered the words and nudged Chaton into a walk. *Oh, Mom, I'm so sorry. I miss you so much.*

Kane loped Bear up beside her and kept pace. "Hey, woman, you're making me eat dust."

When had she started watching Kane with her heart as much as her eyes, loving the way he handled his rangy quarter horse? He glanced at the prairie falcon feather in the band of her Stetson and shot her another grin. They'd found the feather lying on a snow drift beside a cottonwood tree during Christmas break last year. Kane had picked up the feather, stuck it in her hatband, and she'd never removed it.

She held Chaton to a steady walk, crushing the reins in a white-knuckle grip as if it would help rein in her feelings. This was hard.

"Okay, you're way too quiet. What's up?"

She swallowed. "Nothing. Everything's fine." But her voice caught in the lie she told. She looked at him and blinked against the reflected sunlight from the silver cross around his neck. The sudden palpable emptiness that filled her chest wasn't new.

Just shake it off. The ridge was less than a quarter of a mile away, and the trail was wide, safe enough to let Chaton have his head.

"Let's go." Ali shifted her weight forward. The black leapt into the fast gallop he loved, Bear racing beside him.

The trail ahead narrowed, and Ali gave the reins a gentle tug. A small cloud of dust swirled up as they stopped. Chaton reared and pawed the air, snorting his agitation. They reached the ridge and walked the horses the last few feet past the stand of oak and pine trees and into the broad clearing that spread out in front of them. Ali leaned over the saddle horn to stroke Chaton's neck as his breathing slowed.

The horses were as skittish as she was. Chaton whinnied and lowered his head against his chest. Feet away, Bear pranced. Too close.

Ali laughed. "Hey, settle that crazy horse."

"They're both full of fizz." Kane chuckled and put more distance between them.

Standing in the stirrups, she stretched. "It's so good to be out here again. I miss doing this."

But it wouldn't be long before everything would—

"Hey, hold on." Kane urged Bear closer and wiggled the back of her saddle. "Might want to check that cinch. Looks a little loose." Grabbing a handful of Bear's mane, he dismounted in one smooth motion.

Ali moved side-to-side. He was right. If that saddle slid ... She pictured herself upside down, nose to the ground and laughed out loud. Kane didn't miss much. His brown eyes took in everything. Kanen McKenzie claimed a tan complexion, thick black hair, and a fantastic way with people and horses. He'd proven himself many times as a best friend, especially after the accident. He'd always been there for her. Watching him now, her palms grew moist with a sudden surge of something more distracting than friendship.

She huffed and dropped from the saddle to the ground—stubbed the toe of her boot—and fell flat. Embarrassed, she grinned at him. "You think maybe I'm a little out of practice?"

Kane's eyes fastened on hers and wouldn't let go. "Well, you had a pretty good reason." He grabbed her outstretched hand, pulled her up and brushed the dust off her knees and then her nose.

Compassion. Was compassion what showed in his gaze? Kane was aware how much she'd gone through, he probably felt sorry for her. Or was she sensing something else? There'd been a difference in the way he looked at her lately.

Their childhood had slipped away. Shattering change was coming—for Kane—for both of them, in minutes. *Butterflies? Not now.* Her hand covered her stomach and she shoved her emotions into lockdown where they belonged.

Just breathe in the peace of this place.

She reached for Chaton's reins, but Kane already held them. He flipped them around a sturdy branch along with Bear's reins and stood back, watching as she locked the stirrup over the saddle horn and tightened the loose cinch around Chaton's belly.

Six acres and a property line were all that separated the McKenzie's Bar-M Ranch from Shadow Ridge Ranch. Their families had always been close. Vacations and camping trips highlighted every year. She smiled remembering a trip to Big Bear Lake when they were young. They'd entered an archery contest and she'd taken a blue ribbon to his red one.

The stirrup back in place, Ali parked her hat on a log and studied the clearing, silent. Everything had changed. Kane had to know. So why was she stalling?

Because everything happening is so surreal.

She sighed and went to the basin rock formation, one of their favorite spots. The basin brimmed with water from yesterday's rain. She stooped, and serene water mirrored dark brows arched above amber-brown eyes. Sunlight filtered through blonde hair too long past a cut and a somber expression muted the color in her cheeks and mocked her.

Except for the color of their eyes, she really did look a lot like her mother. Once, she hadn't minded looking like or even being compared to her mother. Today the resemblance hurt. Aware Kane watched, she stuck her finger in the pool, the image destroyed in a wave of ripples.

Just tell him.

Ali stood as Kane rubbed his palms on his Levis and sat next to her hat on the log.

He took off his sunglasses, his eyes pinned to hers. "What." The word was more of a demand than a question. Eyes narrowed, he looked at her as if he suspected something was wrong but waited and said nothing more.

Ali's insides twisted. She curled her hands into hard fists and went to sit beside him. He moved closer, close enough that their shoulders touched, and her mind spun with senseless words. *Why did everything have to happen at once?* She'd told him she'd be going with her father, but not this soon.

Concentrate.

"Shadow Ridge … the ranch …" She choked, the rest of the sentence lodged somewhere between her voice box and her lips before the words slipped out. "Dad accepted an offer on Friday, but he didn't tell me until last night when we got home from the party."

Warm against her arm, Kane's bicep rippled and tightened. Strong, patient, and quiet, he was too quiet. Time slowed into long agonizing seconds.

Say something!

She lowered her head into her hands to hide the unexpected tears, furious with herself for being out of control. *Oh, this hurt.* Only once had she cried in front of him—ever—he was six and she was five, and they'd buried her goldfish near a pink rose bush.

Thinking of roses and dearly departed goldfish was *not* helping. She reached to brush dust from the toes of her boots. Her shoulders ached. The reality of their changing lives sank like an arrow into a soft target. *Absorb it. Deal with it.* She had no choice.

She straightened, wiped the tears from her cheeks, and laid her hand on Kane's arm.

"The final walk-through and closing is Thursday, and we're leaving for Brazil next Wednesday."

Kane stiffened but said nothing. She held her breath, watching him. He rose to his feet, blinking hard, his angular jaw clenched.

They'd talked about the ranch being for sale, her father's assignment, even her final decision to go with her father, everything. Neither of them had been convinced the ranch would ever really sell. Her heart cinched as tight as Chaton's saddle as Kane paced, digging his hands deep into the pockets of his jeans.

Ali picked up her hat and stood, helpless as his face darkened with an intensity she hadn't seen before. His eyes snapped with things she was certain he wanted to say but couldn't. He turned and kicked a rock, launching it over the edge of the clearing, then faced her.

"I can't believe this. The place hasn't been for sale that long. I guess I thought Shadow Ridge would take a lot longer to sell." His voice dulled, as if resigned to facts he couldn't change. He stood, unmoving, his head dipped, bowed as if in prayer.

She tried to breathe as annoyance and impatience stifled her. Why did it bother her when he did that? Why didn't he just storm over, take her by the shoulders and shake her or yell or throw something—anything more demonstrative than kicking a rock. Instead, his reaction had kicked her in the stomach, radiated pain and reality as if someone had suddenly died. All over again.

A question cracked the silence as he paced. "So ... how?" Kane raised his head and looked at her. "How did this happen so soon?"

She walked over to stroke Chaton's silky nose and tried to smooth the ragged edges of her voice. "The couple with the little boy who looked at the ranch last month wanted to buy, but only on the condition they could move in right away. Dad agreed. They gave Dad his price and are paying cash. Dad will have the check Monday. Some legal things, then the ranch is gone."

If the man stayed in character, she knew what would come next.

I'm going with him, Kane, please don't argue again.

Kane stopped mid-pace. She tensed as she heard his voice tighten, deep, gentle yet demanding. Her heart shriveled into an ash heap.

"Okay. I can understand your dad wanting to get out of Dodge, but why you? You don't have to go. There's no reason you can't stay."

A sudden mist of doubt blanketed her. Why *was* she leaving? She could surely get through this morass either here or in Brazil. She'd miss Kane, friends, home, everything. She'd be living who-knows-where, doing who-knows-what.

Clarity came with her next breath. She'd made up her mind. She drew her fingers through a handful of Chaton's mane. Some of the tension dissolved, and for a while she just stood there beside her horse.

"There *is* a reason, Kane. We've talked about this. You know why. He needs me. He's been so lost without Mom, and I'm all he has left." She drew in a breath. "And there isn't going to be a senior year for me—at least not now."

Why did she always stop short of telling him she thought a change might help her too? Why couldn't she tell him her tears came too fast and too often, and she couldn't sleep or eat or even think straight? She certainly couldn't tell him how her feelings had changed toward him.

Pressing hard against the side of Chaton's saddle, she willed her heart to settle. "I'll be back at UCSB to finish school next year."

In three long strides, Kane was beside her, putting his arm around her in a tender move that didn't make things any better. Confusion and doubt tried to shove out what reason and logic she still possessed.

She closed her eyes and pushed away from the electric haven of Kane's nearness. Pushed away from his gentleness, the scent of leather, his breath so close to her cheek. If she didn't walk away from the pressure of Kane's arm encircling her, she'd fall apart.

Why was she having these feelings now? She had to go with her father.

Restless, Chaton pawed at the ground, tossing his head, ready to run. A cool wind blew a dust devil over the ridge and her anxiousness followed the wind. She leaned back against Chaton's neck, staring up through the sun-gilded branches of the Coulter pines.

"It's only for a year. California is home, always."

Kane listened, not speaking, and held out his hand. Her heart skipped as he tucked her hand into his warm grasp, his fingers weaving through hers. Silence was a comfort as he pulled her close and they walked to the edge of the clearing, their childhood friendship changing with each step.

His hand tightened, piercing brown eyes locked onto hers. "Registration isn't until—"

She put her hand up to stop him. He was trying. She should too. She pulled the Stetson from her head, took the falcon feather from the hatband, and looked up at him with a mischievous a grin.

"Well, we've got right now." And on her tiptoes, she stuffed the feather into the band of his grungy brown Aussie hat. "I want this back when I come home."

And childhood, for a moment, returned. She smiled up at him. "Ready to race?"

Kane didn't say much as they rode toward Shadow Ridge. He did have a lot to think about and probably some choices to make. She'd made her choices and in the process, had pushed something newly liberated between them aside—for now.

Whitewashed fencing bordered the woods and field grass where Shadow Ridge's gated entrance stood open. Kane leaned over and put his hand on her arm. A blush of tenderness tingled through her and for a few seconds, her resolve wavered. But without a word, he let go, turned Bear, and left her—heading toward the Bar-M Ranch.

Ali watched him for as long as he was in view, then took Chaton through the gate in an easy gallop down the long drive toward the barn.

CHAPTER THREE

Three days left before their flight to Brazil. Her to-do list finally had more things crossed out than not.

Perched on a ladder in the sun-drenched library, Ali swiped her dust cloth across the top shelf of the bookcase, the end of their packing in sight. Near the ladder, Kane knelt on the floor, the muscles of his tanned arms flexing as he filled a box with books.

Ali nearly lost her balance and her train of thought as she gazed at him. All she'd done was mention how she dreaded having to pack the hundreds of books in the library, and Kane simply showed up early this morning. Instead of driving, he rode over on Bear and turned him loose in the pasture with Chaton. She was glad for Kane's help but more so to have him near. "The moving van should be here a little after noon."

Kane glanced up. "Mm, we should have everything boxed up and ready to go by then."

"You didn't need to do this, you, know." She tilted her head at him. "I could have done the whole thing myself."

He pointed at one of her father's heavy botanical textbooks. "Yeah, right, and I'd have left you to lift these books and journals all by your li'l ol' self? You can lift one end, and I'll lift the other." He shot her an impish smile, then ducked as the dust cloth zipped past his head.

"Come on down from there and take a break." Kane grinned up at her. "We've been at this for hours.

She rubbed at her nose. "Good idea. We're almost finished anyway."

Her father's voice sounded from the hall. "Kane, can you give me a hand in the back yard for a few minutes?"

"Sure. Be right there." Kane got up and grasped her arm as she stepped down from the ladder. His hand stayed—warm against her arm. He bent close. "You don't have to go, Ali." He sent her a grin on his way out the door. "See you in a few."

You don't have to go, Ali? *Why had he said that? It's done, settled.*

Unreasonable anger rose and burned in her chest like white-hot lava. At Kane. At herself for wavering …

And the anger was only one of the reasons she had to go.

She stared down at the last book in the packed box. The blood-red book cover snaked its way into her mind and struck. Her head spinning, she reached for the chair, her senses overwhelmed as the scene streaked through her thoughts:

Sounds of a car engine in the distance, the creak of the saddle beneath her, her own voice as she'd called for Gabi to come, Ali telling her mother she'd be right back.

Her mother's fingers smoothed Tango's mane as she spoke. "Gabi's okay, honey. Leave her. She'll catch up. Have you ever known that dog to fail to get to the ridge before we do?" Her mother turned Tango and loped ahead on the trail.

Ali's chin ratcheted up a notch. She reined in the black gelding, turning him toward the ranch. Her mother's words weren't what bothered her, but rather, her mom's condescending tone.

"Come, Gabi—" A wave of panic raced through her. On the deserted highway, a few yards from the trail, a familiar red Dodge Durango veered in her direction, corrected, then blurred by.

Hunched forward, his face a white mask, the driver grasped the steering wheel in a death grip. Greg Steele! A classmate from high school.

Her stomach clenched as if she'd been body-punched. What was he doing? Had he been drinking? His car was all over the road. If he wasn't careful, he'd kill someone.

Mom. The curve! He's not going to make the cur—

Ali twisted in the saddle. "Mom! Look out!" The words left her throat in a scalding scream as her mother jerked Tango in Ali's direction.

Chaton lifted his body in a full rear. His hoofs battered the air then landed in a bone-jarring thud against the trail bed. His muscles tensed to run, and Ali yanked on the reins. Chaton trembled beneath her but held his ground.

Frozen, Ali stared. Tears, stinging bile in her throat.

The squall of tires pierced the air. The Durango fishtailed. Locked in a slide, the vehicle exploded against the guardrail. Scraping metal. Shattering glass. End over end. Airborne.

The guardrail thudded to the ground. Tango erupted in a violent buck, and her mother's scream knifed into Ali's heart. She couldn't breathe.

Time warped and slowed. Her mother's body rose from the saddle. Horror filled her eyes and etched across her face. Her hair spread in a blonde arc against the blue-gray sky. Her arms and legs flailed mid-air, twisting into surreal, unnatural angles.

The car slammed down into the sagebrush, rebounded upward on a course straight toward—

"Mom! No! No!" The words tore from Ali's throat. Her body shook, boot heels digging into Chaton's sides. "Mom! I can't see you!" Was she crushed beneath the car? Alive?

Where are you, God-that-Mom-says-she-loves? Help her!

Tango galloped past headed for the ranch, flashes of red saddle blanket, empty stirrups slapping her sides, and terror widening her eyes.

Disbelief raged through Ali.

The car's engine rasped and chugged, raced, then stopped.

Ali reached the wreckage before the wheels ceased spinning. Air dark with kicked-up dust whirled within the acrid smell of burned rubber, overheated motor oil, and smoke.

She dropped from Chaton's back. Her legs buckled. She fell to her knees beside her mother's still, broken body. Greg Steele's unmoving form lay a few feet away.

Red everywhere. Her mother's red jacket, pools of blood, and the red of the crushed Durango.

"No." The word echoed as the dust settled around her. If she hadn't stopped to look for Gabi. Guilt seized her heart with icy fingers.

Shards of glass hung from the shattered rearview mirror reflecting red. Ali closed her eyes and sank forward, her heart throbbing, her body shaking with sobs.

Gabi's cold nose moved against her cheek. Comforting voices and gentle hands had ministered to her. The hiss of a fire extinguisher, raucous sirens, and unfamiliar scents had assailed her as she had pushed against reality and had struggled to get up.

Her fingers hurt with her grip on the chair. You don't have to go, Ali. Kane's words remained with her as the moments of relived terror faded.

Her back went rigid, the sharp words of objection she wanted to say lodged like fixed bayonets in her throat.

"Ali?" Kane moved through the door, his hand, instantly on her arm, seemed to restrain her as if he tried to hold her back from an abyss. "Ali, are you okay?"

And she was at the edge. He had no idea. She couldn't speak. She was in turmoil.

Still his words resounded, but if she didn't say something …

"I'm okay, just a little dizzy."

Deep, calming breaths. Three of them. Kane's arm trembled as he released her, but she stayed close for a moment as if nothing had happened. Only a bump in their road. She looked at the sea of boxes, books, and a desk covered with computer components and grimaced.

"This place could pass for the city dump. I'll be so glad when all this is over and done with." She slipped away from Kane's disconcerting nearness and sat on the floor in front of the desk.

Kane sat beside her. The man either couldn't take a hint or didn't want to. And either way, his closeness warmed her heart. And that fact obviously certified her as crazy.

"Now, Gabi over there," Kane's index finger slanted toward the dog, "she's got the right idea."

Ali agreed, wishing she could be that serene. The shepherd's ebony and tan fur shone in the patch of sun she'd taken over near a window. Head resting on her forelegs, tail flopping back and forth against the hardwood floor, Gabi's honey-colored eyes stared back at Ali.

"You shouldn't be looking so smug, girl." Ali pulled her knees to her chest and parked her chin on top, eyeing Gabi, glad she'd be going with them. "At least you've stayed out from underfoot."

Kane chuckled. "Don't pay any attention to her, Gabi. Your boss is jealous because she can't loll around in a few sunbeams."

Ali studied his grin and gave up with a sigh.

Her father used to banter with her like that. He'd changed so much since her mother died. Distant and withdrawn one moment, he'd be talkative and concerned the next. Was it normal to feel like she did? Was she acting like her father in her own grief? She had no answers, and she had only herself to blame for the accident anyway.

She picked up the dust cloth from the floor and stood looking down at Kane. Tonight, she and her father would stay with the McKenzie's. Tomorrow, Kane would follow them as they drove their two cars into Solvang. Grandma Dansk's oversized garage would shelter the cars for the year.

"Hey, have I thanked you for all the driving you'll do for us tomorrow?"

He grinned up at her. "Only about six times. Wouldn't have it any other way. Plus, who'd be crazy enough to turn down a free overnight stay in a fancy hotel?" He cocked his head at her. "Even if I do have to chauffeur you around."

She reached to grab his up-stretched hand and pulled him to his feet. After their overnight stay in Los Angeles, he'd take them to LAX for their early flight to Miami.

She pulled the checklist from her jeans pocket with Kane looking over her shoulder at the mangled sheet. "Pretty good progress. Just move those books and the computer stuff over by the door, and we'll be done in here."

Two more boxes to pack. Where was the aspirin when you needed one? Ali pressed her fingers against her temples. "As soon as Dad finishes up in the kitchen, we should have all of it under control." She looked at her watch. "It's almost noon. I hope the movers will be here on time."

Kane tugged on Ali's hand and aimed her toward the desk. "C'mon. This isn't going to get done by itself."

She picked up an empty carton and stuffed it with computer peripherals. "When the movers get here, let's take the horses out for a while?"

"Sure. We can do that unless you want to do some supervising."

"Nope, Dad can deal with it." Her throat tightened. He didn't need to know she couldn't stand to watch a bunch of strangers stuff a truck with a lifetime of her memories and drive away. She yanked the batteries out of the keyboard and mouse and covered them with bubble wrap. "We could use some fresh air, and I'll fix us lunch later."

Kane turned and grinned at her, his expression understanding. "Fresh air sounds good. And lunch? Even better."

She wanted to hug him for that, for not saying the ride would be their last for a long time, for understanding and supporting her even in the little things. No hug, but second best was teasing him. "At least, I *think* there's still some food left in the fridge—no promises."

Her father's cell phone warbled, and she walked into the hallway as he emerged from the kitchen, his voice echoing down the barren walls.

"This is Dr. Lamarque. Hi, Chip." He mouthed *the movers* and wiped a smudge from Ali's cheek before she turned back toward the library, his mood better today. A moment later, he strode through the doorway. "Looks like the movers aren't going to be here until later this afternoon— which may be better for me anyway. I have to go into the office for a while, and I might as well go now. Why don't you two come with me? Five more minutes in the kitchen and it's ready. I can finish a couple of things I have to do at the lab, and we can have lunch in town."

Ali winced. They hadn't gone into town for lunch together since before the accident. "Sounds good to me. I don't think we have much here to fix for lunch anyway." She looked at Kane. "Want to go? We can still take the horses out for a while later."

"Sure. I'll let Mom know what's up." Kane pulled out his phone to make the call, then went to clean up as her father left to finish the kitchen.

Alone in the wood-paneled room, the scent of books, pine logs, and wood smoke recreated childhood memories. Ali sat in a comfortable old armchair in front of the fireplace. Her gaze drifted to the stone mantle. Only hours before, it had held a dozen family pictures.

"How can I leave this place?" A press of guilt and doubt clutched at her chest. She could have just as easily decided to stay and live with Grandma in Solvang until her senior classes began. Grandma loved Gabi, and with Chaton boarded at the Bar M, she'd have nothing left to worry about—except how her father was doing.

No. The commitments were made. She straightened, vaulted herself out of the chair and headed for the guest bathroom to clean up.

Leave the past in the past. Just get through today.

CHAPTER FOUR

The atmosphere in the car bordered on somber as her father drove toward Solvang. Kane leaned against the front passenger side door, his arm draped across the seatback of the Land Rover. From the backseat, Ali studied Kane's profile, the line of his jaw, the deliberate stubble of his dark beard, wanting to cup her hands around his face, to pull him close to her. If she looked into his eyes, maybe she'd find answers about how he truly felt.

They'd talked about plans to store the cars tomorrow and the early flight to Brazil on Wednesday, but the conversation fell flat.

Her father caught her eye in the rearview mirror. He took a deep breath and asked a single question. "How about lunch at Chomp's? One of those nice thick Reuben sandwiches, maybe?"

Tension eased as Kane spoke. "Sounds good to me." He turned toward her, his dark brows arched in a query.

Ali nodded. "And me."

In the rearview mirror, Ali watched the corners of her father's eyes wrinkle with his grin.

She sent him an appreciative smile. His next comment about the Los Angeles Rams' preseason games against two national playoff teams kept them talking for the rest of the drive.

As they reached the edge of town, the June sunshine faded, and a light rain misted across the windshield. Zoran Pharmaceutical Laboratories' campus sprawled out in front of them as they paused at the guard shack to show ID.

Parking lots overflowed with cars, and people were already leaving for lunch. Her father pulled into his parking space close to the impressive structure where he spent the majority of his time.

Entering through double doors into the lobby, they were met by more security. One of the guards nodded at her father. "Good afternoon, Doc. Here on your day off, huh?"

"Hey, Glen. We won't be long. I just need to tie up some loose ends." Her father introduced Kane while the other guard checked their identification.

Glen grinned at Ali. "Nice to see you again, Miss Lamarque."

"Good to see you too, Glen." Ali smiled at the middle-aged man in his black uniform and glanced at the other, very fit, but much older guard, a little surprised at the extra security. *This was new.* Usually either Glen or his rotation relief, Mick, manned the front entrance. *Now there are two?* And the new man-in-black looked like a ready-to-retire fullback for the Rams.

Her eyes dropped to Glen's waistband to the new addition of a metal detector security wand. She looked back at the entrance at a trio of men constructing a unit that appeared to be a state-of-the-art walk-through metal detector.

A chill as cold as the metal unit looked washed over Ali. Was her father expecting trouble?

Glen pointed a pudgy finger at his counterpart. "And this here's Deacon or Deke Regis, new as of last week."

"Nice to meet you, Deke."

Glen walked them to the receptionist's desk to pick up visitors' badges, then to the last security point. Her father entered codes and skimmed his ID card through a scanner before they crossed the lobby to the elevator.

"What's with the heavier security, Dad? And, no pun intended, but he really is one huge guy—is everything okay here? You're making some pretty strong changes."

"We've had a few strange happenings around here, along with more than one threat. I meant to tell you about them last week, but my mind—"

How could "a few strange happenings … along with more than one threat" possibly slip his mind? And what kind of threats? Was he in danger? The elevator door opened with no more time for questions. She'd ask later. They exited on the fourth floor into a windowed reception area. Ali's father put a hand on her shoulder.

"You can wait in here." He motioned to several chairs and a coffee table. "Or you can go down the hall to the break room and wait there. Help yourselves to whatever is in the fridge. I shouldn't be more than about forty-five minutes, then we'll go get some lunch. Save your appetites."

Not even a smile. Just an order? Ali's shoulder tensed beneath his hand, and she bit back a response. Maybe she imagined it, but where before it had been her mother, now her father seemed to be trying to control her life. Her fingers dug into her palms.

She pulled in a breath. "No problem, Dad. We'll be fine. Bored maybe but fine."

Her father's eyes searched hers, and he chuckled. "Okay, I'll be back shortly."

Ali guessed he'd noticed her snippiness.

He went to a door marked *Restricted Area*, entered a code into a keypad, and left them alone.

The unexpected silence was stifling. Ali walked to one of the damask-covered chairs and sat. With high ceilings, thick carpet, and full security, the place was not only big, it was also attractive in a sterile-all-business kind of way. She'd been inside Zoran's fairly new facilities several times, but this was a first for Kane.

Kane wandered around the room, his expression appreciative. "So, this is where your dad spends all his time."

"Yes, more time than ever lately." She reached for a magazine and faked a stricken look at him. "So, what do we do for forty-five minutes? Sit here and look through a boatload of techie mags or wander the halls?"

Kane shrugged. "I'm not crazy about the nerdy reads, but anything else is fine with me."

A couple of white-coated lab technicians nodded on their way to the elevator. Kane walked over and bent close to her, his breath rustling her hair, and whispered, "Just don't let *them* take me away."

Ali shivered at his nearness and laughed. "I should. But it'll have to wait."

And for a few seconds, they were twelve again.

"Speaking of taking you away, you've just given me an idea. There is one place ..." Ali hesitated. *Would he really want to see a garden?*

"Okay, you've snagged my interest. What?"

"I haven't been to Zoran's botanical garden for a while. I wouldn't mind walking through there again." He straightened, and she rose from the chair and stood beside him. "It's not open to the public, and you have to practically go through customs to get in, but I think it's worth the trouble."

The quizzical look on his handsome face made her laugh again. "Yes, Zoran Labs has a garden, but it's not just any garden. It's a combination rain forest, orchid jungle, and herb garden. The focus is on medicinal plants, and it's become a haven for butterflies and a few birds." She tilted her head at him. "It's pretty amazing, and if Jake's there, he'll give us a tour. So, you've got some choices: the break room, library, or the garden."

His brown eyes sparked. "Lead the way—the garden sounds great. So, who's this Jake guy? The gardener?"

"Everyone calls him the gatekeeper ... a teddy-bear of a guy from South Africa. He's worked here since Dad built the place. Actually, his name is Doctor Jacob Masuku, but he's one of the most down-to-earth people I know. You'd never guess the man holds degrees in botany, and chemical and biomolecular engineering. He oversees everything to do with the garden, keeps track of every one of the thousand plus trees, plants, and orchids, and their history. He feeds, waters, and loves them, even talks to them—says they love your exhaled carbon dioxide. He has a terrific sense of humor. You'll like him."

Kane stayed close, and seemingly distracted, while she tried to keep their shoulders from touching as they walked down the wide corridor. They reached a short hallway where Ali led the way to a pair of stainless-steel double doors with the word *Botanicals* on the nameplate. She pressed a button on a small speaker.

"Jake? It's Ali Lamarque … you in there?"

A jovial laugh and a warm "Well, hello!" came from the box. A buzzer sounded, and the doors opened into a wide office area. The dark-skinned man shook her hand, a smile spreading across his face. "C'mon in, young lady." His expression full of interest, he cocked his head and looked at Kane. "And who do you have with you?"

Ali introduced him to Kane, and moments later Jake walked them through two sets of double doors into another world heavy with moist, warm air. The mist held a scent laced with mint, eucalyptus, and a pungent green forest. A vaulted glass and metal canopy encased a jungle of plants, trees, orchids, bugs, birds, and butterflies. Underfoot, a path of red and gray bricks. Every few yards, boardwalks angled away from them in several directions.

Jake pointed to a pale blue, dark-edged orchid. "This blue beauty is from the area of Brazil where you're going, Ali. That specimen has been vital to Dr. Lamarque's work. Came right out of the Amazon. A rare species that's been seen only in certain areas of the Brazilian rain forest."

His expression changed to one of concern. His next sentence was muttered as if to himself. "We're a bit worried this plant is not thriving as it once was in here." Ali studied the blossom. The orchid certainly didn't look quite as healthy and beautiful as it should have.

Jake shook his head and continued with a sweep of his hand as they walked, "Over half the prescription drugs manufactured in the US contain botanical ingredients derived from plants like these."

Ali glanced at Kane, figuring he'd be ready to leave from sheer boredom. Her heart melted at his concentration—he was truly interested in what Jake said as they moved nearer the exit doors.

Kane's arm touched hers and he looked down at her. "God makes some pretty interesting stuff."

She ignored him and checked her watch. They needed to start back.

Half an hour after leaving her father, they started back to the lab, their steps silent on the plush carpet. Kane's hand slipped into hers. His grip, firm and somehow reassuring. She didn't want him to let go. *Ever.*

"I'm ready for a Coke, but I don't think we'll have ti—"

"No!" a woman's voice slashed the air with the single word.

Ali's hand slid up Kane's arm to stop him, her incomplete sentence fading. The open door of the break room was only a foot away. A few seconds of silence hung in the air, then a loud tirade.

"What do you mean you can't tell me where you'll be staying until tomorrow? You had your instructions. Are *either* of you competent enough to follow orders?"

Another brief pause and a sound of the slap of a hand on a flat surface, plus the verbal flood of what sounded like frustrated rage. Kane looked down at Ali, his face expressing what she felt. *Incredulous!*

Ali sagged against the wall. Memories of a dinner honoring her father a month before the accident held the image of an auburn-haired woman in a black evening gown. That voice belonged to Maddy—Dr. Madison Kaarding.

"If you can't handle this job," the woman shouted. "I'll find someone who can." Another pause, then the edge in her voice softened. "Yes."

"All right, you have your orders, and I'll expect your call at seven tonight with your flight and hotel information *and* your itinerary. Call me as soon as you get through customs tomorrow. Understood?" Another hesitation. "Good. And don't call me here! You know how to reach me."

The sound of a phone handset clattering into its cradle reverberated into the hallway.

Ali let go of Kane's arm and they retreated several feet. "That was completely out of character, weird."

"You know her?"

"Yes. Madison Kaarding, a close associate of Dad's, and I'd rather not let her know we heard anything. I don't want to get into a conversation with her right now. It would be too awkward," she whispered. Kane nodded.

A tall woman in a fitted pantsuit, a white lab coat over one arm and a Coach handbag slung over the other, exited the break room. Her face set in a cold glare, she barely hid her surprise as Ali and Kane approached. Instantly, her expression transformed into one of warm recognition.

"Hello, Ali." Kaarding's voice, velvet-smooth. She extended a manicured hand. "Dr. Lamarque is here? I didn't realize he'd be in today." Her eyes slid down Kane, head to toe, and back. "I was just having a quick cup of coffee."

"Dr. Kaarding. This is a friend, Kanen McKenzie. Kane, Dr. Madison Kaarding. And yes, Dad's here, but he won't be for long. He had a few things to do in the lab, and then we're going into town for lunch. I took Kane to see the garden while Dad's finishing up." There. That should explain the direction we came from.

"I see." Kaarding nodded at Kane. "I believe Ali has mentioned you before. It's a pleasure to meet you." She didn't offer her hand, and Kane gave her a cool smile and nod.

"We need to—"

"Well, if you'll please excuse me, I have a dozen things to do." The woman attempted a smile and turned her back to them, gliding away in her stiletto heels.

Kane raked his fingers through his hair. "I don't know if all that was or wasn't out of character for her, but she definitely was rude, not to mention weird. I wonder what the phone call was all about."

"She is eccentric, but Dad thinks pretty highly of her. They've been working together for several years. He says she's a brilliant scientist."

Frowning, Kane shook his head. "Brilliant or not, it sure sounded like she was on somebody's case."

"I agree. Like she's keeping more than one somebody on a short leash. I wonder who they are and where they're going that they have to give *her* their plans and check in when they clear customs." Ali pressed against the wall, trying to shake off the odd sense that something not so good was about to happen.

"Hey, are you okay?" Kane put his hand on her arm—too comforting.

She pushed away from the wall and away from feelings for Kane she didn't want to deal with now and tried to keep her voice even. "It's nothing, and Dad's probably already waiting for us."

The warmth from Kane's hand lingered, but so did thoughts of Zoran's tightened security and her feelings of icy foreboding.

Only days from now, she'd be clearing customs and leaving Kane behind.

CHAPTER FIVE

Time vanished like a sun-warmed sea fog. Three days since the moving van left Shadow Ridge Ranch. Wednesday morning, American Airlines Flight 1222 out of Los Angeles rose above the hot tarmac of LAX and soared toward cruising altitude.

With her father beside her in their First-Class seats, Ali gazed out the window thinking of Kane, along with everyone and everything else she'd said goodbye to.

They had a crazy-long trip ahead of them. The only layover between here and Brazil was Miami, about five hours away. Then they faced nearly ten more hours of flight time to reach South America.

The jet leveled out and the *Fasten Seatbelts* sign chimed and went dark. The gentle pressure of her father's hand on her arm was reassuring.

"I have to admit, I'm happy you decided to make the trip, sweetheart." He gave her arm a light squeeze, his brown eyes softening beneath dark brows. "I know these last few months have been tough."

Well, she'd *insisted* on making the trip, but the warm surge of love for her father had her smiling. "It's been hard for both of us. It'll be a good change."

The flight attendant interrupted with the offer of an extra pillow. Ali stuffed one behind her back, but her father declined, pulling down the table tray to set up his laptop. Understandable. He wanted to bury himself in his project. She sent Kane a reply to his text and opened her purse to exchange the cell phone for her Kindle. Maybe picking up where she'd left off in her novel would help pass the time.

The click of computer keys, rustle of pages, people talking—Ali seemed to hear it all. Reading wasn't going to work. She gave up and stared out the window, watching clouds roil like foam on a soda. The mountainous clouds had been part of the scenery since the pilot announced they'd reached cruising altitude.

They couldn't get there fast enough. She looked forward to the time in Miami to ease the travel kinks, walk through a few shops, and stop at Starbucks for coffee. The five-hour layover before the flight to Brazil looked better and better.

By the time they reached Miami International, Ali's extra pillow had found at least ten new positions. She rubbed the small of her back as they deplaned, anxious to walk somewhere, *anywhere* other than inside this metal capsule with wings.

Her father had scheduled a business meeting during the layover with a professor who worked at the International Center for Tropical Botany at Florida International University in Miami. He wrapped an arm around Ali's shoulders as they neared the entrance of American Airlines' Admirals Club. "Okay, sweetheart, I'll see you at the Ice Box Café at five."

"I'll be there, Dad." She looked down the long concourse and grinned up at him. "A whole lot of stores need browsing 'til then. See you soon."

He smiled and gave her shoulders a squeeze. "Just keep your phone on and call if you need anything."

Ali all but rolled her eyes. She brushed his cheek with a kiss and dragged in a breath. "I will, Dad. See you soon. Hope everything goes well."

She merged back into foot traffic on the busy concourse and walked toward the gift shop.

Something wasn't right. Fourth in line at the checkout desk in the gift shop, Ali inched forward, magazine in hand, uneasiness prickling at the back of her neck.

She studied the profiles of people reflected in the glass display windows. Blurry glimpses. A peripheral view of a male profile. Not once, but twice. Close. Whenever she moved.

Ignore it.

But at the counter, the knuckles of her hand around the magazine had turned white.

Leaving the gift shop, she found a quiet corner to calm her unreasonable concern and deal with the niggling worry. Sheer stupidity. She didn't know anyone here. No one was interested in her or what she did.

Just breathe—you're stressing out over nothing.

Time for a sanity break. She pressed her back against the coolness of the wall where she stood and pulled out her iPhone to check the time and messages. Stefi wanted a status report. Ali texted a smiley and *Later* then sent Kane the promised update, but he didn't need to know about the rest of her silliness.

Even after a leisurely half hour in a book store and looking through a dress shop, the unsettling sensation she was being followed didn't go away until she went into Starbucks.

The coffee break helped. So did checking out Coco-Bay and finding a great pair of sunglasses, but she'd left herself only five minutes before her father would be waiting for her at the café.

Once more they taxied toward the runway for takeoff, this time aboard a wide-bodied 777. Ali glanced through the window to her left at thinning clouds. The sun sparked bits of glitter over the runway, wet from the earlier storms. Main Cabin Extra Seating wasn't full on this nonstop night flight. With seats three abreast and an open seat on the aisle, her father had taken the aisle seat leaving the middle seat vacant as their flight got underway, the plane climbing toward cruising altitude.

What seemed like only minutes later, the cabin speakers crackled to life. "This is your captain. Apologies for the weather delay, but we'll do our best to be in São Paulo right on schedule. You might want to grab the opportunity to take a look outside the windows on your left. We'll be passing the Bahama Islands. The sunset is gorgeous, the weather is cooperating, and we should be making up some lost time. So, sit back, relax, and enjoy the flight."

Ali studied the islands clustered below the southbound jet. *Beautiful.* The islands surrounded by glistening aquamarine ocean took her breath away. Brief colorful spots and then they were gone. Worth the look but reminding her of the path her life had taken. Brief, colorful, then gone, catapulting her into an unknown new direction.

The video display on the seat in front of her suddenly reflected red from the setting sun. Ali pressed back in her seat, threatened with nightmarish replays of the accident.

She closed her eyes and forced herself to think of something else, *anything* else. *Gabi.* Six years ago on her fifteenth birthday, a German Shepherd rescue puppy with amber-colored eyes and an impressive black raven-in-flight marking on her head wiggled and licked her way into Ali's arms and heart. Gabrielle. The shepherd was probably asleep in her kennel somewhere in the depths of the cargo hold. She had used every bit of persuasion to talk her father into bringing Gabi with them.

So many events had led to this trip. "Dr. Matthew R. Lamarque, Founder and CEO of Zoran Pharmaceutical Laboratories, Inc., and noted scientist." That's how the article in the latest issue of *Scientific American* described him. Listing numerous awards and recognition for his research of the medicinal properties of plants and his talent for discovering and hiring innovative young scientists, the magazine stated he "… is poised on the edge of exciting and valuable new findings."

Early last year at her father's suggestion, the board had asked Erick Chance, one of Zoran's top botanical researchers, to relocate to Brazil for a three-year stint. He'd wrangled the invitation from the Brazilian authorities after lengthy discussions. Erick was to work with the Brazilian government at their Center of Biotechnology of the Amazon, CBA, on a business visa. The main reason for his time there was to locate specific plant species that her father strongly felt held the promise of disease-healing properties.

Erick and her father had spoken via Skype or Facetime almost daily as Erick and his guide trekked deep into areas of the rain forest in their search. Following Erick's success, an ironclad agreement had been hammered out with Brazil along with an unusual exception from them to allow Erick to ship the plants to Zoran Labs.

Zoran received several of the exotic species her father thought had strong potential, and his work with a healthy blue orchid already held tremendous hope for healing cancerous tumors in humans.

Ali smiled, remembering a time a few months into the formula's development. Her father had come home late one night, enthused as he paced the floor sharing his news.

"I'm on the verge of a breakthrough, so there may be quite a few late nights for the next few weeks. Then, I'm pulling Madison Kaarding from her other projects to help me finish the formula. I have total support from the board of directors. Financial backing's firmly in place."

Then, another triumph. Zoran Labs pushed through loopholes and several government-sanctioned tests that ended up with the complete remission of two cases of cancer diagnosed as terminal—incurable and irreversible. Forty-eight hours after receiving the new medication, tests showed a large tumor in a twenty-five-year-old man had shrunk to nearly half its original size. Within two weeks, all traces of the disease disappeared, and he returned to work, the cancer in remission.

After an even more remarkable healing and recovery of the second patient, an older woman, Zoran Labs received a generous grant. Additional testing of the formula began immediately in limited clinical trials. Three more patients with the same type of deadly tumor experienced the same amazing results.

Ali opened her eyes and turned to look through the window as clouds and remnants of sunset disappeared into black velvet and mica-chip stars. The cabin lights brightened, and she glanced at her father, thinking of one unhealthy blue orchid and the blow that had sent her father reeling.

The raw formula worked, but her father's efforts to replicate it for less expensive production as a cancer cure had run into a barrier. He hadn't been successful in using either lab or field-grown plants. Every attempt to nurture the plant outside its natural habitat somehow altered it. Probably an enzyme or a protein was missing or changed at the molecular level, as her father explained it. Whatever the cause, his formula failed.

But her father never doubted he could isolate what caused the failure and produce a replica of his cure. "The solution is in the Amazon rain forest," he told his board of directors, "right where that plant is flourishing. I know I'm close. It may take less than a year, but I'll use this year to solve our problem. Let me see what I can do."

If anyone could, her father could. As soon as he worked with plants taken from their original soil or source, he'd find the reason for the failure and turn it around.

Ali sighed. What a fantastic help Erick was. He'd urged her father to come to Brazil and acted as a go-between for Zoran Labs and CBA to make all the arrangements. Her father was more scientist than CEO, and with a competent board of directors running Zoran, his decision was an easy one. He genuinely looked forward to working with Erick on this project.

Not long before they left for Brazil, Erick had briefed them on what they should know while in Brazil. A pro at dealing with foreign travel, he helped them through the maze of passports and customs; he covered everything from language to the dangers for outsiders in parts of the country.

A chill tingled through Ali, as she recalled the warning Erick gave them to be careful. He'd told them some horror stories happening in Colombia—drug cartels, kidnappings, and more—all of his tales had bothered her, but Columbia was far from where they'd be, and she'd nearly forgotten them.

Ali woke to a change in the muffled pitch of the jet engines and the sense of a slower air speed. She pushed up the window shade, blinking at the blue brightness of the higher altitude. In seconds, the plane began descending, surfing the thick gray cloud tops.

"This is your captain speaking. We'll be passing over the coast of Brazil in approximately twenty minutes. You should have a nice view—"

Ali stopped listening. They wouldn't be seeing a lot if it stayed so cloudy. Beside her, her father rested, his computer still on. She thought about a walk to the tail section before the inevitable seatbelt lockdown, but she'd have to disturb him to leave. Instead, she pulled out her iPhone, sent a few text messages, then disconnected from the jet's Wi-Fi.

"Hi!"

Ali looked up. A little boy with curly blond hair and eyes as brown as her own popped up like a Jack-in-the-box and grinned at her from over the seatback. In his one word, he warmed her heart. She hadn't noticed him before. He must have been sound asleep for the whole flight. "Are you going to Brathil?"

Ali smiled, loving his little-boy lisp. "Yes, I am. Are you going there too?"

"Me 'n' Mommy's going back home to Brathil. My sister and my daddy are there already. My thister's name is Caywee, and she has a surprise for me. You can see her too, I promise. I'm tree." He held up three chubby fingers. "Whath your name?"

She swallowed a barely suppressed chuckle at his adorable monologue with its "tree" and innocent question about her name.

"I'm Ali." The iPhone slipped into her lap, and she leaned forward to look up at him. "You didn't tell me your name."

"Oh, I'm Scotty." He grinned again and abruptly dropped from view.

Disappointed, she wanted to know more. She guessed his sister must be around five or six, and her curiosity was piqued about his family.

"He's a cutie." Her father straightened in his seat and stretched. "How are you doing, honey?"

"Not a whole lot of sleep, but I'm okay. How about you? The captain came on a little while ago and said we'd be passing over the coast of Brazil soon."

He cleared a document from the screen and shut the computer down. "Won't be much longer then."

The cabin lights dipped but stayed on as the *Fasten Seatbelts* warning chime sounded and the notice flickered on. Moments later, the flight attendant walked toward them on a routine seatbelt status check. She nodded and smiled as she continued down the aisle.

Ali's father leaned over to stow his laptop. *My cell phone.* She needed to put the phone away too, but two men in business suits following several paces behind the attendant distracted her. The cabin was still lit but so was the seatbelt sign, so why were they out of their seats? No one else seemed concerned, but she couldn't keep herself from staring. The cabin was bright enough to study them. The faces of the two men were a fascinating contrast of landscapes.

A little shorter than Kane, the taller man, maybe in his forties, owned a face full of hills. Rolling swells above his brows, across high cheekbones, and over a narrow nose. A headful of wavy ash-brown hair surged over the top of his ears, curved into sideburns down his jaw, and ended in a longish five-o'clock shadow. Neither man wore a tie, and Ali's eyes were drawn to the heavy silver chain in the open V-neck of the man's shirt. His suit stretched tight over his middle, and as he walked she saw more silver. On his right wrist, light glinted from a wide bracelet of infinity-design links.

The younger-looking man's face held a sun-browned desert of moving shadows. Everything about him was brown and nervous. Almond-shaped eyes darted beneath heavy black brows. A tightly curved beard and mustache rounded his mouth and edged his jawline. Close-cropped hair dipped into a widow's peak that matched the cupid's bow of his thin lips. Two small silver hoop earrings hung from his right earlobe, but his left ear held Ali's attention. Sparks of reflected light flashed from a stud earring in the top of his left ear. *Diamond? Zircon? No way to know.*

As they approached, the taller man pinned his eyes on Ali. Beneath his mustache, a full-lipped smirk shaped an unchanging 'so what' expression and matched the glare from cold olive-green eyes. The man dripped of an attitude that spelled out dangerous and narcissistic.

She quickly turned away as a flash of fear came and went. "Dad!" Ali's whisper went unanswered. Her father continued to rummage through his briefcase. In a few steps, the men reached her father's aisle seat, and just short of passing by, stopped. So did Ali's breathing. Had her glances at them been rude? Too long? Heat burned her cheeks. *Why don't they just move on?*

Her breathing shallow, she sensed them leaving. But the seconds-long event remained seared into her mind with details she couldn't unsee, embedded deep into the recesses of her mind. Were the men part of the Colombian drug scene? Kidnappers? Human traffickers? *Good grief! Why couldn't she turn off her crazy imagination?*

She looked at her palms, reddened with fingernail imprints, glad she hadn't been in the aisle seat. She needed to rid herself of the ridiculous dread she dealt with—more proof she needed this time away. She closed her eyes, let go, and took back the fear-filled seconds.

A look at her father's face as he straightened and tugged at his seatbelt hinted he was oblivious to the whole episode. The men were weird and rude but simply ordinary men on a business trip. She'd read entirely too much into it. She relaxed, her tension easing.

She leaned over and gave her father's elbow a playful nudge. "Well, I think we passed the attendant's seatbelt inspection, but those other two guys gave me the creeps." She shot him a grin.

"Two guys? What two guys?" Her father's expression morphed into a puzzled frown.

Ali wrinkled her nose and tilted her head. "You missed them—the kidnappers, of course."

"Hey, that isn't funny." But he returned her smile. "Seriously, sweetheart, remember the epidemic of kidnappings Erick told us were happening in Colombia? True, we won't be anywhere near there, but we still need to be careful." His eyes misted as he looked at her.

"I know. I was only kidding. They were just a couple of guys out of their seats."

Sort of. She probably shouldn't have joked about it.

Forget the incident. Forget them.

The captain's request to turn off all electronics sounded over the speakers. She slipped her iPhone back into her purse and grabbed the armrests as the plane lurched through a patch of rough air.

The cabin lights dimmed as the harmonic rumble of the huge jet engines changed, and they left the cloud cover somewhere above and behind them. Sunshine sifted through an azure blue sky, poured through the windows, and lit up the interior. Beneath them, the low-pitched grinding whine and thud as the landing gear lowered and locked into place.

Muffled sobs came from the seat in front of them. "Ow, ow, ow. Mommy, my ears hurt." Ali ached for little Scotty. She wished she could do something to ease his pain. Below them, squares and rectangles became buildings. Off to her left, São Paulo mushroomed from the ground in a panorama of hundreds of tall structures. The size of the city that seemed to rise up to meet them was scarcely believable.

Tires met runway with a double bounce as the pilot brought the jet to earth in a bumpy slowdown with roaring engines objecting mightily to being thrust into reverse. Though dreamlike and unreal, they were in Brazil.

CHAPTER SIX

Moving through the sterile corridors of São Paulo Guarulhos International Airport, the rollers on Ali's carry-on were dead-quiet compared to the noise in the Baggage Claim area. She adjusted her purse on her shoulder, taking in the multi-lingual chatter, music, and laughter. She caught her father's eye and shook her head. "This place is a zoo!"

"Zoo? More like a jungle." He smiled and poked at her purse. "Be sure to watch that and keep close tabs on your carry-on. Remember what Erick said about being careful in the airport."

Ali set her jaw. She let his cautious reminders roll over her but did tighten her grip on her purse. As tired as she was, maybe she needed a few reminders.

It might be a while before they could get near enough to the carousel to locate their luggage. Attracted like colorful metal filings to a magnet, the place was thick with people drawn to a revolving track to claim their belongings. The line barely moved. No amount of toe-tapping helped with having to stand here and wait. Her thoughts drifted to Erick's friends, Jeff and Marty Leonard, who lived and worked in São Paulo and knew the city well. Ali recalled the photo Erick had sent of the couple.

"I'm glad Erick is having the Leonards pick us up. Considering what I saw of this city from the air, I wouldn't want to go anywhere without help. Aren't they supposed to meet us here in Baggage Claim?"

"Nope." Her father switched his briefcase from one hand to the other and smiled. "Erick said they'd be near the American Airlines' counter. We have to go through customs first."

Ali inched forward through the sea of people who appeared as impatient as she was. The house Erick rented for them was within driving distance of the Center of Biotechnology in Manaus and wouldn't be ready for two weeks. Since her father had a conference and several business appointments scheduled while they were here, Erick found a bed-and-breakfast where the owners agreed to serve all their meals and was located not far outside the city limits of São Paulo.

Ali watched the conveyor stutter to a halt. "I hope we don't have trouble finding the Leonards. Having their photo helps but spotting them might not be so easy."

"Don't worry, they know our schedule. They'll find us." Her father pointed toward the stalled carousel. "I see one of the bags."

"It looks like yours. I see mine on the other side. I'll get it and be right back."

He looked across the conveyor and nodded. "Okay. Why don't you leave your carry-on here with me ... but watch your purse."

Why not 'Why don't you leave your carry-on here with me?' and forget the 'watch your purse' part! She gritted her teeth, parked her case beside him, and aimed her reply in the direction of the floor. "I'll only be a minute."

She jostled through the crowd and reached the far side of the carousel, getting as close as possible. *Only be a minute? Ha.* Wedged between two heavyset women, Ali scanned the mounds of luggage. The bright yellow ribbon she'd tied around the handle of her suitcase stood out like a sun-washed daisy as the bag lurched nearer. The day before they left, she'd tied the ribbons on each of their checked bags. She and her mother had done the same thing on their trip to France the year Ali was sixteen—an unforgettable summer.

Her father's parents had died together in a rail accident when he was twelve and relatives in the United States had raised him. He'd called the trip a return to roots when he, her mother, and Ali flew to Europe. They'd visited his birthplace near Paris then driven to the graveyard where his parents were buried.

Ali had stepped into the past as she walked between massive iron cemetery gates with her parents. A light morning mist drifted through the treetops and sunshine turned granite monuments to gold. Headstones became images of faith with angels, crosses, and lambs, leaving her to wonder about what she believed in as they found the gravesite.

Her father stood beside the two simple graves with tears in his eyes. But when her mother bowed her head in prayer at the graves of a mother and father-in-law she'd never known, something gentle yet powerful had tugged at Ali's heart.

A still-life mental picture of her mother's resting place beneath the cottonwood trees beside Grandpa Dansk's grave raced through her mind.

Life is strange.

Ali's suitcase slowly closed the distance as she shivered at the finality of life and death. Her thoughts and memories ended when a distracted woman carrying a baby and holding onto a little girl bumped into her. Or had the woman been pushed into her? The accident happened so fast, she couldn't be sure. All she'd seen was the back of a man with a short brown crewcut in a dark blue suit and the glitter from an earring in the top of one ear dart into the crowd.

The baby wailed. Ali's flash of unease vanished with concern for the woman. She reached out toward the mother. "Oh, I'm sorry! Did he hurt you?"

The woman stared at her with a shake of her head. "*Perdão.* Pardon me."

Ali nodded and smiled at the frazzled mother. "*Não foi nada.* That's all right." She hoped her Portuguese had been understood.

The frail little girl with cocoa-colored hair and big brown eyes looked at her with a sad upward crinkle of her lips as if she wanted to speak. Was she hungry? Ali stooped.

"*Ola*," the child whispered. Her small warm fingers feathered around Ali's wrist and she slid her hand down into Ali's. Her touch flooded a tender spot in Ali's heart, and she ached from her chest to her throat as she returned the little girl's smile.

"*Ola*." Her own voice failed into a whisper.

The woman yanked the child's arm and pulled her away. The girl's face crumpled and tears welled up. Ali winced and stood. How could a mother hurt a little one like that? And how could the smile from a child, a single word, and a brushing touch make her feel so helpless? She blinked back tears as the mother and her children moved on.

The baggage carousel jerked, moving forward, and Ali refocused on the bobbing yellow ribbon. She reached to pick up her suitcase—and froze.

"Let me help you." A rugged male voice spoke in passable English, uttering the four short words thick with sarcasm.

Ali gulped in air, her eyes drawn to a familiar silver bracelet encircling the wrist of a muscular arm. The man's arm shot across hers and grabbed the bag.

Ali bolted backward. Her gaze raced up the man's arm to look into cold, disdainful green eyes. An icy tremor traveled down her spine and knotted her nerves. Below his nose—the smirk.

Then the man with the earring might have been the oth—

The ice-tremor morphed to a boil.

Put ... that ... down ... creep.

Without a word, the man studied her with mind-deadening intensity, then set the bag down beside her before he turned and strode away. Ali remained cemented to the floor until she could no longer see him.

The bracelet, suit, his face—one of the men on the plane. Heart pounding, chill bumps rose on her arms.

Dad!

Hands trembling, she looked for him across the carousel. Busy with the rest of their luggage, he hadn't seen the encounter. Automatically, she checked her purse. Untouched.

The draining adrenaline left her steely calm. She was fine, her purse was fine. Naturally, both men would be here to claim their bags. She'd overreacted. The man with the bracelet was only being polite, and the man with the earring? She couldn't be sure. But if they'd meant to hurt her or steal anything, they'd both certainly had their chance. Nothing was wrong.

Ali picked up her bag and returned to her father. Should she tell him—was the encounter even worth mentioning? Not now. He had to be as tired as she was. Maybe she'd say something later.

The beginning twinges of a headache kept time with the beat of her heart. She looked at the signs above an archway, relieved they were through Customs. She pointed to her left. "It looks like we go in that direction, Dad."

He paused, mid-grumble, wrestling the heavy bags. "Okay, but we really need to get some help with these."

Ali smiled. "I think help is just about here." A scruffy-looking skycap with an expectant grin came toward them, his grin widening with every step. The man took over their luggage, loading the bags onto a rolling carrier, then led the way to the main terminal. Her father had him park the bags as close to their airline counter as possible. A generous tip kept his smile stretching from ear-to-ear as he left.

Ali searched the crowd for Jeff and Marty Leonard then looked at her watch. "I don't see them anywhere. Do we need to call them?"

"No, let's wait a while before we try calling. Maybe they had trouble getting to the airport. São Paulo traffic is legendary."

"Maybe." Ali looked toward the American Airlines' desk. "But our plane wasn't late—we couldn't have missed them. I'll check. They might have left us a message."

After an animated discussion in broken Portuguese and shattered English with the man at the desk, Ali understood. No message. This part of their trip wouldn't be as easy as she'd imagined. She returned to her father, shaking her head with the negative results.

A fleeting look of concern crossed his face. "Could be the traffic, but I'm sure there's a good reason why they're not here yet."

"If they don't get here soon, we'll need to check on Gabi. She's been cooped up for so long."

Her father held up a hand. "One thing at a time. She's next on the list of things to do. I have the address of the Galantes' B and B, the place where we'll be staying. We'll just need to line up a taxi."

Ali nodded. Her headache had eased, but she'd feel a lot better when the Leonards showed up. The bright morning sunshine streamed through high rectangles of glass, warming her back as she continued to scan the area.

What in the world? Morse code? Several yards away, amid the crowd and above its owner's silly mustache, sparks of light reflected from an oversized silver crucifix. The cross dangled from a chain in the V-neck of a blue-and-yellow plaid shirt stretched around a large belly. The man's bushy black mustache twirled up in points on both ends. She couldn't help staring—and smiling. He stood out like a big plaid dot on a page of stripes.

Uh-oh. He raked his fingers through his hair, cocked his head, and stared—at her. She wished the floor would open and devour her, hot cheeks and all. The ingrate floor wasn't cooperating and before she could breathe again, he shot her a toothy grin. She wasn't too far away to miss the twinkle in his dark eyes, along with the deep dimple in his left cheek that nearly disappeared when he smiled.

And she stood there, smiling back like a dope, staring back. He stooped to pick up a little boy with a head full of blond curls, hoisting the child high over his head. Their boisterous laughter echoed above the din and confusion.

Ali pulled in a breath, her eyes fastened on the happy little boy. "That's Scotty, Dad!"

"Who?"

"You remember, from the plane. The little guy in the seat in front of us."

From over the heads of the crowd, Scotty glimpsed Ali and crowed at the top of his lungs. "Hi, Awi! Look at me! I'm fwying!" He waved wildly, pointing at her. Plaid slid the boy down into a hug, with Scotty practically sitting on top of the man's belly. Several more American-looking faces turned in Ali's direction, including that of a girl who looked close to her own age. Every one of the faces held a smile.

Scotty squirmed in the big man's arms, jumped down and took off running directly toward Ali and her father. He took all of two seconds to maneuver the distance across the floor.

Ali watched the woman, who must be his mother, jog behind him, scolding him with every step. "Wait! Scott Randall Roberts, come back here! You know better than to run off like that!"

Scotty skidded to a stop in front of Ali. "Come an' see my sister." Along with his demand, he sent Ali the same adorable grin he'd given her on the plane. Before she could say a word, he grabbed her hand and tugged her in the direction of the grinning man wearing the cross.

What sister? Only adults stood in front of her.

Obviously embarrassed at her small son's behavior, his mother gave the three-year-old a gentle swat on the rear. Scotty let go of Ali's fingers, stuck his thumb in his mouth and plopped down on the tiled floor, insulted. His mother looked from Ali to her father, apologizing as she picked up her son and held him.

Ali held up a hand, still smiling. "It's all right. We sort of met on the plane."

Scotty buried his face in his mother's neck. "I want Awi to see Caywee, Mommy," the muffled voice said. "I pwomised!"

"Scotty!" She shook her head and looked at Ali. "I'm so sorry. He's into promising everybody something."

Mr. Plaid and the girl walked over and stood nearby. Ali only had time to smile at them before Scotty's mother turned her attention to her father. "You're here on vacation?"

"Well, not exactly a vacation." Her father wore an amused grin. "We hope to work in some sightseeing, but we're headed into the Amazon River basin at the end of the month. I'm here to complete a research project. It's good to meet someone from the US so soon after getting here. This is my daughter, Aleksia. I'm Dr. Lamarque—Matt."

"Oh, I didn't even introduce myself." Scotty's still-rattled mother reached out to shake her father's hand. "I'm Pam Roberts. Very glad to meet you, Matt, and …" She looked at Ali, her attractive features holding a quizzical expression. "Scotty called you Ali?"

"Scotty's right, Mrs. Roberts. Everyone calls me Ali." Ali shook Pam Roberts' hand, as the rest of those who were with the bouncy little boy surrounded her and her father.

Mrs. Roberts tugged Scotty's shirt down over his tummy. "You and Caylee must be fairly close in age, Ali."

Ali again looked for a little girl that wasn't anywhere in sight. "My age …? But … I …"

Right on cue, Scotty wriggled out of his mother's arms and ran to hug the knees of the older girl standing beside Plaid. "This is Caywee!" Scotty announced, then jabbed a finger toward Ali. "An' that's Awi. I like her."

Caylee grinned and stuck out her hand. "Cay*lee*, but my friends call me Cay."

Ali smiled as she and Caylee traded a friendly "hi." Scotty's sister sure wasn't as young as Ali thought she'd be.

Caylee's friendly, blue-green eyes were intense behind her wire-rimmed glasses. She wore a tan sweater, jeans, and boots. Freckles sprinkled across the bridge of her nose and thick hair the color of roasted chestnuts was pulled back into a ponytail. Ali liked her immediately.

"Sorry about my little brother being so forward. He can wear you out with all his energy. Did he talk you to death on the plane?"

"No, no, in fact, he must have slept nearly all night, he was so quiet. But he's fun. He had me laughing, and I needed that."

Caylee must have guessed she was trying to figure out why the big difference in age. She grinned and nodded as if she knew Ali's question. "He's the best little 'surprise package' our family could ever have received."

A tropical heat wave expanded from Ali's chin to her cheeks again. Had she been that obvious?

"Hello!" A tall, slender man, whose hair and eyes duplicated his daughter's, walked up and introduced himself. "I'm Evan Roberts." He clapped a hand on Plaid's muscular shoulder. "And this is Joaquim Antonio Gaspar dos Santos, self-assigned personal bodyguard, taxi driver, handyman, and friend, all rolled into one good-sized package."

"I am called Jo." Plaid gave Matt a hearty handshake, then raised his bushy eyebrows at Ali and gallantly kissed the back of her hand. His black mustache wiggled as he pursed his lips. At a total loss for words, Ali couldn't help laughing.

"Don't worry, he's harmless," Caylee whispered to Ali with a chuckle. "Best friend anyone could ever have too."

Evan broke in with a question. "Is there anything we can do for you while we're here?"

"Well, there just might be."

Her father's answer sounded as grateful as Ali was.

"Seems we've either missed the couple who was supposed to meet us, or something has happened to delay them. My calls to them go straight to voice mail, and there's been no word. We'd certainly could use some advice about how we can locate them, as well as how to get where we're going."

Evan's face warmed with his smile. "We'd be happy to help with all that."

Ali struggled to keep frustration from her voice. "I'm worried about Gabi too."

Caylee's eyebrows arched. "Who's Gabi?"

"My dog. We haven't picked her up yet, and she's probably going stir-crazy in that carrier by now."

"You're right, that was one long trip for her. And I know how you feel. I miss our dog. We had to leave him in the States the last time we were there on furlough." Caylee pointed to the American Airlines' desk. "You'll probably need to claim her soon. She'll be in a different area, and they have pretty strict time limits on picking them up."

Ali nodded but was distracted, stuck on a one-word puzzle—furlough. No one in the Roberts family looked like they were in the military.

Jo's halting English interrupted her thoughts. "We will get dog for you right before we leave. Dog in Air Cargo area, Miss Ali, and we can help with bags too."

"Thanks, Jo. And it's Ali, please. You don't have to call me Miss." She flashed him a grin, her worries about Gabi melting as he took the claim check her father handed him.

He wore the most endearing smile. *Rescued? Maybe.* She took another quick look behind her. Poked her gaze into dark corners and doorways. No monsters. No *men.* She stretched her fisted hands out and breathed. Overreacting again. Shadows were everywhere. Harmless. Benign. *Right?*

CHAPTER SEVEN

"Dr. Matthew Lamarque, please come to the American Airlines desk."

Ali glanced at the desk as the announcement blared from loudspeakers in both English and Portuguese. "That has to be the Leonards." Her father gave her arm a quick squeeze and headed toward the counter.

The expression on his face when he returned wrenched Ali's heart. Something must have happened to them that wasn't good.

Her father shook his head. "That was Jeff. Not what we wanted to hear." The entire Roberts family and Jo moved closer, concern on every face as he continued. "They've been in an accident."

"Oh, no." Every muscle in Ali's body tensed rock-hard with scenes too painful and recent tumbling through her thoughts.

Caylee touched her arm and turned to Matt. "Were they hurt?"

Her father nodded. "Cuts, bruises, and sore necks, but nothing serious. He called from the emergency room at Albert Einstein Jewish Hospital. They'd stopped for a red light. The car behind them didn't. Their car may be totaled."

Evan turned to Ali, his voice full of reassurance. "Not good about the car, but they're at one of the best hospitals in the country. They'll get good care there."

"Jeff was pretty concerned about us and relieved we had some help."

"And help you have." Evan put his hand on her father's shoulder.

"Can't begin to tell you how much we appreciate it, Evan." He eyed the piles of their combined luggage. "We'll need a taxi as well as the car. I'll call …"

Evan was one step ahead. "There's a line of taxis out front. Follow me. If you'll line up the taxi, I'll get the car and meet you back here in a few minutes. Jo will drive our car and take you, Caylee, Ali, and the dog. Pam, Scotty and I will take the taxi."

"Done." Her father turned to Ali. "You'll need to pick up Gabi—"

"Girls and I go get her now." Jo grinned and pulled out the claim check her father had given him.

Outside the terminal, the taxi moved up behind the Roberts' car. Evan, Pam, and Scotty piled into the blue and white taxi as the driver stowed the overflow of luggage. Gabi behaved as Jo clipped on the leash, staying beside him as they went to the Roberts' car. Ali drew in a breath. Jo had a fan. Gabi had taken to him immediately.

Jo drove the Roberts' older four-door Mercedes with her father beside him in front, and in back, Caylee and Ali rode with Gabi between them. Alert with ears poised at high-noon, the dog's dark amber eyes took in everything.

"We follow taxi. Long drive." Jo peered at Ali in the rearview mirror. "About hour to go nineteen miles from airport to center of city. Lots to see while drive."

Ali craned her neck, looking up as they drove through a concrete jungle of skyscrapers. She rubbed at her nose as the sickening smell of fumes and hot asphalt seeped into the car. Not a good first impression of the city.

Not many drivers paid attention to traffic signals. Horns, the squall of brakes, and the squeal of rubber shrieked from every intersection. Ali bit on her lower lip to keep from covering her eyes and ears.

None of the chaos seemed to faze Caylee, who rocked on with the lurching car, her iPad Mini in hand. Forget any conversation, the uproar was so loud. Would they ever get through this traffic?

Ali stared out the window, disoriented as Jo careened through the busy streets. The first time the midnight blue Vector pulled alongside their car and kept pace, Ali glanced at the vehicle then turned away. The second time the sedan drew close, she studied the dark-tinted windows and wondered how anyone could see through them. But the third time the Vector pulled alongside, the dark windows no longer mattered as the familiar sensation of dread drilled into the pit of her stomach. Whoever was driving the Vector drove too much like the person who had driven the Toyota pickup that almost ran her off the road.

She pushed back out of view, fisting both hands. Absurd. She either had jet lag or she was plain exhausted from the trip.

Jo swerved, mumbling. Ali focused on the back of his head. Had he noticed the car too? As he sped up and pulled ahead, she moved forward in the seat far enough to see the reflection of traffic in the passenger-side mirror. The blue Vector darted in behind them and seconds later, vanished in traffic.

She tried to relax and concentrate on the São Paulo scenery as their speed changed from frenzied to slow-moving. Traffic thinned, and they rounded a lake, its serene surface reflecting a tall concrete monument.

Peace seemed to permeate the car as the traffic noise faded behind them. Her father laid his arm along the seat back with his hand on Jo's headrest and looked over his shoulder at Caylee. "We're grateful you and your family came to the rescue of a couple of stranded travelers."

"It's no problem, Dr. Lamarque, we're glad to help. Actually, this is right on the way to where we live. Besides, it's nice to meet someone else who speaks English."

Jo interrupted with a comment about "city's too-crazy drivers," and Matt turned away to respond. Caylee rubbed her hand across Gabi's shiny coat. "She's wonderful. How old is she?"

"She's three, the same as Scotty." Ali grinned, holding up three fingers. "With the exception of Chaton, she was the best birthday present anyone could ever hope for."

Caylee's ponytail swung as she tilted her head, her expression one of pure curiosity. "Chaton? Okay, what in the world is a Chaton?"

Ali laughed. "My horse—a gorgeous, jet-black gelding.

"I love horses! What's he like, and what does his name mean?"

"He is a fantastic mix of Arabian and American Saddler. I named him Chaton for the Sioux Indian word that means falcon, but it also means kitten in French, and believe me, he can behave like either. I thought I might have to sell him before we left, but my best friend, Kane, volunteered to board him and take care of him while we're gone. You said you love horses—do you ride?"

"Not now, not here, but I did when we lived near the rain forest. Good friends of ours have a ranch there with a stable chock full of horses. I'll have to give you their name and email them about you so you can do some riding while you're living there."

"You have no idea how great that sounds to me. I'm already missing Cha. Maybe being able to ride once in a while will help get me through being away from him."

"Gabi? Chaton? How do you come up with those names?" Caylee asked. "And Kane's name is pretty unusual. Is it short for something else?"

"It's short for Kanen, and he's a great guy, as cool and unique as his name."

Caylee eyes sparkled. "So, a guy. A best friend. Unique. Sounds like he's got a lot more going on than just a cool name, huh?"

Ali checked out her fingernails. Caylee had no trouble picking up how she felt about Kane. "He is more than just a friend." She looked up with a smile and added, "Now, anyway. And the names? Words and their meanings fascinate me, especially Native American names. Online, I sometimes look at baby names. It's really easy to find names and their meanings."

She stroked Gabi's back. "Gabi's name, Gabrielle, means woman of God, Gabriel in Hebrew." Ali glanced at Caylee. "You know, like the angel? My mother had suggested the name since my dad's heritage is French." She paused and swallowed hard. "You said you have a dog?"

Caylee nodded. "Pete. He's our fourteen-year-old shepherd-collie mix. We hated leaving him, but the trip would have been too hard on him. My grandparents are keeping him for us."

Caylee's voice caught as she spoke, and Ali changed the subject. "Have you been in Brazil long?"

"Only here during the summers until I finish college. Mom, Dad, and Scotty have been here in São Paulo six months on this field appointment and will probably be here another year and a half. Since my parents are missionaries, we move to different places, mostly in South America. We were in Manaus for ten years. In fact, I was born there."

Furloughs, field appointments, missionaries—Ali's insides melted with surprise and embarrassment at her assumption.

No Bible in anyone's hand. There hadn't been a clue they were missionaries, and never did Ali imagine these happy-go-lucky people might be religious. Not one of them looked like … and Caylee rode horses and wore boots for heaven's sake! Was she blushing? She *should* be with her preconceived ideas—and making light of angels. She'd been completely off guard and hoped Caylee hadn't noticed.

Caylee continued without missing a beat. "Mom and Scotty have been in the States—actually, near you, in Los Angeles—for three weeks. Aunt Julie, Mom's sister, needed to have surgery, so Mom went back to help out."

A wave of relief gentled through Ali. She'd been able to cover her surprise. "How's your aunt doing now?"

"She's much better and even wants to visit as soon as she feels up to traveling. I'll be starting my senior year this fall at the University of California in LA. I live with Aunt Julie while I'm there. How about you—where are you going to school? What year?"

"I just finished my junior year too, but at UC in Santa Barbara—closer to home than LA. *Or it was.* We'll have to keep in touch."

Caylee looked at her. "What about your mom? Does she plan to join you here soon?"

Ali averted her eyes but not before she could hide her tears, and she couldn't form a single syllable that would make sense.

Her father rescued her. "Mrs. Lamarque died in an accident not too long ago, Caylee,"

Glad he'd overheard Caylee's question, Ali swallowed hard as Cay's hand covered hers.

"Oh, Ali, I am so sorry. I didn't know." Caylee's words left an awkward silence.

Ali struggled against the lump in her throat, fighting to control replays of self-accusation, that her mother's death was her fault. During long seconds of quiet, the bands of pain eased, and she looked at Caylee. She had to let her know her question was okay, that she was okay. But Caylee's head was bowed.

"Please don't feel bad. We just miss her terribly, and you had no way of knowing. It's all right." Ali stumbled over words that didn't seem to come out the way she'd intended. Caylee had to be wondering what had happened in the accident. Maybe another time. No way could she tell her anything more now.

"Looks like this the place," Jo announced. "Two-six-four Valparaiso Avenue."

Behind the taxi, Jo slowed as they approached. Looking at his notes, her father reviewed them out loud as they drove up to a white house with trees and gardens.

"Let's see—large two-story white frame house, set back from the road, whitewashed wood fence and the right numbers on the gatepost—that's confirmation for me, Jo."

Caylee nodded. "I hope this is the right place. How beautiful."

In front of them, the taxi pulled through the open gates into the drive and parked, leaving Jo plenty of room to pull their Mercedes in behind.

The place looked like an old southern plantation house. Ali opened the car door and drew in a breath of perfumed air. Something about that air … "The house is lovely."

Beds of roses meandered down the side of the long walk that curved toward the front entrance. Tangled vines covered with purple and white passionflowers rambled over white house and spacious veranda.

She closed her eyes against a wave of sadness. Her mother loved passionflowers and roses. Gabi leaned in against her leg. Ali smoothed the dog's head, glad for the distraction. They'd be here for at least two weeks—she had to start working through her sorrow. Gabi's leash in hand, she got out and pushed herself to look at the house again.

Only slightly smaller compared with other homes and estates they'd passed in the area, the Galantes' home was a dozen miles away from the bustle of downtown São Paulo. Erick Chance told them the owners, Gina and Marco Galante, had lived in the house for over fifty years, raised seven children here, and now enjoyed renting rooms to visitors. A live-in couple, Jose and Sonia, cared for the house and grounds, but Mrs. Galante did all the cooking. Erick had a huge grin on his face when he warned them to prepare to be stuffed full of her delicious Italian food.

Ali turned at the commotion coming from the taxi and laughed out loud as Scotty tumbled out, tugging at a suitcase nearly as big as himself. Everyone pitched in to help with the luggage. A middle-aged man Ali assumed must be Jose came with a cart to take the baggage to the house.

A screen door slammed, and voices wafted from the porch. Mrs. Galante? Ali smiled as a petite, silver-haired woman, wearing a red print dress and an apron, crossed the porch and came down the steps. And Marco. His smile was contagious, and the color of his hair and beard reminded Ali of Grandma Dansk's pewter ware. Not much taller than his wife, he walked with a cane and followed close on her heels.

"Ola! Hello there. Welcome." The warm, accented words burst from both, instantly putting Ali at ease. There'd be no language barrier. The Galantes welcomed the Lamarques and the Roberts like family, inviting them in for coffee and tiramisu.

Ali tethered Gabi to the railing in the shade on the veranda and joined the others inside. She'd barely walked in before Mrs. Galante placed a china plate holding a generous square of tiramisu into her hands and poured her a cup of strong Brazilian coffee. Ali eyed the caffeine-heavy dessert. She might have a battle sleeping tonight, but the tiramisu looked well worth the fight. The whole scene reminded her of Grandma's ever-ready cookie jar.

Conversation lasted half an hour before Mrs. Galante motioned toward the porch and Gabi. "Would you like to take the dog out into the back for a walk and to get her familiar with where she will be staying? Our two puppies, Rascal and Judge, are in their pen, and there's plenty of room for all the dogs out there."

Ali glanced at Caylee, mouth full of her last bite of tiramisu. "Want to go?"

Pam Roberts stood. "You've been so kind and everything was delicious, but we really should go home."

Both the Galantes rose to offer more dessert and coffee, encouraging the Roberts to stay and relax a few more moments before they left. Almost without hesitation, Mrs. Roberts sat and accepted a refill of coffee.

Caylee grinned at Ali and handed Sonia her empty plate. "Sure. Ready when you are."

The cooler air outside wafted over Ali like a fall mist as she wound Gabi's leash around her wrist. To escape being inside planes, cars, and houses for a while felt refreshing.

"Ready for a walk, girl?" The dog's eager response turned their walk into a fast jog as they went toward the rear of the house.

Caylee stopped to open the metal gate to the rear grounds and laughed out loud. The two "puppies" were in a large separate pen. "Looks like you're going to get to meet a couple of new buds, Gabi."

"Mrs. Galante called them puppies? I don't think so." Ali smiled, but Caylee dissolved into a fresh siege of laughter as a Jack Russell terrier jumped up and down like a yoyo, yipping with every leap. The other "puppy," a big black Labrador retriever, ambled over to the fence with a few welcoming woofs of his own.

Gabi strained at the end of her leash and gave her opinion in one loud bark. Ali glanced at Caylee. "Well, guess which one's the judge! But it doesn't look as if he'll get to have the last word. Calm down, girl." She stooped to stroke Gabi's back, looking over at the yard-owners. "Relax, guys. We won't take over your territory."

"You talk to dogs as if they were people, like I do," Caylee said, still chuckling.

"Don't all dog lovers do that?" Ali grinned up at her and reached to untangle Gabi's leash. She'd never tire of hearing Caylee laugh. There had been so much laughter since she'd met Caylee and her family.

No walls but lots of fencing. The rear gate marked the beginning of a high, slatted-wood fence angled around the back of the property. The grounds behind the house charmed Ali as much as the front had. Multicolored flowers grew at random everywhere and the place had a cheerful, cared-for look.

Caylee gazed at the grassy area. "Mrs. Galante wasn't joking when she said there was room enough for everyone out here."

"No, and Mr. Galante and Jose must spend a lot of time working to keep the grounds so beautiful." Ali urged Gabi through the open gate and held it for Caylee.

As Ali turned to close the gate, a car passed in front of the house … slowly, and not just any car. A rush of apprehension rooted her to the stone walk. She'd only had a quick glimpse of the blue luxury car with dark windows, but one look had been enough.

No. The car was a coincidence before and surely was now. She couldn't have seen the same car. There probably were lots of blue Vector G65 four-door sedans with tinted windows around. But the persistent, uneasy sensation was hard to dismiss, and she had to stop gawking down the street after a phantom vehicle. No, not phantom—she *wasn't* hallucinating. Was she?

Gabi strained at the leather strap and snapped her back to reality. Ali closed the gate and went into the yard, wondering if Cay had noticed the car.

Caylee waved her hand in a semicircle toward the yard. "Anywhere special you want to sit?"

As in several other areas in front of the house, tables and benches also nestled between stands of shade trees in the back. Ali pointed to one. "How about over there? Lots of shade ... looks good."

"Perfect." Caylee left her side to sit on the bench, raising her clip-on sunglasses straight up. "This is great. And don't you dare say anything about me looking like Mickey Mouse."

Lagging behind, Ali looked at Caylee and stifled a laugh. "Don't tell me that's what Scotty thinks when you do that."

"You wouldn't believe how that three-year-old can tease."

"Oh, yes, I would. He's doesn't seem to miss a thing." Impatient, Gabi tugged Ali forward. Suddenly too tired to reprimand her, she let Gabi lead her to the redwood table.

"Lie down, Gabi." The shepherd obediently curled up in the shade. Ali picked up a twig and twirled the wood between her fingers. She had to ask.

"Did you notice the car that pulled up beside ours a couple of times on the way here—the dark blue Vector?"

"No, why? What did I miss?"

"Nothing, really. I just wondered if you'd seen the car. I thought I saw the same car again, going past the house a minute ago. Probably a coincidence. Guess I'm just tired." She shoved the whole scene out of her mind and changed the subject. They talked about Kane and Caylee's on again, off again love life, their families, and their friends.

Bone-weary tiredness set in, and Ali let her mind idle until Caylee was in the midst of saying something about ... Ali straightened, listening.

"God is amazing. Without him leveling a few mountains, I'd probably be waitressing somewhere. I wouldn't be in UCLA at all without the gift of a full four-year scholarship. That was pretty awesome. I never would have been able to go if not for that."

Ali blinked. That Caylee went to the same college, different campus, had been a cool coincidence, but that she was there on a full scholarship and credited God for it was, well, a bit much. "Uh, wow! Congrats on the scholarship. That *is* awesome."

"Thanks. Why don't we get together sometime after you get back home?

Ali's mouth clamped shut. Telling Caylee she wouldn't be going to UCSB this fall, that she would most likely be off another year before she'd begin her senior year, could wait. But she had to say something,

"Sure. Sounds like fun." And would be if she relearned the meaning of fun while she was here. *Talk about anything but college!*

"You said you lived in Manaus? What's it like there? Will I die of boredom?"

Caylee shot her a grin, flipped her clip-on sunglasses down, and looked over their tops. "You sure you want to hear about ten of the greatest years of my life?

And as Caylee unreeled vivid descriptions of her childhood in Manaus and tales of the Amazon rain forest, Ali sat enthralled, visualizing Caylee's fascinating story.

"… but the one thing I'd love to do before going back to the states this fall is to take a long walk into the rain forest."

Adrenalin? Pure excitement? Whatever the emotion was rushed through every cell and atom of Ali's being and scooted her to the edge of the bench. "When are you going? I'll go with you!"

She watched Caylee pick at a fingernail, quiet for a few maddening seconds before she shrugged.

"A hike would be so much fun, but I can't. Honestly, it's only a dream. I've been away so long, I don't really know anyone well enough in Manaus anymore and have no place to stay. More than that, there's no money to get there or to fund a trip."

Ali put her hand on Caylee's arm. "But maybe we could think of a way to work things out. Dreams are the stuff reality is made of, you know. What would you need to get to Manaus? What would we have to do to get ready for a hike like that?"

For the first time in months, life and a future spilled into Ali's thoughts. The air had chilled, but before they went back into the house they'd sketched out plans for a hike into the rain forest.

The Galantes wouldn't hear of the Roberts leaving without dinner, so the family left late that evening, Scotty sound asleep on his daddy's shoulder.

Ali followed Mrs. Galante up the wide staircase and down the hall to her bedroom, glad for her sweater. She could hardly imagine getting used to winter in June in São Paulo. Jet lag was one thing, but season-shock would be an additional challenge. The temperature hovered at a cool fifty-eight degrees and reminded her of crisp, fresh California mornings. She decided to leave the bedroom windows open a little and enjoy the brisk night air.

The bedroom was large and inviting, but she was too tired to care. She didn't bother to unpack her clothes. Tomorrow would be soon enough. She dug a comfy old T-shirt and drawstring pants out of her luggage and crawled into bed. Unfurling the gauzy mosquito netting, she let the draping fall in place around the bed. Mrs. Galante had insisted on her using the netting, which smelled of insecticide, but a slight odor was better than the possibility of malaria.

She wrapped the light blanket around her shoulders and curled up on the too-soft mattress. A soothing breeze blew the filmy window curtains aside and slipped through the netting to ruffle her hair.

Fascinating day. Would the trip be worthwhile—erase a few heart-sinking memories and bring healing for herself and her dad? She lifted the side of the net and gazed out the window, thoughts sent toward the inky star-littered sky.

She hoped so.

CHAPTER EIGHT

The majority of people who lived on the outskirts of São Paulo surrounded their houses and properties with fortress-like concrete block walls for security against rampant crime. Most of the properties on Valparaiso Avenida were no different. Nicolau Cardozo smiled and wheeled the dark blue rental sedan around the corner onto the quiet residential street. Pleased with the darkened environment, he passed several randomly parked cars, switched off the vehicle's headlights, and rolled into a tree-shadowed curve. The Galantes had made his job so much easier with just their flimsy wood fence to contend with. The only walls in sight around their house and grounds were their neighbors' walls.

Cardozo set the parking brake, rolled down the windows, and pushed his seat back before he silenced the Vector's engine. Next to him, his partner, Fernando Velez, lolled against the passenger seat, fiddling with his skimpy beard. Neither spoke as Cardozo looked over the area. They were far enough away from the target house not to be noticed but close enough to accomplish what they were here to do. With no houses on the opposite side of the avenue, a wide grassy swath spread into an area heavy with trees and manicured shrubbery. And behind that, set back about fifteen hundred feet from the street, the towering stone community barrier ran the length of Valparaiso Avenue.

Satisfied with the good vantage spot, Cardozo watched. If everything went as well tonight as it had so far, they'd gain the needed information. Spying on young women wasn't their usual gig, and if not for the money, he wouldn't be sitting here. However, he had to admit, stalking this woman and seeing the look on her face when he'd threatened to shove her off that bridge had been worth it. And getting so close to her in both Miami and São Paulo air terminals a week ago, without her knowing the plans he had in store for her? All part of why he didn't mind. The thrill of the chase. That Velez labeled him sadistic was Velez's problem.

They'd been here a week, settled into an upscale hotel—making it their base of operations—just as the Lamarques had settled into their routine at the bed and breakfast he and Velez targeted tonight. Nearly everything was in place to do what the job called for, but he'd never get used to this heat.

Cardozo rubbed at the perspiration running down his neck. Rotten heat. Despite the cool winter evening, a ring of dampness already circled the edge of his collar. He'd ditched his necktie but should have changed from the suit he'd worn to dinner.

Distant thunder rumbled. Not a good sign. Neither were the clouds. As Nicolau peered through the windshield at the sky, watching a few clouds lumber toward the half-moon. Winter rarely held rainstorms, but this didn't look promising. Maybe they would stay dry long enough to get what they needed.

He switched on the map light. It would create more than enough illumination without giving them away. With a glance at his middle, he unbuttoned the jacket of his gray Gianni suit. *Huh! A little too much dinner.* He should do something about the stomach.

A long-range listening device lay next to a tape recorder on the rear seat of the car. Cardozo grabbed the unit and aimed the receiver in the direction of the white house. In a short time, he'd be aiming the device across the street, balancing the case on his knees, while sitting in a folding chair. The distance to the Galante house was about the length of a *futebal* field with a setback of half that. Perfect. Light poured through the open front door. *Ha. So trusting these dolts were.* He stabilized the dish on the ledge of the open window, experimenting, getting used to the feel of the thing. Maybe he'd use the earphones later.

Velez swore something colorful under his breath in Portuguese about the heat.

Cardozo glowered at him. "Speak up and stick to English. I need the practice."

Velez returned his stare then scowled at the round gadget pointed toward the target house. "You paid way too much for that, Nico." His gaze dropped, fixing on Cardozo's suit.

Cardozo shook his head. "I paid too much for what? The suit or the mic?" No answer. The idiot was still jealous of a suit he could never pull off wearing. His fingers closed around the pistol-grip handle of the parabolic microphone. Maybe the man would think twice about griping if he found himself looking down the barrel of an illegal, unregistered Ruger Cardozo planned to buy and stash in the Vector's trunk tomorrow night. But, no, he needed Velez. He turned his attention to the mic, his impatience with Velez easing. "No pain, no gain; this thing will pay off. Just give it some time."

Mike, their point person in California, had paved the way, providing information until the bugs were placed in São Paulo. During the past week, the Lamarques had settled into their temporary residence, and Cardozo had left nothing to chance. Mike's man in Brazil, Lucas Costa, had slipped in and out of their homes as he'd had opportunity. The man had even arranged for a buddy to install taps in the house where the Lamarques would be staying in Manaus. With strategically placed tiny FM transmitters that doubled for use as both room bugs and phone taps, they wouldn't miss much, if anything, of what they needed to know. The microphone he directed toward the target house now was just one more pair of "ears." Sure, they'd paid a hefty fee, but he had to admit Velez' genius at finding an expert to plug the bugs into both the Galante and Roberts' homes helped.

Yesterday, the transmitter in the Galante house had given them information that the families planned a late dinner and visit. The main reason was to discuss a trip into the Amazon rain forest the daughters wanted to take. What was recorded was enough to make Cardozo want to hear more—firsthand. With talk of both girls taking this little jungle trek, not only would their trip give him the opportunity and the cover he was looking for, but this Caylee woman meant more leverage and more money. The words trouble and nuisance churned through his thoughts, but he shrugged them off.

All was well until the installer tested the transmitter in the Galante home early this morning. The unit had failed, and with no chance or time to replace the transmitter, they'd scrambled to find a parabolic mic and get themselves into position tonight to listen.

With no air-conditioning or breeze, the heat wilted them in their seats. Cardozo checked his watch. "They're late. They should be here any minute. If we get this done, giving Kaarding what she needs will be simple." He snickered, at the memory of staring down Lamarque's daughter on the São Paulo-bound jet. "Once we finish with this, we're on—what do they call it—easy street?"

Velez nodded. "*Sim* … uh, I mean, yeah."

Cardozo leaned back, some of his stress lifted, thinking of the million dollars per man Dr. Madison Kaarding had promised would soon pad their bank accounts. Payment couldn't happen fast enough. Kaarding had FedExed draft copies of the first payment to them a week ago. Two hundred-fifty thousand dollars had been deposited into his Venezuelan bank account, and that proof made Cardozo grin.

He studied the area across the avenue from the Galante house where they would soon set up to listen. Shrouded in deep shadow, the spot gave them the best line of sight he could hope for to use the parabolic. They might miss some of the conversation, possibly all if the entrance door remained closed, but he had to take the chance. There was always a chance if the only obstacle was the screened door and warm nights invited open doors.

Rare movement on the street caught his attention. Cardozo kicked his reverie aside and sat up straight. The heavy, intermittent clouds partially obscured the rising half-moon, and only the light from the Galante house and porch illuminated the grounds. "There she is, and she's got that dog with her." His attention focused on a slender young woman with waves of light-colored hair spilling over her shoulders.

She'd obviously come from the Galante house and gone through the open gate. Somehow, he'd missed seeing her, and she was headed away from them. Hair swinging, she jogged to keep up with the big shepherd trotting along in front of her.

"Katarina," Cardozo said quietly, his eyes riveted on the shadowy scene through the windshield. He wanted to see the dog up close. In fact, he had wanted that amber-eyed dog since he'd first seen her with the girl in the photo Kaarding had showed them.

"Katarina? Where? Who's Katarina?" Velez picked up his night vision goggles, searching the street for signs of someone else. He stared ahead through the windshield. "Huh? She's com—"

"Katarina is what I will name the dog." Cardozo rubbed the bridge of his nose. "It's a good name. I think it suits her." He flicked his silver cigarette lighter, thinking of the cigar he had stowed in his jacket.

"What will *you* do with a dog?" Velez tossed the goggles onto the dashboard and shook his head, plainly disgusted.

"She'll make a good guard dog when she's trained. And … I like dogs." Cardozo looked at him and held back an ugly chuckle. Velez didn't like any animal, much less dogs.

He turned back to watch the pair. They must've reversed direction while he'd talked about the dog. They were moving toward the car now. The dog stopped, pausing for a few seconds. Cardozo tensed. Had the girl spotted the secluded car … had the dog alerted her?

Velez bent forward, pointing toward the two dim shapes moving into the darker area of the Galante property. "I thought for a second there we'd been made, but she's leaving."

"Mm." Cardozo relaxed, watching the girl and dog as they neared the house. He had plenty of time.

Ali walked at a brisk pace behind Gabi as they started toward the opposite end of the avenue. The walls surrounding the four nearest homes on the street made it almost impossible to tell if they were lived in, and tall hedges blocked any view of other homes she knew were there, visible or not. There'd been only a brief reply from Mrs. Galante when Ali asked why their house didn't have any defensive walls. Neither she nor Marco liked being closed in, and Ali completely understood.

They'd gone far enough. "Let's go home, girl." She pivoted to return to the house.

But Gabi strained and bounded ahead of her a few feet before she abruptly halted. The leash went slack as Gabi lifted her head and sniffed the air.

A chill peppered Ali's arms. She tightened her grip on the lead and moved to Gabi's side. The fur on the dog's neck and back stood straight up, and she bared her teeth, growling into the darkness ahead.

"What is it?" The cloud-covered moon and no streetlights didn't help as fleeting thoughts of the men on the plane seesawed through her mind. She drew in a quick breath. She couldn't move, glued to the roadway, heart in her throat, eyes probing the dusky gloom.

Nothing. But with Gabi's reaction, something must be out there, and she didn't want to know what—or who.

Gabi rarely barked and didn't now. Nor did she move. Ali glanced at her shadow. She felt spotlighted even in the dim light. Not good. She yanked on the leash, and Gabi responded with a pull toward the other end of the street. *Oh, we're going to have a tug-of-war?* This might not end as the quick, quiet walk she'd hoped for.

"Easy, gal. Come on, let's get back. Right now!" She grabbed Gabi's collar.

A glint of light sparkled from the blackness that seemed to infuriate Gabi. Ali froze, watching.

Nothing more. Maybe she'd been mistaken. A reflection? Of what? Lightning? Thunder sounded in the distance, and the scent of rain permeated the night air, but no way had that small flash been lightning. A lone firefly maybe? She shivered in spite of the warmth of the bulky sweater she wore. The shepherd jumped forward, straining against Ali's iron-fisted hold on her.

"No, Gabi! Heel." The dog obeyed instantly but then reneged, creeping forward. "Not going to work, girl." She grabbed Gabi's collar and steered her down the street, through the front gate toward the house.

A dull whir, then a black shape dove between the veranda and the two of them. The huge bat swooped low and disappeared behind the house. The distance between the gate and the house vaporized. She sat down hard on the cold stone of the porch steps, panting.

She pressed against her dog, breathless. "We'll go inside in a minute." Gabi nudged her cheek and seemed to settle, but the raised fur on her back said otherwise. Ali glanced at the street and rose. "Okay. No more minutes."

Velez twisted the diamond stud at the top of his ear and looked at the lighter clutched in Cardozo's hand. "I think she saw us."

"Go easy, Fernando. What could she see—a dark street and some parked cars?" Cardozo's abrasive voice hardened. "She didn't see anything, so quit worrying."

The muted buzz of a cell phone set on vibrate intervened, but neither of them reacted until Cardozo snapped an order.

"Well, Ferdie, answer it."

Velez grumbled something unintelligible and set his jaw, the veins in his neck standing out like a pipeline. Nevertheless, he picked up the phone from the console between them. "Ola." He paused and straightened. "Yes …" He turned, held the phone out. "It's Kaarding. What do you want me to tell her?"

Cardozo made no move to take the cell.

Velez' face turned a rotten-peach color in the dim light. "She wants to know when we'll be getting back to her with answers."

Cardozo grabbed the phone. "Ola, Nico here." He stilled, listening. "Yes, they're in place and working." Another long pause. Cardozo gritted his teeth, his lips pressed into a tight, thin line beneath his mustache.

"No, not yet. Yes, I'll call you as soon as we get it. Yes … yes!" Skin hot, palms wet, Cardozo crushed his urge to throw the cell phone through the windshield. The woman expected miracles—yesterday.

Seconds later, he happily punched the face of the phone with his thumb, severing the connection. He tossed the cell onto the floor. Need to know or not, Kaarding would have to sit and wait like they had to. This whole thing was going to be slow and cumbersome, and she knew he could do nothing to speed up the process. The witch just wanted to make them squirm.

Cardozo pitched back in his seat, working with the parabolic for a few minutes until he calmed down. He supposed she had a right to be bossy—she did run the show, and she certainly had made waiting worth their while.

He reached into his inside jacket pocket and pulled out the fat Cuban cigar. They still had some time now that the girl was back inside and Velez had finally shut up. Maybe he could enjoy this thing. He did regret flicking the lighter a few minutes ago. He'd gotten careless. No excuse.

He flicked the lighter and took a few pulls on the stogie, savoring the taste, blowing the smoke out the window, coughing in between puffs. Velez glared at him.

Cardozo returned the glare. "Don't say it … don't even think it."

Velez' head spun toward the windshield. He shrugged, mumbling under his breath. "Those things are gonna kill you, Nico."

The cigar did stink, like Kaarding's attitude. Cardozo held the mud-colored U-boat between his thumb and forefinger, thinking of the first call he'd gotten from Madison Kaarding. He'd been amazed how detailed her planning was.

He and Velez had flown from Brazil to Los Angeles to meet with her several weeks ago. He could still see her entering the restaurant like a commander-in-chief. Except for gold jewelry, everything she wore and carried was black, even the pantsuit that fit her like the casing on a Polish sausage. She was good looking and with her red-blonde hair, pale skin, and green eyes, made a lasting impression.

She was shrewd and smart. He tapped cigar ashes outside the window. A research scientist, she'd worked her way to the side of the lead scientist and CEO of Zoran Laboratories. She seemed to be in-the-know about every detail of the formula Lamarque had developed. Ha. Couldn't shut her mouth, bragging about her position in the company and being Lamarque's right arm.

Kaarding, fluent in Portuguese, had called the meeting for the three of them, which had gone well. Outlining what she required, she provided photos, and described how she wanted the job done. She'd detailed things to the point of giving them a travel timetable and information regarding where Lamarque would be working and staying while in Brazil.

Then … she'd suddenly changed her plan. Lamarque's daughter was going with her father to Brazil. They had a new target.

From the way Kaarding spoke of Dr. Lamarque, the woman could have been jealous of the man's success. Except for money, Cardozo wasn't certain what her motivation was. She did have some kind of backing. Where that money came from, he couldn't care less, as long as he got what was coming to him. Right now, he wished Kaarding would back off some and let him do this job without breathing down his neck.

Cardozo watched as Velez' nervous fingers moved from his beard to the diamond spiked through his left ear. Velez' cheap, navy-blue suit drooped, floppy with moisture. He wiped his forehead with a bandana then returned Cardozo's amused stare with a grimace.

"Shouldn't be long now." Cardozo parked the cigar in the ash tray and returned the parabolic to the rear seat.

Five minutes after Cardozo stubbed out his cigar, the two men ducked out of view as headlights flashed in the rearview mirror and a car passed.

The familiar sedan pulled into the drive of the Galante home, and he and Velez watched as the Roberts family was welcomed inside.

"Time to go." Cardozo grabbed the mic, tape recorder, and a large leather case. Velez pulled a stuffed rucksack and two folding chairs from the back seat. They left the car, heading into the dense wooded area opposite the Galante residence.

CHAPTER NINE

Ali was about to pace the grout lines off the tile floor when Cay and her family arrived nearly twenty minutes later than planned Friday evening. Mrs. Galante wasn't fazed by much of anything, including a dinner delay. The woman amazed her.

"So sorry. Traffic was much heavier than usual." Cay grinned at Ali as she dragged her overnight case up the porch steps. "Don't know what I put in this thing when I packed this morning, but it feels like I'm hauling rocks instead of a weekend's worth of clothes."

Ali had been tackled by Scotty and his Star Wars toys before she was able to greet Mr. and Mrs. Roberts and jog down the steps to help Cay. "You're here. That's what counts."

Cay tilted her head toward the case and laughed. "I suppose part of this load *could* be the two books in there you wanted to borrow."

"Heavy reading, huh? Thanks for remembering to bring them." Ali grabbed one of Cay's bags and led the way upstairs. Halfway down the wide hallway, she pushed her bedroom door open wide and stood on the threshold to watch Cay's face.

"*This* is your bedroom? Ooh, it's gorgeous!"

Cay eyed everything from ceiling to floor. Four wood-bladed overhead fans circulated night air coming through partially open windows. Oil paintings hung on every free wall space. Nearby, chairs with ottomans, mahogany end tables, a magazine rack, and reading lamps sat on a green and white area rug. Oak flooring shone between several other large oval rugs.

"So beautiful." She pointed to a vase of dark green ferns and white roses. "I love green and white. I can smell those roses from here."

Cay seemed as impressed as Ali had been when she first saw the room. "Dad's room is even larger than this one. Looking at the house from the street, who'd ever dream it would be this pretty inside?"

Mom would have loved—Stop it.

"I'm loving that you're going to be here for the whole weekend!" Ali motioned to one of the two queen-size beds where delicate mosquito netting cascaded over the canopies. "Just throw your stuff on that bed. We can unpack later. The bathroom is right through there." Ali pointed to the door between two of several tall bookcases dominating one wall.

She shot Cay a mischievous grin and motioned toward the mirrored dresser. "I want you to know you have an entire dresser drawer to yourself. Plus, I left you a three-inch-wide space in the closet."

"Gee, thanks, girl, but I don't even see a closet."

"Right over here." Ali walked over to a large mahogany wardrobe.

Cay shook her head, laughing. "Are you absolutely sure you can spare that much space?" She put her overnighter on the floor and tested the bed. "I won't have any trouble sleeping tonight, this is so comfortable."

One of the French doors opening onto the balcony stood ajar, moving in the light breeze. Ali adjusted the doorstop then sat on the edge of the other bed.

"Seriously, go ahead and spread out. Use as much space as you need. I hope you brought your swimsuit."

"Right in here." Cay tapped her case. "There's no way I'd forget my suit after you called me this morning. So, how in the world did you ever wrangle an invitation from your neighbors to use their pool—their heated indoor pool yet!"

"Easy. Their son, Carlos, drove by and saw me walking Gabi. She's magnetic north to anyone who's never seen an amber-eyed dog with a black bird marking like she has on its forehead. He actually stopped his car and got out to look at her." Ali smoothed her hand over the silky duvet.

"The family is Portuguese, but they speak English. I have an idea you'll like Carlos." Ali chuckled. "There's nothing like having a heated pool *and* a stable full of horses."

Cay's eyes shone with interest. "Sounds like a very interesting guy." She leaned forward, elbows on her knees, palms cupping her chin. "Have you seen them—the horses? Is there a place to ride?"

"He is, not yet, and yes—in that order. Ali got up and went to the chest of drawers. "Listening to Carlos, the place sounds massive. So … behind those imposing walls at the end of this street is a breeding ground for Peruvian *Paso Finos*. They're a family business. Several generations have raised and sold them. They have a training ring, a big stable, and riding trails all over their property."

"Paso Finos? I don't think I've ever heard of them."

"They're gorgeous horses with a fantastic gait. You'll think you're on a rocking horse when you ride one." Ali spritzed cologne inside her elbow and rubbed her nose, trying not to sneeze. She looked at Cay over her shoulder and grinned. "When I told Carlos I had a friend coming to spend the weekend, he asked if we'd like to ride with him. By the time we'd finished talking, he'd suggested we come over and spend the day—to ride, have lunch, and use the pool."

Ali opened a drawer and pulled out a pink sweater. She cocked an eyebrow at Cay. "Still think you'd like to go?"

"Are you kidding? Can't wait to see all that … and meet this Carlos guy. But you need to know I have parents who are stone-age over-protective. They're going to want to meet your terrific neighbors first."

Ali shot her a grin. "Something else we have in common. I could be thirty-one, and Dad would want to meet them, so I'm a step ahead of you—or rather, Carlos is. He's bringing his parents over for a few minutes tonight. They'll be here around nine-thirty. They sound like fascinating people."

Cay rolled the band from her ponytail, letting her dark, red-gold hair bounce around her shoulders. She stood and idly twisted a strand, nodding, her expression thoughtful. "We are going to bring up the hike over dinner first though, aren't we?"

Ali's muffled "Absolutely" came from beneath the sweater she was pulling over her head. "Like I said this morning, I think Dad's more open and ready to talk about the hike tonight, but I'm sure getting a bunch of static about us wanting to go on our own. I'm hoping he only needs to hear how well you know the area before he feels comfortable about the trip."

Ali stood brushing out her hair, studying Cay's reflection. "How about you? Have you had any feedback?"

"We've talked about the hike some. They want to discuss arrangements with your dad, but I don't think we'll run into any problem with them." Cay glanced at the computer on the desk across the room. "Have you had time to get online yet?"

"Yes, I emailed Kane for the first time this morning." Ali freshened her lipstick and went back to sit on the bed. "When I finally had time to get everything set up and checked out, there must have been ten new emails from him." She smiled, more to herself than at Cay. "… says he misses me, at least once in every email, and Chaton is doing fine." She studied the lines in her palms and swallowed hard. If she looked at Cay, she'd come unglued. She missed Kane so much.

The thought of him being three hours behind her in the strange warp of time differences suddenly overwhelmed her. She grabbed the chest of drawers, glad Cay was focused on filing her nails.

The scent of tomatoes, herbs, and olive oil wafted into the room, and Ali looked up as Marco Galante's elfin frame appeared in the open doorway.

"Gina says dinner in five minutes." He cocked his head and put a hand over his heart and smiled at Ali then Cay. "And please call us *Nonno* and

Nonna Galante, Marco and Gina … you will make us very happy. Now, don't be late, lassies."

Ali had to smile at his fond, far-from-Italian, "lassies." And calling themselves Grandfather and Grandmother? Her heart warmed. "Thanks, Mr. Galante, um, Marco. There's no way we'll be late." The aroma already made her stomach growl. He sent her a grin and left.

Cay sniffed the air. "Garlic and fresh bread? I don't think waiting five minutes is an option."

CHAPTER TEN

Lunchtime in downtown Solvang was an explosion of activity with the summer tourists. So was Paula's Pancake House as Kane McKenzie breathed in the mixed aroma of breakfast and lunch. He took off his hat and raked his fingers through his hair as his eyes adjusted, then scanned the popular restaurant for a place to sit. Good. An empty stool at the far end of the lunch counter.

Nearly every table in the place vibrated with the buzz of people talking to each other or typing away on their laptops. In the midst of the noise and familiarity, he missed Ali. They'd grown up often having breakfast or lunch here with their families. Weird to imagine her three hours ahead of him in time and in a foreign country. She stayed on his mind as he strode toward the stool, passing the busy single row of tables lining the wall opposite the counter.

Nice. The last seat was as close to being in a private corner as he'd find. Might be a shade quieter there. Dealing with errands and iffy brakes on his old pickup today, or any day for that matter, was time away from the ranch. But the projects he worked on with his dad could wait. He needed his ride safe, and they needed the concrete mix and extra horse feed.

Whoa. Is that Dr. Kaarding? Kane nearly tripped on his boots, staring, but kept walking. Her back was to him. Couldn't be her. Could it? He took a breath.

Yep. No way to miss that red hair—or the stilettos. A little overdressed for this place. He couldn't recall having seen her in here before. He didn't want to acknowledge her presence—just to eat and go. But could he avoid it? Well, either way, he wasn't leaving.

Chill. No big deal. Everyone needs to eat.

Ali'd said Dr. Kaarding was her dad's associate—close associate. He should have asked Ali what she meant by close. He hadn't liked the woman from the second he'd heard her on the phone at Zoran. Didn't like the way she'd looked him over either.

The woman faced the wall, cell phone in one hand and menu in the other. Most likely taking a lunch break from her work at Zoran.

Kane set his jaw and claimed the stool, plopping his hat on the end of the counter. No mirror across from him. She probably wouldn't see him, maybe wouldn't even hear him order. If he moved a little to the right though ... he could see her reflection in the clear glass of the dessert cooler perched on the island in front of his counter.

Her head bobbed, yelling something into her cell phone. Curiosity planted itself firmly in his mind and had him wondering who she was raising her voice to now. Maybe the same person she'd talked with in Zoran's break room? The waitress interrupted his thoughts.

"Good to see you, Kane, the usual?" She tilted her head. "By yourself today, then?

Kane flashed the fifty-something Ms. Lucy a smile and nodded. "Thanks, Lucy. That's exactly what I want. And, yep, flying solo this afternoon." Another easy grin came his way as she set a mug of hot coffee in front of him and left.

Living in one place all your life had its perks. A refill of coffee and a club sandwich on sourdough toast were in front of him in five minutes. He'd grab a Danish for dessert on the way to get his truck, as soon as they called to let him know the brakes were working again. He said a brief, silent blessing and dug into the thick club.

Kaarding was on and off her phone with three separate calls. She obviously didn't give a rip if anyone heard. Kane shuddered at her acidic tone of voice.

He leaned forward and studied her reflected image behind him again. Kaarding checked her watch then looked toward the entrance. What now?

What now turned out to be a sarcastic welcome.

"Have a seat. Better late than not at all, I guess. Glad you could make it, Mike-the-bug man. This won't take long."

Bug man? Kane kept watching as a tall, balding man appeared in the glass, shook Dr. K's hand and sat beside her. Kane swallowed a bite of his club. None of this was any of his business, but he didn't exactly have a pair of earplugs handy. There was no tuning out what the man said.

"Everything is in place here, and Lucas is taking care of the other location. Things are working with no glitches, so you should have all the info you need when you need it."

Huh? Kane gave an internal shake of his head. That was cryptic. She had *two* places with problems? What kind of bugs did she have? And what kind of bug spray had off and on glitches? The woman made his skin crawl, but what the guy had said was downright strange. He shrugged, maybe he'd missed something with the noise in here. He finished his lunch and reached for his wallet.

Behind him, he heard the rustle and mini-commotion of people leaving the table next to Kaarding's.

Kane turned back in time to see Kaarding's reflection handing "Mike" an envelope as he left the table. Seconds later she was back on her phone with a familiar intensity in her voice.

"Call me tonight, ten o'clock *my* time."

Close to the same orders he'd heard her throw out befo—

The phone in Kane's pocket vibrated. A text. The repair shop had a question about his truck.

And he had plenty of questions about what he'd just seen and heard. With every step he put between he and Kaarding, thoughts of the man, an envelope, and the word "bug" had him suspecting, with no proof, that someone was about to experience an electronic invasion.

CHAPTER ELEVEN

Ali tilted her head as a whisper of soft evening air brushed her cheeks. Gina had opened a few windows and the front door to the comfortable breeze. Sitting in the dining room at the table with both families, Ali couldn't stifle her feelings another second. "Dad, I have enough experience with all the camping and hiking we've done. And Cay grew up in Manaus, she's been into the rain forest many times. There isn't anything she can't handle on a hike. We don't really need anyone else." And, there *was* no one else.

Dinner had been enjoyable until the subject of the hike had taken a stormy twist that threatened to shipwreck their plans. Studying her father's expression, she fingered an earring until her earlobe hurt. Would he *ever* accept that she was just fine with handling things on her own? The rigid lines of his face told her he was no longer listening, and judging from the past, he probably wouldn't be changing his mind. They were a matched pair at this impasse. Stubbornness was a shared trait.

The mirror across the room returned her stony expression, reflecting eyes dulled to thunder-gray and cheek color that matched her sweater. Waves of emptiness surged in her stomach. She didn't like what she saw or the frustrated anger churning her insides as uneasiness crept around the table like a slow-moving tsunami.

Evan Roberts cleared his throat, and his calm voice cracked the murky silence. "Your dad has an extremely valid point, Ali. Accidents happen, and there have been too many cases of abductions in South America lately. I know you'd be careful, but I'm with him on this one." He turned to Cay. "I'm sorry, but unless you find an experienced guide, there won't be a hike."

Evan placed his napkin on the table with such finality that Ali knew the discussion was over. Cay obviously didn't think so.

"I know bad things can happen anytime, Dad, but most of the kidnappings have been in Venezuela and Colombia. Here they mostly happen in big cities like Rio and São Paulo now, not in the Amazon rain forest. We'll be careful. We're not wealthy, and I can't think of any reason someone would want to bother with us."

Ali glanced at her father. In answer to Cay's last-ditch effort, his icy expression, unchanged, held the silent statement "No." Ali sighed. Remembered childhood roadblocks rose in her mind like track hurdles.

A few uncomfortable moments slipped by as tension rose and quietly settled in like sea fog. Nobody said anything as Pam got up to take a restless, squirming Scotty outside. Gina pushed back her chair and began clearing the table. Marco wiped his chin with his napkin several times.

Jo had listened to the entire conversation without getting involved. He caught Cay's eye, then Ali's. Rocking his chair back onto two legs, he folded his hands over his belly, his black mustache nearly touching the sides of his nose as he grinned at them.

Ali opened her mouth.

Ow! She pulled back from a sharp kick against her shin and looked at Cay. Cay's eyes said, "*Wait!*" Ali did exactly that, as Jo lowered his chair and leaned forward, his eyes fixed on her dad.

"I will go with them on hike. Just trust Jo. I make sure they safe. We be fine, the three of us, and we take dog!" He added his last words with a flourish.

Ali's breath left her lips in an incredulous *swoosh.* "You'll go with us?" A hike certainly hadn't been part of his plan. Earlier he'd mentioned he wanted to spend the summer with his sister and had been planning his trip for weeks.

Jo nodded at Cay, and with a big wink, he looked at Ali, his dimple cratering his cheek.

"Won't cost single centavo, either. Free guide." Jo's contagious belly laugh took the pressure off. Ali slapped four fingers across her mouth to keep from bursting into a chuckle and watched a wave of humor ripple around the table. Pam brought Scotty and a fistful of cookies back to his chair. Marco laid his rumpled napkin on the table, and Gina rejoined them, looking relieved.

Jo had immediately turned things around. Ali relaxed as Evan quizzed Jo on whether he really wanted to volunteer for this "mission." He needn't have asked. Jo was so full of ideas for the hike that Ali wondered if he hadn't truly wanted to go with them all along. Everything he said built confidence in both sets of parents they'd be safe.

Jo's memories of Manaus took over the balance of their conversation. He told them of his sister, Maria de Mello, and her husband, along with their six children, living on the Amazon River northwest of the city. The only family he had left, he hadn't visited them for three years. He missed them and spoke of how much he wanted to go back.

Guilt of a new sort crept into Ali's mind. By going with them, Jo would give up precious time with his sister. But he had changed everything, and her appreciation for his offer grew.

Ali's pulse raced, listening to the plans evolve. Everything sounded so doable. Jo had made the journey from the city through the rain forest to his sister's home many times previously, and though they wouldn't be going as far as Maria's, he seemed to look forward to the hike. He sketched out a map of where they would be and an approximate timetable. And, as they continued to talk and plan, a thrill of excitement covered her arms with goose bumps—for them and for Jo. They'd take a full twelve-hour walk into the forest and back, but Jo decided that when they returned to

Manaus, he'd go by river boat to visit his sister. Ali could have hugged him for the way he helped them smooth out so many details.

Thunder sounded in the distance, and the topic changed to the weather. With dinner finished, they moved from the dining room to the veranda for dessert. Ali added the last plate to the dishwasher, then went outside with Cay to rearrange the porch chairs into a semi-circle.

"Looks good. I'll check to see if they need help in the kitchen. Want to come?" Cay opened the screen door to go in.

Ali stood. "You go ahead. I'll be there in a few minutes." Cay must have sensed she yearned for a few minutes to herself.

"Okay. Want me to leave the porch lights on?" She sent Ali a smile.

Ali tilted her head. "Off is good."

Cay went inside and the lights flicked off. Gabi curled up on an old blanket and stayed put, her leash fastened to a hook on a porch post. Ali stooped to stroke the shepherd for a moment then went to the opposite end of the veranda. She leaned against the railing and let the cool night air embrace her. The half-moon and clouds floated in a black backdrop scattered with stars. The beauty of the scene instantly took her back to California, to Kane, to everything she'd left behind. Tears blurred the stars and she pushed away from the rail.

Lights flashed on, and the screen door squawked as if it hadn't seen an oil can in a century. Gina came out carrying a tub of vanilla ice cream and put the container on a table. Cay followed, carrying a huge tray of dishes, spoons, napkins, and hot fudge. Everyone else trooped out behind her.

"Yum." Scotty squealed and climbed up on the chair nearest the ice cream, grabbed a serving spoon and plunged into the frosty dessert before anyone could stop him.

Ali dashed over to rescue him—and the ice cream—from disaster. "Oh, no, you don't. Not yet, you little rascal." She ruffled his hair and tickled him, trying to make him give up the spoon.

Giggling, Scotty's brown eyes twinkled up at her, and he handed over the ice cream-covered spoon. She stuck the spoon into the carton and scooped him up into her arms. Warmth infused her as she hugged him, and his little arms hugged her back. He tucked his head into the curve of her neck, his curls brushing her cheek. She closed her eyes tight, giving him an extra squeeze before she put him down. Her heart filled with the joy of borrowing a little brother for a moment.

"I wuv you, Awi." His whisper sounded sweet as he jumped out of her arms and stood, looking up at her.

"Wuv you too, Scotty." She whispered in return, tousling his hair.

"Does anyone *not* want chocolate fudge on their ice cream?" Pam Roberts asked.

"No one in this family!" Cay picked up two dishes of ice cream, covered with a ladleful of Gina's homemade hot fudge, and handed one to Ali.

"Thanks. But you know neither one of us is going to sleep tonight."

"Sleep? Who needs sleep? We've got way too much to talk about."

"Let's go sit out there." Ali pointed to a bench bathed in porch light and moonlight.

Cay dipped her spoon into the dish of fudge and vanilla as they went to the bench. "You know—I really don't mind having Jo for company on the hike at all. He's a lot of fun to be around, and he knows the rain forest so well."

"I'm thrilled we'll have him with us. Without him, I'm not so sure we'd be going anywhere. Only one problem, though." Ali licked her lips and grinned. "We won't be able to quit laughing."

Cay chuckled. "Hadn't thought of that. It could turn out to be a major problem."

"I also like his idea of taking Gabi with us." Ali nodded toward Gabi on the porch. "She's a good guard dog."

"What are you planning on doing after you get settled in Manaus?" Caylee asked between bites.

"Well, besides our hike, I've been invited to go to the bio center with Dad to observe. Other than that, I loaded the Kindle with books to read. I'll bring the two you brought, and besides my iPhone, Dad gave me a new digital camera before we left. I plan to do a lot of walking and taking photos. What about you? Anything special you'd like to do while you're there, besides the hike and us doing some shopping?"

"Maybe checking out a couple of places I used to go, but we won't have a whole lot of time to do very much."

Terrific segue. Along with the hike, she and her father had talked about another possibility.

"What do you think about staying with us in Manaus for a while instead of only a week for the hike? You could spend most of July and the first or second week of August maybe. That would still give you time to get back to São Paulo and pack for college."

She raced past the possible question she might face about when *she'd* be leaving for the States and college, and continued. "You could show me where you grew up, and if there's time, we could see if we could do some riding at your friends' ranch."

Ali had the distinct sense that Cay wanted to jump up and hug her, but she didn't move. Instead, her eyes misted and she looked down into her bowl of melting ice cream.

Cay blinked back tears as she smiled. "Ali, you have no idea how much that means to me. I've thought about Manaus so much since we moved here. I love the idea of going back there again, but I never dreamed I'd have a chance to spend more than a few days."

Ali held her breath. *This might happen!*

"We'd have plenty of time to canoe and fish, and I can show you some of the places I used to go. I learned to canoe on the Amazon when I was little." Cay paused and added, "I didn't tell you about Miss Tess, but I doubt I'll ever see her again."

"Miss Tess? Who's she? And, by the way ..." Ali narrowed her eyes. "I could teach *you* a thing or two about canoeing and fishing. I learned to do both on Big Bear Lake where we went camping when *I* was little."

"So, you're not such a greenhorn after all." Cay laughed. "And Miss Tess? She's a nutty little wooly monkey with an attitude. They only live seven to ten years. She'd be pretty old by now, if I could even find her. Oh, have you ever heard of pink dolphins?"

"Pink? I didn't know they made them in that color." Ali shook her head. "The only ones I've ever seen are Pacific dolphins."

"We might see some when we get to the river. God's creations never stop amazing me. He created the pinks with an interesting amount of intelligence. The Indians have a lot of legends about them."

Cay's mention of God staked an instant claim on Ali's attention. Cay talked about God as naturally as if he were a close friend. Ali's hand flew to her chest, to cover a twinge—a totally illogical pull on her heart. She shoved back hard against the sensation, barely hearing as Cay continued.

Ali looked up at a sky alive with heavy clouds. Lightning tracked across the navy-blue expanse followed by rumbles of not-so-distant thunder. Not brilliant to be under a tree. The breeze died and the moonlight faded as her eyes were drawn to the shrubbery opposite where they sat. Shadows? Silhouettes? More than bushes moved the rustling, stirring branches. Another flash of something light colored that was *not* lightning. Some wild animal? Ali held her breath, staring at the now still bushes. Nothing more as the wind picked up again.

Cay rose from the bench. "We're in for a storm!"

Another brilliant shard of lightning painted the grounds around them in vivid shades of green as an almost immediate gust of wind and blast of thunder sent them racing to the veranda.

"Run or we're going to get drenched!" Ali grabbed their dishes and didn't look back. Cay raced right beside her, and they reached the porch just as the storm dropped sheets of heavy rain.

Cay dropped into a chair beside Ali. "Won't last long. They never do in the winter."

Her father looked at his watch, then at the dark wet street. "Looks like it's already letting up. Our neighbors should be here anytime."

Matt Lamarque needed a break, some time to think. He glanced at Ali and picked up a stack of empty dishes to take inside. He hadn't seen

Ali this happy since before Ann died. Maybe this hike she was so fixated on taking was a good idea for her, but he couldn't get rid of the dread in his gut.

The quiet hallway was a relief from the chatter outside as he went into the bathroom. The expression of the man in the mirror was grim and bordered on being haggard. He locked the bathroom door and sat on the edge of the tub.

Something was off—no—just about everything was off and not just with him and his irritating gut feelings. The relentless, need-to-know questions of why his formula had failed after its tremendous success continued to plague him.

His concern for Zoran's entire campus after the break-in had increased, even following the heavier security additions. Solvang PD had no suspects, no fingerprints, no nothing to go on. The damage to the rear of the building had been minor and the botanical garden, untouched. But Doc. Jake's desk had been rifled through. That bothered Matt more than anything. Jake's desk was always a mess. No telling what he had in there, so it was no surprise he'd not been of much help in determining whether or not any vital records or information had been taken.

Then there was Madison Kaarding's attitude—for months now. She'd changed. Edgy, more abrasive than usual, taking a lot of time off to travel. Not at all the close teamwork they'd enjoyed in the beginning of her employment three years ago. He shrugged. She'd always been eccentric.

But the call today from Zoran's Security Division reporting attempts to hack their computer systems had left him with the sense of walking the edge of a cliff. This non-physical invasion felt to him more like a diversion, a smoke screen to cover something up, and he couldn't put his finger on what.

Being this close to completing his formula, keeping all the final steps committed to memory, he was vulnerable. Knowing the compound's value and having Ali here with him ... He should send her ho—

Voices in the hall. Muscles tense, nerves on edge, heat rose in his face. Never enough time, even to think.

The whine of a golf cart and voices sounded from the street. "That storm didn't delay the Batistas any. They're right on time." Ali glanced at Cay as the golf cart turned into the Galante's driveway. "Want to walk with me to meet them?"

Minutes later, the intermittent moonlight cast short shadows as a heavyset man stepped from the golf cart. Carlos was right behind him, and the two men helped a slim, stern-looking middle-aged woman. With Carlos and the man on either side of her, the woman strode toward Ali and Cay. She wore riding jodhpurs, a tailored shirt, boots, and carried a riding crop in her hand like a scepter. Ali thought she looked downright regal.

Carlos moved ahead of the older couple and stopped in the driveway in front of Ali, chuckling. Heat rose in Ali's cheeks. He had obviously noticed her studying his mother.

He leaned in close and whispered. "Mother waves that thing around when she talks, so you may have to duck once in a while."

Ali was a little embarrassed he'd read her that easily, and she was glad to see the porch deserted and everyone coming down the steps to greet the Batistas.

Isabele, Paulo, and Carlos Batista stepped up onto the veranda like royalty and dominated the evening with their conversation in between the cookies and coffee Sonia served. Ali listened, fascinated, as Paulo and Jo exchanged histories and life stories unfolded.

Like Jo's grandfather, Carlos's great-grandfather had been one of the *bandeirantes*, brutal slave traders from São Paulo usually born of Indian mothers and Portuguese fathers. They hunted down and sold the Indians of Brazil as slaves. They pushed back the borders of their country and got rich from their discovery of gold, emeralds, and other precious stones.

Paulo Batista suddenly paused and leaned forward, his eyes filled with emotion. The intensity of his expression had Ali on the edge of her own seat anticipating what he was about to tell them.

"My grandfather, may God bless him, was saved from death by a missionary." His dark eyes locked onto Evan's, and his accent thickened as he spoke. "I would not be here to tell you this now if it weren't for Father Benedict." He made the sign of the cross, then sat back about to say more but looked at his wife instead.

God. Again. Ali also moved back from the edge of her seat and followed Paulo's gaze.

Statuesque Isabele Batista frowned, then nodded at her husband and rose from her seat. "But, Paulo, that is a tale for another day." She looked at Ali and Cay and waved her riding crop in a wide arc. "We will expect you in the morning?" She didn't wait for a reply. Raising her arched eyebrows, she abruptly turned to thank the Galantes for the refreshments.

Lightning flashed and thunder rolled through more gathering clouds. Carlos grinned at Ali, then at Cay, as he got up to follow his parents. "We're in for another shower. See you in the morning."

The Roberts left half-an-hour later with an exhausted Scotty asleep on his daddy's shoulder.

Upstairs, Ali stacked two huge pillows against the headboard of her bed and took her shoes off.

Cay plopped down into a lotus-like pose on the bed opposite her. "You know, if we could stretch the hike by a couple of days and spend the night with Jo's sister before we come back, we'd get to see a lot more."

Ali propped herself against the pillow pile with a shake of her head. "I'm not going to try. We've already had to fight just to go out there for a dozen hours. Are you sure you want to ask?" But the idea of spending more time hiking was intriguing. With so much to see and do, she'd have something to take her mind off ... other things.

Silence. She turned to look at Cay.

Cay studied the ceiling fan as she spoke. "Well ... if we did want to go, we'd have to radio Maria from Manaus."

"Radio? She doesn't have a phone?"

"No, not out there, it's way too remote. They use a ham radio to keep in touch with the outside world." Cay grinned and pulled a nail file from her purse. "We'll sort of be inviting ourselves, but I know she'd love having us, and I don't think Jo will object since he planned on going there anyway. He would save time and a boat trip. I've been there before, she has a beautiful place."

Cay paused and pushed her glasses back up on her nose. "And the best part—if he wanted to, Jo could stay, because instead of him having to take us back to Manaus, we could take a boat back. Maria gets most everything delivered by boat. They're always glad to take on paying passengers, and the trip doesn't cost much."

"That could work. What do you think about waiting until after everyone gets used to what we've already decided on, though? There's plenty of time."

"Knowing my parents, you're probably right. Let's see how the weekend goes, and then bring up the subject when they come for me Sunday, or we could save the question until later in the week."

Ali pulled in a deep breath and mentally crossed her fingers. "Sounds good to me either way." A black blanket of negativity wrapped itself around her throat. She couldn't smother Cay's excitement, but what if they pushed too hard? What if her father changed his mind? Things could explode between them. She could simply defy him and …

She bit down on her bottom lip. What if he changed his mind about everything? He'd done so before, and he could just as easily ruin things again. Like the progressive party after her senior prom and the ski trip that didn't happen in her sophomore year of college. Her mother had been there to reason with him, to work out a compromise, to help rescue her plans.

But this time her mother wasn't here. She wasn't coming back. *Not anymore.*

A wave of panic left her trembling. What would happen to her if she didn't take this hike, this walk she depended on to … no, that she *knew,* would heal her? Without the hike, would she ever heal from the pain and guilt of her mother's death? Would the color red always split her heart and drop her onto a trail of never-ending tears?

Saturday morning in the hotel restaurant, Cardozo stopped short of calling their breakfast, brunch, even as late as it was. He tucked a napkin in his belt and washed down a huge bite of butter-covered banana cake with *média*, half black coffee, half milk. Across from him, sleep-deprived Velez was having a hard time finding his mouth with his forkful of *Pão francês*, French roll and ham.

This week, transmitters at the Galante's not only left them with more good intel about the hike, they provided information about the Lamarque woman and her friend's acceptance of an invitation to go horseback riding today at the Batista's. Learning of this had positioned them to get Cassara closer and more involved—a move that would make Kaarding happy.

Even after the transmitter's failure yesterday, and the rain nearly wiping them out last night, the parabolic mic had worked well. They'd been up past midnight phoning in their report to Kaarding and discussing what would happen today.

Lucas Costa had been working closely with Kaarding. As soon as they learned of the bed and breakfast Erick Chance had found for the Lamarques, Lucas had checked out the neighborhood and nearby residents, several of whom ran businesses from their homes. There was no coincidence that another man involved in the project, the wealthy gallery owner/horse enthusiast, Vicente Cassara, would be purchasing a stallion from the Galente's neighbor today.

Cardozo looked at his watch and pulled out his cell phone, setting it on the table. Cassara had probably already seen the women by now, and …

He looked down as his phone vibrated. He shook his head. "Huh. Like we need these. Probably Kaarding's idea." He shoved his phone toward Velez. "Cassara sent photos of the women, Lamarque and the other one."

Velez leaned in to look and raised his eyebrows. "Easy on the eyes, both of them." He pushed back, jaw tensed, and fisted his hands. "They'd just better not give us any trouble."

CHAPTER TWELVE

"Are you ready for this, sleepyhead?" Cay's head poked in under the white waterfall of mosquito netting draped over Ali's bed.

"Of course," Ali mumbled from beneath the covers. She snaked a finger out to push the sheet away from her face. "But it can't be six yet."

"Alarms don't lie." Cay laughed. "Come on, get out of there."

Ali sat up, sniffed, then dropped back down on her pillow. "Do I smell coffee and bacon, or am I dreaming?"

Cay closed her eyes and breathed in. "You're not dreaming. That heavenly smell woke me up right before the alarm went off."

Gabi's wet nose nuzzled Ali's hand. Last night, Gina solved the problem of Gabi and Judge not seeing eye-to-eye on the ownership of the rear grounds and allowed Gabi to stay in Ali's room. "Are you hungry, girl?"

Gabi ignored her and followed Cay through the French doors onto the balcony. "Sorry, pretty amber-eyes, but you won't be going with us today." She reached down to rub the dog's ears.

Cay's voice wafted in on the breeze. "It's gorgeous out here."

"Mm." Ali grumbled her acknowledgment, wishing she had two more hours to sleep. Chocolate and sugar had done their job by keeping them awake and talking last night. Overhead, fans cooled the room as the beginnings of a rose-colored sunrise edged the treetops.

"Sun's coming up!"

"Okay, okay." Ali pushed strands of hair back from her face and smiled at Cay's rare impatience. "I'll be there in a sec."

Showered, the girls pulled on jeans, boots, tee shirts, and sweaters, layering for a chilly ride on the Paso Finos this morning. The canvas bag holding their swimsuits swung from Cay's shoulder as they walked toward the wrought iron gates of the Batista estate. Ali looked over at Cay and smiled. Interesting that Cay had chosen to wear her contacts. She went back and forth between her glasses and contacts, but today, only sunglasses perched on her nose. Carlos, maybe?

"I never imagined I'd be anywhere near a horse for at least a year." Ali's palms were damp with perspiration as they neared the twin towers supporting the tall metal gates. Only weeks into their stay in Brazil, she was minutes away from riding again.

Above the entrance, an arch proclaimed *Batista Casa do Sol* in large black letters. Sand-colored stonework covered the towers while dark green hedges extended out from either side, continuing along even taller cement walls.

"That looks like a security camera." Cay motioned toward a white box on top of the left tower.

Ali looked at a square of audio grillwork built into the stanchion to her right. "And if Carlos doesn't show up on time, we can always use the intercom."

Beyond the gates, trees lined both sides of the wide drive, their branches meeting in a foliage canopy. The driveway meandered away and disappeared around a curve. The surrounding lawns unfurled like green carpet for as far as Ali could see. "I can't see the house. Can you?"

"Not from here. Carlos said he would meet us at eight, right?" Cay checked her watch. "It's pretty close to that now."

A *whir* sounded from the white box. "Well, somebody knows we're here." Ali nudged Cay's arm and pointed to the top of the pillar as the camera adjusted its aim with a slight downward movement. "I think we're being watched."

Cay blocked the sunlight with her hand and looked up, her ponytail nearly reaching her waist. "You're right. They'll probably open the gate or send someone."

"Looks like they already did." Ali gazed at a horse that moved like liquid silk coming toward them. Carlos waved and slowed as he neared the gates that seemed to drift open of their own accord, one to either side. With no reply from Cay, Ali smiled as she noticed Cay's eyes fastened on the horse's handsome rider. Isabele had mentioned his age as they'd talked on the veranda. "He's too old for you," Ali whispered.

"Twenty-six isn't *that* old." Cay tugged at her hair, adjusted her sunglasses, then sent Ali a good-natured scowl.

"Ha. You *were* listening … and that is one beautiful horse."

Carlos rode up and reined in the feisty mare. He seemed to note their appreciative expressions. "So you like her?" He smoothed his hand down the glistening neck of a horse the color of buttermilk and smiled down at them.

Ali put her hand on the horse's neck, unprepared for the familiar scents that instantly painted her thoughts with vivid memories. She drew in a quick breath and closed her eyes. How could a simple scent be so full of reminders—her last ride with Kane, Chaton's nose against her cheek, saddle soap, worn leather, and the sun-warmed plank walls of the barn?

Lightheaded, she concentrated on keeping herself in check. "She is absolutely gorgeous." Her voice trembled, and she continued to stroke the mare's neck until the feeling passed. "I've never seen a horse this color."

"She's a palomino roan. Right, Quista?" Carlos dismounted and stood beside Cay, running a gloved hand through the horse's long, snow-white mane. The compact mare's head rose and fell as if she knew exactly what Carlos had asked her.

"She's beautiful." Cay rubbed the mare's nose. "Can she have a sugar cube? Mrs. Galante gave us a handful before we left."

"Of course, and you'll make a friend for life." Carlos nodded.

Good. Neither Carlos nor Caylee had noticed her lapse of attention. "Is there more to her name?"

Cay grinned and sent her a knowing look.

Carlos nodded. "Yes, she is *Conquista del Dorado Pantera*. It means Conquest of the Golden Panther." He tugged at the wide brim of his hat and continued. "Her sire is *Castillo del Diamante Pantera*, Castle of the Diamond Panther, and her dam is *Conquista del Dorado Rosa*, Conquest of the Golden Rose. We took parts of her parents' names to come up with hers." He turned to Cay and smiled. "Probably more than you ever wanted to know, but interesting, *sim?*"

Cay pulled her ponytail over her shoulder. "Very. But those are all Spanish names. Then they aren't related to the *Mangalarga Marchador* horses?"

Ali raised her eyebrows. Caylee knew about a breed she'd never even heard of?

Carlos' smile widened. "No, and that's why you don't see many Paso Finos around here. Mangalargas are the horse of choice in Brazil. Here, we raise the Pasos to sell locally by word of mouth and on the internet where horse breeders are likely to look for information. We stay rather quiet about them."

Carlos's explanation was interrupted by the loud, *slap-swish* beat of helicopter blades as a small white craft flew low overhead, passed above the stand of trees and disappeared from sight.

"Sounded like it landed somewhere very close." Ali had seen and heard helicopters in the area almost daily, but this one could have landed on someone's estate, the sound was so close.

Carlos pointed down the drive. "There's a helipad behind the house. The copter landed there. We're expecting one of our buyers this morning. He has an appointment to see my father."

An electric golf cart wheeled up behind them and stopped. Carlos chuckled looking at their expressions. "Your transport, ladies. I've no intention of letting you walk all the way to the house. You've already had one walk this morning, and you certainly don't need another."

"Thanks, Carlos—this is great." Ali grabbed a support and swung herself into the cart with Cay following.

"Mother is waiting for us at the house. We'll go there first, then I'll show you around the ranch. You'll get a good look at the helipad when we take the horses out." Carlos vaulted into the saddle and rode Quista beside the golf cart as they moved toward an imposing two-story house.

Palatial is the word. Ali took in the white-stucco structure from the terra cotta barrel-tile roof to the wide verandas and countless windows. Stonework showed everywhere as did white wrought-iron grillwork. A gardener pulled weeds from a flower bed and another man trimmed shrubbery. Both waved as they passed.

An older man came from behind the house and strode toward them. From the way he was dressed, Ali figured he must work with the horses. Carlos signaled the driver to stop the cart and dismounted, leading Quista to the man and handing him the reins. They stood there for a few minutes talking.

Ali could still hear the helicopter's idling engine. She shook her head and glanced at Cay. "First, dive-bombing bats. Now choppers!"

Cay nodded. "At least you can hear the choppers coming, but the bats they have here are another story."

The helicopter's engine noise abruptly ceased and Carlos returned. A uniformed woman emerged from the front entrance, took the canvas bag and helped them from the cart. In the foyer, Carlos dismissed her with instructions to put the bag in a guest room where they'd change later. The servant ascended a wide staircase and vanished into the cavernous house.

The interior reminded Ali of a medieval castle—large and cold and oversized. Furniture, fireplaces, paintings, even the entrance doors looked overpowering. She felt doll-sized and out of place in comparison.

Carlos led them down a hallway. As they were about to pass the open doors of what looked like a sitting room, Ali fisted her hands and cringed. Red. Done in crimson, gold, and black lacquer in an oriental theme, the entire room struck her as odd. The back of her neck tingled, and she paused with a sense of being watched. She glanced upward. Eyes. A gaudy painting of two Chinese Foo dogs stared down from a wall canvas.

Ali turned away, walking fast to catch up. Why did she feel so antsy? Cay didn't exactly appear to be bowled over by the immensity of this place, only quietly curious, taking everything in.

She fell in line behind Cay, hearing the last of a comment Carlos made—something about Chinese art. The disquieting sensation of unease returned and crept down her spine.

Let it go.

Isabele Batista gave them a warm welcome as they entered a homey sunroom at the back of the house. A sense of peace traded places with Ali's edginess when she went to the windowed wall showcasing the rear grounds. Footpaths, fountains, patio gardens and in the distance, a stable filled her vision. To the left and well behind the stable, she saw the white helicopter, its rotors unmoving. A golf cart pulled away from the pad and moved toward the house.

Ali sighed. She needed a few more days like this to feel more like her old self.

CHAPTER THIRTEEN

Dr. Madison Kaarding wheeled her white BMW from her parking spot in front of Zoran and headed toward downtown Solvang. She'd had a nice, quiet morning alone in the lab but not a full work day this Saturday. She loved the autonomy of setting her own hours when Lamarque was away. Leaving the lab early this afternoon would give her time to do some errands, have a leisurely dinner, and get ready for tonight's video call from Dr. Shin—a call she looked forward to. They'd be tying up loose ends as time grew close to the day *the project,* as they'd been calling it, would be completed. Matt Lamarque had made no secret of the news that his reformulation and final evaluations, though still incomplete, were in process.

Shopping finished, she'd done everything she'd intended to do and had a quiet dinner alone. Kaarding shut the garage door, loaded her arms with several shopping bags, and went into the kitchen to put things away. "Enough, Paxton!" The dog insisted on making her trips to the pantry next to impossible. Kaarding huffed and stood, glaring down at the maddening spaniel that wove himself around her ankles, refusing to leave her alone.

And suddenly, neither would the memory of the frail little girl who wrapped her arms tightly around the legs of the man she adored. The man had wrestled her away from him, thrust her into the dark place that smelled of moth balls and winter coats and slammed the door, leaving her to her tears.

Her fingernails bit into her palms, fiery hatred burning through her for the five seconds she allowed it. Even from the distance of all the years that had passed, the event reached through when she was least guarded, and struck. "No!" She tore her mind from the wretched memory, forced herself to stop shaking, to focus.

Kaarding pressed hard against the wall, her lingering emotions dissipating as the phone call she'd made to Cardozo ten minutes ago replayed word-for-word in her head. She'd never trust men. Always excuses. Couldn't trust them to listen, to follow instructions, or to believe she knew what she was doing better than they did. They were unbelievably sloppy in getting anything done on time or in letting her know their progress. Too late, the expensive listening device Cardozo had Lucas plant in the Galante's home had stopped working. Cardozo ended up having to gain vital information using an unreliable plastic mic. She'd call him again later tonight for an update.

She opened a chilled bottle, poured herself a glass of the pale rosé and took several swallows. Unbuttoning her suit jacket, she paced, her stomach churning as the drink hit bottom, Paxton still underfoot. *Blasted dog!*

"Go, get out! Get in your bed!" The dog's tail drooped, and he crept through the arched entry into the hallway. She refilled her glass and followed the toy Cavalier King Charles into the living room, berating herself for having added him to her menagerie. At least her cats stayed out of her way until she chose to hold them. Pax always wanted her attention, climbing all over her, sitting in her lap, interfering with her work at the computer—needy!

She sighed and set her glass on the desk to scoop Bella into her arms. The lights of Solvang began to flicker on as she went to the wide front window. Watching the dark red and orange rays of sunset fade, Bella's warmth and rumbling purr soothed her threadbare nerves.

Calm and in charge. That was the demeanor she wanted to have before she spoke with Feng Shin two hours from now. Her notes were ready, and freshening up for the Skype video call wouldn't take long. She could take some time to relax.

She'd made a good choice moving into Coyote Creek, into this condominium unit. Here she had her safety and fantastic views. With a housekeeper and pet sitter on her payroll and on a regular schedule, she was free to work and play as she pleased.

Kaarding scanned the luxury surrounding her and smiled. Her favorite art originals covered the walls, and all her beautiful furnishings fit in perfectly. She was a smart, attractive widow and wanted to travel. Her dead husband had left her wealthy, and though her position at Zoran paid well, she was about to do much better.

Bella still in her arms, she settled on the antique silver and gray damask sofa, her thoughts turning to the night she'd met Feng Shin and his wife, Lihwa. She'd been dining with a friend at Hadsten House Restaurant in Solvang when Shin had literally bumped into her, spilling red wine on her ivory pantsuit. He'd profusely apologized, insisting on buying her dinner as well as paying for dry cleaning her pantsuit.

Their friendship had an unusual basis. They had something in common. As Kaarding had, both the Shins had doctoral degrees in chemical engineering. The couple were in the area, touring, and while there, Kaarding had invited them to join her for dinner on two other occasions. Through the ensuing months, they'd kept in touch and the project had been born.

She was still in control but had to admit she had a deep sense of being manipulated by something much bigger than the small project that had rooted and taken on a life of its own as the months passed. She'd chosen to ignore that sense. It no longer mattered. Might even have been a relief. Beau jumped up beside her, likely jealous of the attention she was giving his Himalayan twin.

A chill of pure excitement swept through her from the power of the knowledge she had. In a matter of days, she'd be consoling Matt, who would be suffering due to his daughter and her dear friend's horrible disappearance in the Amazon rain forest. She'd be by his side just as she had been after his wife had so tragically died.

Kaarding picked at a piece of lint on the sofa, another smile pulling at her lips. She'd also be by his side to console him when he fell prey to a very clever international scheme. Though to him, for a foreign firm to have beat him to the punch would simply be devastating, when they introduced an extraordinary and effective cure for deadly cancerous tumors.

And then, she'd ease out of his life and her career to do something she'd wanted to do since her college days. She'd spend her summers in Austria, in a chalet she was already set on buying, and half the winter, she'd spend in a villa in Provence in the south of France. The balance of the winter, she'd revel in the warmth of the North Shore of Oahu, in a Waikiki beach penthouse.

Staying in place in her position at the lab for a while, in order not to raise any suspicions, would be a challenge. Kaarding checked her watch wondering if she possessed the patience and tenacity it would take to wait. She rose and went to the desk to nudge the Mac Pro awake. Feng Shin would be initiating their Skype video call any minute.

No people or plans had been mentioned during the call, and Kaarding made notes on certain words that Shin used. Those words were coded topics involving how the project would be handled or how it was progressing. She'd cover each topic in detail, encrypting and emailing them to Shin sometime tomorrow.

The face-to-face live conversation went smoothly as they kept their communication light and friendly. Twice, Lihwa had hovered over Shin's shoulder with additional comments. Although she was fascinating and brilliant, Kaarding thought the woman possessed a ruthless side to her personality. And as their conversation continued, Kaarding had quickly made a note of one statement in particular that Lihwa had made, to think about later.

She had a few more things to do before she could get some sleep. Kaarding turned off the desk lamp, and went into the kitchen, Paxton on her heels ready for his nightly walk.

The dog came back inside full of energy and raced around the kitchen like a brown and white rabbit the second she'd removed the leash. Skidding to a halt, he trotted around her legs in circles, begging for attention. "Stop it, Paxton!" Cute or not, he was going to make her fall if he didn't stop. He'd become a nuisance, getting under her feet and on her nerves.

Again? He'd nearly tripped her! Rage fisted her hands. She gave him a violent shove with the tip of her shoe—hard enough that he yipped in pain as the kick sent him sliding across the marble tile floor. He stood, unsteady, looking at her with his pathetic brown eyes, wagged his tail and returned to lay at her feet. Someone else might feel sorry for him, but she did not.

She opened a container of peanut butter pretzels, poured herself a drink, and sat at the breakfast bar mulling over Lihwa's cold, flat comment and precisely what she meant.

The Shins had no intention of leaving witnesses.

CHAPTER FOURTEEN

"Come, girls, sit down over here." Mrs. Batista motioned to a couch near her in a shaded area. Ali noticed the riding crop "scepter" lay on a table in the corner. This room certainly made up for the coldness of the rest of the house, and she sank into the soft cushions of a loveseat.

Cay sat beside Ali and turned to Carlos. "This is such a comfortable room."

"Thank you." Carlos took an armchair next to his mother, across from Cay.

Mrs. Batista clasped her hands in her lap. "Paulo will stop in for a moment, but he has a business meeting this morning. I hope you don't mind. He'll join us for lunch when his guest leaves."

Ali shook her head. "No, of course not, we don't mind at all."

"Of course not." Cay echoed, nodding.

A woman carrying a tray of glasses and a frost-covered pitcher entered the room. "Luana, please serve the young women." Mrs. Batista motioned toward Ali and continued. "We're glad you could come, and we look forward to having you spend the day with us."

The hum of the electric cart increased and then stopped. Ali glanced up as Paulo Batista and a second man got out. Carlos excused himself and left to greet them. Minutes later, he reentered the room. Behind him, the elder Batista stuck his head in the door, his eyes darting from Ali to Caylee and back. "Welcome. I am sorry I cannot spend time with you this morning," He nodded at his wife. "Vincent Castle has arrived. I should not be long."

Mrs. Batista smiled. "I trust all will go well, Paulo. Perhaps we will see you at lunch."

Carlos returned to his seat. "Father will sell one of the stallions today. In addition to owning an art gallery in São Paulo, the buyer breeds horses and has decided to purchase a Paso Fino to pair with one of his Mangalarga mares."

"Enough horse talk, Carlos." Isabele Batista raised an eyebrow at him.

Carlos smiled. His dark eyes glinted as he ignored the reprimand, eyeing first Cay, then Ali. "Would you like to see the stable?"

Ha! As if he had to ask. He already knew their answer.

His mother rose and picked up her riding crop from the corner table. "I'll accompany you to the stable, but you must ride by yourselves; I have other things to attend to." She turned to Carlos. "Lunch will be served in the dining room at one o'clock. You must bring them back early enough so they have time to freshen up."

Ali's eyebrows lifted. She wouldn't have been anywhere near as diplomatic and patient. If Carlos was annoyed with his mother's commands, he didn't let on.

On their way to the stable, Mrs. Batista gave them a walking lecture on the casa's history, then left to return to the house. The double doors to the stable were open, and Carlos ushered Cay ahead, pointing down a wide passageway. Ali paused on the threshold, closed her eyes, and breathed in the familiar scents. The place bustled with activity, and as they walked between the stalls, she yearned to ride again.

Cay waved her arm in a wide arc. "This place is huge."

Carlos grinned, his pride obvious. "It is big. Fifty-five regular stalls and eight double birthing stalls in a separate mare barn."

"That's the heated wash bay." He motioned to a large open area where several horses stood being groomed. "And over there is the indoor arena. No matter what the weather, training and exercise can continue."

Ali half-listened to Carlos's monologue as he and Cay passed a tack room devoted to show leather. Ali stopped and checked out the array.

"Ricardo," Carlos called to a stable hand. The man, about to toss a pitchfork full of straw, came toward them instead. "Ricardo, can you take us to see our newest addition?"

Carlos turned to them. "Born this morning." They followed Ricardo to the mare barn and into a roomy stall at the far end that housed a mare and her foal.

"Oh, he's beautiful." Ali's heart warmed as she watched the foal nurse. She glanced back at Carlos as Ricardo left. "May I go to him?"

"Of course, go ahead." Carlos smiled his consent. "Donia is a gentle *mamae*; she will not object." Ali moved slowly toward the mother and baby with quiet words of admiration. She stroked the mare's nose and spoke to her, then slid her hand down the horse's side. The foal stopped nursing and tossed his head but didn't back away. She held out an open hand to him and scratched gently between his ears. He lowered his head, allowing her touch for a moment before scampering behind his mother. Ali couldn't help laughing as big, curious brown eyes peered at her from behind the mare's shiny rump.

Ali rejoined Cay and Carlos. "He's such a handsome little guy."

Ricardo brought three Paso Finos to the barn door.

"Ah, you brought the best, Ricardo. Thank you. I'll take over from here." Portly Ricardo bared stained teeth in a ready grin and handed Carlos three sets of reins.

"Are you ready for a ride?" Carlos gave Ali the reins of a spirited roan mare and passed Caylee the reins of a gelding whose gleaming chestnut coat matched her hair.

Carlos showed off the outdoor arenas as they rode toward the wooded area behind the stable, and Ali was instantly at one with her horse's rolling gait. As they passed the helipad, she noticed landing lights around the perimeter of the asphalt circle where the helicopter sat like a calm white dove in the center.

"You use the helipad at night too?" She motioned to the lights.

"Yes, often. The helo is our main means of transport into the city lately."

Caylee's gaze stayed on the helicopter. "Have you had the helo long?"

"About a year. Most of the families living outside São Paulo have them now. With so many pads on the tops of buildings in the city, we can stay out of the constant snarl of traffic. We do keep a car in town to make transportation easier when we land there though."

Cay pushed at her sunglasses. "The 'copter is a lot smaller than it looks in the air."

"Yes, very compact. With the rotor blades and body made of composites, the machine is amazing."

"Do you fly?" Ali asked.

"Not yet. Right now my father has a pilot, but I will fly him when I finish training and get my license in a year or so." He looked at Cay. "I will take you both up sometime if you would like to go."

"We'd love that," Cay said with a vigorous nod in Ali's direction.

Ali grinned at her. "Sounds like fun."

An hour later, walking back to the house, Carlos showered them with compliments on their horsemanship. Paulo Batista and his client, who apparently liked to use his cell phone camera, shortened the distance between them in the golf cart piloted by an expressionless driver.

A chill rippled down Ali's arms, her fingernails drilled into her palms as the cart slowed and circled around them. Batista hadn't bothered to acknowledge them, but his client lowered the cell phone aimed in her direction and fastened his eyes on hers as they passed—an all too familiar invasive gaze that only distance and her stumble broke.

"Are you all right?" Carlos sent her a quizzical smile, and she nodded.

"Good," he said. "Apparently, my father will be with us for lunch. They must have finished their transactions."

Transactions? She'd like to transact an interrogation! Why would what's-his-name-Castle stare at her like that? Worse, why hadn't she looked away?

CHAPTER FIFTEEN

On the tenth floor of a twenty-eight-floor high-rise apartment building in São Paulo, Nico Cardozo sat, glass in his hand, stunned. He listened, staring at the man who strongly resembled a slightly taller Nicolas Cage, pacing the floor across from him.

A helicopter? I'm risking my skin doing this just to buy a weapon?

"… not my choice. Kaarding wants it done her way, and I've got no beef with that. I'm not transacting business here in town. Not this kind of business," the man continued.

Cardozo stiffened in the recliner and stopped listening. Passenger jets were one thing but being airborne, at night, in a tin can with a pinwheel on top had Cardozo's hands damp and his eye twitching. He didn't have time for this. He was here to pick up a gun not joy ride in a chopper.

He'd gotten here early to pick up the package Kaarding had arranged for with this guy, Lucas Costa, her contact in Brazil. Costa had done the job of placing the listening devices but taking Cardozo for a night ride in a helo … never had been mentioned.

He sucked in a breath, shook his head and glared at Costa. "A pilot. So, you're a pilot. Not interested. What's wrong with hailing a taxi?" The growl of his own voice echoed in his ears. Sweat crept around his collar, formed on the nape of his neck.

Costa's head swiveled toward Cardozo. He stopped pacing, blue eyes narrowed, darkened, pinned Cardozo into the brown leather recliner, his words slow, monotone and deliberate. "Taxis are why I keep a chopper on the roof of this place. *I'm* not interested in spending my time in traffic. Flying will take fifteen minutes each way instead of an hour plus—if we're lucky. Kaarding's stamp of approval is on this and if you want to make the purchase, we do the job my way, or you can—"

Cardozo glanced at the dead-white knuckles on both Costa's suddenly fisted hands. "Okay, okay. I got your point. Let's get this done. What is it, 'wheels up in ten' or skids up? Stop wasting time."

Cardozo downed the few drops left of his drink, pounded his glass down on the table beside him, and rose. He might as well get this over with. He'd decided on a Ruger, needed to have one in his hands long before the day the Lamarque woman and her friend hit the trail. And this 'copter ride looked like the only way out.

Cardozo's head pounded as he stepped from the rooftop elevator and faced his demons. The sleek four-passenger Squirrel Eurocopter sitting on the well-lit helipad reminded him of the white beluga whale he'd seen at Sea World. His stomach lurched. *Nothing like being in the belly of a whale.*

Costa checked Cardozo's seatbelt and handed him a headset. "Cuts the noise if we need to talk. Put them on."

Cardoza donned the headset and forced himself to focus on the money he'd soon be stashing in his off-shore account. And—if he didn't die in this flying pod—plans on how he'd finish the job.

Lamarque and his daughter were flying into Manaus on Thursday. The next day, he and Velez would take the private jet Kaarding had chartered for them into a smaller airport near Manaus. At least he didn't have to put up with Velez's constant spew of complaints tonight. Velez was good with most of the tech stuff and was picking up the satellite phone they'd take with them and getting instructions on using it. The phone was a critical part of getting the ransom demands communicated from where they'd be on the Amazon river to Lamarque in Manaus. They'd meet later at the hotel to finalize plans on how they'd handle the two women and convince Lamarque's daughter to pass on their demands to her father. Putting together the details of what they wanted her father to do was something Cardozo had already committed to paper.

Things were moving fast. They were scheduled to meet with the native guide in Manaus—canoes had to be rented and gear bought. The guide had plans in place for the time they'd be on the river, but they'd only have a week to perfect all the other details.

Twenty-five minutes later, Costa set the helo down in a deserted landing field and shut down the engine. The circle of lights around the makeshift helipad flicked out and Costa motioned Cardozo to follow him toward a dark-colored SUV with its headlights on. Cardozo's nerves were on fire. He'd do a lot better by himself than let this jerk issue orders. But he didn't know these people. He had no choice but to do what he was told if he wanted to get through this without getting himself killed.

"Shorty speaks English, but his bodyguard speaks with his Glock 19. So stay cool. Follow my lead. I'll do the talking." Costa moved toward the headlights and the two men standing in shadow. "You know what you want. Look over what he shows you, keep your mouth shut, and pay him when he and I come to terms."

The short fat man shoved a stainless-steel Ruger revolver toward Cardozo. "You won't find a better deal anywhere in Brazil. It's loaded and ready to fire. Give it a try."

Cardozo lifted the gun from the piece of plush carpet on the hood of the SUV. The weapon fit his hand like a glove. Felt good. A comfortable matchup, this killing device and him. He turned to the row of empty bottles serving as targets, took aim, and fired four bullets. Four bottles shattered.

With the explosion of the first shot, Cardozo's mind exploded with slow motion images of the Lamarque woman, bullets thudding into her upper left torso sending her twisting backward ...

Smiling at his pilot, Cardozo turned back to the seller and 'the hulk' beside him, and sent him a slow nod. Then, in quick succession, he fired the two remaining shots.

CHAPTER SIXTEEN

Monday. Again. Ali sat up in bed, lifted the netting and gauged the day outside the French doors. Sunny, beautiful, probably cold. And all of that could just stay out there. She flopped back, twisting between the sheets, like her mind—restless after a bad dream—irritable, and with zero desire to climb out of bed. Three days to go before she and her father flew to Manaus.

Cay had left yesterday afternoon, and Ali's talk with her father last night about their idea to stretch the hike and spend time at Maria's crashed. She expected a negative response and got one. She'd pushed too hard—they both had. She should have known not to ask for more time out of his sight and protection this soon after losing her mother. She misread his good mood and ran headfirst into the "no" zone. In a way, she understood. She'd live with his decision. As long as she lived at home, she'd deal with boundaries and the mixed emotions, but she did *not* have to like the restrictions.

Too late to phone Cay to let her know, she'd gone upstairs yearning to feel Kane's nearness and hear his calm voice. She curled up with her iPhone and poured her heart out into a long email to him.

As she was finished with nearly all her packing, there didn't seem to be much reason to get out of bed. She shut her eyes against the gold shafts of sunlight that sailed through the door glass and sifted through the mosquito net. The day was shaping up to be a long, boring day alone.

Get up, lazybones. Instead, she added a mental note to her things-to-do list. *Call Cay after breakfast.* Maybe Cay would have another idea to get her father to agree to the additional days. They still had time. Cay and Jo would fly to Manaus on July 14th, and Cay would stay through the first week of August.

She untwisted from the sheets, threw on her robe, and opened the balcony doors. The whining *whir* of a golf cart sounded from the street. Much earlier, her father had knocked, told her to have a good day and blown her a kiss. One of the Batista's staff had arrived to pick him up. Paulo Batista had business in town, and as her father also had a meeting scheduled in São Paulo, he'd offered to take him in the helo.

She shaded her eyes and waved at her father as he left. Two chirpy birds landed on the balcony railing where she'd laid sunflower seeds last night. She watched them feast until memories of her mother filling bird feeders in early morning California sunshine clutched at her heart. She buried her face in her hands, unmoving as the noise of the cart faded into the distance.

Long minutes passed before the hum of the helicopter sounded low over the house and headed toward the city. Beside her, Gabi nudged at her leg. Ali sighed and sat on the floor to pet her, glad the Galantes hadn't objected to having Gabi in the house.

"You didn't sleep much either, huh, girl?" Gabi's amber eyes studied Ali, her tail flopping against the plush carpet.

"Telephone for you, Miss Ali," Sonia announced through the closed bedroom door. The old Princess phone on the bedside table hadn't rung since she'd turned off the ringer the day they arrived. One loud jangle of the phone, and one noisy ring had been enough.

"Thanks, Sonia. I'll pick it up in here." Ali reached to answer. "Hello?"

Cay dove headfirst into Ali's lethargic morning as Ali listened. "You're kidding. They think alike. Dad said the same thing." A disillusioned pause.

"There's no way, then." Ali closed her eyes. They would not be seeing Maria. The fire of a good idea died. She slid off the side of the bed and stood.

Cay was saying something about being thankful for what they had now. Ali couldn't think of a single positive word except … She grinned into the receiver. "Oh, by the way, Dad came up with another small requirement." She listened to Cay groan, and laughed. "This time it's a good thing. When we get to Manaus, he's leasing a satellite phone for us to take—just in case. Really, it's not a bad idea."

Cay agreed, then made Ali's day when she suggested they go into São Paulo to shop for hiking shoes. Ali wanted to buy a pair for the hike but had planned to find them in Manaus.

"Great idea. Gives me time to break them in before the hike." Ali paced beside the bed as their conversation colored a sunnier side to her morning.

"Jo's driving. We'll pick you up in about an hour."

Ali hung up and grabbed Gabi's leash. "Come on, girl. Let's hit the backyard. If you want to take a walk, it's now or never. I need coffee!"

Jo had several errands in São Paulo, and they planned to meet for a late lunch. He nosed the car in close to the busy sidewalk to let Ali and Cay out.

"Okay, see you at two-thirty at Gero's?" Jo pointed over his shoulder down the avenue at a colorful blur of buildings.

Ali peered down the street. "Sounds okay to me, but what is Gero's?"

Cay laughed "You'll like it. Great food. It's a really cool place not far from the boot shop we want to check out."

"We'll be there, Jo." Caylee shut the car door.

Jo moved out into the line of traffic but not before he was nearly sideswiped by the second midnight blue Vector Ali'd seen since they'd left the Galantes. She sighed, relieved there was no accident, and she'd been right. Blue Vectors *were* a common car here.

She looked at the lineup of stores. "Looks like we're about to work up an appetite. So where do we start?"

Cay motioned to a store. "Right over there, and it doesn't look too busy."

The shop's display window held a dozen or more pairs of boots and hiking shoes in several styles. Cay pointed to a pair of hiking shoes. "We're not going to have to look far. If I'm right, those are exactly what you need."

The store sold every type of hiking and riding shoe and boot imaginable. Ali drew in a breath, relishing the rich scent of tanned leather as they walked in. She'd left her ratty attitude in her bedroom, and the cup of strong, honey-sweet tea Sonia handed her at breakfast hadn't hurt either. With every sip, she'd promised herself nothing was going to ruin this day with Cay and Jo.

"What do you think about these?" Cay picked up a pair of two-tone gray and teal ankle boots. "Except for being a whole lot newer, these are a lot like mine. Comfortable, and they should get you through our jungle walk and more."

"How much are they?"

"Expensive, but on sale, and they're worth every penny." Cay read the price aloud. "Waterproof, good traction, the works."

"They look solid. Kane likes to hike, so I can use them back home too."

Cay spoke to an enthusiastic sales clerk in Portuguese, and twenty minutes later, they were out the door with a boot-and-sock-filled shopping bag.

Cay pointed at the bag. "Those won't even need breaking in. Mine didn't either."

The balance of their time as they worked their way toward the restaurant morphed into a leisurely wandering walk and talk of the things they needed for the hike. Fascinated, walking in and sometimes through the various shops had Ali dragging her feet … until she came to a complete stop in front of a larger shop. She couldn't read the black Portuguese lettering at the top of the sign above the door and barely glanced at the

English translation below. The words beneath them both interested her far more:

Native Brazilian and Rare Asian
Art and Sculpture

A mental composite of Paulo Batista's client and a São Paulo art gallery filled her mind.

Probably not his gallery.

Nothing really indicated this shop was anything special—no reason to connect the two. She turned her attention to a sculpted figure in the store window.

"Cay, take a look at this … um … *thing* in the window." A masculine shape with slanted, bulging eyes gaped back at her through the glass. Red-orange lips, curled upward in a grotesque grin. The figure of a man-monster with its arms forever raised above his head in triumph. The body of an enemy lay suffering beneath the conqueror's foot slammed across his belly.

Cay grimaced. "*Thing* is right. It's hideous."

"Nope." Ali grinned at her. "It's ancient Chinese art."

"Art? Should I be impressed?" Cay stooped to take a closer look. "How can you be so sure it's ancient and Chinese?"

"The piece is scary enough to give you nightmares for one thing. But last year, I wrote an essay on Chinese culture. When I was researching, I saw a photo online that could be an exact double for this … well, art form. The caption said the statue was photographed in the Museum of Xinjiang, so this one's probably a copy."

She paused and leaned closer to the window to look past the glass into the shop. "You know, I don't think this is any ordinary store. Much more like an art gallery. Let's go in. They've got some interesting stuff in there—I'd sure like to look around."

Cay checked her watch. "We could. We still have time."

Long shadows of late afternoon stretched across Erick Chance's desk in his office at the Center of Biotechnology of the Amazon in Manaus. He studied the three reports on his desk—shipping information regarding the three new specimens ready to send to Zoran for testing. His desk phone buzzed, yanking him away from his number-crunching, indicating a call on a dedicated line that he felt hadn't been very dedicated or secure lately. The line was rarely used since he and Matt had decided to do all their communicating via encrypted email when discussing their business activities. Maybe Erick was getting paranoid, but what they worked on at Zoran and the successes and growth they were experiencing had become much bigger than the existing security.

Security was one topic they'd talked of when they'd had lunch together at a little dive around the corner from the bio centre yesterday. He'd encouraged Matt to plug the gaps in all areas of his company—fast, especially after Matt let him know about the attempted hack of the company's computer systems.

Erick picked up the phone on the fourth buzz. "Erick Chance here …

"Erick! So good to hear your voice. It's been a long time. I hear you'll be returning to Solvang soon! Wonderful news. I hope things are going well for you there. We miss you here."

He blinked and swallowed. Madison Kaarding. Nothing wrong with the woman's "hello," but she hadn't bothered to breathe or let him say a word—and if he was supposed to be returning home soon, it was news to him. She'd caught him off guard, at a complete loss for words. Except for inner office calls, she'd rarely called him when he was in the States, or here.

"Erick?"

"Yeah, I'm here, just um, ah, it's good to hear from you, Maddi. How have you been?"

"Ohhh, I apologize, I've called you at a bad time."

Apology? Nope, not going there. And as for the news update, was she fishing for info? She'd never cared where in the world he was before. "No, no, your timing is fine. As a matter of fact, I've been thinking about you. I understand you've been doing some traveling. You should've come to see me while you were in São Paulo, you were so close."

Silence.

Then she didn't know he knew about her trip to Brazil last month. Or maybe she was trying to recall *which* trip. Amazing. But word did get around.

"Oh. Yes, I did do a little personal business there last month, just taking a few vacation days off. Well, I'm calling because I wanted to give you a personal invitation."

Erick's interest spiked. Invitation for what? The only time they saw each other was either at Zoran, conferences, or during holiday business gatherings. He'd been happy with no more than that amount of frequency, but he listened as she continued.

"I'm hosting a private dinner party at my home to celebrate our success! I'll text you the details when we're certain of when the announcement will come. I'll schedule the party for the following weekend. You and Susan should have plenty of time to firm up travel plans. What do you think?"

Erick's leather desk chair creaked as he rocked back and took a breath. Ha! He knew what Susan would think, but he was curious since Maddi never had been terribly social. At least she'd been smart enough not to mention the formula on the non-secure phone line. He told her he'd let her know if they'd be available to attend—after she'd set the date. They chatted a while longer and hung up.

The whole conversation left him interrupted and thinking about how much he'd prefer she wasn't associated with Zoran at all. He'd been uncomfortable around her since Matt had taken her on to work with him three years ago. Erick did not trust her.

Ali pushed the door open and moved through the entranceway of the gallery. Every step propelled her into another world that took her breath away and filled her nose with the scent of exotic spices. The aroma permeated the air as if incense was burned in every corner. The door shut behind them, silencing the busyness of outside. Beside her, Cay whispered "Wow." That strange, tingling sensation covered Ali's arms as her eyes adjusted to the dim interior spoke of mystery.

No customers or anxious sales person were anywhere in sight. Ali eyed the walls where drawings and paintings hung bathed in indirect lighting and looked as if they were of recent vintage. Hand-woven baskets sat randomly placed among the Chinese works.

Drawn deeper into the large room, Ali noticed a dozen or more small spotlights that punched bright holes into the dusky atmosphere. Beneath the spotlights, each glass case featured a single piece of art. Among the pieces, a bronze Buddha, a rose quartz jar, a carved wood cup, and a porcelain hawk perched on a rock, and ... two familiar ceramic Foo dogs. All the art pieces sat on seats of red velvet inside their transparent glass prisons.

Ali pointed to the Foo dogs. "Do they remind you of something you've seen recently?"

Cay had paused several feet away beside one of the glass cases. "Mm—they look identical to the dogs in the painting we saw at the Batista's. The painter could have used them as models."

In the center of the gallery, Ali fixed her attention on the tiny statue of a gold horse, not quite two inches high. Spotlighted, but not under glass, the horse was in a full rear, front hooves beating the air. Information was printed on a small folded placard, one side in Portuguese and the other side in English. Ali read:

> **Chinese Stallion $4550.00**
> **Miniature sculpture of a rearing horse**
> **18k gold Height 1 15/16**

So, there were items for sale, if you could afford the prices. She turned to speak to Cay, but Caylee was looking at the bronze statue of a seated Buddha. Ali joined her and studied the ornately dressed figure. The face, with tightly shut eyes, held a serene expression and a meditative smile.

Cay touched the simple cross on her necklace. "How great to know and love a God who created and loves us and is alive forever."

Listening, Ali let Cay's words settle into the back of her mind and stay there. Maybe she'd deal with the whirl of negativity she felt later. *Time for a change of subject.*

"A weird combination—Chinese and Brazilian—these two cultures under the same roof."

"True." Cay's gaze moved from floor to ceiling at the variety of works. "A whole lot of the Brazilian art in this place looks like what I've seen in the Museum of Modern Art right here in São Paulo."

A rustle and the tinkle of beads came from a doorway in the far wall, and an Asian woman, petite and exquisitely dressed, emerged. Her jet-black hair gracefully covered most of her forehead and swept back into a cluster of curls at the nape of her neck. With perfect posture, she appeared to glide toward them.

She wore a *cheongsam*, a slim, ankle-length dress, bright blue with bursts of white flowers that accented her slim waist. The woman studied them with piercing dark eyes as she neared, but there was a complete lack of any expression of welcome on her face.

Ali couldn't stop staring, intrigued with everything about the place, including this woman whose eyes trailed down Ali from head to toe. Ali set the awkward shopping bag on the floor beside her. Really? She'd decided to wear these grungy blue jeans and slouchy navy Los Angeles Rams sweatshirt today?

"May I help you?" The woman spoke English with a heavy Asian accent.

Cay took a step forward. "No, but thank you. I hope you don't mind. We were only looking around."

"It is okay." The woman's gaze drifted from Cay's gold cross to the bronze Buddha, then up at Cay. With a wry smile, her tone thick with sarcasm, she added, "You like Buddha? He from Ming Dynasty. Good condition. Only thirty-five hundred American dolla. Better to put Buddha in your house."

Witch! Ali stiffened and opened her mouth to defend Cay. Cay stopped her with the touch of her hand on Ali's arm and smiled at the woman, her expression as gentle as ... Ali sucked in a breath. *Gentle? How could Cay respond like that?*

Cay locked her aquamarine eyes onto the woman's black ones, her words slow and clear. "Buddha is like my cross, a symbol to remind me to pray. Buddha lived and died and is dead forever ..."

Cay's voice sounded soft yet firm. Ali took a step back, watching as warmth rose in her face. *Cay! How can you speak to her that way?*

Cay didn't hesitate.

"... but the God I worship is alive, and he sent his only son, Jesus, to be born on earth. God's son not only lived, he gave up his life and died—"

Cay paused, and in that split second the woman's almond-shaped eyes narrowed, her expression charged with frustration, sorrow, and crushing anger as she hurled word-shaped daggers at Cay.

"Ha! Same as Buddha! Husband die. Death always end of things."

"For some, yes. But something more happened." Caylee continued to look into the woman's eyes, never letting go of her gaze, speaking as if each word told a story. "God's son came alive again, because evil and death could not hold him. He is still alive, and if you believe in him and ask him, he has a place for you to be with him also, so you will be able to live with him in paradise—forever." Cay reached out her hand and touched the woman's hand.

Caylee ... But Ali couldn't move or speak as she watched.

Cay's voice remained even and sincere. "He loves you ... and I love you too."

The woman stared at Cay for long seconds before her face crumbled, drained of belligerence, and her dark eyes brimmed with tears.

Ali's hand found the side of a display, her knees unsteady as she held her breath. She'd been padlocked into a moment of time where only the three of them existed. Yet there was something else. She rubbed her arms, arms cool even beneath the long sleeves of the sweatshirt. And inside, something deep within her shifted, radiated a sense of comforting warmth.

The fragrant air inside the shop enveloped Ali, seemed to hold her, steady her. The Asian woman's eyes blurred, and through tears that spoke before the woman did, Ali saw a spark of longing, of hope, of a yearning to believe in something more. Cocooned within the moments of silence, Ali absorbed the woman's unspoken emotions and glimpsed a clear, unsettling reflection of herself.

"You ... go." The woman's voice cracked, its edginess softening as she nodded and brought her hands up to cover her face. As if deliberately turning her back on the unmoving Buddha, she walked away.

Crystal. She was crystal. Fragile. Fearful she might shatter at any sound, her hands trembled. Ali looked at Cay not knowing what to say or do. Cay sent her a reassuring nod as she turned toward the door. Ali picked up the shopping bag and followed.

Cay paused in the entrance, put a hand on each side of the doorway, and lowered her head for a few seconds.

Ali's heart stirred, warmed. Anywhere else, any other time, she would have been embarrassed at such an obvious display of praying in a public place. Here and now, admiration rose that Cay prayed without the slightest hint of concern for what she looked like to anyone else.

They stepped back out on the street, blinking hard in the sunny brilliance of daylight. "Cay—what just happened in there?"

Cay turned to her as they walked toward Gero's, "God touched her heart and spoke to her spirit … and she answered."

Ali looked over to reply and instead looked into the face of coincidence as a third blue Vector sedan crawled by the shop like the viper the vehicle had become to her.

CHAPTER SEVENTEEN

No way was she able to sleep. Gabi trailed her as Ali left her bedroom behind. She moved quietly down the stairs and flopped onto the glider, alone on the Galantes' veranda.

Stars shone overhead. She drew her knees up under her chin and snugged her lightweight robe around her. Still, it wasn't quite warm enough against the cool night air. Winter in July in Brazil simply didn't jibe. Her thoughts kept returning to what happened in the art gallery, even as she fought to keep the scene out of her mind. None of what happened could possibly mean anything to her. Ali shivered and folded her arms close to her body.

The sweetness of Kane's last kiss and the heart-wrenching sense of his closeness flooded her thoughts. What did the future hold for them? Thinking of him had kept her awake countless nights. So had making yet another change—for better or for worse—the move to Manaus.

She patted the seat beside her. "Up, Gabi." The shepherd willingly jumped to the comfort of the glider and put her head in Ali's lap. She wound her arms around Gabi's warmth and nearness. At least her father was more at ease than she'd seen him in the months since her mother died. After three intense business meetings in São Paulo, he'd become wrapped up in his work again. His life and attention seemed to spiral away from Ali, the time he spent with her was less and less.

Loneliness pressed in trying to surround her, along with her struggle of hope against the descending depression. The relief that her father was no longer inconsolable only left her confused about how she fit in. Maybe she didn't anymore.

In less than two weeks, the Galantes had become more like doting grandparents than temporary landlords. With Gina's cooking, Ali regained a few lost pounds. She even fit into her favorite jeans again. And Marco's endearing way of teaching the art of caring for roses would be with her forever. Saying goodbye to them tomorrow would be hard. After São Paulo, what would Manaus be like?

Ali laid her hand on the cold, wooden arm of the swing and gazed up at the night sky. Would the hike ever really materialize? So many times her plans had failed and disappointed. She licked a salty tear from the side of her mouth and wiped her eyes with a sleeve. Tears felt strange against, meandering down her cheeks. She hadn't cried since she'd left California.

Why did life seem so empty?

She shook her head, trying to remember what her mother used to say. "With God all things are possible." How could that be when God couldn't even keep her mother from dying? Something pushed gently at the edge of her mind, and she pushed back, trying to ignore the annoying nudge and whatever it meant. She wiped her cheek with a fist.

I handled spring in California, and I'll handle winter in Brazil.

"Come on, Gabi. Back to bed." Climbing the stairs with Gabi at her heels, she didn't really believe sleep would come. But sleep did, in fitful swatches of time, filled with confusing dreams and replays of the art gallery encounter. She awakened more than once, restless and questioning.

She *was* right. Goodbye was hard. The Galante's generous invitation to stay with them again for a few days on their way back to California helped lessen the sadness of leaving.

The drive through São Paulo to the airport was hectic but uneventful. Flashbacks of businessmen and blue sedans came and went. Except for asking Cay if she'd seen the car, Ali was glad she'd decided not to mention any of what had happened to anyone else. She'd simply been exhausted, frazzled. She would be glad to relax and settle into the house in Manaus, go to the bio center with her father, and get ready for the hike.

The flight from São Paulo to the Eduardo Gomes Airport in Manaus had been bumpy and warm and uncomfortable. The two airports were a dramatic contrast. Manaus's terminal was a tiny smudge on the landscape compared to the sprawling Guarulhos International.

Erick Chance had forewarned them about how winter weather in São Paulo differed from the hot, humid climate of Manaus in central Brazil. They'd dressed in light clothing and carried sweaters. Great advice, except the arrival and departure halls in the terminal were air-conditioned. In spite of her sweater, she shivered but outside in the melting heat couldn't wait to take it off.

Jo had asked his good friend, Jaco Chavos, to meet and drive them to the house her father rented in an upscale suburb of Manaus. Jaco's old pickup was about as reliable as his broken English. But the truck with its covered bed held everything, including Gabi. As they bounced through town, Ali gained a new appreciation for comfortable cars.

Beautiful—another big two-story house. Ali fell in love with the place the minute she walked through the front door. For the next few days, she threw herself non-stop into unpacking and adjusting to where everything was. She had a lot to do before they'd pick Cay and Jo up at the airport next Thursday. Only days after that, they'd leave on the hike. She kept her mind and heart busy letting those two events stop her from dwelling on how her life had changed. Maybe if she talked with Cay about all that had happened, that would help. Maybe Cay would have some ideas about pushing through all the high and low emotional waves. More and more the thought nudged at her.

In stark contrast to the darkness outside, before long, light shone from nearly every room in the house, including Ali's bedroom. She was restless, the uneasy merger between anticipation and excitement formed wisps of dread in her chest. Was she really up for heat and bugs and unknown wild things? She rolled over, groped for the flashlight to turn off the noisy alarm she'd set for two-thirty.

A chuckle and a click. "Looking for this?" A bright ray of light shone on the clock-radio and lit the area between their beds as Cay held the light out to her.

"Mm-hmm, thanks." Ali took the flashlight, grinned as she switched off the alarm fifteen minutes early. "Glad you're up. I'm too antsy to sleep." And yes, she was up for all of whatever the hike held. Being with Cay and Jo would be fun and good for her.

Great. Self-talk? She really *did* need this hike.

"I know, me too. We've got a few things to do yet, but we've got plenty of time."

Sometime within the next hour and a half, they'd leave for the outskirts of Manaus and begin their walk into the Amazon rain forest. They had enough time to finish stowing their food, water, and gear for the hike.

Half an hour later, Cay pulled at the zipper of a backpack and chuckled as Ali's stomach growled. Ali's appetite was stoked with the tantalizing aroma of fresh coffee, frying bacon, pancakes, and sweet syrup.

A day after they arrived, her father hired both the cook and housekeeper Erick had lined up for him to interview. This morning he and the cook put together breakfast for them.

Cay sat on the edge of the bed and checked her headlamp. "Your dad must be making sure we don't die of starvation with his plans to stuff us before we leave."

Ali moved her pack from the bed to the floor and nodded. "Breakfast may be our last decent meal for a while, and my stomach is more than ready to be stuffed." She tucked an extra pair of socks into her already heavy backpack. Heavy, humid air wafted through the open doors of the balcony, and stars still winked in the dark mid-July sky.

Jo and Cay had flown into Manaus two days ago and had quickly adjusted to the heat. Ali wondered if she ever would. Sleep had been sketchy. Too warm. Thoughts of the hike. Missing Kane. All of the rambling thoughts kept her midnight kitchen run to cover half a banana with the cook's homemade chocolate nut-butter interesting.

Jaco and his wife, Luisa, lived in a small bungalow in Manaus on the edge of the Rio Negro a few miles north of the Port of Manaus. Jaco offered to take them upriver in his longboat to Manaquiri near the trailhead, and pick them up there when they returned. An hour ago, Jaco had driven up in his old king cab truck, and they invited him to have breakfast with them.

Time dragged, filled with small talk as Ali finished the last bite of her pancake. Her patience stretched, she nudged Cay's shin with the toe of her boot and shot her a "Let's get out of here" look. In the midst of a heavy discussion of futebol scores, they left to check the gear in the truck against Ali's master list.

A gentle breeze rustled through the garden as they walked back to the house. Ali listened when Cay called her parents, her staccato replies punctuated every step back to the house. Ali smiled and watched as Cay looked up and closed her eyes.

"*Okay*, Dad … I will … Yes, I know. I love you too. Love you too, Mom."

Sharp, painful heart-stabs of no longer having a mom to say "I love you" to almost doubled Ali over. She fought to keep from biting her bottom lip in two and looked away.

Okay. She needed a scenery change.

Ali sprinted ahead and picked up two extra bottles of water from the porch. On the other side of the screen door, Gabi, with Jaco behind her, paced and whined, knowing something was going on out there.

"Ready to go, girl?" Ali opened the door, laughing as the shepherd bounded to the truck like an oversized puppy. "Guess that answered my question." Jaco followed Gabi, letting the dog jump into the cab with him while Jo and her father joined the group.

Her father pinned his eyes on Ali's. "You have a mighty happy dog there, and she's not the only one. I'm pretty happy she's tagging along with you."

"Dad, we're going to be just fine. Don't be such a worrywart. Jo knows the area better than anyone." Ali hugged him, trying hard to keep her thoughts to herself, as he continued with half a dozen last minute reminders.

Squeezed into the king-cab, along with Jaco and Gabi, they drove the few miles to Jaco's home. Jaco pulled the truck onto a dirt track toward the river, passed a house, slowed, then stopped close to a dimly lit dock. Ali could barely make out the wooden longboat moored beside the pier as Jaco parked and helped them unload their gear. Lights from the modest house came on, and a sleepy Luisa emerged from the back door. She greeted them with a big Thermos filled with strong coffee, some foam cups, and a bagful of warm sweetbreads for their trip.

Ali was the last to climb aboard as Jaco keyed the engine. The old, but he guaranteed, reliable Evinrude outboard roared to life. Luisa smiled and waved them off as they left the dock, heading south on the Rio Negro. Turning westward into the Amazon, Jaco took them upriver.

As they reached the lush vegetation covering the low bluffs, Jaco let the longboat drift back into a small cove near Manaquiri. The shallow inlet boasted nothing more than a rustic wood structure stretched out over the water. Jaco left the running lights on, cut the engine, and tied up to a pole that strongly resembled a stripped tree trunk.

Ali's heartbeat and breathing quickened as they unloaded their gear. Her father had been right to insist on a guide. Now, even with the deep thrill of this rare experience building within her, the forest felt strange and lonely as she watched the lights of the longboat fade in the distance.

Deathly quiet and deserted, the nearly mile-long walk on the dirt road seemed never-ending. The trees thickened and the jungle began in earnest before the road completely eroded into a rough path. They took a short break. Ali pulled out the satellite phone to call her father and let him know approximately where they were and how they were doing. They wouldn't call him again until their return to the trailhead.

Jo set up a brisk pace in the still dark morning, instructing them to turn on their "headlights." The headbands with attached lights circled their heads like tight halos and bounced yellow shafts of brightness wherever they were directed. The mosquitoes would be around until the sun came up, but they'd used plenty of repellent, worn long-sleeved shirts, and their jeans were tucked inside their ankle boots. Gabi seemed unusually obedient, and Ali didn't bother to use the leash, as the dog remained close beside her while they walked.

To lessen the risk of inhaling bugs and to conserve energy, they didn't talk. Ali didn't want to talk anyway as she breathed in the moist, earthy scent of oxygenated air and listened to the raucous sounds of the rain forest edges. The deeper they penetrated the jungle, the more exhilarated she became. Would this time away truly make a difference in her life? Was Kane thinking of her as she thought of him with every step she took in this place?

Hours had passed since they'd left the house. She wanted to see the plants and native wildlife Jo and Cay had so endlessly talked about. She looked forward to daylight, but dawn would be a while coming beneath this dense green umbrella.

Jo continued to lead the way, machete in hand, hacking at the underbrush and overgrowth that occasionally blocked the little-used path through the jungle. He'd told them he had navigated the trail many times during his boyhood in Manaus. Even though the last time he used this foot trail had been three years ago, he didn't look to Ali as if he'd lost his keen sense of the territory.

Their three bobbing headlamps washed an eerie glow of light onto the trail ahead, making dusky gray shadows jump and writhe in their wake. Jo stopped short and shook his head. He turned and faced them with a mischievous grin, his face bathed in the light of Cay's lamp. "Must watch step carefully. Might step on things that not want to be stepped on—lots of things that come out when dark."

Ali looked down hoping she wasn't about to squash one of those "things."

Cay laughed out loud. "Ignore him. Any self-respecting 'thing' will run the other way faced with death by machete! He's teasing, plus it's almost daylight."

The trail meandered for what seemed like miles, only interrupted by a few bats overhead and a spiny rat that scurried across the path in front of Cay's foot and made her squeal—much to Jo's delight. Except for an occasional sniff, Gabi paid little attention to the skittering wildlife and stayed close to Ali.

Bending under the weight of the heavy knapsack, Ali mentally made a count of all the things she could have left at home. Thanks to Jo, she wouldn't have the extra weight or drop the satellite phone again. After her call to her dad, the phone had hit the ground hard when she'd tried to stuff it back into her pack. Jo had found space in his own backpack.

She looked toward Cay, her headlamp illuminating Cay's bulging canvas sack. "At least we *tried* to get in shape for this," she said with a grin, thinking of their practice walks with their packs stuffed full of books.

"You call this 'shape,' huh?" Cay grimaced and focused her lamp on Ali's face. "I should have taken a class in heavy breathing."

The farther they walked, the darker the forest became. The trees grew in dense clumps with the leafy roof overhead hiding what little daylight was available. The trail closed in, overgrown with bushes and overhanging vines. A chorus of croaks, chirps, and cricket noise came from every direction as they concentrated on moving deeper into the rain forest, getting more familiar with the terrain.

The path led west following the Amazon River, weaving through both sparse and dense vegetation. Jo told them that not too long ago, the river had flooded and this trail had been underwater. They walked across several of the many narrow inlets of dark water, crossing on fallen trees, some of which Jo said had been rolled into place by prior hikers.

Ali touched the button on her watch to illuminate the time. Eight-thirty. They'd been walking for three hours, keeping up a fast, steady pace.

"Okay, switch off headlights." Jo tossed the instruction over his shoulder, hacking at an overhanging, web-covered branch, then added, "Watch for spiders."

Ali took off her headlamp. She glanced up at the webs and let Cay go first. The insect repellent worked well, and the few gnats and mosquitoes that came near were only an annoyance. Gabi snapped at a lizard but didn't bother to follow as the reptile disappeared beneath some moss.

Constant noise made the river impossible to hear from where they stood, and they hadn't seen it yet. As more and more sunlight filtered through the trees, she checked her watch again. Almost eleven-thirty. Time had flown by. They'd stop to eat something soon. She readjusted the extra water bottle hooked to her belt and caught Cay's eye. They had to be close to the river by now.

Cay must have thought the same. "We should see the river anytime now."

"Good. It's really getting bright." Ali shaded her eyes with one hand and dug into a side pocket to search for her sunscreen with the other. "It's surreal we're finally doing this."

"For me too. I've haven't been in the rain forest for so long." Cay shook her head and smiled. "It feels like only yesterday we hatched this crazy plan."

Ali rubbed sunscreen onto the back of her hands as Cay stowed her headlamp. "It really is hard to believe."

Jo glanced back at the two of them. "Better believe and keep eyes on alert. Very close to river now." He took a wide, slicing swipe at the heavy foliage blocking the way in front of him. "Never know what you see out here." He pulled out his sunglasses and adjusted his hat.

Ali didn't miss the twinkle in his eyes through the shaded lenses as he chuckled and added, "Maybe even see snake or two."

Cay glanced at Ali. "Only if they're friendly. And Jo, don't you start teasing her!"

"No way, no thanks, no snakes, not even a friendly one," Ali said.

"Okay, okay." Jo laughed. "I keep all snakes away."

Gabi's cold, wet nose touched Ali's hand, and she jumped. "Not funny, Gabi!" She bent to ruffle the fur on Gabi's neck then wiped perspiration from her forehead with a sleeve. "I should have brought a sponge."

Jo paused and looked back at her. "Here. Got this for you." He pulled a new bandana from his pocket and handed the cloth to Ali. "Everyone in Brazil has bandana. Better than sleeve of shirt for drying sweat."

"Thanks, Jo. I'll fit right in." She took the bright blue and white bandana from him and stuffed it into her jeans pocket. "But when did you find the time to go shopping?"

He grinned. "You go for boots—I go for bandanas. Good for lot of things, bandanas are. Wiping brow, wrapping things, tying up ponytails."

Ali laughed, glad to have her own long hair out of her way in a ponytail.

Jo slowed his pace. "River not far away."

Gabi left Ali's side and bounded up beside Jo. With a rare bark, she spun toward the right side of the trail. Jo kept walking, shushing the dog. Ali quickened her steps and moved forward to scold the shepherd but listened. Was she was hearing the river? It couldn't be far from where they were.

The dog suddenly halted in her tracks, growling threats deep within her throat. Her head shifted, and she fixed her gaze onto the trail in front of them. Jo stopped short beside her.

Ali chuckled. "That's enough, Gabi. Be still. It's only a jungle out there." She stood on the other side of Gabi and stroked the dog's neck. But the fur on Gabi's back raised. She looked up at Ali with a whine and turned back to the trail. In seconds, with another sharp bark, she bared her teeth and continued to growl.

She's telling us something is wrong. "What is it girl? What's the matter?" Ali straightened enough to look in the direction that commanded Gabi's attention, but kept her hand on Gabi, a sense of dread moving up her neck. Time to grab her collar. "Stay, Gabi!"

Cay put her hand on Ali's arm. "What's wrong? Is she sensing something?"

"I'm not sure. She's really upset." Ali reached to unhook the leash from her backpack, but Gabi abruptly crouched, jerked away from her, and lunged out in front of Jo. The dog paused for a split second then took off at a dead run. She raced away from them in silence, swallowed up into the green-brown foliage and trees as the trail took a twist.

No! The last time Gabi ran off ... Ali froze, forcing the words from her throat. "Gabi! Come!" But Gabi was gone. Every muscle in her body tensed, ready to run after Gabi, but Jo held out his arm as if to stop her.

Panic edged in as Ali watched Jo's face change from an amused expression into an iron mask of seriousness. "Dog knows something we don't. Too quiet. Wait here. I go check it out."

She took a step forward, Cay beside her. "No, let Jo check first."

Ali's shoulders sagged. Why hadn't she put Gabi's leash on sooner? She should have been listening, paying more attention to the sounds. When had the birdsong stopped? And why did Gabi point like a hunting dog toward the river? Why did she go up the trail instead of toward the river?

She watched Jo fast-walk up the rough track, glancing back, keeping them in sight until the trail turned. An icy feeling of dread moved up Ali's spine with glacial slowness. Something was really wrong. When the dog reacted like she had, she had a good reason.

"Cay, Jo's right. Gabi knows something we don't, and it isn't good." She looked down, gripped with regret. "I should have kept her on the leash. Are there any animals out here that might mean trouble for her—or us?"

"Caiman or an alligator, but they stay near the water." Cay rubbed her shoulders as if they ached. "Could be a jaguar, but they're rare, they're not seen very often. I suppose any one of those would set Gabi off."

"If they were close and meant harm. Yes, in a heartbeat."

"Well, Jo shouldn't take long to find out if there's anything we need to worry about."

"Listen. Sounds like Gabi." Ali grabbed Cay's arm. Gabi's sharp bark had turned vicious.

"She *never* barks that much." Ali couldn't steady her voice. "We have to make sure Jo is okay. Gabi wouldn't bark like that if nothing was wrong!" With every fiber of her being she wanted to run, to see for herself, to make sure, but Cay stopped her, holding her back.

"No, Ali. You can't go yet."

As she spoke the words, Gabi's bark became several pained snarls, and then fell silent.

Ali felt the blood drain from her face. Cay loosened her grip but didn't let go, and Ali stared as Cay bowed her head for a few precious seconds.

We don't have time. Ali pulled away. "Gabi! Jo! Are you all right?" Her voice was a strangled blend of terror and hope. She desperately wanted to see Jo and Gabi come back down the path.

Run! But fear paralyzed her legs, and she couldn't move.

"Wait. We have to be careful." Cay's voice was maddeningly calm as Ali tried to listen to her. "Jo will take care of Gabi, and we don't know what's there or what's happened. It won't do either of us any good if we get hurt."

"No. We have to go. Something's gotten Gabi. Something awful has happened …" The words screeched from her throat, but even as she spoke, Cay's warning did make sense. They couldn't run—they needed to be careful.

She listened for a few more seconds. Nothing but the noise of the river and their breathing. No sound from the trail. The noiseless forest sent chills through her. Shadows formed menacing shapes across the path, and not a breath of air moved through the trees towering over them with their green parasol canopy.

Her backpack clung to her like a huge parasite, draining her of energy. A sense of eerie, disconnected reality encased her as she stood close to Cay in the middle of the narrow trail.

When had they started to move? She'd become mechanical, deliberate. Ali watched foliage pass her by in slow motion. She made herself look down at her legs. Somehow they held her upright and moved her—not the trees—forward. Sick with dread at what they might find, she didn't try to stop Cay from leading the way.

Within minutes, she stood gaping in horror at the scene in front of her, her boots grafted to the path. Gabi lay in a black and tan heap on the ground, mouth open, pink tongue lolling to one side, her breath coming in quiet little gasps.

She's alive, but is she hurt? Ali's own breath came and went in short, convulsive gulps, and she forced her eyes away to look at the rest of the strange scene that floated in waves around her.

Jo lay next to Gabi, unmoving. She couldn't tell if he was breathing at all. He lay face down on the path, as still as if dead. Blood oozed from somewhere beneath his thick black hair and rolled down his cheek. On the ground next to him, his sunglasses. Littered with leaves, his cowboy hat lay near his feet. A gaping rip zigzagged up the side of his shirt—the same plaid shirt she'd first seen him in at the airport in São Paulo. His hand still held the machete he'd used to carve through the vine-choked trail. Flipped up onto his arm, the silver cross he always wore glimmered in a shaft of sunlight. Ali stared at Jo's head, at the crimson-red blood. Bile rose, burning the back of her throat. Cay's hand grabbed hers.

"Ali, there's a *dart* in Gabi's side." Cay's whisper sounded strained and shaky.

Ali stared. "Oh, no—"

A twig snapped. A rushed shuffle of underbrush behind her.

She opened her mouth in an empty scream. Her body jerked, vised in the wide grip of heaviness encircling her waist.

Kicking. Twisting.

Arms pinned to her sides. Breath huffed from her lungs.

Softness across her nose and mouth. Firm unrelenting pressure. Reeking, nauseating stench.

Death?

CHAPTER EIGHTEEN

Desperate to reach the surface, Ali struggled through a sea of black cotton, grasping tentacles and tugging riptides that kept her from the shore.

Why couldn't she see? Was she dying? She swallowed, forcing words to her lips "Kane? Dad? Where are you? Please. Help me."

Her head throbbed, her mind hazy. Bones, muscles, even her skin ached as she fought off the blanket of nausea and confusion suffocating her. Something restrained her hands. Something had a tight, viselike grip around her head.

Flashes, memories stabbed at her. Gabi, Jo, blood, Cay's voice. A dart. Sounds behind her. A wrenching grip around her waist. Something soft and damp slammed against her mouth and sucked at her breath. *The smell. No … no … no …*

Wake up! She had to wake up, open her eyes again, breathe …

Only darkness. She lay still, her heart thudded with terror, threatened to explode from her chest.

Think. Slow breaths. Listen. Reason this out. She certainly wasn't dead. Pain told her that much. But where was she?

The vice around her head—a blindfold—but why? The straps of her backpack no longer pulled against her shoulders. Gone, with no memory of taking it off.

Fear snaked around her chest. She had to gain control, to assign some reason to all this.

Breathe. Listen.

She lay on her side on something hard, curled up like a child with a tummy ache. A bench? Sounds. Someone behind her? *Clack, clack.* Wood against wood? Water slapping against something solid. An oar? A paddle? Was she in a boat? The rhythmic forward motion matched the sounds.

Her head hurt. Dizziness made whirlpools of her thoughts. The stench she'd smelled before morphed into a strange mix of water, new wood, vinyl, and rancid sweat. Damp air, permeated with oppressive heat. Another wave of nausea shook her.

Ether! That was the awful smell. Whoever grabbed her had used ether. That's why she was so groggy and sick. Her father's words etched themselves in white lightning against the darkness of her thoughts: "… an epidemic of kidnappings …"

Kidnapped? No, that can't have happened. She struggled to breathe again. The universe orbited, swirled around her, yanked her backward, absorbed her into black oblivion.

She lay unmoving, regaining consciousness. Slowly aware, she listened, tried to unravel the chaos of what was going on. A light breeze swept the rancid air aside. She pulled in a deep breath and held it to clear her head.

"Cessar!" Ali tensed as a male voice boomed from behind her. Had she heard the voice before? All forward motion slowed, and the boat became nearly stationary in the water. That sound. The noise of a paddle scraping against a gunwale? A chill of fear shot through her.

What are they doing? They? Why did she think there was more than one person? She allowed the air to seep slowly from between her lips. The voice spoke again, more foreign words sounding as if they were directed toward her. She battled against another blackout as rough hands gripped her arms and jerked her upright.

Her blindfold tightened then abruptly loosened, untied. Ali dipped her head against the sudden glare of sunlight. Her hair, freed from the ponytail, fell around her face, a welcome curtain of shadow against the piercing brightness. She blinked hard, her eyes gradually adjusting. The outline of a canoe formed in her blurry vision.

Gabi. The shepherd lay quiet at her feet—too quiet. Rigid with a wave of dread, Ali nudged Gabi with the toe of her boot. Except for the dog's chest rhythmically rising and lowering, Gabi remained still.

The dart. Gabi must still be feeling the effects of a drug, but at least she was alive, her breathing, easy. Relieved, Ali straightened, forcing her attention outside the canoe. Maybe she could figure out where she was.

Impossible. She had no clue where she was. Her spirits sank with the realization. Deadly, monotonous views lay in every direction, water beneath her, dense, green jungle to her left, and an empty horizon to her right. She wouldn't take the chance of looking behind her yet. Another good-sized canoe moved along several yards ahead, and she strained to see the occupants.

Cay! Caylee sat in the center of the green-hulled canoe, a man positioned slightly to the side behind her. Only part of her friend's back was visible. Cay's backpack was missing too, she had no blindfold around her head, and she didn't look as if she'd been hurt. Relief poured through Ali, easing more of the paralyzing panic. Enough to know they were together and not hurt.

Had both men been in on their abduction, yanking them bodily off the trail? How many minutes—or had it been hours—ago?

The man in cut-offs and tee shirt behind Cay looked vaguely familiar … A spark of light flashed from the left side of his head, igniting the glimmer of a memory. She blinked and looked again, but whatever the connection eluded her. Ali shook her head. Her mind. Her thoughts. So fuzzy. She watched him pause from paddling and lean over, picking up a bottle. He held it up for Cay to drink from. Ali raised her roped hands and touched a finger to her own dry lips, overwhelmed with pangs of thirst.

Gabi yipped. "I hope that's a good dream, girl," Ali whispered, but as she watched her sleeping dog, her hands curled into angry fists. How had she not noticed the ugly muzzle covering Gabi's mouth? Tears of frustration and helplessness came, but she was grateful Gabi slept.

Ali swallowed hard. Her tears were useless. She stared down at chafe marks on her wrists. She'd been working to undo the ropes soon after the man had removed her blindfold. The ropes had rubbed the skin nearly raw in places. She pulled at the bonds to test them. A spark of hope kindled. The gap between her wrist and the rope had widened a little.

Moist heat hovered over the river like the atmosphere in a sauna. If her captor didn't give her water soon, he'd have a dead captive. She shivered, tried to shut down thoughts of death and watched the shoreline for anything unusual. Maybe Cay did the same. If they could remember anything that even resembled a landmark … but that was laughable. Most of the riverbank looked repetitious, except for an occasional house or dock. Would Cay recognize any of the area or know where they were? And if she did, would she know where they might be headed?

The two-boat fleet stayed far enough away from the riverbank that she could hear more than watery gurgles and splashes and forest noises. Again, she concentrated on listening. She hadn't been imagining the additional sound. There *was* something more. From behind them, she clearly heard another paddle, dipping in and out of the water, but no voices.

Another boat. Ali tried to squash the huge temptation to turn around and look, but the urge wouldn't go away. She had to take the chance. The man behind her might not notice.

Inch by inch, she turned to try for a glimpse. She received a shove and harsh words in Portuguese for her efforts. Understanding nothing he said, she had no intention of trying again. From the tone of his voice, he'd likely knock her out of the canoe if she did.

Tiny tremors shook her insides. Again, something about his voice sounded familiar. No way to know why. No choice. She had to be satisfied with what she could see going on in front of and beside her.

The two slender canoes slid expertly driven through the water, and occasional noise from the third boat gave proof it continued to follow. These were new or fairly new boats and looked identical, at least sixteen or seventeen feet long. Similar to the lightweight river touring canoes she'd seen. So far, everything looked as if their abduction had been carefully planned.

Kidnapped. She had to face the fact. She and Cay had been abducted and would probably be held for ransom, exactly like what was happening elsewhere in South America. Staring at the frayed ropes around her wrists, she stifled another avalanche of sheer terror.

She had to do something—anything—useful. She continued to feel his eyes on her, but the constant challenge of carefully picking at the ropes calmed her and kept her mind alert. The unnerving surge of fear ebbed, dissipated into temporary resignation. But not trying to get free would be giving up, and no way would she ever give up or give in to this.

Gabi strained to stand, then sat, resting her head on Ali's knees. Ali shut her eyes against fresh emotion, glad to see her dog up and moving. The ropes might as well have been chains. All she could do was rub Gabi's head to pet and reassure her. As much as the shepherd hated muzzles, she wasn't fighting the one over her nose now. The tranquilizer hadn't completely worn off. Still dazed and confused, Gabi looked up at Ali and gave a muffled whine, finally flopping against the side of the hull.

Ali studied the back of the man in Cay's canoe. His oar strokes, methodical, dipping in and out of the unruffled water, mesmerized her, reminded her of when she was little and first learning to canoe on Big Bear Lake. Her mother and father, soaked and laughing, struggled to right their flipped boat. Wearing a lifejacket, Ali bobbed in the water nearby, trying to figure out how she had gotten so wet, so fast. It happened in shallow water near the dock, and though nobody ever said who was at fault, Ali learned standing up in a canoe wasn't smart.

She smiled at the memory, a precious moment of relief. So different, the changeable gray-blue waters of the seemingly endless Amazon and the brilliant indigo waters of Big Bear Lake—each had its own beauty and risks. Had Cay enjoyed as much fun canoeing with her family when she had learned in these same waters? Could their childhood experiences pay off in this mess? What they'd learned as kids might come in handy. They only needed to get free, to have a chance.

Would Jo have a chance? Would he be able to get help? Was it possible he was in the third canoe? Ali clenched her jaw and closed her eyes, shaken by the thought of how hard Jo must have been hit.

"Jo ..." But his whispered name was lost in the warm breeze that feathered her hair away from her face. If he were still alive, he had to be terribly hurt. She hoped he still had the satellite phone her father insisted they bring with them. Jo had buried the phone in his backpack. He'd use it if it worked—if it hadn't been found and taken. Thoughts of the men rummaging through the pack and discovering the sat-phone gripped her like the ropes around her wrists.

Kane's strong, handsome features seemed to float before her. Would she ever see him again? She'd gotten to see him graduate. Would she be alive to see her senior year? To graduate? To follow in her father's footsteps, work beside him at Zoran? Would there be marriage and children or any future for her at all?

Queasiness twisted inside her along with a new onslaught of fear and anguished regret. Her father was right about the hazards out here. Why had she ever insisted they'd be okay on a hike into this wilderness, even with Jo? She'd made yet another poor decision. Now she'd caused fear and heartache for more than just her father. Cay and her parents would suffer too.

Her thoughts careened out of control with imagined reasons she and Cay had been taken. Had it been random? Everything in her screamed, "No!" Too much coincidence. Too many familiar tweaks she couldn't splice together yet. Ransom was all about money. That had to be what the men wanted. But did they know whether or not her father could pay—would pay?

Her father stood to benefit from his work if one day he marketed the formula. But he hadn't, at least not yet. They were comfortable but not wealthy. Life held no "sure things." None. For no one. She'd learned that. Or was this somehow about Cay? Would her parents be faced with a ransom and maybe the loss of their daughter as well? She shook her head against the pointless conjecture. There was way too much she didn't know.

Splashes on her right drew her attention to the water where a fish the color and texture of a Pink Pearl eraser swam beside them. With stubby flipper-like appendages the fish had to be one of the pink river dolphins Cay had wanted her to see. A welcome diversion. She watched, fascinated by the creature with its long, bottleneck nose. Crisscrossing in front of the bow more times than she could count, the mammal seemed to be playing with the boat.

Cay had said the Amazon was one of the few places on earth they'd been found. The one that now swam lazily beside them had to be at least eight feet long, and looked powerful enough to flip the canoe. The dolphin ventured close with its round, black eyes that appeared to look up at her.

"Boto! Boto! Abdicar!" A bass voice coming from behind her growled out the anger-filled Portuguese words.

He's mad at a dolphin? So strange, sounded funny—abdicar, like abdicate—he wanted the animal out of his way. The dusty pink creature dropped back but continued to play in the ripples spreading from the bow of the canoe.

"Good for you." Ali sighed, envying his freedom. The man grumbled and spewed a few more sentences directed at the boto, which did glide silently away. Ali watched the water, and seconds later saw a brief reflection of the man behind her, polished wood paddle in hand, glaring after the dolphin.

Jolted as if she'd been shocked by a live wire. The sunlight and a smooth patch of water had revealed him. His hair was pulled back into a messy stub of a ponytail, but the mirrored face was familiar, and combined with the voice, pricked at her memory. She'd seen and heard him somewhere recently, but where? When? She must still be groggy, out of it. He probably reminded her of someone she knew. She put him out of her thoughts and checked Gabi. The dog's position hadn't changed; she'd slept through all the commotion.

The sun wasn't as intense now. The men must be getting tired, and Ali wondered how long they'd be on the river. As if in reply, the man in the first canoe ceased paddling and looked toward her boat, allowing his canoe to drift closer. She didn't want to look at his face, but she couldn't stop herself from staring. Again a shard of light reflected from the top of his left ear.

That spark of light before … a diamond earring … his face. Cold chills traced down the length of her spine with the revelation he was one of the two men she'd seen on the plane. Her heart sank as his gaze transfixed her, and she instantly lowered her head. Then the man who sat behind her now was the other man on the plane, the same man who picked up her suitcase in the São Paulo terminal. That's where she'd seen him.

Panic built with a backwash of vivid scenes flooding her mind, one after another. The baggage claim encounter; three, maybe four, sightings of the blue Vector, the strong sense of being watched the night Gabi alerted her to danger on Valparaiso Avenue. Even the feelings she'd had during their flight layover in Miami? She stiffened. The white pickup on the canyon bridge? Had they been …?

The truth leered at her from two canoes in the midst of the Amazon. They'd been stalking her even in California. She was the one they wanted. Cay was either collateral damage or a bonus.

Now that she'd seen one man's face, they had to know she'd recognize them both. She and Cay were surely expendable. Beyond her understanding was why the two men bothered to prevent them from seeing them at all.

They were planning to kill them, whether or not they got any ransom.

She groped for something good to think about so she wouldn't scream with terror. Biting down hard on her bottom lip, she held onto the fact, so far, they hadn't been hurt.

The steady swish of the paddle from the third boat slowed, and the man behind them spoke what sounded like instructions. Both of the other men responded as if agreeing. Hoping he was directing the small armada where to take a break, she looked up again to find out what was going on. She raised her head enough to see the man behind Cay in the lead canoe. He ignored her but nodded at the person in the third boat. Cay's canoe drifted closer, and a burst of words erupted from Ali's captor. Ali watched in disbelief as Cay was blindfolded, and with a sloppy splash of the paddle, Cay's boat headed back into the main current. Seconds later, a cloth shut out sight from Ali's eyes.

Why the blindfolds again? She lodged a mental protest, fresh anger and indignation clarifying her thoughts. She and Cay had already seen the men. Was it a control thing? Or maybe they simply didn't want their hostages to know where they were going?

The canoe picked up speed, and she felt the boat lean as they rounded a bend. Cay had talked about the hundreds of large and small tributaries piercing the riverbank. They must be entering one of them. Gabi sniffed the air and moved her warm body against Ali's legs as they slid through the water. The jungle closed in around her. Filled with shrieking birds, monkey chatter, and insect song, the atmosphere changed, intensified in the afternoon heat as they left the river behind.

The canoe slowed and a gritty sound emanated from beneath as it ran aground. Ali heard the second boat grinding ashore, but no other. She'd heard nothing from the third canoe since they'd been blindfolded and assumed that one must have gone somewhere else.

"*Vamos!* Move! We don't have all day," the raspy, accented voice of Ali's captor demanded. And the first word of English confirmed once more he was the man who'd grabbed her case in the terminal. Rough hands tugged her up and out of the canoe. Her boots sank into soft sand at the edge of the water then gained traction as he shoved her, stumbling, up an embankment. A second voice directed at Cay echoed the order to move.

Seconds later, the earth under Ali's feet grew firmer. The man stopped, grabbed her by the shoulders and turned her, pressing downward as if to tell her to sit. She sat on a hard, wooden surface. A wooden chair? No. Maybe a wood bench beside a tree. The roll and roughness of tree bark ground through her shirt. If it was a tree, it offered no shade, as relentless heat-filled rays from the sun shot earthward with only an occasional cloud to diffuse them.

A light breeze ruffled her hair, and somewhere nearby dry leaves rustled. Hope rose for a shelter of some sort, maybe with a roof of dried palm leaves. She'd seen dozens of huts and wooden shacks like that along the river's edge.

For the first time since they'd been taken, the man tied her legs. She held her breath until he left—not stopping to check the ropes around her wrists.

"Drink!" The sip of offered water refreshed her parched throat and cracked lips. He spoke again, and the two male voices mingled with the crunch of brush as they walked away.

She had no idea where Cay was, and didn't want to risk speaking. Cay had tried once when they were still in the canoes and was quickly silenced.

Moments later, Ali heard Cay cough as if to let Ali know where she was. The sound came from the same direction as the rustle of the dry leaves. Ali cleared her throat in reply, relieved Cay was close and hopefully had more shade than she did.

Except for a deep growl before she'd left the boat, she hadn't heard Gabi since they came ashore, wherever "ashore" was.

Her thoughts returned to Jo. Had he been in the third canoe, or was he still lying on the jungle floor where she'd last seen him? What had become of him? Was he dead or alive?

Footsteps. Her worries interrupted, she pulled herself upright, bracing for what might come next.

Gabi's throaty growl. A loud, angry stream of Portuguese. Ali recognized the voice of the man in Cay's canoe. She dipped her head to hide her smile. Gabi was okay.

She turned her head toward the *crinkle* of paper. More footsteps closed in. The same man who'd lashed out at Gabi's growl abruptly spoke to her in

English. His breath, rancid and hot, grazed her face. His voice, threatening as barbed wire, shaped her breath into a strangled gasp and froze her in place.

Deke Regis tugged at the jacket of his black uniform, patted his sidearm, and went down the hall toward Zoran's security offices. His new job had been not only interesting during the last few weeks but a challenge. He liked the people here, the place was fairly new, most of the security was state-of-the-art stuff, and the business was growing fast. No surprise they'd tightened security around here though. Just not in the right places yet. He rubbed at his chin.

From his experience, the place was a target for all kinds of theft, particularly intellectual and digital theft. After two employees had felt threatened by phone calls and the botanical garden was broken into, he'd recommended upgrading the alarm system and more surveillance cameras. Dr. Lamarque's secretary had scheduled a meeting with the newly appointed Director of Security, to discuss suggestions Deke had made for other safeguards. He and Glen Porter would be on hand and ready to discuss more improvements.

The new employee orientation session had given him an education on why they'd required top secret clearance here, and he liked the challenge of supporting their rigid requirements.

A solid résumé and his skillsets had gotten him hired. They not only appreciated him, his age and background, but also for a suggestion he'd made for periodic building sweeps for bugs.

He was old, not dumb. The FBI had been a great place to work—and to retire from. But keeping his mind active and his body in shape? Well, being a Walmart greeter wouldn't work for him. Solvang, Zoran Labs, his new apartment, the whole atmosphere … perfect for an active widower who liked things balanced between solitude and busyness. Besides, he was nuts about the town's Danish pastries. *One more reason I need to stay active!*

This morning, he'd notice some lax security on his rounds before hours and headed down to Security to let Glen know before they opened the entrance doors. Glen sat in front of a bank of security monitors, mug of coffee in hand, as Deke entered.

"Morning, Glen. Just finished rounds—"

Glen and Deke's radios chirped simultaneously, and Mick's voice sounded. Deke keyed his mic. "What's up, Mick?"

"Deke, you and Glen need to get down here. It could be a false alarm, but someone's left an unmarked package beside the steps out front."

He looked at Glen. "Ten-four. On our way." He shook his head. "Too much of this happening lately. Feels like harassment, but why?"

Glen shrugged, his coffee sloshing over the rim of the mug as he put it on the desk. "Yep. Probably nothing, but let's check it out."

CHAPTER NINETEEN

"You! Repeat words I say … after me." The voice reverberated in Ali's ears, issuing commands in loud, halting English.

What words? Would they tell her why she was here? She cringed, nodding, hoping she could understand and parrot the words he wanted her to repeat to him. His accent was heavy. This wouldn't be easy. If he'd simply let her look at the paper and read, repeating would be so much simpler. But it most likely wasn't written in English. Everything in her screamed, *"Take this useless, rotten blindfold off me!"*

"You understand? Answer!" He yelled the demand. She jumped and mumbled a "yes." Her captor, Cardozo, must have been near, listening. Ali heard his derisive, sarcastic laugh fade with his footsteps as he walked away.

A sharp, firm clap of hands and the gruff voice sounded again. "You! Listen!"

"Yes."

She might be blindfolded, but she knew who Fernando Velez was now. She'd heard them use each other's names frequently, both first and last names. It wasn't difficult to figure out who was attached to which name as the men conversed. Why they had made no attempt to hide their identities before was frightening—one more reason to fear they would not survive this abduction.

From the direction of his voice, Velez either sat or stooped in front of her as he insisted she repeat the words of a ransom message. With every sentence, her heart sank as it became clearer why she'd been taken. How these men knew so much terrified her, filled her with confusion and more unanswerable questions. Cay was extra insurance for them, but why had they bothered with Gabi? Why hadn't they just put her out of commission with the dart and left her there on the trail, which it seemed more and more likely they'd done with Jo?

Over and over Velez harangued her, forced her to recite the ransom demands. Moments later, the jagged, husky voice of Nico Cardozo joined Velez, coaching and correcting her until she could say the words without error.

Her neck, arms, back, everything, ached. Exhaustion crept into her mind, obliterating her thoughts, one by one. They must have been at this for at least an hour.

When they seemed satisfied with her "performance," Cardozo left them. Velez gave her a moment of peace and placed a water bottle in her hands. She drank as much as she could before he took it from her, his rough hand touching her arm. Startled, she jerked away. Velez had never come this close to her before.

"Hold still!" He still spoke in English. The repulsive acrid smell of sweat swept around her, leaving her breathless. Close to nausea, she twisted away, coughing and tried to bury her nose in her shirtsleeve. She wouldn't forget Velez anytime soon.

He muttered a few words in Portuguese then grabbed her wrists and untied the ropes. Her heartbeat raced. Would he notice how loose they'd gotten? If he had, he ignored it. Pressure around her shoulders. More rope? Heavy rough cord wrapped around her, pinned her upper arms painfully against the trunk of the tree. She rubbed at her chafed wrists, relieved to have the ropes gone, but doubted he removed them because he saw rope burns on her wrists.

Common sense said the men had a satellite phone they were preparing her to use. She'd be repeating their demands soon. Would it be her father's voice she'd hear, the one she'd say these terrible things to? Why didn't one of them do it? But maybe it was a shrewd move. When her father heard her voice …

Movement. Velez was leaving. The crunch of brush underfoot faded, immediately replaced by other heavy steps coming toward her. Cardozo. A light breeze moved around her. Within it, his scent arrived at her nose before the wafting stale cigar smoke did—a failed cover-up of some unknown men's cologne mixed with grime and sweat. His shadow cast coolness between her and the bright sun.

She tried to keep her head down as much as possible to keep her face shielded. The shadow helped. His rough fingers fumbled with her blindfold. She went rigid, closing her eyes and bracing for the brilliant light that would blind her for a few painful seconds.

The dirty red and white cloth fell onto her lap, and despite the intense sunlight, it was good to have the blindfold away from her face. Tears stung her eyes. She lifted her hands against the brightness. Cardozo backed away. She lowered her hands to her lap and curled them into fists. If she let go, she'd lose what little composure she had left.

Concentrate. She pushed back against the anger, fear, and frustration. *Think.* What could she do? Cardozo stood in front of her. If she lifted her head, this would be the first time she'd seen him face to face since she stood beside him in the terminal in São Paulo. She steeled herself and looked up.

His back was toward her. He appeared to be studying something he held. A series of muffled chirps. He was punching numbers into a phone— the satellite phone she had anticipated they'd have.

Her courage left in a landslide to her toes. *Wimp!* She dipped her head as he faced her. He moved closer, becoming nothing but a cast shadow again. But the shadow continued to move forward.

Cardozo grabbed Ali's hand and shoved the phone into it. The bulky phone was cold and awkward. Fear emerged, a creeping paralysis. She stared down at the black rectangle. What did he want her to do? The man changed positions, and the sun's incessant brilliance and heat hit her.

"*Fala!* Talk!" Cardozo shouted the order. His gravelly voice snapped her emotions into line. Fear vaporized, righteous anger slammed into its place. How dare he do this to her, to her father, to Cay? *Detestable man!* And his voice. She had no desire to hear it now or ever again.

Sweat ran down the back of her neck. Her tongue suddenly didn't belong to her. Her throat was stuffed with thick, dry rage. But she was a cardboard figure, restrained, unable to move. Cardozo grabbed her shoulder and squeezed hard. Ali winced with pain. She still hadn't looked him in the face. Couldn't. Not yet. The slow-moving sun mercifully hid itself behind the lush forest canopy.

"Talk." The command came again. She couldn't defy him. She was to recite the ransom message, and she knew exactly who would answer this call. She held the phone to her ear—already ringing—twice, three times.

Please, please, Dad, pick up.

Jo's frantic phone call at two-forty-five that afternoon flipped Matt Lamarque's world. Behind the closed door of his second-floor home-office outside Manaus, he paced—gut-wrenching agony of spirit, heart, and mind tearing him apart. Periodically he sat, his head in his hands, perspiration covering his forehead, his stomach in knots. He'd asked the staff not to disturb him but told them he would answer any phone calls. He refused to eat but accepted a large pot of coffee from the concerned housekeeper as he waited, hoped, and prayed for word of the two missing girls.

Mid-pace, he paused in front of the expanse of windows. His gaze darted from the walled grounds below to the iron barriers, gates closing him off from the world. Somewhere beyond those gates, beyond the city, in the wildness of the Amazon forest, his daughter was in trouble—more than likely in life-threatening danger—and he could do nothing to help her.

This wasn't supposed to happen, not to Ali. He never would have come to this inhospitable country if he hadn't been so selfishly absorbed in his work. He never should have brought her here. He'd tried to discourage her, keep her focused on finishing college, and to stay with her grandmother, but Ali was as stubborn as both he and Ann combined. With Ann gone, he hadn't had the heart or the fight in him anymore to try to change Ali's mind.

Since boyhood, the assertive "in-charge" man rarely prayed and only halfheartedly believed in God. Ann had always been the one who prayed, the one who'd taken Ali to church and Sunday school. Then, there had come a time when Ali no longer wanted to go with Ann. His little daughter had looked up at him with adoring, trusting amber-brown eyes and refused to go with her mother because "Daddy's not going."

When they tucked her into bed each night, he'd simply kissed her and left while her mother stayed to hear her prayers. He'd had no time nor seen the point in any of it—religion or prayers—and there had come a time when tucking her into bed ended with bedtime stories instead of prayers because "Daddy will stay with us."

He had won, and he'd felt a comfortable smugness that his little girl wanted to be like him. Not anymore. He had cheated her of having something he silently envied Ann for having but never allowed near his own life. Maybe he'd cheated himself too.

He raked his fingers through his hair, cradled his head in both hands and shut his eyes. Guilt filled him. He'd missed so much—had caused his daughter to miss so much. Loneliness and emptiness gnawed at his insides. A deep knowing he'd been wrong overwhelmed him with regret. With Ali's disappearance, everything suddenly spun out of his control. Faced with unfamiliar fear, he found himself imploring God for his daughter's safety.

It took forcible effort to inject calm into his thought processes. He walked over, eased himself down into the leather executive chair at his desk, and attempted to mentally review the steps he'd taken following Jo's phone call.

Jo hadn't been able to reach the Roberts' at home or on their cell. Fearful of the possibility of the satellite phone failing, Jo had asked him to call the Roberts to tell them what had happened. They'd spoken for close to ten minutes when Jo's phone went dead. Matt had immediately placed a call to Evan and Pam in São Paulo, thankful to catch them as they returned home. While his own voice shook, Evan's reaction wasn't the fear, anger, and frustration Matt expected. Instead, Evan's voice was measured, laced with a peace and a confidence that spoke reams of a rocklike faith and reminded Matt of Ann's faith. Evan would be on the earliest possible flight to Manaus to meet Matt. He would radio Maria to let her know he and Matt would rent a boat and start searching as soon as possible. He'd also tell her Jo was already on his way to her home. Pam would stay with Scotty in São Paulo to receive any phone calls, and Matt was to contact her if he received any demands from whoever took the girls. They would keep each other in the loop on where they were and what they were doing.

A small photograph of Ann and Ali standing beside their horses sat on the polished wood desktop across from him. He stared at it, longing to sense his wife's deep calm again, to hear her trusting prayers, to watch her live her faith. She was gone. Would he lose Ali too? He wondered if his prayers would rise above the roof—if God was even listening.

The desk phone broke the silence with its jangling ring and he froze. Fear of what this call might hold entangled every nerve and fiber of his being. As if his arm pushed through thick mud, it wasn't until the third ring he grabbed the receiver. He reached for a pencil and pad of paper and pulled in a deep breath.

"Matt Lamarque." He said his name, listened, then bent forward as a mix of disbelief and joy surged through him, knocked the breath from him. Not the male voice of one of the kidnappers he'd expected, the voice on the other end belonged to Ali.

"Dad?" Ali choked back tears that threatened to mutate her voice into something garbled and unfamiliar. She took a deep breath and began again.

"It's me, Dad. No … we're really okay, and you have to listen. They won't let me say this more than once.

"Please, Dad." But he continued to press her for details she couldn't give him. She chose her words quickly. He had to pay attention, had to remember every word. "They haven't hurt us, but you have to listen carefully." She paused, waiting until she could be certain he would follow the instructions she was about to give him.

Matt glanced at the desk clock. Three-fifteen. He needed to pay attention, listen to her. He drew in a breath, clutched the pencil in his right hand, poised to write. "I'm listening, sweetheart. Go ahead. I'm making notes." Quaking inside, he kept his voice even and as reassuring as he could. As if she knew he was ready, he heard her voice strengthen with confidence.

"They'll let us go when you give them your formula." Ali laid out the statement and paused.

Matt sat back in his chair, shocked. Not money? They didn't want money. They wanted his formula. It hadn't crossed his mind anyone would want the new compound. How did anyone even know the formula was complete? Very few people knew why he was in Brazil, let alone what he worked on while here.

His mind flew back through the months and days, searching for someone, anyone, who might have known more about the formula than he realized. With the exception of his assistant, Dr. Madison Kaarding, he had developed the compound alone. She'd been informed on almost every step and had been instrumental in solving the problems they'd run up against in the early developmental stages. She'd been involved in everything but the final analysis, and he'd just finished that analysis while he was here in Brazil. Had she somehow betrayed him?

He'd never committed the final resolution of the chemical process to either paper or computer, nor had he informed anyone else about how he resolved the problems. Nothing would be released until the final testing was complete. He could think of no one else who knew. He was stunned, yet the single fact stood out—Madison Kaarding could have something to do with his daughter's kidnapping. Confusion and disbelief assailed him.

Something niggled at the back of his mind. He rubbed his forehead. He *had* told someone.

Who? Think! His brain and memory were rigid with stress. The day he'd solved the problem with the formula, Erick had been away from the bio center and had called that evening. He'd told Erick … and he'd used this phone. And the things Erick had said—the warnings of kidnappings, what he knew … he'd made most all the arrangements for when and where they'd stay—and about the hike.

No, not Erick. Erick was a good man. Coincidence. He couldn't be involved. But now was not the time. He couldn't think about the possibility. He had to listen.

Ali's voice. He shook his head to clear his thoughts, to bring himself back to what she was telling him. His total concentration had to be on getting Ali and Caylee back as soon as possible, whatever the cost. While anger built in his chest, he struggled to keep his wits about him, to listen and comprehend.

"Dad, are you there?" The pause had been too long, and Ali cringed as the man standing beside her took an edgy step toward her. She sighed relieved as her father responded. But her voice failed, quivery and broken as she blurted out the first few words.

Cardozo bent over, leaning close, reeking of stale cigar smoke. She turned her head and breathed clearer air, trying not to panic. She watched his hand form a fist and his knuckles whiten. Clearing her throat, she pressed out the words, reciting the precise, detailed list of instructions.

This was the performance of a lifetime and had to be her best. Her voice strengthened as she spoke, and she did a little ad-libbing to help smooth out the stilted English the men used. Showing no reaction, they didn't seem to notice.

"I am being held for ransom. In exchange for your new formula, if you follow instructions, Caylee and I will be released alive and unhurt. You will not contact anyone. If you do, they will kill us. You are to do this alone."

With the word "kill," she heard the force of her father's breath exhale as if he'd taken a blow to the stomach. The abrupt, staccato sentences she spoke sounded strange. She hated to say these things to him, but she had no choice.

"Here are your instructions. You are to copy the entire formula for the medication onto a flash drive. Leave nothing out. It will be verified. We will be held until it is. At seven o'clock tomorrow morning, take the flash drive to Porto de Manaus. Go by taxi. Tell the driver to wait for you. Be on time. A security guard will meet you. Do not speak to him. Only show him your passport and identity papers. He will give you directions. Follow them exactly."

Molten fear made Ali's insides burn as if she had swallowed liquid lead. She'd pleaded with Cardozo to no avail, told him the formula was not complete. It *couldn't* be verified. It simply wasn't finished.

Unless ... A possibility knifed into her consciousness. What if her father *had* completed the formula and hadn't told her—or hadn't had time to tell her? Did it matter now? She'd already done everything in her power to convince Cardozo her father needed more time. Cardozo had been deaf to her explanation, ignored her. She and Cay were as good as dead.

The words Ali spoke reverberated in her ears, empty, expressionless, as if someone else were saying them. The phone in her hand shook, her arm quivered with tension as she went on.

"There will be a boat moored at the place the guard tells you to go. The name *OMarineiro* is painted on the stern. No one will be on the boat, but you will be watched. Go aboard. Go into the cabin. Find a black briefcase.

Put the flash drive inside the case, and put the case back where you found it."

The heavy cord dug into the aching muscles and flesh of Ali's shoulders, and the bark of the tree cut into her back. Perspiration stung the rope burns on her still-aching wrists. Her palm was so slippery she could barely hold on to the phone. She swiped her free hand across her jeans and switched the phone from one hand and ear to the other. This part of the message, Cardozo had told her, she had better make very clear.

"Dad, you have to listen carefully to this part. From the boat, you must go straight back to the house and wait for a phone call. Remember, do not to contact *anyone*—you will be watched constantly. They will know if you contact the authorities or anyone else. If you follow the instructions exactly, and the formula is verified as complete, you will be called and told where to find Caylee and me."

Ali paused, hating to repeat what came next. "And if the formula is not verifiable, you will not see or hear from us again." She swallowed against a deep, wrenching sob.

"Oh, Daddy ..." She was his little girl again, and into those two words she poured all her love for him. A sandpapery hand slapped across her mouth.

"Cessar! Stop!" He snatched the phone from her hand and terminated the call. Shaking, her head dropped forward. She could do nothing. Tears of anguish and fear fell into her open palms, making tiny, dirty puddles. The words "they will kill us" repeated like a canyon echo.

Cardozo released the rope from her shoulders, retied her wrists, then joined Velez. He seemed rushed as she watched his sweaty shirt cling to the roll of his belly as he moved. The men stood under the makeshift shelter with their backs to her, talking. Moments later, Cardozo moved away from Velez and dialed a number into the satellite phone and began to talk. He stood too far away for her to hear what he said, but he was animated, and even through her tears, she saw a smile of satisfaction cross his lips as he hung up.

She gulped in several deep breaths regaining calm. She figured he'd phoned someone else to tell them "the call" had been made. Obviously, more than these two men and the man in the third canoe were involved in this. Not far from where Velez stood watching Cardozo, Cay sat on a rough, makeshift seat appearing to have been cut from a log. Her blindfold was off and the ropes were still around her wrists. Ali was glad the men had put Cay in a shaded spot. Any sunscreen they'd used this morning was long gone, and with Cay's fair complexion, sunburn was inevitable.

Cay must have felt her gaze. She sent Ali a smile and two distinctly separate expressions that let Ali know she was okay and hoped Ali was too. Ali nodded, not trusting her roller coaster emotions. But when Cay closed her eyes and bowed her head, Ali shook hers. Cay really did believe her prayer would be heard.

An instant vivid vision? Memory? It all but erased the doubt she'd just felt about Cay's belief in prayer. Grandma Dansk sat beside her bed, or had it been a crib? Ali had been so sick, so hot and feverish, until her forehead cooled with the touch of a gentle hand and she watched her grandmother's serene eyes close and her head bow, just like Cay had bowed hers.

Matt Lamarque hung up, dealing with blind hatred for these men who held his only child, and terror at what was more than any human being could handle. The passion of his emotions struck him like a battering ram and he hit the floor on his knees, uttering the most agonizing prayer of his life.

Not knowing how long he had prayed, Matt rose with new strength and a calm resolve. His formula had long ago been displaced, relegated to second in importance, and he had much to do. Ali's voice still reverberated in his mind. So did the last two loud, gravely words from a man he assumed was Ali's abductor. The instructions she'd given him quickly went from memory to more notes, no detail too slight not to matter.

Evan had been correct in what he'd written in the encrypted email he'd sent Matt after they talked this afternoon, and from that moment on, everything Matt sent, he encrypted. All the houses, phones included, were probably infested with listening devices. He'd already begun to accept the probability Ali's abductors had overheard his conversation with Erick, and who knew how many others, for how long.

The knowledge was both a relief and frightening as he sat staring at the photo of Ali and Ann on his desk. His formula *was* now complete. It *could* be verified. If he was being watched as they'd said, the possibility existed conversations were still being monitored. He toyed with the idea of checking but discarded the thought. There could be fingerprints, but he didn't have time nor did he know the extent of this crime-in-progress or any idea how many people might be involved.

"It will be verified." The words Ali had spoken echoed in his ears. Verified? He doubted it, but if Kaarding was involved, then, maybe. "You will be watched." He wondered about that too. Should he ignore the warnings and call the police? If the phones were bugged, they apparently didn't know he'd called Evan. They'd said nothing about that. They could be deep in the rain forest, but they did have communication. With Caylee's involvement, he decided to wait and make plans when Evan arrived. Confused, he shook his head, praying for clarity on how to proceed and not further endanger the girls.

Trust. Take one thing at a time. Words and phrases Ann had used over their years together formed in his thoughts. He wondered again at her faith—hoped he had enough.

Talons of frustration wrapped around his heart as he turned to the computer screen, but he was already mentally composing what he'd send to the Roberts. He opened a new email then looked at his watch, recalling how within twenty minutes of communicating with Evan this morning, Evan had emailed him. With no commercial flights into Manaus until late tomorrow morning, he'd contacted a close friend and entrepreneur, Max Sykes, who owned a Gulfstream G450. Max had agreed to fly Evan to Manaus. The only problem was the jet wouldn't return from a business flight until after midnight. The jet's minimum turnaround time was an hour. They'd gain an hour with the time difference between the cities, and with the jet's capability, he'd make it in about three hours.

Evan would arrive around four-thirty or five in the morning Manaus time and they immediately had to decide whether or not to involve the authorities. Evan had contacts in Manaus, having spent so many years here, but they didn't have the luxury of much time to plan.

Matt finished the email to Evan, pressed *Send*, then checked the notes Ali had given him of the kidnappers' demands. Would he have enough time? A wave of fear gripped him. The balance of the formula still had to be written out and added to the whole before he could even begin the transfer to the flash drive.

Intent on following his daughter's instructions to the letter, he opened the file drawer holding several new USB flash drives and the wireless electronic keypad that opened the wall safe and removed what he needed. He'd meet Evan at the airport, but the flash drive had to be at the Port by seven o'clock tomorrow morning. At least the thugs had given him tonight. He typed in the password to open the document containing the formula. Timing was precision-tight. Could he do this and do it right?

CHAPTER TWENTY

The sun played games in the tops of the trees, aiming dusty rays of sunlight at Ali. Cardozo headed toward her in a fast walk. What did he want now? A noise to her left and she turned as Velez leaned over Cay, jerking at her ropes. He seemed rushed, jumpy, acting in a way that made Ali's skin crawl. Was something about to change?

Cardozo's scent reached her before he did. He poked at the ropes around her wrists, pulled at them and muttered something in Portuguese. She still couldn't bring herself to look him full in the face. His shadow fell across her. She yelped in pain as he grabbed her hair and yanked her head up.

Not again. Ali squeezed her eyes closed as the still-damp, dirty cloth serving as her blindfold covered them. A breath of wind swirled its way past her with some cooling relief as his rough hands tied the cloth around her head.

Cardozo pulled her up from the bench and forced her to walk down an embankment. Her legs weak and shaky, she stumbled, and fought to keep her balance.

She must stay calm. Listen. Pay attention to everything. The sound of water gently slapped the sides of the canoes. Not far away, Cay cleared her throat and Velez immediately grumbled over something. Ali took another tentative step. Soft soil beneath her boots. That was it. They were about to be forced into those boats again.

Why would they leave this place? Had it only been a pit stop? Her fingernails dug into her palms at the thought of getting back on the water. Was there another place they'd be permanently held? If so, logic said the only reason they'd stopped here was to make the phone call before it got too late. It did make sense to get it done during daylight hours.

Her chaotic questions weren't helping. She was guessing at all of it, but the idea they might be on the water at night shot a wave of terror through her. If there was another place they were to be taken, hopefully it wasn't far and maybe would be better than this forsaken excuse for a camp. Being hot, hungry, and thirsty made her dizzy and lightheaded. She struggled to concentrate on her footing.

"Get in!"

Cardozo's sudden terse command set her nerves on edge. She halted—couldn't move. Get in where? She couldn't see. His hand steadied her, and she took a wobbly step forward in an attempt to enter the boat. Her boot hit the side and she nearly fell.

She clenched her teeth to keep from screaming. Both boots left the ground as muscular arms lifted and deposited her into the pitching canoe. She sat down hard, her heart beating a violent tattoo inside her chest. The canoe rocked as she heard the heavy man climb in behind her.

She listened for other sounds as she slowed her breathing. Where was Gabi? She heard no voices except for Velez's continued grumbling. Seconds later, Gabi's cold nose rubbed against her arm. She gulped down a sob, relieved.

"Hey, girl, you okay?" she whispered. Gabi responded with a soft whine and her head found Ali's lap. Ali bent forward, picturing Gabi's amber eyes. She laid her cheek against Gabi's sleek fur, the tension easing at the simple joy of her presence. The pungent scent of new leather made her nose prickle. That dratted muzzle.

"I'm so sorry, girl. I know you hate the thing." She wove her fingers through Gabi's soft coat. "Good girl. Lie down." Ali kept her hands on the dog as she settled into the small space in front of the center seat.

Moments later, they were back on the water. The itchy strip of cloth, damp with fresh sweat and tears, remained securely in place. Despite Gabi's nearness, being confined in the canoe with the rope around her wrists again, Ali couldn't remember ever feeling so hopeless or helpless.

Deep breaths. She fought off waves of anxiety that threatened to turn her mind into a sandbox. She couldn't think about what she was feeling. Must do something constructive. She changed positions as often as she could to keep her blood moving and leg cramps away, then tested the ropes circling her wrists. They didn't feel quite as tight. Had Cardozo seen the mangled mess her wrists were in and felt sorry for her? Probably not. So far, he hadn't shown any compassion toward her. Not once. She shouldn't expect any either, the way he pushed and shoved her around.

Cardozo's rasping voice sounded from behind her over the noise of his paddling, and in a rush of regret, she wished she'd told her father about what had happened in the São Paulo airport. She shook her head. How could she possibly have imagined anything like this happening?

She deliberately deflected her thoughts to Kane. Had her father let him know about what had happened? Like a fist to her stomach, wrenching pain of imagining how she'd feel if Kane were in danger, pitched her forward with her face against the rough ropes wrapping her wrists.

No. She had to keep it together.

The boat jerked and leaned to starboard and she struggled to steady herself on the seat. He was changing course to go back into the river. That meant they were headed in the same direction as before, upriver. Ahead, she heard the clacking noise of a paddle against a gunwale. Were they being joined by the third canoe?

The paddling paused for a moment, and Cardozo fumbled with untying her blindfold. He removed the cloth and barked an order to someone. She kept her head down against the sharp glare of bright light as the canoe slowed and drifted. Velez' response, from behind them this time, sounded loud and sarcastic. Wishing she could figure out what was said didn't help. Did they know Cay could understand and speak Portuguese?

It made good sense to take off their blindfolds out here. If any of the other boats got close enough to see them, it would create suspicion for the men to be seen on the river with two blindfolded women. She blinked hard against the brightness of the setting sun. Cooling air caressed her forehead. She lifted her arms to wipe her brow on her shirtsleeve but kept her head down until her eyes adjusted.

The kidnappers continued to talk, and the order of their voices affirmed what Ali finally raised her head to see. The third canoe, identical to the others, moved up to take the lead with the guide, Cardozo and she were next, in the center position, with Velez and Cay behind them in the third canoe.

The lead boat slowed and for a moment came close enough for Ali to get a glimpse of the interior. Along with other items she didn't recognize, she saw both their backpacks and all the hiking gear she and Cay had brought, including Gabi's dog food. She stared at the familiar bags. Apparently, the men left nothing behind on the trail except Jo and his backpack. Probably too much trouble for them to take his from him. The memory made her cringe. That had been the last glimpse she'd had of Jo. She fixed her gaze on the river and willed her tense muscles to relax.

The sound of her father's voice replayed in her head, and she could see him again as he cautioned them to be careful before they left. Remembering his image and concern comforted her, and then the words he'd managed to squeeze in before Cardozo had ripped the phone away from her: "I love you, honey. Do exactly what they say, and I'll see you soon." Straining against the confining wrist restraints, her hands curled into fists.

The men continued their loud discussion then settled back into the business of getting to an unknown destination. The canoes moved fast, and Ali distinctly understood. Their rush was against the loss of daylight.

Other boat traffic on the Amazon didn't appear to pay any attention to the three-canoe convoy hugging the riverbank. Most of the boats were the riverboats Cay had told her ferried tourists to small hotels and sightseeing spots. None came close. She studied the fast-moving watercraft. It would only take one, but because of the distance they were away from the other canoes they'd probably never be noticed. Were they ghosts on this maddening river?

Hopelessness swept over her, and she swallowed dread of what might be next. She looked down at Gabi, glad to be rid of the blindfold, her thoughts drifting back to Kane. She listened to her uneven breathing, sensed her quickened heartbeat as pain that she might never see him again overwhelmed her.

She was still surprised at how her feelings for him had changed—how she'd seen their friendship suddenly evolve, deepen—or thought they had. She could picture him so clearly, as she recalled the last crisp, chilly morning they'd spent on the plateau and the sweet, tender way he'd held and kissed her at LAX, as if he never wanted to let her go. What if she'd imagined his extra affection, or what if he'd just been 'testing the waters' or she'd misread him?

How could this happen? He was Kane, her friend, yet so much more. Could she really risk thinking of Kane as more than just a friend? What if he didn't want more than friendship? Could she ever go back to just being friends? Would she ever know? Ali shut her eyes with an agonizing stab of fear that she might never feel the warmth of him close to her again.

She tried to rest, an hour dragging by before she checked her watch and lifted her head to look up at the open sky above the river. Daylight faded by the minute and the setting sun cast multi-colored rays, the scenery fading from vivid colors to muted pastels. Beautiful, but the beauty didn't change the deep exhaustion pushing at the edges of her being. Her arms and legs trembled. Her emotions rose and fell in uncontrollable waves. Were they going to be on the river all night?

Cardozo yelled to the man in the lead canoe. Startled, she scooted forward on her seat. The stocky, dark-haired guide replied. He looked like a native with his dark skin. He must live out here. He probably acted as a guide for their kidnappers from the beginning. Without a guide, the men most likely wouldn't have the slightest idea where they were. Kidnapped *and* lost? She shivered. And what if their canoes became separated out here? She suppressed another wave of fear. That wouldn't happen. It couldn't.

Restless, Gabi moved around, rocking the canoe, and looked up at her. "It's okay, girl. Settle down." Ali whispered, her words, threads, woven through the breeze. Gabi had to be as miserable, hungry, and thirsty as she was. Having given them enough water to stave off heat prostration, she'd bet those barbarians were deliberately keeping them thirsty so they wouldn't have to bother with rest stops.

Their canoes pulled into a wide tributary. Within moments, the water became turbid and sluggish, the trees a dim emerald arch above them. The guide said something to Cardozo, and Ali dared to glance back at Cay as they rounded the curved bank. Velez had taken her blindfold off too, and her face shone with perspiration. Some of her hair had escaped her braid, and she looked as hot and tired as Ali felt. Tired or not, Cay managed a brief smile before Ali turned back.

The guide motioned to a clearing coming up on the right. It looked about as large as two tennis courts, and in the midst of the open area, a weathered, thatch-roofed house, perched on short, rickety-looking stilts, sat back from the riverbank. A narrow deck ran around its perimeter and widened into a larger, porch-type space in the front. A long wooden dock extended from the porch, jutting out over the water.

Openings, looking like glassless windows, periodically pierced the reed and timber walls of the house. A swath of limp, dirty cloth, which Ali supposed represented a curtain, lay flopped out of one window. A flimsy door hung from broken hinges beside a dark opening gaping back at her from the center of the house. Glass, screens, and sturdy doors didn't seem to exist in this rugged jungle.

She couldn't see anything beneath the house except piles of timber and stacks of what looked like future thatch. Maybe someone was getting ready to repair the old place. Several large bottles of water sat on the porch, and a hammock hung at one end. She ran her tongue over her parched lips, hoping some of the water would soon slip down her parched throat.

The house looked like a ghetto reject, a smaller version of many others she'd seen along the river. This house had much shorter stilts and sat farther back into the encroaching forest, more on land than on water and probably got flooded every rainy season. Could this be where they'd be held? More than ready to get out of the cramped canoe no matter what the house looked like inside—she'd welcome staying there—anywhere but on the water with night falling. The canoes slowed and headed toward the riverbank near the dock.

She watched two wooly monkeys scamper from around the house, past a dead campfire, up the large tree trunk notched with steps that served as stairs, and onto the porch. Scrambling around the water bottles, chasing each other, chattering and screeching, their race ended with a comical dive into the hammock. The havoc abruptly stopped, and they picked at each other's fur as if they'd been doing it for hours. Ali heard a chuckle from Cay as they both watched the scene, a strange contrast between the two carefree animals and the two imprisoned girls. Simply hearing Cay's laughter lightened Ali's stress.

Instead of tying up to the dock, Cardozo and Velez nosed the boats onto the beach-like embankment. They climbed out and pulled the canoes up behind them, side-by-side. The guide beached his canoe on the opposite side of the dock, and Ali watched him pull a beat-up white foam cooler from the boat, setting it on the dock.

Cardozo's eyes fixed on Cay's canoe. "Stay there. Don't move." The big man pointed a menacing finger at Cay and then at Ali. "We will not be far from here, and we will be watching you." Cardozo barked the warning at them in English. Uneasy over the loud, grating voice, Gabi stood, the hair on her neck raised.

Ali held her breath. If he came at her … Gabi hadn't been trained to attack. But would she?

For the first time, Ali looked Cardozo full in the face. He pulled off his sunglasses and blinked down at her. His scowling olive-green eyes were in shadow, his brown mustache spread in a wave above his perpetual smirk. Though every inch of her body ached, she had no plan whatsoever of moving. Along with being exhausted and having her hands tied, if she tried to move on her own, she'd end up face-first in the mud. Cay nodded, indicating she'd stay put too.

Ali stared at Cardozo. "We won't move." Without thinking, she'd risked a reply. The ponytailed kidnapper casually reached up, replaced his sunglasses, and studied her. He seemed surprised she'd spoken, or maybe he wondered because she'd spoken with respect. A guess, either way.

She chose not to lower her eyes but was careful with her expression—she had no desire to anger him. Ali hated being intimidated by the man, imposing, frightening figure or not, but did it really matter? Her stomach churned as she wondered what his reaction might be. There was none. Nico Cardozo simply turned on his heel and walked toward the house.

Ali glanced over at Cay and saw a look of admiration. With one exception, neither of them had dared to say a word before now. The men had made clear they didn't want any trouble, and Velez had made his point with violence to insure there wouldn't be any. He'd backhanded Cay the first and last time she tried to speak. She'd found out the hard way talking wouldn't be tolerated. The dried blood and bruises remaining beside her mouth gave mute evidence of his short temper.

For the first time in hours, Ali's eyes met Cay's in a silent exchange. But the fear piercing the distance between them from her own eyes was returned full of something far different. The assurance in Cay's eyes spoke peace. She sent Ali a hint of a smile and a nod that seemed to say they'd be all right.

Ali shivered and shrugged off the notion. All right? How could they possibly be all right? They were in the middle of nowhere with two brutes who obviously couldn't care less if they hurt anyone as long as they got what they wanted. Her fingers clenched into balled fists. How could Cay be so calm?

Especially knowing they could die.

Praying, Kane jogged to the corral and watched Chaton lope the circumference of the enclosure. He shared the horse's smoldering disquiet. Had for hours. Beside him, Bear was his usual calm self, but Chaton had been restless and agitated off and on all afternoon—as if Ali's horse sensed something wrong. Kane did, and he couldn't shake off the feelings.

His prayers were for Ali's safety on the hike. There was no good reason to think she was not okay. This guy, Jo, she talked about knew the rain forest well, and he'd been the one wanting to take Gabi with them. That gave the man some points. "Just a long walk," she'd said. Sure. Twelve hours qualified as a long walk—and he had to admit, if he'd had the chance, he'd have taken that side trip too. In a heartbeat.

Cha trotted up to him, bobbed his head, and nickered. Kane rubbed the horse's neck and ran his fingers through Chaton's thick forelock. "Glad to see you slow down a little, fella. Our favorite girl's gonna be fine. No worries."

But he hadn't been completely convinced. Neither had Chaton. Minutes after he'd returned to the house, the call had come from Dr. Lamarque—the call that had nearly laid him out in pain and fear for Ali's life. Now a jet couldn't get him there fast enough. His heart ached for Ali and for news. *Just keep her and her friend safe, and get me there in time to help, please, Father.*

CHAPTER TWENTY-ONE

Several feet away from the porch, the resurrected campfire cast light through the open doorway. Finally freed from the confines of the canoe, Ali sat on an uncomfortable wooden chair inside the dirty house watching the firelight pirouette in eerie shadows across the walls. Sounding as if they were on the far end of the porch or by the fire, the three men talked, probably arguing, from the tone of their voices.

Ali stared at the opening to the room where Cay had been taken, hoping she was all right. No way to know. Tears of weariness, frustration, and worry brimmed in Ali's eyes, and for long moments, she fought against the sobs that would drain what little energy she had left. She shook her head, forced a few deep breaths, and tried to focus on the rest of her surroundings.

The air hung heavy with the scent of insect repellant. Tattered blue and white striped curtains waved and curled with the breeze moving through the openings in the wall. Suspended from the ceiling, mosquito netting draped over each of two rusting metal bed frames that looked like refugees from a city dump, their thin, lumpy mattresses torn and filthy. Between the beds, an upended crate, serving as a bedside table, held a single, half-burned candle. Across the room a short stack of what looked like folded gray-white sheets sat on top of a rectangular table.

Ali studied the light and shadows, overwhelmed by a sudden memory. She sat at her father's desk in the library in Solvang, faced with writing a short story for an English literature assignment due the next morning. Unable to come up with a subject, she'd idly stared at the fireplace watching the flames from the dregs of a fire. The title, *Dance of the Firelight*, and an idea came to her full-blown, a young girl taken against her will while in a foreign country.

Strange to recall the assignment after so many years. She never dreamed she'd be living a story so close to what she'd written. Firelight had danced in her imagination then, as it did now, against these crude, unfinished walls.

Taking advantage of being alone a few precious minutes, she wiggled and twisted the rope around her wrists, trying to ease the tightness. She had managed to loosen them more when the doorway darkened, filled with the presence of someone new and unrecognizable. Ali stilled her hands and sat—frozen—not knowing what to expect.

An older woman with straight, short black hair, sullen black eyes, and dark skin walked into the house. She carried a tray-like board with food-filled bowls and several thin wooden plates covered with wide green banana leaves. The faded red and white flowered sack of a dress she wore hung from her slight frame as if she were a clothes hanger, and on her dirty feet she wore something resembling sandals.

Without a word, the woman set the tray beside the sheets on the long, roughhewn table. She lit the kerosene lantern hanging on a post near the center of the room, then went to a far corner of the room to fill and light a second lantern. Placing the light on a crate near an open window, she took a third lantern to the porch. Except for the light that shone through the open doorway, Cay's room remained dark.

Ali relaxed a little, watching. The delicious scent of food made her stomach roll and complain with hunger pangs. The woman bent over the table, straightening things, not paying any attention to Ali. She lit the wicks of several squatty candles and placed them on the table, then methodically picked up the sheets and shook them out, spreading them over the mattresses, tucking in the excess.

The two men and the guide came inside and stood near the table, continuing their conversation. Ali nearly choked as Cardozo blew smoke from his cigar in her direction, then coughed until his face flamed red. He flipped what was left of the fat, chewed-up cigar stub out the front doorway and spoke to the guide. Ali caught the word *amanha*, morning. What would happen in the morning?

For the first time, the woman spoke. She mumbled a few unintelligible phrases to Cardozo and pointed in Ali's direction. Ali's muscles tensed and her senses heightened watching the cryptic scene. Cardozo said something to Velez. Nodding, Velez went into the room where Ali had seen them take Cay. A moment later Cay came out, her hands still bound, Velez directly behind her. He steered her toward the woman, who, with lantern in hand, took Cay outside.

Helpless to do anything, gripped with fear for Cay's safety, Ali searched her heart, desperate for a prayer she could neither find nor verbalize.

She closed her eyes, tears burning behind her eyelids until she heard excited monkey chatter and the scuffling sound of feet on steps. Cay glanced at her from the doorway, scrunching up her face in a look indicating something smelled worse than awful out there.

Understanding where she'd been, Ali's fear melted into a smile. But her smiled turned to anger as Cardozo grasped Cay's arm and jerked her back into the other room, mumbling something about ropes.

Jolted, Ali heard Cay's sharp protest of pain. Cardozo came out of Cay's room, chortling to himself over some private joke, and sat at the table.

Evil and ugly personified. Bile rose in Ali's throat, sick at the sight of him.

Velez bent to loosen and remove the ropes from Ali's legs and went to the table. He'd left the rope around her wrists, and it looked as if she'd be going outside next.

The woman walked to Ali's side, her back to the three men, and helped her up from the chair. She looked straight at Ali, her dark piercing eyes and the expression on her face held both a warning and compassion. Puzzled, yet strangely comforted, Ali went with her through the door and down the rickety tree-ladder. The woman held her arm and steadied her as they rounded a corner of the house onto a worn path dimly lit by the kerosene lamplight from inside the hut.

The smell assaulted her senses, and in the sallow wavering light from the lantern, Ali saw the small structure a few yards in front of them. The woman quickly took Ali and the lantern inside and left.

Glad she'd taken a deep gulp of air, Ali held her breath as long as she could. Having her wrists tied made the process difficult, but she managed. She picked up the lantern in an awkward, two-handed grip and raced outside. Immediately the woman's firm, bony hand grasped her arm, stopping her in her tracks, pulling her into the shadows, out of sight of the house.

The woman grabbed the lantern and set it on the ground. She looked at Ali, pressed her lips together and putting her hand over her own mouth, shook her head. The entire gesture conveyed the concise message, "Don't say anything."

She took Ali's hands, lifted them, and carefully, deliberately, loosened the ropes, leaving them tight enough to appear as if they'd not been disturbed. Ali stared into the old woman's eyes, and with every ounce of drama she could muster without speaking, mouthed the words, "Thank you."

She must not approve of what the men are doing. The woman had taken a huge chance in trying to help. Lightheaded, considering the possibilities now open to her, Ali's thoughts spun into nets of ideas for escape.

She'd hoped for a glimpse of Gabi as they returned to the house but didn't see or hear the shepherd in the heated blackness of the night.

Inside, Velez took over, shoved her into the chair, and swiftly replaced the ropes around her legs. He gave the ropes on her wrists only a cursory glance, and his carelessness about checking them sent a cascade of relief through her.

The guide spoke with Cardozo a few minutes then motioning toward the rear of the house, followed the old woman outside. Ali listened to the sound of their voices fade in the direction of the jungle behind the hut—not toward the tributary waters—as they left. The woman and the guide bore a strong resemblance. Was it possible he could be her son?

Velez dragged Ali's chair up to the table, and she stared down at the spread of food, her stomach in knots. After so many hours without eating, it looked like a feast. Cardozo picked up a plate, leisurely piled it high with food, then looked at her with his usual smirk stretched wider as if to taunt her with the fact she wasn't free to eat.

As Cardozo took his heaping plate onto the front porch, Ali stared at his waistline, stunned. She'd paid so much attention to the interesting terrain of his face, she nearly missed noticing he'd hooked the satellite phone onto his belt. She hadn't seen it since he'd taken it from her hours ago. Visions of hitting him on the head with a two-by-four, grabbing the phone, and running to the canoes with Cay made her smile.

Somehow, she must try for the phone, but unless she had time unobserved and could focus on working to get the ropes off, there'd be no chance at the phone, freedom, or escape. They needed to sleep sometime, and if she could stay awake …

Velez sent her a questioning look and she wiped the smile from her face. He spooned a lumpy substance onto one of the plates and stuck it in front of her. She tensed, certain he was going to untie her hands, but instead, he drove a spoon into the heap of rice and lifted it to her mouth.

Velez glared at her. "You eat!"

The relief he hadn't touched the ropes was palpable. She quickly opened her mouth as he shoved the spoon of rice toward her, feeding her between taking bites of food from his own plate.

Ali ate everything he stuffed into her mouth, happy the spoon's handle was between her lips and his grimy hand. The rice, black beans, and a banana, tasted good, but he barely gave her time to chew and swallow, and her jaws hurt with the effort to rush. Exhaustion and a mind-bending stomachache followed the last bite of fruit. She closed her eyes and steeled herself. Neither the pain nor her emotions would reel out of her control again.

As soon as Velez finished, he piled food on another plate and disappeared into the next room. Food for Caylee. Good. Drawing a breath, she forced herself to get a grip and unfurled her fists, her jumpy nerves easing with him leaving.

Cardozo returned, barking orders into the other room at Velez then strode to the table. He snatched up a banana and sat opposite Ali. He must be looking at her, but she kept her eyes averted, not at all comfortable with what might be going through his mind. The gorilla of a man was apparently still trying to figure her out. A chill shot through her in spite of the heat. He was probably conjuring up the most efficient way to rid himself of two college students.

Not funny. If only he'd stop staring.

He finished the banana and got up, towering over her. Grabbing the back of her chair, he dragged her a few feet away from the table, out of his way. She kept her eyes on him as he walked to one of the beds and picked up a bag. Reaching inside, he took out a gun, glanced at her then dropped it with a clatter onto the box between the beds.

Ali gasped at the sight of the weapon as it hit the top of the crate, spun, and stopped, the polished stainless-steel barrel pointing right at her. She squeezed her eyes shut, every muscle, nerve, and fiber tight with fear. Would she feel the bullet thud into her torso?

Nothing happened—no explosion, nothing. She opened her eyes as he retrieved the gun and laid it on the mattress at the head of the bed, barrel toward the wall. Her breath expelled in a weak, quavering sigh. What else did she expect? Of course, they wouldn't be out here without a gun, but the reality and shock of seeing one … She fought to stop trembling. Was a gunshot the way he'd get rid of them?

He looked over at her, his dull green eyes mocking, the corners of his mouth and mustache twitching in an upward curve. Hate slammed into her chest like a sledgehammer, and she battled against the foreign bitterness.

Cardozo went back to digging through the bag and pulled out two long lengths of netting. He threaded the top of one net through a metal loop and hung it on a hook screwed into a roof support. With gnats and mosquitoes already finding their way to places on her skin where the repellent no longer had an effect, Ali hoped the net was for her.

He closed the space between them in three strides and jerked her chair across the floor, centering it near the sidewall of the house where he'd hung the net. Positioning her chair beneath it, he dropped the mesh tent over her. She held her breath, wishing she could hold her nose. She didn't know which stink was worse, him or the net reeking of insecticide. As if he'd heard her thoughts, he turned and left.

Velez sauntered in and dropped an empty plate on the table. He took the net Cardozo shoved into his hand and went through Cay's doorway.

Ali was grateful they'd have the protection, but why bother, unless they didn't want to put up with hostages sick with malaria. Unsure whether from the food or the smell or both, her stomach roiled.

If they weren't going to be killed, would they be sold? A common practice was for women to be sold anywhere in South America. Her thoughts filled with terrifying images that tackled her mind—tried to hold it captive.

Enough! She blinked hard. Too much research, too much reading. It had gotten her nowhere but scared to death. She strained to see through the netting to study the room from her new vantage point then tested the loose ropes. Her position was perfect. Even though the netting gave everything a fuzzy appearance, her view wasn't cut off. From where she sat, she could see more of Cay's room, out the back window, and through the front door. *Señor* C didn't know how much better he'd just made things for her.

Velez dragged the foam ice-chest up to the table and dug into it, pulling out cans and bottles. Cardozo sat and grabbed a long-necked bottle of beer as the two men got into a heated discussion over a futebol game. Lapsing in and out of English, they settled into a steady pace of drinking, the strong smell of alcohol and cigar smoke permeating the stale air of the house.

Openly eavesdropping, Ali heard bits and pieces about the phone call, the flash drive, the formula, and the mention of money—lots of it. Neither of the men seemed to have any interest in trying to be discreet as they spoke. It didn't seem to matter. Maybe because she and Cay eventually wouldn't matter either.

She hadn't thought to check her watch and had no conception of how much time had passed. She had to have watched them play cards and lift cans and bottles one after the other for several hours.

Dozens of rounds of cards later, their noisy talk grew quieter, their speech thickened and slurred. With one last blitz of chatter, they doubled over with laughter about something hilariously funny—to them.

Whatever was so funny failed to bring a smile to Ali's lips. She watched them stumble to the beds and collapse onto the clean sheets, not even bothering with their mosquito nets. In moments, their laughter changed to snores and heavy breathing. They'd drunk themselves into a stupor.

Ali fought against sleep, hovering between dreams and reality, keeping an eye on the two sleeping men and the open door. Flickering shadows and intermittent moonlight combined to create images of monsters with fangs and claws. They crept around the room on stealthy feet, ready to attack her from every corner, howling and screaming.

Screaming—hideous screams? Startled, roused, heart racing, she lifted her hands to cover her ears. "What's happening?" She couldn't break the locks chaining her hands together. Panic rose in her throat before fear dissolved into reason. Ropes, not chains. *A dream?*

Those terrifying howls hadn't been in her dreams. She leaned forward, rubbing at her forehead. Cay had told her of the howler monkeys and their deafening night shrieks. She strained her eyes, staring into the semidarkness, wondering how long she'd slept, or if she really had ... *The men!* Another rolling wave of fear engulfed her. Were they still asleep?

The men stayed quiet, sprawled on the beds, and the menacing shapes dancing against the walls became simple silhouettes of tree branches.

Nightmares remained, asleep and awake, but the few moments of rest had helped. The adrenaline of fear infused her with a burst of energy, and she turned to concentrate on the ropes around her wrists. Working at them, biting and picking at them, Ali studied the dusky sight surrounding her. The fire had reduced the wood to embers, and the light the nearly full moon offered, dodged clouds and sifted through foliage.

She could have hugged the old woman for what she'd done. The knots in the rope weren't tight enough to hold for long. The men still slept while Ali tugged on the ropes in earnest.

Countless cans and bottles littered the floor. Minutes after they'd collapsed on the beds, the lantern hanging over the table had sputtered and gone out. The others flickered, fuel ebbing. Moonlight gave her some illumination. Her fingers and arms ached as she struggled to untie herself. Ali rested a moment then inspected the ropes. *Almost there.*

A super-sized bug scrambled across the room and out the door, and she caught a glimpse of the porch monkeys. She hadn't heard anything out of them in a while. She didn't blame the little guys. Maybe they'd been trained not to come in, or maybe they were afraid. Either way, the two stayed hunched outside, just beyond the threshold, never venturing inside.

Her thoughts returned to the ropes and escape. If she and Cay could get loose and out of the house, should they follow the trail the woman and the guide took and stay on land? Or being this close to the river, should they take a canoe? And Gabi—was she okay? Where did they have her? Would the dog stay quiet enough not to wake the men?

She must have been right about the guide. He hadn't returned, and if he did live out there, he'd probably gone home. Without him around, maybe there really would be a chance they could get away. Ali stared at her captors, draped over their beds, twitching with the effects of the alcohol. Her many questions had no answers, and time was running out. She bit and pulled at the fast-loosening bonds with her teeth and then picked at them with her fingernails.

"Finally." Ali breathed out the words along with a sigh. The noise of the forest absorbed her whisper as the ropes succumbed, falling with a rustle to the floor. Her back hurt and her arms were stiff as she rubbed her wrists and forearms. She wanted to yell to Cay with joy. Instead she leaned forward and put her head down toward her knees, stretching her shoulders, rotating them to ease the kinks.

She had yet to deal with the ropes around her legs. At least her jeans and boots had saved her legs from the same chafing her wrists and arms suffered.

Yanking and pulling, she struggled until the restraints dropped from her legs to the floor. Hope rising with each passing moment, she moved her legs, massaging them until she was certain she could walk without falling. Putting her hands on her knees, she pushed, helping herself to stand and stretch out.

She had to see if Cay was okay—they had to get out of there. She picked her way around the trash. Inching forward, a foot away from the beds. Cardozo snorted and changed positions. Terrified, her heart pulsed hard against her ribs, she stopped bolted to the floor, not risking a single move. Seconds crept by until the man's breathing became steady and even. She relaxed as much as she dared then continued toward the open doorway. Moving as fast and as silently as possible, she maneuvered around the two sleeping heaps of drunken humanity toward the other room. The floor creaked, and an ember in the campfire snapped, but the men remained passive and unflinching.

She reached the doorway and peered around the corner, blinking hard, trying to see. A threadbare sheet hung over the single window, letting a skimpy amount of light into the room. The house had surely tasted river water when the Amazon flooded. The atmosphere in the room was thick and warm and smelled damp and of spoiled food. She gagged, longing for fresh air, desperately wanting to run across the room to the window, to lean out and breathe in something cooler and fresher.

She steeled herself and stepped forward, adjusting to the lesser light. Where was she? Eyes darting, looking for any movement, she searched, frantic to see any sign of Cay.

A blurred triangle of gray-white netting spread from ceiling to floor in a darkened corner. She took another step.

Caylee?

She covered her mouth to suppress a scream.

CHAPTER TWENTY-TWO

Cay sat slumped in a chair, her arms drawn behind her. Her legs crossed at the ankles, ropes wrapped around them, woven through the chair legs.

With the sensation of a violent punch to the stomach, Ali's heart thudded within her chest, fresh terror swept hope into oblivion. From where she stood, she saw no detectable signs of life in her friend.

Had she passed out—or worse? More thoughts of death raced through her mind. She half-turned, wanting to run. More unearthly shrieks from the howlers. Her hands flew to cover her ears and she went to her knees on the filthy floor.

Stop it! She bit her lip to keep from screaming the demand to the shrieking monkeys. Echoing howls shot tremors of worry through her. What if they woke the men?

Still in stark fear, she got up but moved in slow motion. She crept deeper into the room toward Cay, not taking her eyes away from her lifeless form.

"Cay?" She whispered as loud as she dared, desperate to find any trace of life through the mosquito netting. With Cay's head drooped, the sides of the chair back pressed into the flesh of her upper arms. Ali winced and blinked back tears.

Wait. Ali held her breath. Had Cay's head moved? "Cay, are you all right?" In a slow, deliberate roll, Cay twisted her head, hair escaping from her disheveled French braid flipping from one side to the other.

Ali choked back laughter. Cay stretched out the best she could to relieve the cramping. Moments ago, she'd done exactly the same thing. Ali closed the space between them in seconds.

"You scared me to death, girl." Ali leaned close and hissed the whispered words. "I thought you were *dead,* flopped over like that." Cay managed a soft, pained chuckle as Ali lifted the net out of the way and stooped behind the chair to untie the knots at Cay's wrists. "We've got to get you out of this mess."

"I can't wait!" Cay tried to squeeze her hands closer to give Ali some slack.

"Hard to see back here. Just a sec." She tiptoed to the open window and tucked the ragged curtain up. The improved light helped as she went back to work on Cay's ropes. "Velez was rotten to have tied your arms behind you! Did the woman loosen your ropes?"

"She tried, but she barely moved them. Velez didn't seem to notice and retied them in back of my chair anyway, so it was a good thing she didn't loosen them much. They're really tight—hurt like crazy. Then Cardozo jerked the ones around my legs even tighter. I hope you can get them undone. Ow!"

"Sorry. I should have them off in a second."

"Did the Juma woman untie your hands?"

"*Juma* woman? No, but she definitely loosened the ropes. No way I could have escaped them otherwise."

"Thank God for her." Cay whispered. "They're good people, the Juma Indians. They're native to this area, and not many of them are left. I think she and the guide—and I'm sure that's what he is—are related." Cay paused. "I didn't even ask about you. Are *you* okay?"

"Stiff but good." At least the night noises covered their hushed conversation. "There." Ali stood up from where she'd crouched behind Cay, victorious in her war with the ropes. "Your arms okay?

"They're all right, but my hands feel like they're asleep. Where are the men? I heard a lot of talk and noise, but I wasn't exactly sure what was going on."

Ali grimaced. "Both of them are smashed, totally unconscious and snoring. As much as they drank, I think—I hope—they'll be out for hours."

She rubbed Caylee's shoulders and arms. "Do your hands feel any better?" If only they could run …

Cay lifted her arms and shook them then massaged her hands and fingers. "A lot better, thanks. Thank God for long pants and good boots though." She leaned over and pulled at the rope around her legs. "My hands aren't co-operating; I don't think I …"

"I'll get them, no problem." Ali knelt to attack the knotted cords. "Cardozo really did a job on these. They're awfully tight. It's going to take a while."

Cay moved her legs a little and rubbed them. "I've been thinking about how we could get away. Not much else to do while here."

"I have, too. It's been a long time since I last saw the guide. I saw him leave with the woman who brought the food—the Juma woman."

"Yes, he seems to know his way around here." Caylee pointed to the doorway. "And it's a good thing he does. Those two don't seem to know anything about where they're going."

"True. And there's more you need to know, good and not so good." Ali looked up and rubbed at her own chafed wrists for a moment. "The guide and the Juma woman left, but on foot, not by water. They went into the forest, so the guide's canoe must still be out there by the dock. Not such good news is he's supposed to come back here in the morning, and who knows what the men will do then."

"Well, your bad news says we'd better move fast. Hopefully all our gear is still in the canoe."

They continued to speak in soft whispers as Ali pulled at another knot. "If we can make it out of here, do we try to get back to Manaus, or would it be quicker to try for Jo's sister's house? And whatever we decide, how do we get there—stay on land or the water?"

"Definitely the water. The river leaves no trail and will be far safer and faster. I've tried to keep track of where we are. The way I figure, we're much closer to Maria's than Manaus."

"But wouldn't it be quicker to go downstream using the current?"

"I don't think so. We're way too far west, upriver now. Even going against the current, we'll be safer trying for Maria's than going downstream, especially with them following us—which they *will* do." Cay pointed past the doorway toward the sleeping men.

Ali nodded. "Okay. Whatever you decide. You know the river. They'll know we're on the water when they see one of the canoes gone—um, make that all three of the canoes gone after we set two of them adrift. I'd sink them if we had time! And unless there's another canoe stashed around here, they won't be going anywhere."

Cay sent her a half-grin. "There is at least one more canoe. I saw it when the woman took me outside. And as soon as we push them off the bank, they'll drift toward the river. It'll be a slow float and there's always a chance they could get stopped by roots or logs, but us shoving them off the bank? Priority on my list too!"

Ali almost laughed out loud. "Well, whether they wait for the guide to get here or not, it'll take them time to put a boat in the water, and then, they'll have to guess which way we went. Maybe they'll figure we'd take the easy way, going with the current. Right now I don't really care which direction we go, just so we get away from here."

Cay rubbed her wrists. "Those guys mean business. They won't give us up easily. Based on the phone call they forced you to make, we're nothing but dollar signs to them."

"Didn't you say Maria has some kind of a phone or a two-way radio?"

"No phone, and she's too remote for a two-way. But they do have a ham radio they use all the time. We can get help that way."

Ali's hope spiked. They had to get to Maria's.

"What about Gabi? I haven't heard a sound out of her all night."

"Neither have I. No telling what those trolls did with her." Ali failed to crush the angry tremble in her voice. "She still had the muzzle on the last time I saw her. That might be one reason she's been quiet. I hope she's slept off the tranquilizer, and they didn't give her any more of the stuff. It'll be hard to manage her if they did."

The ropes dangled from Ali's hand as she stood. "Okay, your legs are free, but go slow."

Cay made a wobbly attempt to stand, and Ali helped her sit again.

"You might want to stretch your legs out for a minute. After I untied mine, I still nearly fell when I first got up, so take it easy."

Cay nodded and stretched her legs out, rotating her ankles as precious seconds flew by.

"Do you think you can walk? We really need to get out of here." Ali gritted her teeth with impatience, anxiety lacing through her words.

Cay didn't move. Moonlight still filtered through the open window, casting dim light into the room. She'd bowed her head, and Ali couldn't help hearing her.

"Thanks, God, for helping us get loose. Please keep us safe and show us the way we need to go."

What was the matter with her?

Ali's shoulders sagged. Why wasn't Cay flying apart?

Like she was?

Ali chewed her lip and waited as Cay took her time getting up from the chair.

Cay wiped her glasses with her shirttail, put them on and looked at Ali. "We are going to make it out of here."

She made the statement with such confidence that in any other circumstances, Ali might have believed her.

"We'll be lucky if we make it out of this house in one piece." Ali hissed the words in response.

How does she know if we'll make it or not?

"Come on!" But Cay held back, staring at the unconscious men. Ali assumed she might be praying again and grasped her hand. "Cay, we really have to go." They had to make some fast decisions—and the first was to find Gabi.

Outside, Cay took the lead. She crept farther out onto the porch, slinked down the ladder, and ran straight to the canoe the guide had beached on the opposite side of the dock. Ali shadowed her every step, as they quietly made their escape.

"Thank God for moonlight." Cay glanced up at the white orb glinting through the trees. "It would be like moving through a tar pit without it."

"Yes, it helps. We need to check to see if our gear's still onboard."

Cay pointed. "I see both packs."

Ali pulled her backpack from the boat. "Not exactly intact. Looks like they've been tossed. The plastic bag with my iPhone in it is still here, but my camera is missing. It doesn't look like anything else is gone."

Cay grabbed her pack and replaced the scattered gear. "I don't think anything's missing from mine. We need to lash both packs in here good and tight." Ali found an old plastic raincoat hanging from a nail on one of the dock's support stilts and some rope to secure the packs.

Minutes later, Ali stood. "Can you finish up? I've got to find Gabi."

"Go ahead. I'm almost done with this. I think we're ready." Cay paused, staring at the canoe. "Except ..."

Ali followed her gaze and, unbelieving, completed Cay's sentence. "No paddle." They double-checked all around the canoe. "I don't see any sign of paddles anywhere, and they've done something with Gabi's bag of food. I don't see it in here."

"It's probably wherever she is. Go ahead and look for her. I'll grab the paddles from the other canoes, if they're not gone too."

Ali shot her a grin. "Good, and while you're at it, maybe you could give those canoes a shove into the trib. That should help slow them up. Gabi's most likely in back of the house. I'll check for paddles back there, too."

"We'd better hurry. We don't know how much time we have."

Ali hoped their whispered conversation wouldn't carry inside. She kept low around the house and spotted Gabi as soon as she rounded the corner.

The shepherd lay in a pen several yards away, the bag of dog food on the ground in front of the gate. It was a wonder some animal hadn't hauled it away. The abominable leather muzzle still covered Gabi's mouth.

"Come, girl!" Ali stooped in front of the gate and held out her hand. The dog stood, unsteady, whining, and wagging her tail, but she was much too subdued.

In the darkness of the jungle behind her, one of the howler monkeys decided to challenge another to a hoot-and-howl duet. Ali's fingers were as wooden as the peg she fought to remove from the metal loop to open the gate. They were running out of time.

Gabi did look as if she had been dosed again. She was so unsteady, but at least she was up on all fours. Tranquil or not, she might try to bark if she heard something close by. The leash hung from a hook on a fencepost, and Ali left the muzzle in place, clipping the leash onto Gabi's collar. She picked up the dog food with her free hand and urged Gabi forward.

Halfway around the house, she was glad for both the muzzle and the leash. She crouched, cautiously passing beneath the open side window of the house. Gabi suddenly pulled against Ali's hold on her, and a guttural growl sounded from deep within her throat. Verging on panic, Ali yanked back on the leash.

"No, Gabi. Hush!" She gave the command in a loud whisper, and for the first time she could remember, Ali asked God's help. Gabi stopped growling and settled.

They were nearly at the corner of the house when words Cay had said to her days ago came to mind.

All you have to do is ask and believe, Ali. God listens and answers prayer.

Cay had the guide's canoe ready to push off when Ali and Gabi rounded the side of the house. "I found a couple of these." Cay's voice was low but triumphant. She stood, grinning at Ali. Reflected moonlight sparking from the finish of the two wood paddles Cay held, one in each hand. "And if I had found any extras, they would have been floating down the trib right now—like the two other canoes are!"

"Brilliant! Except for Gabi, I came up empty-handed. I'm sure glad you found those." Ali waited until Cay put the paddles into the boat and then held up the bag of dog food. "Can you stow this, and I'll get Gabi in?"

Gabi took one look at the boat and decided she was not happy about canoeing again. Ali put a hand on Gabi's rear and pushed her toward the boat. The shepherd tensed her haunches.

"Come on, be a good girl," Cay whispered from the canoe. "This boat's not going to hurt you."

But Gabi refused to move, planting her rump on the shore. "I'm going to need some help, Cay. She's still out of it—stubborn as a mule."

After several tries, Gabi gave up her attempts to jump back out of the canoe, laid down and closed her eyes.

Cay touched Ali's arm. "Ready to push off?"

"More than ready!"

The canoe slipped easily through the water, as they sliced their paddles deep into the turbid tributary. With every stroke, the distance between the canoe and the shoreline lengthened. They passed the two drifting canoes. With every foot they gained, Ali's hope they would escape grew stronger. Maybe their combined experience was paying off.

The banks of the waterway blurred as Ali concentrated on paddling. But minutes later, she gave in to a worried urge to turn and check behind them.

Beside her, Gabi moved, restless. A flash of light reflected on the black water, and Ali's hands instinctively tightened on the paddle.

A reflection? Of what? The moon? Had the men heard them, found a paddle, followed them? And if they had, how far would they go without the guide—or would they have even left without him?

Had she imagined the flash? Should she tell Cay? *No. And don't look back.* Instead, she looked up. Overhead, only the charcoal silhouettes of tightly embraced tree limbs glowered back at her in the low light of early dawn. Her rocky emotions ratcheted toward panic. They clutched at her throat. Her hands hurt. She was choking the paddle.

Another glint on the black waters. She pulled in a deep, ragged breath.

CHAPTER TWENTY-THREE

Their movements were almost robotic. Ali angled her paddle, synchronizing it into a smooth rhythm with Cay's who matched her stroke-for-stroke with her own strong, even pattern. She hadn't seen or heard anything more behind them. They made their way down the dark tributary, their headway nearly soundless, sliding through the water toward the river.

Watching the sun edge up in the eastern sky, sparking through the thinning foliage, lessening the shadows with every moment, calmed her. Forest noises changed from subdued night sounds to a storm of birdsong and monkey chatter.

Crimson shafts of light rose like spires piercing the cloudless sky. Her mother would have loved Brazil. She would have come on this hike with them in a heartbeat. She had such a beautiful, free spirit.

Ali swallowed against the tightness in her throat. Her emotions soared and dipped. She needed to focus on the water ahead. But more than a few minutes sifted by before she trusted her voice.

"Hey, you're good." Ali smiled as she spoke without whispering for the first time since the phone call to her father.

Cay interrupted her paddling and turned around, her complexion silvery in the misty morning light. The corners of her mouth lifted in a grin. "You, too—we make a great team."

Ali glanced up at the sharpening tree silhouettes. "I've never been so thankful to see daylight." She tugged at the paddle as they continued pushing themselves with the help of the currents. "I still can't believe the Juma woman wanted to help us. She took a huge risk. I hope she doesn't get into trouble with those thugs."

"I don't think they'll bother with her. They can't know what she did. She sure was an answer to prayer for us though."

"Those two aren't going to be very happy when they wake up and see we're gone—I agree with you though. They aren't going to let us go without trying to find us. We mean money to them. And there's something else worrying me. If they knew our plans for the hike and all about what Dad's doing, they may know who Maria is and where she lives. That puts Maria in danger right along with us."

"I've thought about that too. Hopefully they don't know about her. And if I were them, I'd figure we would make a run for the city, that we'd think that route would be faster and easier—to go downriver with the current."

Ali pushed straggles of hair away from her face, continuing her measured paddling. "My thoughts exactly. And they wouldn't have any problem catching up to us either. But, we can guess about it all day and we still won't have any idea what they'll end up doing. So, if you're right, we *should* do the opposite and try for Maria's."

"Yes, and as soon as we hit the river and head west for a while, I should be able to tell a lot more about where we are. I know I've been much farther upriver than this, and if we can make Maria's, we should be okay."

"I hope so." Ali's cynicism translated into much harder pushes with the paddle, and the canoe responded with a fast-forward lunge.

Cay's long red-gold braid swung and her shoulders moved in a shrug. "Even if they do know, there's safety in numbers."

Gabi changed positions and Ali paused to stroke her head. "True, but they've got at least one gun. And there's something else I thought of. If Jo still has our satellite phone, he'll call Dad to get help and let Dad know what he plans to do."

"We've got some pretty serious ifs to deal with." Cay slowed her paddle strokes again and studied the water in the inlet. "The river is ahead. The water's changing a little, gotten brighter."

They paddled in silence for a while, and Ali continued to listen and glance back every few minutes. She wouldn't feel good about anything until they reached the river.

"I don't know how much money is in this for them, but if they lose us, they've got nothing." Ali looked at her watch. "Unless Dad gives up his new compound this morning at seven. There's one other thing in our favor. They have to have a guide. Thanks to you, we don't need one. They probably would have waited until the guide came back before they would leave. And if that happened, it should give us an edge."

"Guide or no guide, with money at stake, they definitely won't give up." Cay shook her head.

The idea of being back in the hands of the two men chilled Ali to the heart, but Cay seemed to know enough about the Amazon they might have a chance—maybe even a good chance. Long minutes had passed as if they'd been hours with the fast-moving current carrying them toward the river.

"Here we go." Cay pointed ahead.

Ali's heart warmed at the welcome sight of the majestic Amazon as the canoe emerged from the inlet. They pulled away from the banks and made the westward turn. Ali's arm muscles ached as they headed upriver, but she kept silent as Cay studied the shoreline. Maybe Cay would spot some signs of where they were.

"Yesss!" Cay crowed moments later. "I know where we are. It'll take us awhile, but we should be able to make it with no problem."

"Won't there be more houses along the river before we get to Maria's? Couldn't we find someone with a two-way radio or a phone?"

"There's very little chance of that. The people here are too poor, and Maria has mentioned before that hers is the only ham radio for miles in either direction."

"Probably not a good idea to take the time anyway."

Cay's attention was fixed on the riverbank. "We'll have to keep our eyes open. There aren't any more inlets for at least another mile or so after Maria's. If we miss the marker at the mouth of the tributary we need to take, we'll be in even bigger trouble than we are now."

Not another tributary. Ali groaned but kept her thoughts to herself. She'd had her fill of the dismal, muddy inlets. However, working the paddle was much more difficult against the current, so she concentrated on what she was doing.

Her hands and arms hurt as they slowed for rest, and they'd lose precious distance if they let the canoe drift. Cay paddled while Ali stretched out, arching her back to relieve some of the pain. Gabi sat up, whining, and pawed at Ali's knee. Ali took off the muzzle. "Time to get rid of this thing." Unfastening Gabi's leash, she put them both in the bottom of the canoe. She might need them. She dropped her paddle back into the water. "I've got it, Cay."

"That should make her happier." Cay stretched out then pulled up the three flasks of water they'd had hooked to their belts when they'd started the hike. "Here, these aren't full, but they were still in the canoe." She handed Ali two of the bottles and fastened one on her own belt loop. "Better clip these on. The heat is getting miserable again. We're probably going to need them."

They switched off sides, digging their paddles into the river water. After several deep strokes, the boat skimmed forward.

"So, what's the final plan, and where do you figure we are?"

Cay's reply blended with the light breeze. "If we're where I think we are, we may be able to make Maria's house before noon. Along with trying to figure out what we should do, I've been trying to imagine what Jo would do. He was hurt, but we don't know how badly. He can navigate this forest in his sleep. If he can, he'll get some help—for himself, and to find us."

Thoughts of the terrifying scene they'd walked into invaded Ali's mind. "Jo doesn't know what happened to us, but he'd have to assume we were taken. Just thinking back on the way everything looked, Jo was facedown beside Gabi. I wonder if he had stooped to see if she was still breathing and was hit hard from behind. The canoes had to have been hidden somewhere nearby, so there might be some evidence of them Jo could have found."

"Right, and we were about what—seven hours or so into the hike?"

"At least, if not more. When I last looked at the time it was close to noon, and I figured we'd be stopping to eat soon. They sure pinpointed where we would be and when. But I haven't been able to fathom why they would take us upriver instead of back to Manaus."

Cay glanced over her shoulder and grinned. "I think there's an easy answer to that. The river traffic around Manaus is constant and heavy. No way they could risk someone seeing two bound, blindfolded women in a convoy of canoes in broad daylight."

"And you think Jo would realize that and keep going west—upriver—to look for us?"

"Yes. If he isn't too badly hurt, I think he'll go straight to Maria's," Cay said, never pausing in her even oar strokes.

"I sure hope he made it that far." Ali slowed her paddling and used her shirtsleeve to wipe the sweat from her forehead. She smiled, thinking of their escape, doubting Jo would ever imagine they could have escaped from their captors. She could scarcely believe it. If Cay's prayers were answered and they did make it to Maria's, Jo was going to be one surprised man.

Cay looked back at her. "For us, Maria's is logically the closest, safest place to go. From where we were at the house last night, we were well past the halfway point between Manaus and Maria's."

They glided past an tangled maze of trees, holding not only birds and monkeys but also huge snakes—including the one Ali looked at now. Her paddle left the water, suspended mid-stroke and she tapped Cay's shoulder, pointing toward the river's edge.

"Another snake, and he is big!"

Cay pulled her paddle inside the boat and turned to look. The canoe slowed and meandered lazily in the current. "Anaconda. He's not all by himself, either. He has lots of relatives around here. They like to wind themselves around low hanging branches over the water and watch for their next meal from there."

"Well, I hope he's well fed." Ali shoved her paddle back into the gray water.

Cay grinned, picked up her paddle and followed Ali's lead with her paddle. "They do have big appetites."

"Scary."

"See that?" Cay pointed to the angled skeleton of a branch, bobbing several feet farther out in the swifter current. "That branch could be attached to a log submerged right under the surface. The river's full of them."

Ali watched the limb float by in choppy water, silvery-gray beneath the cloud-shadow and wondered what else the silt-filled river might conceal.

Cay nodded toward the shoreline. "We should stay fairly close to the bank. It's risky, but it'll make us harder to see. We still need to keep away from the overhanging branches and underwater roots though—the paddles can get caught on them."

"Not to mention overhanging snakes." Ali slapped at a bug, glad most of the mosquitoes and gnats kept their distance from what little bug spray still covered her.

Working against the current, they leaned into the paddles, staying a few yards away from the bank and taking turns to rest every few minutes.

Both had rolled up the sleeves of their shirts, and the fuller light of dawn revealed deep purple marks on Cay's arms. Ali's heart went out to her. The men had been far from gentle. Ali's own arms, sore and aching from the ropes stretching and pulling on muscles, bore bruises too. Simply paddling the boat hurt. At least, neither of them had any serious cuts.

She shivered. This wasn't the friendliest place on the planet. The river nurtured some really ugly residents. Cay had laughed when she said the "saber-toothed" piranhas wouldn't attack unless there was blood and they were hungry. But there were always the gators.

Ali blew out a breath, wishing she could turn off her vivid imagination. With each passing moment the jungle noise increased. A thin, mist dissipated into the morning light, evolving into a stifling blanket of moist heat.

She watched as the sun rose into the azure blue of the Brazilian sky. The warmth made her sleepy. They must stay alert to any sign of the men. In front of her, Cay's head dipped and her paddle slowed for a second.

Cay straightened and chuckled, glancing over her shoulder, catching Ali's eye. "Only a few thousand more miles and we'd be running the rapids near Colombia. Wanna try?"

Ali laughed and shot back. "Oh, sure. We're in great shape for a white-water run." Laughing felt good. The backbreaking and constant battle against the current was exhausting, and Cay's attempt to stay awake and take their minds off the work helped.

"But I wouldn't go to Colombia on a bet," Ali said. "It's not a great place for tourists to be right now. Even people who live there aren't immune from kidnappings. A friend told us what happened to a seventeen-year-old Colombian guy a year or so ago. He was taken, and his father ended up paying a ransom of over a million dollars."

"Then they got him back?"

"No. The kidnappers shot him anyway. The people who do the kidnapping use the money to finance some kind of a revolution."

"I heard something similar about a few men who worked for a company there." Cay mopped her face with a sleeve. "They were hijacked right off the street on their way to the job, and one was killed."

Ali sighed. "How did we get so lucky to get away?"

"I don't know about luck, but we've sure got a lot to be thankful for. Neither Cordozo nor Velez were very smart—and thank God they weren't. They underestimated us, but the biggest miracle was our Juma angel. The story could have been completely different. Your dad's formula must be worth a lot of money."

"It must be for them to do this to us. And that's why I can't believe it's over yet." Ali pulled her paddle from the water and wiped her forehead with Jo's gift bandana. She blinked back tears recalling how his dimple had deepened with his grin as he'd handed the cloth to her.

"Cay, can we rest for a minute?" Ali sighed, sinking past an edge of despair. Had she ever, ever been this tired and hurting?

"I heard that sigh." Cay twisted around on the seat and nodded. "Sure. It's okay with me." Cay's smile vanished and she squinted through her glasses.

The expression on Cay's face caused Ali instant terror, exchanging her exhaustion for adrenaline. She followed Cay's stare.

"Is it a canoe or some other kind of a boat? I can't tell." Cay's voice shook.

Ali strained to see. "I'm not sure of the boat, but it looks like there's only one person in it." The distance between the two watercraft shortened by the second, and she blinked hard, straining to see more. "Canoes! It looks like there's another one right behind it, and I think there are two people in that one."

"If it's the men, we'd better get this thing moving." Cay picked up her paddle. Their canoe had already turned and drifted several feet back downriver.

"It just can't be them!" Two canoes. So familiar. Lightheaded with fear, Ali thrust her paddle into the water as they furiously propelled the canoe ahead.

"Wait!" Ali yelped. "My paddle! It's caught!" Her paddle had caught on something beneath the water near the bank. She gripped the paddle sensing the canoe lean precariously close to flipping. The paddle began to slip from her hands.

They worked frantically to steady the boat, to free Ali's paddle, finally yanking it loose from the grasping roots. "Are they still behind us?" Ali's breath came in short gasps.

Cay looked back. "Whoever they are, they're gaining on us. Are you okay, we've got to move ... *now!*"

"I'm all right. Let's get out of here." They maneuvered out a little farther from the bank and sank the paddles into the river again.

They had passed several narrow inlets before they'd seen the other boats. Ali hoped they'd see another—soon. She glanced back. As the two canoes grew closer, she tried to stay close to shore and keep her paddle free while matching Cay's rhythm.

Then, amid monkey screeches and birdsong, Ali heard Cay's prayer. *"Please, God, help us."*

Their canoe shot forward with the increased pace. Too slow for Ali. More frustrating than trying to run in waist-deep water. She saw no waiting inlets where they could hide. Two river dolphins neared them, racing beside them in the wake of their slim boat. Ali watched them cross in front of the bow, effortless in their skill of sliding by with inches to spare. Their pink bodies flashing in the sunlight looked as satiny smooth as a new baby's skin. Seeing them there, playing, eased Ali's frayed nerves. Then, as quickly as they came, they disappeared.

"They sure left in a hurry." Cay's paddle smacked hard against something in the water. "We're too close to the bank again, we've got to get farther out than this." They wrangled the boat into deeper waters but steered clear of the swifter currents.

"Far enough." Cay let her paddle slice through the water. "I think we're good here."

Gabi lifted her head and jerked herself upright. Ears straight up and body tensed, she looked toward some unknown, fascinating sight behind them. Despite the heat, Ali's skin iced with fear.

Please, God, help us. The words Cay had spoken echoed one by one in her mind. She took a breath then took a chance, glancing backward to check the distance between them and the two other canoes.

But she saw no canoes. Her breath left in a huff and without missing a paddle stroke, she gawked at the open river. Shocked, disbelieving, she stared down at the rivulets of current their canoe left in its wake. She had not been mistaken. No boats, no nothing. Could they have gone into one of the tributaries? Could we have put that much distance between them so fast? Maybe it hadn't been the men at all? She answered her own silent questions with a nod.

Staying with the traditional, nearly mechanical pull of her paddle, she studied the riverbank, allowing common sense and logic to surface. They'd been on a straightaway for a while, with not even a bend in the river where they could hide. Nevertheless, there wasn't any way to know for sure if they'd lost them or if it really had been their captors.

She'd wait and check once more before telling Cay the two boats following were out of sight and, hopefully, gone. Her palms stung. Blisters? Oh, not now. She drove the paddle into the water deeper. They couldn't afford to take any chances.

Cay seemed to sense Ali's renewed energy and matched the speed of her strokes. The sleek canoe responded, flying arrow-straight through the dusky Amazon waters.

Boom!

A deafening thud and a long, hissing, scraping slide. No warning. She reached, desperate to grab the sides of the canoe.

The boat lurched, launched into a sickening upward spiral.

Cay screamed, terrified. Time split into jagged, horrifying seconds.

Thrown into the gray-blue waves, Ali's screams were strangled by river water as she stared, helpless, at the canoe, airborne, turning, twisting—descending.

CHAPTER TWENTY-FOUR

Lord ... please ... help.

Every breath held a prayer as Caylee struggled, clawing at the water, desperate to reach the surface and air. Bursting up, treading water, coughing and choking, trying to regain her bearings, she opened her eyes to inky blackness and the helpless sensation of being pushed along by the river's current. Had she come up under the canoe?

She kicked her legs to keep her head above water. Raising her arms, her fingers made contact with the smooth inside of the overturned boat. She ran a hand down along one side, touching the edge, trying to figure out what part she had come up under.

The center supports. She grabbed one smooth crossbeam with each hand and took in a huge gulp of air, praying there'd be enough trapped in here to keep her up and breathing.

With every heartbeat, her jumbled thoughts came in staccato half sentences. *Thank God, the water's not too cold.* The paddles. Probably gone, but she had the canoe, and she didn't think she was hurt. Her thoughts changed to whispered prayers echoing through the darkness as she took precious seconds to catch her breath. "Please let Ali be okay. Help us find each other."

Moving one hand away from a brace, she made a quick search for her glasses then sighed with relief. They'd remained safely attached to the slender metal chain around her neck. No point in putting them on now.

A firm jolt beneath her feet swept fear through her. It was too deep here to have been the riverbed. They'd taken the canoe much farther out after nearly capsizing near the bank.

Please, God, don't let it be a log.

A single limb could catch her clothes and pull her under, leaving slim chance for escape.

Again she felt a push, and this time she sensed its size. Something large and very much alive had bumped against her. Visions of caimans and alligators assailed her. She bit her lip to keep from screaming, praying as the sensation of it sliding down along her leg vibrated along every nerve. Thoughts came of all those she loved.

"Oh, dear God, no. Not here, not in this part of the river." She closed her eyes, bracing against the pain and horror that could come next. Desperation cracked in her voice, and her words sounded hollow and strange in the dark underside of the canoe. She steeled herself, forcing herself to be still, to trust.

A single verse, spreading beautiful words in a gentle wave throughout her heart and mind, calmed her, reminding her to believe. *"He will give his angels charge over you."*

The frightening sensation changed, and whatever it was beneath her feet appeared to try to buoy her up. She was moving—she and the canoe!

A dolphin? Legends and stories of dolphins actually helping people, raced through her thoughts. She held her breath, feeling a swift movement crosscurrent, and prayed she was heading toward the bank. She had no way of knowing. Seconds later the rapid muscular movements under her feet ceased. Whatever had carried her vanished, leaving her alone and not knowing whether to cry with relief or send up a prayer of thanks. She did both—hot tears coursing down her cheeks and thanksgiving on her lips.

She kicked hard to keep herself from sinking, her legs beginning to burn with the effort. There'd been no time to take off her boots. They were expendable if she stared death in the face because of them, but she had to try to hang onto them. Bare feet were not an option when she got to shore. She had to find Ali. "Lord, how am I going to get out of here?"

Push the canoe over and duck.

The command popped into her mind, unbidden, and she didn't waste time wondering why. Letting go of the supports, she put both hands on the top edge of the upside-down canoe. Shoving upward and back with all the energy and strength she could muster, and pushing herself down as she did, the slender craft, still heavy with their backpacks, flipped upright and settled.

How had she—? No way she could have done that. But there wasn't time to think, to reason it out.

Fighting back up out of the water, attempting to dog paddle her way forward, she blinked hard to clear her eyes. Through the blur, the riverbank looked to be only several yards away. Something *had* pushed her closer. She was out from under the boat but moving fast downriver.

The canoe! She could lose it. The fuzzy form of the mooring line attached to the bow of the canoe floated out in front of her, nearly out of reach. Her leg muscles ached from trying to stay afloat. She quickly shook the wetness from her glasses and put them on. Lunging forward, she grabbed the line and wound it around her hand, searching the surface of the water for any sign of Ali and Gabi. Neither were anywhere in sight.

"Ali?" Yelling wouldn't work. Her voice was too weak to carry far, but she tried again. "Ali, where are you?" No answer. The only sound she heard was the rushing of the river. "Ali!" Still no response. How far had the river taken her?

Oh, God, let her be all right. Somehow, some way, help Ali to get safely out of the river. Save her.

Caylee's sobbed plea wrenched from deep within her, tears blending with river water in her eyes.

A pair of dusty-pink river dolphins cut through the water a few feet from her and sounded without a ripple. The animals looked to be six or seven feet long. An instant rush of fond memories warmed her like a comforting hug. As a little girl she'd loved the river dolphins and played endlessly with them, racing them in her small canoe. A boto—a pink guardian angel? Had one of them kept her head above water?

The canoe rope tugged at her hand. She didn't have time to think about anything except getting to shore. The river's edge held her attention. A few yards downstream to her left, a small open area on the bank looked promising. As far as she could see, it was the only area free of heavy foliage. She might be able to get to it. Ahead of that the river curved, probably woven solid with trees and thick overgrowth and impossible to tell if there would be another space wide enough to be safe. Exhausted, legs cramping, if she didn't make this embankment, she might not make it out of the river at all.

CHAPTER TWENTY-FIVE

Ali pushed her way through dense black clouds, her breathing ragged and labored. A faint, faraway sound. Was someone in pain? The moan penetrated the walls of her prison. Who was hurt? Her chest hurt. Had she made the sound? Nothing made any sense. She fought against the blank walls that held her thoughts captive as she tried to think.

Her body was sluggish, at war with her determination to move her arms and legs. Her nose tingled with the pungent scent of damp earth, and the ground was sandpaper-rough against her cheek. Dripping strands of hair covered her face.

Why did everything feel so wet?

The river. She must listen. Forest noise. Watery gurgles and ripples. The river sounded close. Her eyelids heavy, she blinked hard watching the current curl its way around the root-tangled bank. Her shirt twisted behind her back and her pants clung to her legs. She moved her toes. Her socks were saturated inside her boots, and water flowed over her legs. She battled to pull herself up and away from the sucking source of wetness.

What happened? What was she doing here? She tried to keep her eyes open, to see something—anything—but her head hurt. She tried to change positions and put her hand to her forehead into her hair to touch the lump. Pain pulsed and stars danced behind her eyelids.

Again, awareness came and went, rolling over her as if she were trapped in an angry surf. Sounds vied for her attention. Someone pleaded with her in short, staccato cries. Was someone else in pain? Did they need her? She pressed out of the darkness toward the sound.

"Gabi?"

The cries became more insistent and distressed. Ali's chest tightened. "Gabi. Oh, please, someone help me to help her." The fog that had claimed her mind lifted. She opened her eyes to a blurry, watercolor scene and stretched her arms out toward the whimpering dog.

"What's the matter, girl? Are you okay?" Pushing herself closer to Gabi, she stroked the dog's wet fur and took in the surroundings. "Where are we? How did we get here?"

Inches away, the Amazon meandered by, licking at the soles of her boots. Beneath her, the hardpan deck of the clearing made a wide semi-circle, free of the lush growth of the encroaching jungle behind her. A long line of cutter ants, carrying emerald colored leaves, marched from one end of a fallen log to the other. Above her deep green branches reached out from the forest edge and offered shade that shifted in the breeze.

Light-headed and shaking, she pushed herself into a sitting position. She had to slow down. Maybe if she rested her head against her knees.

She looked at Gabi, lying in full sun, on her side, panting with exhaustion.

"No." Ali recoiled with shock. Gabi looked as if she'd been in the fight of her life, her beautiful coat matted, wet, and filthy.

"Oh, Gabi. I can't remember what happened." Ali leaned over to touch the shepherd again, trying to comfort her. The whimpering stopped and the dog's breathing seemed less stressed.

Ali didn't see the blood until she lifted her hand away, unbelieving as she stared at her palm, studied it, and then looked back at the dog. She hadn't been wrong as she'd looked at the sight of the bright redness smeared on her hand. Gabi raised her head and pulled herself closer.

Where did the blood come from? Ali's eyes burned with fresh tears that dripped onto Gabi's wet fur. How badly was she hurt?

Terror gripped Ali, anxiety squeezed at her throat and threatened to spin her out of control as memories of the accident crept into her mind. She clenched her fists with the effort to shove them away. If she didn't, they'd shove her instead—right into hopelessness.

One minute at a time. Concentrate on Gabi.

Blood seeped from a wide jagged gash. Ali's stomach knotted. "Easy, girl, you're bleeding. Let me look." The dog moved her head to lick Ali's fingers as she gently explored Gabi's hind leg. The shepherd whimpered and twitched but didn't object to her touch.

"Nothing's broken, but this must really hurt."

The edges of panic faded from her nerves. She searched her pockets and pulled out the blue and white bandana Jo had given her. It was all she had but would work. The cloth dripped with river water. She wrung it out and pressed the edges of the wound together as best she could, then tied the cloth firmly in place. Maybe it would help keep the cut clean and stop the bleeding. The shepherd whined and tried to stand.

"Stay, girl. It's okay." Ali paused and looked from Gabi to the river and back again as flashes of what had happened raced through her mind.

"You pulled me out of there, didn't you, Gabs? You kept me from dying in that river." Still unsteady, she crawled to the water and rinsed the blood from her hands, shuddering with visions of piranhas. So far, she hadn't seen any of the flesh-eating fish, and she didn't want to see them now.

She stood for a few seconds then shook the water from her hands and returned to sit beside Gabi. As she reached to put her arms around Gabi's neck, a collage of images engulfed her. Boats behind them. Digging their paddles into deeper waters. The terrifying, explosive thud. The canoe flipping, airborne. Cay, tossed like a ragdoll …

Caylee!

The vivid image of her friend slammed into her mind and she jerked upright.

"Cay." Ali's voice caught, twisting the word into a garbled murmur. "Cay, where are you?" She tried to stand and nearly fell. Instead, she stayed beside Gabi and held her head to press the pain and fear away.

She had to find Cay.

CHAPTER TWENTY-SIX

Caylee struggled toward the shoreline, the canoe trailing her like a bouncing puppy. Currents pulled at her and every muscle hurt. Terrible grinding tiredness seeped into her entire being, but the intermittent feel of river mud under her feet gave her fresh hope. She dog-paddled a few more yards before her boots caught on underwater vegetation and the firmness of the river bottom welcomed her. Scrambling toward the embankment, she tugged the canoe behind her.

The thin, long-sleeved cotton shirt and jeans she wore didn't hold her back, but her ankle-high hiking boots did. Filled with silty river water, they weighed her down and slowed her progress. Pushing wet hair away from her face, she wiped the fog from her glasses, her breath coming in short gasps as she concentrated on getting onto dry land.

A tree root, poked out of the bank in an arch and gave her a place to tie the mooring rope, securing the canoe until she could hide it. She scanned the thick greens and browns of the dense forest a few yards in front of her, wondering if she'd be safe and out of sight here. She'd had no other choice. At least the small open spot gave her room to rest, dry off, and figure out how to find Ali.

A thrill of praise and thanks for the dolphins and this small haven filled her as she studied both sides of the clearing. Anaconda territory, heavy with trees and foliage that gripped the shore and hung out over the water. None draped in the trees now.

Double-checking to make sure she tied the canoe well enough before she left the river, she looked over the interior of the boat. Inside, the hull was wet but not holding water and intact, with no breaks or splits. Outside, the bow did show evidence of having hit something large and rough—probably one of the underwater logs she'd been concerned about. One more thing to be thankful for. With a strike that hard, the canoe could have split and gone straight to the bottom of the river.

Both paddles had disappeared. She hadn't seen either of them anywhere. Their packs and gear had stayed put, stowed in place in the stern. They'd been wise to have taken time to cover and lash them into the canoe. She uncovered her backpack and pulled it out of the boat, breathing prayers of thanks and another plea for help in finding Ali and Gabi.

Caylee dragged herself up out of the river and looked for recent animal tracks. Not much showed in the hard-packed clearing. She dropped the heavy pack beside her, sank to her knees and laid flat on her back on the sand. Gasping for each precious breath, she rested, waiting for her heartbeat to slow before sitting.

Between the heat and the sporadic breeze, her shirt was already beginning to dry as she unbuttoned it. She took off her boots and socks remembering Ali and their interesting boot-hunting day in São Paulo. She'd had as much fun helping Ali decide on her new Ahnu hiking boots as getting a new pair for herself would have been. They'd never imagined the boots might be tested like this. Until the canoe capsized, it had been a good thing they'd worn sturdy boots, but if Ali's had weighed her down— Caylee forced the thought from her mind. She picked up her socks and wrung the water from them.

A noisy splash erupted from the river. Ali? Caylee stood, full of hope, scanning the surface. Nothing but a boto broke the water with a playful leap, and a chill of disappointment surged through her. Only a dolphin. But a second chill held the thought the splash might easily have been Cardozo and Velez instead.

Instantly, she dropped to the sand. She needed to be more careful. Her thoughts turned to Ali and the medals she said she'd won for how well she could swim. Being a strong swimmer might save her life now.

"Please watch over Ali, Lord. Keep her safe and out of danger." Caylee sent the prayer heavenward, and within seconds, an unusual quiet settled around her like a lowering fog.

She looked toward the forest. Her surroundings looked normal, but except for the gentle lapping sounds of the river against the shore, nothing sounded normal. Two monkeys swung on slender green vines between the trees not far from where she stood, but their usual chattering had stopped. A yellow-billed toucan stared down at her, completely unafraid of her invasion into his territory, though the clacking of its huge beak and its high-pitched peeping call had fallen silent.

She watched a pair of vibrantly colored parrots sail from tree to tree then into the forest without a sound. A lizard the size of her hand ignored a fly and crawled into the landscape. Even the occasional light breeze from the river had ceased.

Why is it so still, Father?

An animal? The men? Were they coming through the jungle instead of on the river? Caylee scrambled to crouch beside a palm tree, buttoning her shirt as she did, certain something or someone was poised to leap out of the forest. She had no sooner reached the palm to hide when a mournful wail came, not from the forest, but from somewhere downriver, a sound so faint she almost didn't hear it.

"Caaaayleeee!"

CHAPTER TWENTY-SEVEN

Still dizzy, her head spinning, Ali walked as close to the river as she dared, searching the water and riverbank in both directions. Neither Cay nor the canoe were anywhere in sight. She stumbled back to the harbor of shade and leaned against a tree. Gabi scrambled to her feet, limped to Ali's side, and leaned against Ali's leg.

First her mother and now this. Another accident that was her fault. If she'd let Cay know the boats were gone—if she hadn't begun speed-paddling. The weight on her chest crushed hard. A sea of staggering guilt broke over her, flooded her limbs, left her weak.

"Dad. Will I ever see him again—or Kane?" She spoke to the wind. A deep sob shook her and hot tears seared her eyes and rolled down her cheeks. Would she lose Cay, too? She pushed back hard against the tree trying to breathe, hard enough for the pain in her chest to transfer to her shoulders. She *had* to see them again, and Cay *had* to be okay.

"Caaayleee!" Her tears blended with river water on her shirt. The strange sound of her long, mournful cry faded into the pulsing noise of the river.

Nothing. Desperate, she called out again, and again, moving away from the tree, pacing up and down the muddy bank, Gabi limping along behind her, following in her footsteps. "Please, Cay, be close enough to hear me. Please, please, please!"

No reassuring voice in answer. The forest mimicked her cries, mocked her with an eerie, evil-sounding laughter all its own. A shiver of fear rattled her frame. She stumbled and sat down beside Gabi to take off her boots. She couldn't let fear overcome her. She drew in a breath of the moist-hot air and stripped off her socks. Wringing the water from them, she forced herself to think about what had happened.

The canoe had turned over. They'd rammed into something, but what unseen thing had they hit big enough to flip them—to send them both flying? One of the logs? Cay had pointed to the timber submarines with their up-periscope limbs. They'd passed some right before the accident.

Ali's thoughts instantly fixed on the men. Cardozo and Velez were after them. They had to get away, as far away as possible, as fast as they could. They'd been paddling furiously—the canoe sliding through the water like dry sand through fingers. They had to have hit a log. But from there, she recalled nothing. Not pain, not how she got to this place, nothing.

How long had it been? She lifted her wrist to look at her watch. Ruined, useless. She shoved the watch into her jeans pocket.

She scrutinized her clothes and inspected her skin for any sign of injury. The backs of her hands were sunburned, wrists red and tender, her palms blistered from the paddle—and her head thundered with pain. Running her fingertips through her wet hair, she gingerly explored the painful lump on the crown of her head then checked her hands for any sign of bleeding. No trace of blood, no open wounds.

"The boat must have hit my head when it went over, huh, pup?" She looked into an unblinking pair of serene, dark-amber eyes. "Thank God, nothing is bleeding or broken."

God?

She set her lips in a thin line. But she had no sarcasm left within her. A fresh round of tears sprang to her eyes, and she shook her head. Gabi put a paw on her knee and Ali rubbed her dog's fur.

Both water bottles were still clipped to her belt. Thirst made her tongue thick, her throat and lips, parched. She poured water into her palm and offered it to Gabi. The shepherd lapped up every drop, and Ali filled her hand twice more before tilting the bottle to her own lips to take long greedy pulls of water.

She hoped Cay still had water, but what if she was hurt? Maybe she was lying somewhere nearby, unconscious, or maybe—

No! Ali wouldn't think of it, she couldn't. She jammed the cap on the bottle and returned to the river, sweeping thoughts of death from her mind.

Again she called Cay's name. No answer as she listened. Instead, a gradually settling silence as raucous birds and chattering monkeys quieted. Periodically she called out, the single word skipping across the water as if laughing at her.

Uneasy with the expanding quiet of the forest, and fighting off sheer terror, Ali paced, retracing her steps over and over. Would her life end out here in this forsaken place? Her twenty-one years of life suddenly stood out in stark comparison with Cay's. Cay's life counted, but Ali had done nothing significant, nothing that mattered, and there would never be another chance. Twice, and maybe more, she'd avoided death in a single day. Why wasn't it over?

Emptiness and pain rose in her chest like searing hot lava, the same pain that burned through her when her mother died. She stopped pacing and held her breath, sensing someone near. The presence was so tangible, so real, she turned to look through the trees into the jungle beyond.

"Is anyone there? Cay?" She spoke the words, daring to hope. But no one stood behind her, only the now-silent rain forest.

The words Cay had spoken to her only days ago rose in Ali's mind. She'd wanted to know how Cay could be so serene, so centered no matter what happened. And Cay had answered as if she understood. Ali had never stopped blaming herself for what happened to her mother.

"Jesus promised us his peace. He even heals broken hearts, Ali. He's always right there with you, especially when you're in trouble."

Ali couldn't imagine Cay ever having a broken heart or being in any kind of trouble. She'd banished the words from her mind, telling herself Cay didn't really know how she felt. How could she? But Cay had said more.

"God wants you to believe in his Son, Jesus, and to ask him into your life. He loves you, Ali. The same Jesus who forgave and saved me will save and forgive you too. He died for us, but he left death behind, and he lives again, for both of us, and for everyone who believes in him."

Ali shook her head, her fingernails digging into the palms of her hands. Again, tears came, this time with twisting regret she hadn't done what Cay had asked her to do right then and there.

Cay's remembered words whispered in a breeze that moved her hair around her shoulders like a soft hug. "He's closer than breath, Ali. You won't ever be lonely. He wants to help and comfort you, and he will never leave you. You only have to ask."

Ali gazed at the beauty and wildness around her. She stood in the middle of Brazil, alone with Cay's words radiating in her heart. At the time, she'd heard only with her ears. Now, Cay's words melted like snow beneath a warm wind and touched the depths of her spirit. With all her heart, Ali wanted to know God like Cay did, to walk with him, to have the peace of mind and heart Cay had with Jesus.

"Please, God, help Cay."

She shivered—with joy? A prayer, but she needed to do more. Not because she had to, but because with her whole being, she *wanted* to.

Gabi looked up and wagged her tail as if to reassure her. Ali fell to her knees barely able to see through her tears as she ran her fingers through Gabi's fur.

"I'm not sure how to do this, Gabi."

Dark eyes studied hers as if to say, "Yes, you do."

Ali closed her eyes and took a deep breath. She was small, so insignificant in this huge, silent forest.

"Lord ... Jesus, I've been so stubborn and hard-headed, I haven't listened, even when in my heart I knew I should. I've done so many things

I'm sorry for, so many things that were wrong. Thank you for loving me in spite of all that. Thank you for Cay's friendship. Please keep her safe, and help us to find each other. Please, heal Gabi's cut." She kept her eyes closed, the breeze cooling the tear-trails on her cheeks, and lifted her face toward the sky.

"God, I don't want to feel empty and alone anymore. Mom loved you. I know she's in heaven, and I want to know I'll be where she is when I die. Thank you for giving your life so I can be. Thank you for my life, my friends, my family, and thank you for never leaving me, even when I turned away from you. Please come into my life now."

She paused, still on the ground. She closed her eyes and waited, not knowing what she waited for.

She was unsure quite when the warmth enfolded her—so gentle and comforting she didn't want to move. She kept her eyes closed and remained motionless, breathing in scents and sounds and indescribable peace. She didn't try to stop the smile or the deep joy that bubbled up inside and covered her arms with chill bumps. Hope grew and transformed into a knowing. She truly was not alone.

"Jesus, thank you."

Gabi sat beside her—quiet while Ali prayed out loud on her knees on the bank of the Amazon River—but she moved now. A little shaky, the big German shepherd stood and licked Ali's face.

Ali put her arms around Gabi, stroking her, thankful the dog could stand at all, but Gabi didn't appear to be favoring her leg. Ali loosened the bloodstained bandana, letting it slide off so she could check the wound.

"Oh, girl, that's a lot of blood … but this can't be. Where is it? What's going on?" She held her breath and got closer, spreading the dark red, matted fur out in every direction, searching for the gash, blood covering her fingers.

"I don't understand."

Gabi held perfectly still, while Ali examined every inch of her. Blood still covered the dog's leg, but Ali saw no evidence of the injury anywhere on

Gabi's entire body. Still sitting beside the shepherd, Ali stared skyward—awed as the truth became clear. She hugged Gabi and laughed out loud.

"You healed Gabi! You healed her cut, God. It's gone. It's really gone!"

A cascade of thoughts piled against the edges of her mind. If she hadn't already seen the wound with her own eyes, she might have doubted. If it hadn't been for the blood coating the fur right down to Gabi's skin, she might have doubted. She might have believed the blood was from her own head, but there was only a lump. She hadn't a single open wound, only scrapes and bruises. How could she possibly doubt any longer?

A butterfly with rainbow-colored wings that reminded her of stained glass church windows flew in a lazy circle above them then disappeared into the trees.

Her mother would have said seeing a butterfly right then had significant meaning. Ali drew in a slow, deep breath, scanning the beautiful creation that was Gabi from her head to her tail. Had God known then the little rescue puppy she held in her arms so long ago would save her life today? She sat there, filled with memories of other events in her life. Each took on new dimensions. She saw God's hand in them all.

Ali got up and walked to the edge of the water, absorbed in the wonder of the last few moments. A cooling breeze swept around her along with the sense of being free. The color red no longer held fear. The heaviness of guilt no longer weighed on her. She was changed, and still changing second by second.

"Jesus—I think I love you." Her whisper feathered out over the murky majesty of the Amazon. "Cay calls you 'Lord.' It took me awhile, but I'm so thankful you're my Lord too."

CHAPTER TWENTY-EIGHT

Anxious, and listening, Caylee stepped forward, her bare toes digging into the river mud. "Ali?" With the stress of all that had happened, she could be hearing things.

"Caaayleeee!" A sudden, quickening wind blew over the surface of the river, twisting the sound of her name into an eerie, ghostly moan. Her heart in her throat, Caylee could not mistake the voice. Ali called to her.

"Ali." Caylee breathed out the name, shivering as much from the cool breeze as from hearing the sound it held. The strange quiet couldn't last. The jungle was never quiet for long, and she was desperate to hear more.

"Ali, I'm here. Are you all right?" She yelled the words back into the direction she'd heard Ali's call, praying no one else but Ali would hear them.

Oh, God, let her be okay.

"I'm okay. Are you?" Faint but audible, Caylee caught Ali's answer as the wind died along with the final notes of Ali's voice.

"Oh." Caylee choked out the word, tears of relief and joy spilling down her cheeks. "Thank God. Thanks, Lord, for watching over us—both of us."

Precious seconds passed before she swallowed hard and responded. "I'm okay too. Stay where you are. I'm coming." With the words barely out of her mouth, her final call seemed to reawaken the forest. The noise returned, drowning out any hope of their hearing one another again.

Ali couldn't be very far away. Hoping she'd pinpointed the direction she needed to go to reach Ali, her thankfulness and relief dissolved into a groundswell of ideas on how to get to her. Her thoughts became prayers for insight, and ideas formed as she paced the width of the shallow clearing.

They'd passed an open spot a few minutes before the boat capsized, one animals probably used to get to the water. It was possible Ali could be there. She sat down at the base of a palm tree near where she'd laid her backpack. A fat yellow and green water lizard inched toward her left foot. Deep into trying to figure out what to do, she chuckled as the little reptile settled beside her bare toes and sat there, brazenly looking up at her.

"I've got to decide the best way to get to her—fast." She gazed at the attentive lizard. "She's downstream. I could try finding the footpath, but taking the canoe would be quicker, plus we'll have it to use to get to Maria's. But with no paddles, I'm not going anywhere."

She paused to push her glasses up on her nose. "Oh, great, now I'm talking to a lizard." With a shake of her head, she reached over and picked up her wet socks, flipping them over a sun-dappled bush. "There isn't going to be much time for these to dry out. What do you think, Liz?" The lizard zipped sideways and skittered toward the other side of the clearing.

"Something I said?"

Something sharp pinched the back of her arm then gently scratched it. Caylee stifled a scream and yanked her arm away, jumping to her feet, ready to run. A short, black blur scampered around in front of her, and a large pair of brown eyes stared out from a fuzzy, round face. The face tilted up and looked at her with its teeth bared in a silly grin.

Caylee laughed out loud, relaxing as the tension drained from her nerves. The tiny wooly monkey's expression changed as if insulted, and it screeched at the top of its lungs.

"No wonder Liz hightailed it, you rascal!" Caylee shook her finger at the monkey. "You scared the life out of both of us." The animal squalled again and held out its arms, as if asking Caylee to pick her up. Caylee lifted her arms, but before she could even complete the offer, the monkey catapulted herself into them.

"Unbelievable. You look exactly like Miss Tess. What are you doing out here alone?" Caylee scanned the tree branches at the forest edge but saw nothing. "You can't be very old. Where's your mother?" The baby wallowed in her arms, making satisfied, cooing noises.

Attempting to put the monkey down, the little creature clung to her. "Okay, okay, *macaco*." She kept her voice calm. "I'll hold you for a minute more. You're one lonely little girl, aren't you?"

But big brown eyes held hers and small fingers wrapped tight around her forearms. "Well, okay, you can stay, but you have to behave. You sure aren't going to be of much help, but you do have one saving grace—you've given me something besides a lizard to talk to. My guardian angel has a great sense of humor, but *this* is over the top."

She shook her head and smiled down at the baby macaco. "You have to have a name. I'm christening you *Anjo*, for angel. From now on you've got no choice except to be angelic. I do *not* have time for monkey mischief."

She gave Anjo a few more seconds, then set her down to search through her pack. The Swiss army knife she'd stuck in the side pocket would work. The clump of fan palm trees to her right held the branch she needed. Reaching the branch looked impossible, and she scanned the shallow clearing for a solution until she realized she was sitting on one.

Except for putting up with Anjo's antics beside her, rolling the lightweight log over to the trees was the easiest part. She shoved it hard against one of the palm trees, wedging it in tight to steady it. She opened the knife and stood on tiptoe to grab a branch large enough to become the "paddle" she envisioned. Separating the palm frond from the tree was a mini-battle, and the whole effort left her trembling, her strength slipping away. They'd eaten hours ago; hunger clawed at her stomach. She pulled a package of crackers from her pack, and sprinkled the leftover crumbs for the tiny monkey as she worked.

Using the log as a workplace, she trimmed the long green leaves of the fan-shaped frond. Anjo climbed into her lap as Caylee whittled away sharp edges from the rigid branch.

"What do you think? Will this make a halfway decent paddle?" The monkey looked at her from her cozy spot and curled her lips back into another silly smile. "Okay, goofy, now I know what you think. I think it will not only make a fairly good paddle, but it will also make a perfect rudder. We'll float downstream with the current."

Help me find Ali, Lord, and keep her safe.

Moments later, along with the stubborn little monkey that wasn't about to stay behind, Caylee finished loading the canoe. Using the new paddle, she pushed off from the shoreline and stayed as close to the bank as she dared. Anjo wrapped herself around Caylee's boots and fell asleep.

She had to keep from wanting to sleep too. If Ali could hear her, she couldn't be too far away. But would there be any second chances if she overshot the place where Ali was?

CHAPTER TWENTY-NINE

She's coming! Cay's voice, carried down on the wind from upriver, sent flashes of hope through Ali. Beside her, Gabi's ears pricked up and she raced in circles around the clearing, prancing back to Ali's side, her tail wagging.

"Thank God, she's okay." Ali breathed the prayer as if her new relationship had always been in place, as if she'd been in a two-way conversation with God all her life. "Thanks, Lord, that she's coming. I'd never have been able to get to her."

"Did you hear what she said, pup? She's okay!" Gabi gave a rare, sharp bark in response and paced the ground around the spot where Ali stood. Ali quickly raised her finger in warning. "Hush, girl. No more noise. If Cay heard us, the men might be able to find us."

The matter-of-fact calm in her voice surprised her, as she realized the unreasonable panic was gone. The presence she'd felt as she knelt by the riverbank remained with her as she stayed near the water's edge, listening. The warmth of being held close with love hadn't changed, and she hugged herself with quiet joy.

She gazed out over the river, huge and forbidding, thankfulness sprinkled through her thoughts like a gentle mist, gratefulness that fear no longer gripped her. She took a deep breath. The world felt fresh and new and wondrous. The image of her mother's serene face came to mind and with it an even deeper peace.

Thoughts of Kane filled her heart, and a new tenderness of love for him welled up within her. Bits and pieces of their shared childhood rose in her memory. Little things he'd said to her as they'd studied together, played together, and rode together—things she'd ignored or paid little attention to suddenly held tremendous significance. Her mind tumbled with fresh questions. She had so much to ask him, to share with him.

The wind increased and brushed through the trees with a final sigh, leaving moist, listless air behind. Ali held her breath with thankfulness and awe as the jungle stopped holding its breath and burst back into life. Rising in a crescendo from every direction, the air filled with monkey chatter, screeches, and birdsong. She turned back toward the forest. Gabi settled down and stood beside Ali, nuzzling her hand with a wet nose.

"You sure are feeling better." Ali stroked the shepherd's back. "My head's fine, too, thanks." She chuckled and reached to touch the lump on her head. "Let's see if we can find a safer place to wait rather than standing out here in the open."

Ahead of her lay the evergreen darkness of the jungle, while behind her was the risky openness of the riverbank. She must find a place to hide and still be able to see the river. She couldn't take any chance she'd miss Cay, and Cay had two possible choices on how to reach her. Land or water. She looked down at her faithful friend.

"All right, Gabi, you're the only one I have here to talk this out with, so listen up." But she hesitated with the realization what she'd said was not true.

"No. There is Someone else to talk with now." She shook her head in wonder at the strange, but welcome, new direction her life was taking.

She smiled down at Gabi. "Okay. This is new for us. I'm talking things over with the Lord, and you get to listen." Gabi's tail flopped back and forth. She lifted her head and sniffed the air. Her eyes fastened on the narrow trail from the clearing that disappeared into the trees and brush, as Ali continued, thoughtful and reasoning.

"If Cay was able to save the canoe, she'll float back down with the current. If not, if she can find a trail, she could come on land." But finding any trail didn't look like a good alternative as she looked at the dense growth.

Without warning, Gabi uttered a low, menacing growl. Ali instinctively grabbed her collar as the fur on the back of the shepherd's neck stood straight up.

"What is it?" Ali stooped beside Gabi, looking in the direction of the jungle—and froze at a new sound. A distinct, piercing snarl and a series of throaty grunts came from close by.

An icy chill traveled the length of Ali's spine. Jaguar. She and Gabi could be in serious trouble. Her grip on the dog's collar tightened. They'd come across a lot of wildlife, but they had not seen a jaguar. Jo mentioned, though he'd often heard them, he'd only seen two in all the time he'd lived out here. As rare as they were, this one had just announced its presence. Gabi growled again.

God, please help. Keep her quiet, and make that thing go away.

"Quiet, Gabi." Ali made the demand in a firm whisper. She pulled at Gabi's collar, forcing her to the side of the clearing and into the thick growth to hide. Crouched beside the dog, she looked out over the open area and, for the first time, saw tracks in the softer earth near the path. The large, indented prints stood out in full relief from the rest of the smaller ones. Why hadn't she seen them before? This place had to be where animals came to drink.

She looked at Gabi, tugging the heavy shepherd back farther into the trees and ferns. Concerned about piranha, she hadn't taken Gabi to the river to wash the fast-drying blood from her leg, and she couldn't remember what she'd done with the bloodied bandana. Now she had to face the fact the scent of blood could be drawing a hungry animal straight to the clearing.

Her prayers intensified, filled with fervent pleas the cat would be full of food and only want water, that their scent would somehow be carried away and they'd be ignored. But the grunting sounded closer and exactly as Jo had so vividly described it. Her heart pounded as she kept praying for their safety and kept a stranglehold on Gabi's collar.

A light breeze picked up, blowing tendrils of Ali's hair around her face. The wind had changed direction, wafting out from the jungle. Pungent and rich with the smells of damp earth, it blew over and away from them, taking their scent out over the river. If the breeze continued, maybe the cat wouldn't be able to tell they were there.

Another loud snarl, a rush of birds and monkeys abandoning the nearby trees and bushes, then silence.

God, please help me keep Gabi in check. Don't let her jerk away from me.

Finding a strength and presence of mind she didn't know she possessed, she held Gabi's collar with her left hand and reached over Gabi's quivering body with her right arm. Placing her hand palm up, beneath and around Gabi's jaws, she enforced silence and restraint. Ali held her breath, thankful Gabi didn't fight her, and kept her eyes locked on the worn path emerging from the woods.

Seconds later, a majestic jaguar with jade green eyes made a graceful entrance into the clearing. In awe, Ali gazed at the magnificent, jet-black animal. A faint but unmistakable pattern of spots covered its muscular body, its shiny coat glistening in the sun. Padding over to the water's edge, the cat drank its fill before ambling back into the forest.

Thanks God, for changing the wind.

For long moments, Gabi trembled under Ali's intense grip as they remained quiet and in place.

"Stay, Gabi." She released the dog and stood. The shepherd obeyed, her attention remaining strictly on Ali. Ali gazed down at the alert, yet submissive, dog with a vividly clear impression. If the giant cat had turned and made a single threatening move toward her, no power on earth could have—and no Power in heaven would have—restrained Gabi from protecting her.

And if she didn't do something to fill the time, she'd be a fidgeting mess. It seemed forever since she heard Cay call to her. She had to be here soon. Ali paused and closed her eyes.

Help me to be patient, Lord, and to keep trusting.

She reached into her pants pocket, her fingers closing around the small, flat pearl-handled jackknife Kane had given her the Christmas they were ten. Glad she'd brought it—and that the men hadn't found it—she pulled it out and flipped it open, using it to rip a long vine loose from a tree. She made a makeshift leash for Gabi then cut another vine, stripping it into three lengthy strands. Maybe useful, maybe not, she braided the strands into a rope then sat on the edge of the clearing to form the rope into a lasso. Brush helped to hide her as she worked and watched both the river and trailhead for signs of Cay.

A bobbing dot in the distance grew to canoe size as Ali strained her eyes to see. She stood and grabbed Gabi's collar, backing toward a cluster of trees. A boat … but who? It was coming from the right direction. Someone waved.

"Ali."

Tension huffed from Ali's lungs and melted from her body. "Cay, over here." Ali let go of Gabi's collar and ran to the bank, waving.

Cay battled to cross the current and nose the boat into shore. What she held in her hand didn't look much like a paddle and it wasn't moving the canoe nearly fast enough. The lasso. She dashed the few yards back to get it, coiling it as she returned.

"Here, catch this." Holding on to one end, Ali threw the lasso toward the bow of the canoe. Her first cast fell short, and she raced against time and the current to coil and throw it again. The second attempt landed across the bow of the canoe.

The canoe rocked as Cay snatched at the vine, missed, then grabbed again. "Got it! And am I ever glad to see you." She hung on to the braided vine while Ali pulled the boat closer to the bank. "Hey, this makes a great rope. You've been busy."

"You have no clue." Ali smiled at her. "And you're a sight I wondered if I'd ever see again." She continued tugging on the rope, and seconds later, a foot away from missing the clearing, the bow of the canoe dug into the shoreline. Gabi barked once and plunged into the water toward Cay.

"No, Gabi. Come." A telltale swirl of blood trailed the dog and Gabi didn't waver in her track toward the canoe. Anxious, Ali searched the water that washed away the evidence of Gabi's injury, but no hungry, razor-toothed fish were in sight.

Cay's grin faded as she stared at Gabi then at the dark swath in the water behind her. "Is she bleeding? Was she hurt?"

"She's okay, I'll tell you more aft ..." But Gabi's happy greeting evolved into an uncertain growl as a wooly little head with two large round chocolate drops for eyes, popped up and peered over the side of the canoe. The eyes widened, and a tiny body as black as a charcoal briquette flew up and grabbed Cay around the neck.

Ali clapped her hands. "Easy, Gabi. Come here to me!" The dog retreated to the bank, the black and tan fur on the scruff of her neck still ruffled. She shook the water from her coat and stood uneasily beside Ali.

"What in the world is *that?*" Ali laughed, yanking the watercraft farther up onto the embankment.

"Ali, Gabi ... meet Anjo." Cay smiled, trying to untangle the octopus-hold the monkey had around her. "She found me, and I can't believe how much she looks like Miss Tess. She must have been born in captivity, she's so friendly."

"Well, hello there, Anjo. I have an idea it's a pretty big compliment you look like the famous Miss Tess." Ali reached over to steady the canoe, grabbing Cay's hand as she stepped out.

Gabi behaved but stood her ground, keeping a minimum of three feet between herself and the strange, wide-eyed creature.

Cay studied Ali. "Are you okay?"

"Other than a little bump on the head, courtesy of the canoe, and an encounter with a big black pussy cat, I'm great.

"You saw a jaguar?"

Ali grinned, watching Cay's eyes widen in surprise behind her glasses. "A black?"

"Thankfully, it was only thirsty, and we were downwind, but yes, coal black and beautiful." Ali looked Cay up and down. A rip in her not-so-white shirt, wet boots, and some mud stains on her jeans were all that told of the accident. "No cuts, bumps, or bruises when the canoe flipped?"

"Some overstretched muscles and a couple of bruises but good other than that. And rescuing the canoe was a miracle all by itself. Right now, I'm just really tired."

"There's a downed tree over there in the shade with your name on it."

"That sounds so good. We can risk taking a few minutes, I guess." Cay looked at the now empty spot her watch used to occupy, shrugged, and grinned at Ali.

Ali smiled and patted her jeans pocket, nodding. "Guess both our watches are toast." She eyed the backpacks secured in the rear of the boat. "I can't believe all our supplies and packs are still okay." But neither the muzzle nor Gabi's leash were anywhere in sight. She glanced at the makeshift vine-leash. It would work for a while. "Tying them in there tight sure paid off."

"Your idea of using the plastic raincoat worked too. Kept things dry." Cay pulled the canoe completely out of the water. She reached in to undo the cords holding the backpacks and handed Ali hers. The monkey, her long arms around Cay's neck, slid over Cay's shoulder to her back and peeked around at Ali.

"So you named this little guy Anjo, Portuguese for—?"

"Angel. And she's been one all the way here too. Speaking of angels, I think ours were on special assignment today. Are you sure your head's okay? No signs of a concussion?"

"Nothing more than a goose egg. Swelling's already going down. It'll be fine." Ali leaned over to hug Cay, screeching monkey and all. "Here, I can carry both packs." Ali took Cay's pack, and they walked deeper into the clearing toward the fallen tree.

"I can't remember when I've been happier to see someone." Ali smiled. "I have so much to tell you, I hardly know where to start. But before I do, we probably need to figure out where we go from here. Just because we haven't seen those guys doesn't mean they aren't still somewhere close." Ali dropped the packs onto a patch of rough ground cover and sat on the log.

"Without us, they have no ransom, and I know they won't give up trying to find us."

"I don't believe they will either. We've got to get to Maria's. We'll be safer there than anywhere."

"We have to get help for Jo, and we might be able to catch Dad before he gives up the formula. The faster we can get to some kind of communication, the better." Ali's stomach gnawed at her insides, and she looked over at her pack.

"You need to eat." Cay opened her pack and pulled out a plastic carton of crackers and cheese. "Here, I've already had something."

Ali didn't argue. She ate between sentences and dug into her backpack during the pauses. "You know, we haven't taken the first photo yet. My camera's gone, but I've still got this." She took the plastic bag holding her iPhone and held it up. "Just wish we had the time …"

Ali froze, and the bag slipped from her hand to her lap as several tumultuous splashes instantly focused her attention on the river.

Dark. So was the SUV that seemed to shadow her as she drove home tonight. Annoying! Madison Kaarding pulled her car into her driveway and pressed the garage door opener on the visor.

Her Skype conversation with the Chinese couple left her with the strong impression they would not be leaving any witnesses. That suspicion plagued her thoughts.

She turned off the engine, shut the garage door, and sat, hands grasping the steering wheel. At three in the morning, two days after she'd talked with the Shins, she'd wakened from a violent nightmare, unable to breathe, suffocating, a pillow pressed against her face. The furry weight had been nothing more than Beau using her head as a footbridge to reach his favorite sleeping spot. But if she faced the facts, nothing would stop the massive wave of fear she'd set in motion. She'd started it, she was in the midst of it. The Shins didn't need her anymore.

Minutes later, only the street lights illuminated the dark living room as she sat with Belle and Beau on either side of her and Pax at her feet. Fear she hadn't experienced in decades spilled down her backbone, spiked with ideas on a dozen ways she could survive. Threatening the Shins with exposure was pointless. Sheltered in a foreign country, they would deny everything.

"No!" Both cats scattered as Kaarding straightened, rigid. Pax raced to the safety of the hallway as she abruptly stood, went to the window, and paced. The sudden thought she might have made a wrong assumption took her breath, yet steeled her thoughts.

The SUV had looked more official than one the Shin's might have arranged for. But whether the vehicle held a hit man sent by Shin or a detective hired by Zoran or agents from the FBI, she'd handle it.

Kaarding stopped pacing and smoothed the upswept sides of her hair, smiling. She'd figure out how to protect herself, finish playing her part, collect what was due her, assume her new identity, and disappear, probably much sooner than she'd originally planned. But before anything else she had to make herself indispensable to the Shins. This project would end— as intended.

CHAPTER THIRTY

Cay gasped. "The men!"

Ali echoed Cay's terrifying words then dared a glance toward the water.

But her breathing slowed, her heart calming as half a dozen pink-and-gray shapes roughhoused in the river with wild splashes, moving steadily nearer to the bank. She stood, laughing, and pointed toward the river. "Right. Pink men."

"That is one weird mental picture—men in pink." Cay's contagious laughter had her close to hysterics as they shared their relief. No men in canoes anywhere in sight.

"What in the world?" Ali jogged to the water's edge, motioning Cay to follow. "Cay, look at what they've got." The river dolphins played, and their toy looked familiar. "Am I seeing things or *is* that a paddle they're tossing around out there?"

"You aren't imagining things." Cay squinted in the sun, trying to get a better look. "That is a paddle. I've heard of them playing with things they find in the water, but I've never seen it happen."

"I can't believe it." Ali shook her head. "This has to qualify for *Ripley's Believe it or Not.*"

"Wish we could get a shot of this. Just look at them." Cay stepped closer to the waterline.

"Wait a minute. That's pretty strange." Ali stayed, locked to the water's edge, still watching the playful animals. "It's *almost* as if they want us to have the paddle." She stared at a fast-approaching dolphin. "And that one is pushing the thing toward us!"

"You know." Cay's tone changed to somber, "that paddle is the only way we're going to be able to move the canoe against the current. The one I tried to make is no more than a rudder."

Ali nodded. "Mm, not exactly jet propulsion. We'll need at least one good paddle to get anywhere with any kind of speed."

"Without it we might as well find the trail and walk to Maria's house." Cay paused as a huge pink boto leapt into the air, splashed down and vanished beneath the blue-gray water. "They're coming closer. I think I can get to it."

"What if they really don't want us to have it?" Ali envisioned botos furious at the loss of their new toy.

"I'm not sure, but I don't think we should wait. If I don't get to it, the current will take it. I'm going after it." Cay already had her boots off and waded into the water.

"Can you reach it? Want me to get the rope?"

Cay didn't answer. She swam straight out to where the wooden paddle floated within an arm's-length distance from her. Ali held her breath as Cay moved into deeper water, lunged forward to grab the paddle, and struggled against the current to the riverbank.

Cay shot her a triumphant grin. "It's the paddle I used before. Same big chunk out of its side. How about this for an answer to prayer?"

"Unbelievable." Ali's whisper matched the sense of awe and protection surrounding her. Something only hours ago hadn't existed within her.

"Thanks, guys," Cay yelled over her shoulder.

River water drenched Ali all over again as they shared a hug. She stood near Cay and looked out over the waters of the Amazon River, watching the pod of dolphins leap and sound until they swam out of sight.

"You might not believe it, Ali," Cay said, "but I honestly think one of them pushed me toward the shore after the canoe went over."

Thoughtful, Ali looked at the paddle, then at Cay. "I do believe it, and I'd say we have a lot to thank God for." The hint of surprise on Cay's face made Ali smile. "Like I said, I've got a lot to tell you." But she couldn't have continued talking even if she'd wanted to. Anjo scampered over to her instead of Cay, her long tail and furry little arms clamping on to Ali's leg.

Gabi bounded up, chasing after Anjo. "Hey, you two, you're having way too much fun. Settle down, Gabi. We've got business to take care of." Ali picked up the wiggly monkey, juggling her with one hand and with the other, reached for Cay's socks and boots.

"Hear that, earth creatures? You have to let us concentrate on finding our way out of here." Cay wrung the water from her long hair and then finger-combed it back, knotting it into a semblance of a ponytail as they walked back to the edge of the clearing. I've got to rest awhile or I won't have enough strength to make it anywhere." With every step Cay slowed, and Ali watched her energy drip away like the water from her clothes. Anjo extended one lanky black arm, making soft noises in Cay's direction.

"I think she's worried about you, Cay. I am too. You'd better sit." Cay gave her a weak nod and sat on the fallen tree trunk. She opened her arms, accepting the baby Ali handed to her. Holding Anjo close, Cay rocked her and whispered to her as though she were an infant. Ali sat beside Cay, stroking Gabi's head, watching Cay work a small miracle. The wooly bundle in Cay's arms fell sound asleep.

Ali shook her head in admiration. "How did you *do* that?"

"Practice. Miss Tess used to do the same thing when I whispered to her." Cay continued the rhythmic rocking for a few more minutes. "Jo taught me how to soothe them a long time ago." Ali saw tears well up in Cay's eyes, and the vivid memory of Jo lying injured on the trail, returned.

She put her hand on Cay's arm. "I've been praying for Jo."

Cay's tears spilled over and dripped onto the monkey's fur. "Me too." She took a deep breath and wiped the wetness from her cheeks.

"You know, without a machete we're not going to stand much of a chance of finding or using a trail." Cay chuckled as Anjo woke, jumped from her lap and sat beside Gabi. "If those trails aren't used enough, they get overgrown, especially since not much sunshine gets through the canopy. The canoe is going to be our fastest and easiest way."

"Especially since we have the paddle. Using the canoe makes more sense to me, too. It'll be slower going than before, but maybe we can still make it."

"If we're as close as I think we are, and we leave soon, we should get there long before dark." Cay rubbed her stomach. "We should eat something more than cheese and crackers before we go."

"I'm dying for a burger and a Coke, but I'll settle for some beef jerky." Ali eyed Cay's wet hair and clothes. "Looks like you could use a few more minutes to rest and dry out anyway."

Cay nodded. "The clothes won't take long to dry in this heat, but we still need to hurry. No telling where those guys might be by now." She brushed debris off her feet and put on her socks and boots.

They spent precious minutes splitting the beef jerky and repacking the canoe. Concealing any traces they'd been there, they laid down branches to hide the tracks they couldn't brush away.

As Cay bent to pick up some limbs near the end of the log, Ali caught a glimpse of her expression as it went from earnestness to puzzlement. Her eyes had locked onto something.

"What is it?"

"There's something—Ali, isn't this your bandana? There's blood all over it. Oh, you *are* hurt." She straightened and whirled around to Ali, her face filled with concern.

Ali covered the three steps between them in two, and put her hands on Cay's shoulders. "No, Cay. Really, I'm not hurt. It was Gabi, and she's fine now. So much happened, I forgot to rinse it out." She reached over and picked up the cloth. "I'll take care of it on the way, but we've got to get out of here."

Much of Cay's strength seemed to have returned as they loaded the canoe. With Cay in the front, Anjo was happy to be in the bow, and a not-too-enthusiastic Gabi was content to stay in the center with Ali behind her.

Underway, planning to take turns using both the rescued paddle and the makeshift substitute, they made slow progress upriver. Ali wrapped the rinsed bandana around the handle of the paddle to keep her blisters from getting worse, but Cay didn't mention the bandana again.

Since they left the clearing, they had talked in brief spurts, swapping stories of how they each found safety after they capsized. Ali told Cay almost everything, except about when she'd knelt at the edge of the rain forest and her life had changed … and about Gabi's leg. She'd save those things for some quieter, calmer time. Every muscle and tendon in her body ached, and she doubted if she'd make much sense anyway. Cay must know something had happened to her, that she'd changed, especially when she occasionally glanced back with a look of curiosity in her eyes. Ali couldn't seem to quit smiling in spite of how tired she was and the mess they were in. But Cay never pressed.

For several hours, the sturdy canoe cut through the water, moving steadily upriver. Ali pulled the bandana off the paddle, dabbing at her forehead as sun basted the treetops with sizzling rays.

"There." Cay rested the handmade paddle and pointed to a narrow inlet in the riverbank. "That's the tributary marking the place we were watching for. Maria's house is in the next one, not very far from here. We're going to make it."

Near exhaustion, Ali lifted her paddle and let the boat drift for a few seconds, enjoying the brief respite. "Do you have any idea how much time?"

"My best guess would be about twenty minutes, if we can keep up the pace." Cay pushed at her glasses and turned to Ali. "Can you hold out a while longer?"

"I think so." Ali looked at her hands, glued to their only good paddle. Maintaining the pace would put them at Maria's in the early afternoon and Cay seemed stronger at paddling.

"My turn. Let's switch—here you go." Ali handed Cay the good paddle and took the makeshift paddle from Cay. "You're as tired as me, and you've been battling this thing long enough."

"Thanks."

Cay smiled and sank the paddle into the water, heading the canoe back upstream. Ali did the same, and the boat responded with a forward lunge.

"There it is." Cay thrust her arm toward the bank. Ali barely nodded, her energy fading with each paddle stroke. The muscles of her arms burned, and the minutes slogged by as if being dragged through mud. They turned the canoe into the mouth of the inlet, and Cay pointed to a long wooden dock on a far bank, poking into the wide tributary like a peninsula. "We did it."

Ali stared in awe at the spacious house surrounded by a rambling deck. If she hadn't known better, she'd think she was hallucinating. They'd passed countless shanties and tumble-down houses on stilts along the way but nothing like this. The sheer size took her breath as she looked at the house. What looked like the lengthy trunk of a large tree with steps carved out angled toward the deck serving as a staircase.

Supported by a dozen or more thick poles and dozens of thinner stilts, the house sat back from the bank, rising high above the water. Smooth, level hard clay covered a wide area beneath and extended far beyond. All the way to the river's edge, the ground had been packed down and swept clean of every twig and blade of grass. There would be no danger from the mounds of fire ants or parades of cutter ants rampant everywhere else.

Despite the heat, a shiver of amazement moved through Ali. As her gaze rested on a leaning coconut palm tree near the house, she sensed yet another change God was leading her through. As if to test her, the tree trunk was covered with a vine full of purple and white passionflowers in full bloom. *Mom.* Memories of her mother's love for them flooded her mind, but serenity filled her heart.

"We really did it," Cay said again.

"We did. Thank God, we really did." Ali breathed out a long sigh as they eased up on their paddling, gliding into the quiet waters of the inlet.

Four brilliant blue-and-gold parrots perched on the crossbars of poles, bands and small chains securing them. "*Tchau, tchau, tchau!*" The Portuguese word for "see ya" erupted from one followed by a second, echoing its goodbye "*Adeus, adeus, adeus!*" The rest of the quartet flapped and squawked, announcing the arrival of the two intruders.

Ali gazed up at the heavily thatched roof, cleanly built walls, and sturdy base. "This place is a palace compared to the shack we were in last night."

"Maria!" Cay yelled, drawing the name out. She looked back at Ali with a grin. "All you have to do is wait a second, and this place will explode with life." Cay didn't need to explain further. Six squealing, raven-haired, brown-bodied children swarmed all over the front porch area of the deck. They came from every direction, three of them carrying monkeys, two of the boys with fishing poles in hand. They bent over the railings, waving and chattering as loudly as their pets, and the color yellow was everywhere.

"They look like a bunch of daisies, or better yet, like black-eyed Susans." Ali had to smile. Yellow covered the lower half of most of them, but the smallest one sported only his birthday suit.

Cay adjusted her glasses and grinned. "Yellow is Maria's favorite color, and she makes everything they wear. Get used to seeing sunshine. Maria is as beautiful as Jo is funny. You'll love her and her husband, Mauro."

"I love her already." Ali couldn't take her eyes from the children.

"Mauro manages a huge ranch not very far north of here. We may not get to see him, though. He comes and goes as he has time."

"Why does he do that with all he has here?" Ali asked as the distance between the boat and the bank shortened.

"Maria says he's got wanderlust and is as restless as the Amazon. He seems to like to live at the ranch for a while then come back here to the peace and beauty of this place. He loves the river and built this home for them."

Cay's words slowed as her self-generated enthusiasm wound down. "Mauro's one of the Amazon River people called the *Caboclos*, part

Portuguese and part Indian. He's smart, self-taught, and speaks nearly perfect English. The whole family speaks both Portuguese and English." Cay paused and then added, "Thank God, we're finally here."

Ali whispered a nearly inaudible, "Amen."

The entire cluster of yellow-clad children raced down the slope toward them. With Anjo clinging tightly to her arm, Cay waved.

Ali focused her energy on steering the canoe toward shore, barely strong enough to follow Cay and climb out of the canoe. She pulled Gabi out, took a few steps then stood, shaking and exhausted.

"Be a good girl, Gabi. Sit." Gabi obeyed, her tail wagging, ears forward, whining with anticipation. The children slowed their approach and stared.

"Ola, Cay," a frantic, worry-filled voice called from above them. Maria came running down the steps, her eyes never leaving the two girls. "Caylee, Caylee. We thought we might never see you again." She put her arms around Cay and hugged her for a moment, then put a hand on Ali's shoulder. "You are Ali? I'm Maria ... thank God, you are both safe."

Safe? How did Maria know they might not be? How did she know they were coming? Had Jo contacted her? There had been no contact she knew of before or after their plans to visit had fallen through.

Ali tried to smile at her, so tired, she wasn't sure if her response would even make sense. "Hi, Maria. We're so thankful to be here ..." She paused, and as if she understood, Maria quickly continued.

"Jo called your fathers yesterday afternoon to tell them you both were missing—that you had been kidnapped." Maria crossed her arms over her chest.

"Then, Caylee, your father radioed me."

Ali looked at the slender young woman with long dark hair, and the breath squeezed from her lungs. So, Jo was okay.

Everything began to fall into place as Maria supplied more unexpected answers.

"Your dad said he would be leaving on his friend, Max's, jet for Manaus as soon as he could, Caylee."

"Max flew him here?" Cay's eyes misted. "Thank God for that man's generous heart."

Maria put a hand on Cay's arm. "Yes, they took off sometime after midnight. Mr. Roberts had the pilot radio me right before they landed in Manaus very early this morning."

She looked at Ali. "He and your father, Ali, planned to rent a boat as soon as possible and start looking for you on their way here." Maria shook her head, pain flashing across her face. "He didn't say anything when I asked if he'd gone to the federal police. And that was the last call I was able to receive or send. The radio has been giving us trouble for the last two weeks. Mauro will have to fix it when he gets here." Maria's voice betrayed her distress.

Then they were completely cut off from any communication. Ali's heart sank at the reality of their isolation.

"It's okay, Maria, he couldn't say anything to you about the authorities, whether he went to them or not. I had to tell Dad the kidnappers would kill us if he did that."

Maria nodded. "So many things can happen. We tried not to believe the worst." She paused, her eyes filled with tears. "God is so good. We never stopped praying. It is a miraculous thing. We had hope, but we didn't ever think you would be able to escape."

Ali's heart absorbed the faith and love and trust of this beautiful woman who'd prayed for them. It *had* been miraculous, God in every detail. And the best possible news—both of their fathers were coming.

The smallest of the boys ran to his mother, grabbing her hand, diverting Maria's attention to Gabi. Ali looked at Cay. Her face expressed the same relief that flooded Ali, knowing Jo's injuries hadn't stopped him from calling for help. But an undercurrent of concern filled her as she realized Maria didn't know Jo had been injured. Ali was uneasy. Jo probably hadn't told anyone he was hurt, possibly because he didn't want to worry them. That would be so like Jo, he was such an unselfish, giving man. *But Maria needed to know.*

"I thought she knew." Cay whispered as Maria bent to speak to the excited child. "Jo must not have wanted to add any more bad news to worry anyone."

Ali gave Cay a weak nod. "That was my guess too."

Maria straightened as the boy ran back to where Gabi basked in all the attention. "You are not hurt?" She scanned them from head to toe.

Cay smiled and put her hand over her sleeve-covered arm, the arm Velez had struck and terribly bruised. "Rope burns, mosquito bites, and a few bruises, but the men didn't harm us, Maria. We're okay."

Maria's eyes filled with wonder. "We've been praying so hard for you, that you would be safe. How did you ever escape the people who took you?"

"So many little miracles, Maria, but we got loose while it was still dark this morning. There were two men and a guide, and I don't know what would have happened to us if we hadn't gotten away from them. They were sleeping, and we took a canoe." Cay's voice weakened with every word. Still holding Anjo, she stumbled forward, pulling the canoe farther onto the shore.

"Cay!" Ali watched, helpless as Cay's head drooped and she sank to her knees like a wilting flower.

Maria grabbed for Cay's arm. Two of the older children bounced into action, one running to Cay's side, and one of the older boys taking over the mooring rope, fully beaching the canoe and hauling out their two backpacks. Anjo jumped into the arms of one of the younger girls, clinging to her as if she were a long-lost friend.

"Caylee? We need to get you out of the sun and this heat." The concern in Maria's voice was balm to Ali's ears. Exhausted, unable to help or move another inch, the last day and a half caught up with her too.

"We're just *so* tired." Ali's voice mingled with the compassionate little voices surrounding Cay and her. The young faces, reflecting such genuine concern touched her heart. She forced a smile and added "Don't worry, we'll be okay." Small, caring hands and a pair of gentle, larger ones helped the two girls to their feet and to the stairway.

Everything in the house ran on batteries, propane, or candlepower. On the wall in the kitchen a small clock, hanging below a large wooden crucifix, read 6:30. They'd been at Maria's for hours, and Ali had never in her life had so much attention. They soaked in tubs of warm water, ate, then rested beneath light blankets while Maria took their muddied clothes to wash.

Comfortable and in fresh clothing, they sat in the large room that served as the kitchen, dining, and living area. Maria's gas generator hummed behind the house as batteries recharged and more water heated. They had yet to tell Maria about Jo. Cay looked at Ali, took a deep breath and turned to Maria.

"Maria, right before we were taken, someone attacked Jo. He ran ahead of us, trying to get to Gabi. When we found him, he was lying on the ground, bleeding from a place on his head. The best we can figure, one of the men that took us had hit him hard with something heavy enough to knock him out."

A pained gasp escaped Maria's lips. Her hands flew to her cheeks as she looked at them, fear filling her brown eyes. "But your father didn't say a word about Jo being hurt."

Cay leaned close, took Maria's hands in hers, and gently held them. "He probably didn't know Jo was injured, but Jo has to be okay or he wouldn't have said he'd be coming. And you know how he is, maybe he didn't want to tell anyone, didn't want anyone to worry."

Maria sighed, relaxing as Cay released her hands and the paleness faded from her face. She looked down, picking at threads in the hand towel on her lap. "You are right. Jo didn't want to take the focus away from getting you back."

Ali laid her hand on Maria's arm. "Or cause you to worry. I think that's one of the main reasons he didn't tell you."

They talked of Jo for a few moments, then Maria told them what she'd done to try to locate them after Evan Roberts radioed her yesterday. He'd told her they'd been abducted, and Jo was on his way to Maria's to meet them to search. She'd put out a call on the ham radio to the few houses in the vicinity able to receive one, alerting them to watch for anything suspicious and to let her know if they saw Jo. No radio contact since then, and Maria was trying to coax the radio into working again when she'd heard Cay hailing her from the canoe.

A heavy strand of worry wove through Ali's mind as their conversation continued to focus on Jo. He should have been here by … Ali turned toward the open door as sounds outside the house changed.

"Maria!"

A familiar voice.

Maria stopped speaking mid-sentence. Beside her, Cay grabbed Ali's hand and gasped.

CHAPTER THIRTY-ONE

"Maria!" The stern, resonant voice filled with apprehension. Maria rose from the bench and went through the doorway onto the porch. Breathless and perspiring, Jo hugged her close, then held her an arm's length away, shaking his head. "I am making mess of you."

"Do you think I care?" She grinned at him, handed him the small towel she'd been folding, then pulled him to her. "Thank God you're here, and safe. We've been so worried after Mr. Roberts radioed me yesterday."

He hadn't seen them yet, as they stood together in the dim kitchen, waiting. Tears stung Ali's eyes as she watched him, his eyes never leaving Maria's face. Still breathing hard, he dabbed at his face and followed his sister into the room. "I move fast since daylight." He put his hand on her shoulder. "Caylee, Ali—the girls—gone." He looked at Maria and shook his head.

"No. Jo, the girls …" But Maria's words were lost as Jo barely paused.

"Took so long." Jo choked, his face etched with pain and worry. "Jungle overgrown … thick. Had to rest. All too much." He pressed the cloth against his eyes, rubbing at them.

Gabi strained forward. Ali didn't bother waiting a moment longer to release her hold on Gabi's collar or to whisper, "Go, Gabi."

The towel dropped from Jo's hands as the shepherd bounded to his side. "Gabi?" His expression filled with disbelief. He reached out to put his hand on the dog's head then looked up. "Caylee? Ali?" A blend of surprise and shock registered on his face, and then, overcome, tears of obvious joy flowed from his gentle brown eyes as he saw them. His concern gone, his expression instantly transformed, he blinked hard as his eyes adjusted and Maria practically pushed him through the doorway.

Ali didn't hesitate. Neither did Cay, and with tears of their own, they rushed to him.

"Oh, thank God, you get away. God answer Jo's thousand prayers for you." The big man with the bushy black mustache, though filthy and disheveled, opened his arms and gathered them into a huge bear hug. The overzealous hug knocked his black hat to the floor, exposing the bloodied bandana he'd tied over the wound.

"Jo, your head. Is it going to be all right?" Ali backed a few inches away to study his face and the cloth wrapped around his head.

"Let me look at that, Jo." Maria fluttered around him with sisterly concern. "Mr. Roberts only told me you'd been attacked, the girls were missing, and you were on your way here. He did *not* tell me you were hurt. The girls had to tell me." She shook her finger, scolding him as if he were one of her children.

Gentle, patient Jo. Ali smiled, watching Maria sit him down at the long plank table, gathering antiseptic, cotton balls, ointment, and bandages, fussing over him. Half-a-dozen curious children encircled their uncle, all talking at once, and in between Maria's first aid he hugged each of them. He accepted the glass of water Ali offered. Jo looked over the heads of the milling children at his attentive sister, his eyebrows knit in a concerned line above his eyes.

"Trouble coming by river. Three." He clenched his hands and shook his head. "Two canoes pulled up on bank in short trib. Men who attacked me. I saw them in clearing, eating, long time ago."

"You *saw* them?" Her words and expression incredulous, Cay gripped the table's edge and dropped down onto the bench beside him.

"Yes. Saw them—they did not see me. I listen. Did not know they were ones who took you 'til hear them talk of Maria's house."

His shoulders sagged, drained of energy, and he nodded at Maria, who stuck a plate of food in front of him. "Watched men eat like pigs, drink like drunks they are, then fall asleep. We may not have much time to get ready. Don't know how long they slept, but good for us they did."

He turned to Maria. "Please put kids in back bedroom. Tell them not come out till you say. Sarena, please, take dog too." Jo beckoned, instructing the tallest girl in the stair-step lineup of children.

Ali gave the hand-woven leash to Sarena and watched Gabi follow obediently behind her. Anjo, still clinging happily to her new friend, set her wooly black face in a grin and tossed some animated monkey chatter in Cay's direction.

"Caylee, Ali—you really okay?" Jo eyed them as if he couldn't believe they escaped unscathed.

Cay smiled at him. "Sunburn, a few rope burns, blisters, bumps, and bruises, but we made it."

Ali nodded, as Maria shepherded the children toward the rear of the house. "We have lots to tell you, but we're okay, Jo. I'm not so sure about you, though." Ali looked up at the bandage Maria wrapped around his head.

The tips of Jo's mustache lifted with his grin. "Covered with jungle dust and head dented, but they can't keep good man down long."

"Are you sure?" Cay got up, still looking doubtful, her eyes scanning him from head to toe.

Jo stood and put his arms around them. "Looks to me like Jesus watch over us all."

Ali's heart ached as she glanced at the beautiful crucifix dangling from its chain around Jo's neck and thought of Kane. Kane wore a cross given to him by his grandmother. He'd worn the symbol for so many years it had simply become a part of him. What did it really mean to him? She'd never asked.

There was so much she wanted to change now. One change involved a necklace, a small gold cross her mother had given her long ago. Lying unworn and all but forgotten in her jewelry case, but not for much longer.

"But Jesus got more watching over to do." Jo added, interrupting her thoughts. Warmth filled Ali as Jo repeated His name. She took a step backward, knowing she needed to say the words to her friends—now. There might not be another chance.

She turned to Cay, silent until their eyes met. "Cay, I wanted to wait to tell you at some special time what happened to me after we got separated and I was alone. But with what we're facing with Cardozo and Velez, there's no better time than with you and Jo both here right now." She kept her eyes on Cay's, but sensed Jo listening. Drawing in a breath, she paused, praying for the right words.

"Exactly the way you told me he would, Cay, Jesus came into my heart this morning."

Cay reached out and grasped Ali's hands in hers, her face alight and her eyes brimming with joy.

She squeezed Ali's hands, hugged her tight, then stood back still holding her hands. "You have to tell me all that happened."

"Hah! Jesus faithful. Answer prayers," Jo crowed. The dimple in his cheek deepened with his smile.

Jo's tone held a strong touch of urgency. This wasn't the time to share details. "Oh, Cay, there was so much more. When we're on the other side of all this, I'll tell you how it happened, but right now, we'd better do everything Jo wants us to do to get us out of this mess."

Cay nodded. "Okay, Jo, we're ready for anything. We've got armies of angels on all sides. We'll get through this."

Jo pointed to a large chest against a far wall. "Cay, remember bows and arrows in that trunk? Better get them out."

He looked Ali in the eye. "Ali can use them too?"

"I can." Ali hesitated, appalled at the thought of fighting the two armed, threatening, and dangerous Brazilians. "But you know for certain they were the men you saw and heard?"

Jo held up a hand, his mustachioed smile spelling out utter patience. "Yes, I sure they are men I saw before lights went out in my head. Your father says houses and phones bugged. Men have guide with them now. They know of Maria's house, and maybe they know lots more."

Ali's new faith faltered. But if the Lord could keep her in all she'd been through, how could she doubt?

Jo had followed Cay to the chest. He lifted the top, pulling out the lightweight bows and quivers full of arrows.

"Do you really think we can stop them, Jo? With those?" He'd been serious about her archery skills. "Then Maria doesn't have a gun?" Ali stared down at the flimsy arsenal Jo placed on top of the trunk. "Those guys do. We saw one, and I don't know if there were more."

"Mauro keep gun with him." Jo frowned. "Mauro not here, surprise is best weapon for us. Bow and arrow will do job fine. Did you see kind of gun man had?"

Ali swallowed hard and nodded. "Yes. It looks like Dad's Ruger Vaquero, the six-shot revolver he used on our ranch."

"Good. We count good things, and thank God for good thing that man does not have ten-shot automatic." Jo grinned. "We have advantage. We surprise them." With his calm assurance, he already had Ali's agreement, and Cay sent him a firm nod and a smile.

"At least we know we've got help coming." Ali looked at Cay. "Your dad told Maria yesterday my dad would rent a boat and leave the Port of Manaus sometime this morning. She said he and Cay's dad were coming straight to Maria's to start looking for us."

Maria walked back into the room. "Yes, Jo, they could be here by sometime later tonight."

"Battery in satellite phone die after I call Dr. Matt yesterday." Jo looked at the clock. "Getting dark. Men could be here any time. No help from phone. Maybe your dads will come soon. Say prayers they come *very* soon." He grasped Maria's hand. "Okay. Hold hands … pray. Put on God's armor first."

Ali stood between Jo and Cay, soaking up the way they trusted God. She reveled in the warmth of the hands that held hers—hands of friends who'd become mentors of faith for her—and she bowed her head and heart.

Ali watched wisps of red and gold light from the leftover sunset glint through the trees as the four of them waited in the shadows. Jo had asked them to dress in dark clothes so they'd be harder to see. Then, minutes ago, he positioned Cay and Maria around the house near a stash of extra arrows, ropes, and flashlights, while Ali stood beside a tall, thick-trunked palm. All of them were armed with bows and arrows. Jo had taken up a spot near the place where he assumed the men would land their canoes. A single gas lamp shone like a beacon from the deck. Except for a small light in the room where the children stayed, Jo had ordered all others extinguished.

Foolish. That's what she would have called herself a day ago, standing there in the gathering darkness beside a monster palm tree with a quiver full of arrows draped over her back and a bow in her hand. She might even have disintegrated facing the emotional, mental, physical stress, and terror of becoming a captive again. But men with guns and plans to lay their hands on her again were on the way. And between today and yesterday, a single decision made everything as different as the land from the sea—her new-found faith in Jesus.

Ali's eyes continued to adjust to the thickening darkness, a tender reminder from deep within her about adjusting to change. She nudged a tree root with the toe of her boot, wondering over all the thoughts filling her mind. Strange how differently she perceived the world now—a peaceful perspective, easy within herself, calm. But how would she react when the kidnappers actually pulled boats ashore right in front of her?

She glanced at Cay huddled beside one of the big poles beneath the house. Cay smiled and shot her index finger toward the heavens, sending Ali reassurance of her own faith.

The wait could take hours. Did she have the stamina to wait? She remembered Cay telling her that life was still her life but with a huge difference; she didn't have to do life alone anymore.

Ali stretched her shoulders. Jo would let them know with a hand signal when the canoes approached. Each of them knew their target, and with a second signal, he'd tell them when to let loose a volley of sharp-tipped arrows.

A dusky gloom cloaked the inlet. It would be hours before the moon showed itself. Ten minutes passed, then ten more. Tension edged into their voices as they spoke to one another in low tones. Ali swatted at a mosquito and leaned against the palm tree, shifting her weight to relieve the cramping in her legs.

"Shh." Jo hissed with caution, dropping his right hand and patting his knee.

They were coming. Dangerous, armed men, intent on harming her and her friends. Ali held her breath and prayed as the old familiar wash of fear swept over her. Her grip tightened on the bow. No way were the men—or her fears—going to take her again. She wiped sweat from her forehead and slowed her breathing, fresh strength rising in her. She listened, concentrated on the *clack* of paddles against the canoes, the odd contrast of sound above the noise of the forest behind her.

She lifted her head, along with the bow, and nocked the arrow. Cay matched her motions. Ali glanced to her right where Maria loaded her bow and took aim. Two canoes holding three men, paddles now silently lifting and dipping, neared the bank.

Jo had instructed them. "Aim for arms and legs. Cause hurt, not death. We take wind out of sails. Get them first." Jo waited until the men beached the canoes and stepped out before he made a move.

Eerie silhouettes of Cardozo, Velez, and the native guide on the inlet surface. The gas lamp shed enough light for the four to easily see their targets. Seconds after the last man set foot on the bank, Jo's right arm, bow in hand, reached for the stars and then immediately dropped as he positioned for his shot.

Arrow already nocked, Ali raised the bow, drew, took aim, and let fly. Maria and Cay did the same. In spite of the jungle's unceasing serenade, the unmistakable *whoosh* of their arrows slashed the air, splitting the darkness. Thuds and yells proved their marksmanship.

Jo's strategy and the element of surprise worked. Ali's arrow tore into Cardozo's shirt, piercing the fleshy part of his right arm. Her gaze left him for a split second and fell on Velez. He hadn't been struck. Cay's arrow passed through his shirtsleeve, missing its target. Like a slow-moving statue, Velez's head turned, followed the projectile's track straight toward Cay. Fully aware he was under attack, his face changed from shock to a mask of fury and indignation. Snarling words in Portuguese, he barreled up the bank, heading toward Cay's position. She gasped and grabbed a second arrow.

As soon as Ali let fly with her first arrow, she'd nocked another. *Help, Lord!* She took deliberate aim at her moving target and launched the second shaft into the night air. Only a few feet away from Cay, Velez screamed and dropped to the ground, grabbing at the arrow buried in his thigh. Yelping with pain, frantic, he fishtailed himself back toward the inlet.

Still on the bank, Cardozo, fit and strong despite his belly, brushed the long-shafted barb from his arm as if nothing but a pesky bug. Ali quickly nocked a third arrow and aimed at him again. But before she could shoot, Jo's next arrow scored its objective, sinking deep into Cardozo's right shoulder. With a maddened bellow, the muscular man jerked out the arrow, flipping the shaft behind him into the water, and in one smooth motion reached for his gun, ripping it from its holster.

The jungle reverberated as Cardozo took four potshots toward the base of the house. One ricocheted off a metal shovel. The bullet whizzed by Ali's head. She dropped the bow and hit the ground. The jungle went silent. Cardozo fired two more wild shots.

The gun should be empty, and unless he reloaded … Ali clearly heard the *click* of the hammer several more times as Cardozo tried to shoot. How was he using his right hand with his wounds?

Grasping at the arrow that had found its mark in his shoulder, the native guide raced past Ali and vanished into the jungle. She remained on the ground, raised her head and reached for her bow. Velez lay on the bank, moaning, his hands around the shaft of the arrow protruding from his thigh.

Metallic sounds came from Cardozo's direction. No! He was reloading the gun. She touched the quiver, ready to grab an arrow. Just as quickly, she froze, watching Jo, mesmerized.

Jo dove at Cardozo from the shadows and tackled him around the waist, knocking him into the water. A wrestling match ensued as the two large men grappled and punched. Jo proved the stronger and yanked Cardozo back up onto the bank, yelling at Maria to bring him the ropes. She was by his side in seconds and threw him one of the ropes. Whipping the heavy cord around the brawny man's hands and feet, he hogtied Cardozo.

Face down, Ali stayed pinned to the hardpan, eyes glued to Jo's actions, heart beating hard against her ribs. Velez lay on the ground still holding onto the arrow in his leg, groaning. He didn't look as if he'd be going anywhere under his own power for the next few minutes. She rested her head on her outstretched arms, her eyes still on Jo and Maria.

Jo took the second rope from Maria as they went to the spot where Velez lay. Deftly tying Velez's hands behind his back, Jo stood over the rope-restrained kidnapper catching his breath before leaving Maria and returning to check Cardozo.

"Maria? Jo? Are you okay?" Cay called out.

Jo waved. "We are not hurt. I do not know about Toro-the-bull, here." He touched Cardozo with a boot tip. "Out of commission, and he does not look so good."

Jo glanced through the darkness toward the palm tree where she'd been standing. "Ali is okay?"

"Ali! She was right there … no, she's down! I'll go see." Cay jumped out of the shadows and raced toward the tree and knelt beside her. "Ali, did you get hit? Are you all right?"

Ali jumped to her feet. "I'm okay—so thankful you and everyone else are too!"

"Thank God! I thought for a minute you'd been—" Cay shook her head and reached to hug Ali.

"I'm still shaking but really thrilled not to be Swiss cheese with all those bullets flying." Ali brushed herself off then cocked her head toward the black waters of the tributary. "Do you hear that? Someone's coming. A boat, maybe more than one. Our dads?" She glanced at the two trussed men. Were they about to get free of these gargoyles?

The rumbling drone of diesel engines rolled across the wide inlet. The bright running lights and brilliant blue and white strobes of a large watercraft shone through the darkness and laid silvery tracks on the water. The sound ceased as the diesels shut down, and the police launch continued moving toward the dock.

Lights popped on all over the house, streaming through the open windows. The children filed out onto the porch, eyes wide and watching in silence. Behind the police launch, a slightly smaller craft with twin inboards roared up, switched off its engines, and glided silently toward the opposite side of the dock. One of the three officers on deck tossed heavy ropes over the side of the police launch and secured the boat to the pier. Two other men followed, one running to help Jo with Velez, the other checking on Cardozo.

"Maria?" Evan Roberts called out from the twin-engine yacht, his voice echoing across the embankment.

At a dead run toward him, Cay called out to her father.

Ali ran with her, echoing her call, her eyes scanning the area where the second boat had docked.

"Ali? Ali! Thank God you're safe. How …?" Shock registered in her father's voice and across his face as she ran to him. He leapt from the deck of the yacht and caught Ali up into his open arms.

Ali fell into the warm safety of her father's hug, tears flooding her cheeks, mixing with his. All her fears and frustrations blended with her joy at simply being whole, alive, and with him.

Ali and Cay moved their gear from the dock to the yacht as Inspector Roberto Vega of Interpol approached and introduced himself, then spoke with their fathers. What? Why was Interpol involved?

Ali was grateful that at her father's request, Vega had agreed to conduct all his interviews at the Lamarque home instead of Manaus Federal police headquarters. He'd meet with them at the house the following afternoon. The idea of going through a debriefing, being required to relive all she'd experienced, wasn't something she looked forward to. Exhausted, her head ached with thoughts of how she'd get through the interviews.

Two hours had passed since the waterfront skirmish resolved with the capture of Cardozo and Velez. Everyone except Ali and her father gathered on the porch above, while they stood under the house near one of the thick pole stilts. She wanted to watch all the intense activity on the dock alone.

"Why don't you join the others on the porch, honey? You've been through enough."

Ali smiled and shook her head at her father's urging. He returned her smile, his arms surrounding her in a hug before he turned and walked down to the dock.

Glad for the solitude, she couldn't leave, couldn't stop watching. She'd lived and walked through too much with these men threatening her for so long. How could she close the door on this if she didn't see the ending?

From the dock, Inspector Vega's voice came loud and clear, wafting up on the breeze from the inlet. Ali watched the Manaus FP detectives search and briefly question the two handcuffed men before they were taken aboard the police launch. She stood listening as Vega debriefed another detective and two officers he'd sent on a routine but unsuccessful search for the missing guide in the forested area surrounding the house. Vega's comment echoed in her mind. "I don't expect he'll ever be found."

Inspector Vega and her father were deep in an animated conversation as the diesel engines of the police launch rumbled to life. Ali left the base of the house and started toward the dock.

"Wait up. I'll go with you."

Ali stopped and turned as Cay scrambled down the steps and jogged up beside her. "Something you didn't want to miss either, huh?" She smiled, understanding Cay's clenched hands.

"Nope."

They watched the departing police launch, loaded with its imprisoned human cargo, headed toward the river and Manaus. The faint scent of diesel engine fumes wafted back toward her and the others on the shore. She swallowed hard and pressed the clean bandana over her nose, staring at the winking strobe lights until they disappeared.

Maria had allowed the children to come down to the docked rental boat as Ali and Cay boarded with promises to return someday soon. Cay held Anjo, whispering into her ear for a few seconds then handed her back to little Marissa to keep.

Jo wouldn't be staying with Maria as they' had both hoped. An eye witness as well as a victim in the case, Vega's work wouldn't be finished without Jo's statements and corroboration of facts. Jo didn't hesitate. He'd return—after he made sure Cardozo and Velez were permanently "put away."

Jo led Gabi below into the cabin to rest. Evan Roberts drove the boat, Cay at his side. The craft pulled away, engines revving, blending with the night noise of the jungle and steadily moving them away from the dock. Near the railing beside her father, Ali watched Maria's brightly lit home fade to black in the distance behind them.

The small cruiser reached the mouth of the tributary and angled out into the river making the turn east toward Manaus. The running lights illuminated their path, and the speed increased, putting the boat on a smooth plane. The warm breeze tousled Ali's hair and swept tendrils against her sunburned cheeks.

She looked up at her father's strong profile in the dim light of the rising moon, but Kane was in her heart and on her mind. "Dad, does Kane know about what happened to me?"

Her father put his hand on her arm. "I felt you'd want him to know. I called him a few minutes after I spoke with Evan yesterday morning. Kane was pretty upset, frustrated he wasn't here to help us look for you." His eyes met Ali's, and he smiled. "He made very clear to me that he cares for you a lot more than I was aware."

A flush of warmth flashed through her, quickening her heartbeat. The image of Kane's face as their lips parted after his kiss at LAX floated before her as if he were there. Everything in her ached for him to hold her again.

She gripped the rail, trembling, hoping her father wouldn't notice. Kane was so far away, and she was standing here on a boat not knowing how what she'd been through would affect her future—or her father's.

How safe was the project her father had worked on so hard, for so long? "Do you think the police got to the flash drive before Cardozo's contact picked it up?"

"We won't know for sure until tomorrow, honey. But even if they did get to it in time, nothing is more important to me than having you back safe and sound. That little flash drive ranks way down there below dirt in comparison."

His smile and eyes filled with a tenderness that had her eyes swimming with tears of love. "Thanks, Dad." She smiled and leaned her head against his shoulder for a moment. "Well, at least they didn't get the *complete* formula."

He looked at her, his expression wavering somewhere between a frown and a smile. "That isn't exactly the case, honey. If they got the flash drive, I'm afraid they have the whole thing."

Ali's head jerked up, and she stared at him. "Everything? How could that happen?"

His eyes focused out over the water. "The answer I came here expecting to find was close but completely eluded me until one morning early last week." He paused, rubbing at his forehead. "That was the point when I finally narrowed down the chemical properties I'd been looking for, thanks in large part to some excellent equipment in the biotech lab. And, to make a long story short, I had a lot of head knowledge but couldn't for the life of me pinpoint the actual process until that moment."

Ali studied the waters that flowed like a black satin sheet past the hull. Her head dipped with a twinge of disappointment. He hadn't said a word to her about the formula before they left on the hike. She watched his expression, knowing there was no way he could make the long story short as he continued.

"It was one of those rare serendipitous moments when everything fit, and I nailed it—proved the efficacy beyond question."

He looked at Ali, his eyes holding a twinkle, looking like a kid who'd just hit his first home run. Fascinated, she nodded, waiting for him to tell her more as he seemed to search for words to simplify his explanation.

"When broken down far enough, the key to the whole thing is pretty remarkable, a perfect relationship between the epiphyte—the orchid plant—and fungi on the host tree."

As if to make his point, he folded one hand into a fist, placing it into the palm of his other, his eyes seeming to hold the memory of the moment. He looked at her. "In a way unlike any I've ever seen, Ali, the ingredient we needed is nurtured within a symbiotic relationship between the orchid and the fungi, a lichen." He paused and grinned at her. "They play very nicely together, and this unusual type of leafy lichen thrives along with the orchid on the host tree. The orchid takes nothing from anywhere but the air, and minute, unique changes take place within the orchid stems and roots. Their cells absorb airborne nutrients from the lichen as the orchids grow in their native environment."

Ali felt like a privileged lab assistant and had to smile at his enthusiasm as he continued, lost in the excitement of his success.

"There is a lot more involved, but it's enough to say, I duplicated the process in the lab and recreated what was missing. There's no doubt in my mind we'll quickly and easily be in a position to manufacture and mass produce a high-quality synthetic copy."

He stopped, thoughtful, and more to himself than to her, he added, "There was only one person I talked to about my findings, and that was Erick Chance. He was in the field for several days and called me. I'd just finished compiling the data. He was thrilled I'd finished, and couldn't wait to observe the test results first hand."

"Dad, that's wonderful. I know how much it means to you. So many people will be helped. And Erick phoning you on that particular night was a real coinci … really amazing. Had he called you for some other reason?"

He looked down at her and grinned. "He was checking on us—you and me, honey. He wanted to hear how we were doing and to find out if I'd heard from you on how the hike was going." Her father's eyebrows met in the middle as he frowned. "When I told him about the formula, the thought never occurred to me the phones might be bugged."

Ali shook her head. Thoughts about anyone breaking into the house and compromising the phones, and who-knew-what-else, rocked her emotions between happiness for her father and worry for his finished formula. "I still can't believe they were listening in on our calls."

"Well, that's not happening any more, thanks to the Manaus PD, but it's not the end of the story. You'll hear quite a bit more about everything tomorrow."

Ali hesitated to change the subject, but she had something she wanted to share. No holding back. He was looking at her, and as their eyes met, she prayed he would understand the depth and breadth of what she was about to say to him.

"Dad, I've been praying. I prayed so hard the flash drive would be safe." She paused, waiting, unsure of how he might respond.

His eyes glistened, never leaving hers. He smiled and put his arm around her. "I'm learning how powerful prayer is too. I've prayed about a lot of things during the last two days." He gave her shoulder a loving squeeze. "Having you standing here next to me is the answer to one of those prayers."

A warm sense of love and contentment filled Ali, and she hugged him. Months had elapsed since he'd said so much about his work, and he'd never told her he prayed. "I love you, Dad."

"I love you too, honey."

Her father kept his arm around her as they both looked out over the Amazon. Ali was intrigued and enthralled with what he'd shared about his discovery—and thrilled he would tell her of his prayers.

Lord, let there be a right time and place when I can tell him about my faith, about Jesus.

Had it been yesterday, or was it the day before, when she'd knelt on the riverbank? Events ran together. Her thoughts tumbled with a dozen questions she wanted to ask him, but exhaustion turned them to fuzz. The little energy she had left trickled away.

What she wouldn't give for a long hot shower. In spite of the tub-soak at Maria's, she smelled bad and looked worse. Maybe tomorrow would hold answers. Tonight, having her father close filled her with thankfulness.

Ali watched Cay's dad kiss her on the cheek, then bodily turn her in the direction of the hatch leading below deck. Cay didn't object, and as she passed Ali heading toward the opening, she grabbed Ali's hand and sent her a tired, lopsided grin.

"The Admiral says the crew needs sleep. Orders. C'mon, crew."

"I have to say, I think he's right." Her father gave her a hug and a nudge of encouragement to follow Cay.

"No argument from me. I could sleep on a rock, but if there's room enough below to lie down, I'm there."

Before they went down the short companionway, she saw her father go forward to stand beside Evan Roberts. Had he made as much of a difference in her father's life as Cay had made in hers? Maybe God had allowed this whole trip, even down to them being kidnapped. Cay had said God was in every detail of life.

Arms and legs as wooden as the deck planks, Ali closed her eyes as soon as she laid her head on the small pillow, asleep … until a *thump* against the boat jolted her awake. Port Manaus so soon?

CHAPTER THIRTY-TWO

Ali woke well before dawn, fear and panic rising within her. The men. Ropes. Blindfolds. Gunfire. Sheer terror. A stampede of violent images. Every nerve and fiber of her being on fire, she clutched at the sheets and clenched her jaw in the dark silence of the bedroom. Do *not* scream.

Dear God, please, no more.

Ali.

So gentle. As if the air itself had whispered her name.

Be still. Breathe.

Remaining motionless, battling a desire to run, she breathed.

O God, thank you. Thank you.

With every beat of her pounding heart, she whispered thanks. Lying in bed, wide-awake in the darkness, she prayed, a growing sense of peace filling her as her heart regained rhythm.

A birdcall broke into the quiet, and she couldn't stay there another moment. Near the window, Gabi whimpered in her sleep but didn't wake. Ali slipped out of bed, letting Cay sleep.

Light streamed through the window as Ali pulled a brush through her hair. Gabi looked up at her from her sentry spot in front of the bedroom door. "Good morning, girl. You want to go with me?" Ali whispered the words, glad for Gabi's company. Gabi stood and put a paw on Ali's foot, her tail wagging, her amber eyes fixed on her mistress.

Gabi stayed several feet behind her as she left the house and walked the short curving path into the side garden. She was glad to be safely back in Manaus and at home—as close to a home as she had anywhere in the world right now.

Every shrub and flower shimmered with still-clinging dew in the soft light, drawing her into a fairyland of color and scent. She reveled in the freshness of the air, staying on the narrow walkway, reflecting on memories of her mother, her grandmother, and Kane. Life had taken such a bend, as if she'd suddenly changed centuries or walked through a time warp.

Near a bower of pink and white bougainvillea, she leaned against a tall palm tree, catching a glimpse of the setting moon.

Something moved on the arm of the nearby bench. In a flash of iridescent white wings, a delicate bride moth lifted off, a wisp of air beneath its wings. An empty brown cocoon rolled and dropped to the ground. She watched the flitting moth. Had she literally morphed into something other than what she had been? Was this what her mother had tried to impart to her so often as she'd grown up?

Petty things she'd been so upset about, problems she'd feared would ruin her life, had become inconsequential. She'd placed them in God's hands. And being sincerely thankful for simple things, things she'd come "home" to that days ago she hadn't given a second thought about—her father, good friends, safety, hot showers, and even clean clothes—all now took the form of gifts.

Truly everything I have is yours, Lord.

More than anything, she wanted to share every detail of what had happened to her with Kane. She stared at her feet, regret sweeping through her. There was a side to Kane he'd been forced to hide, even to protect, from her. Her chin dipped to her chest.

I'm so thankful he cares for me, Lord, but will he ever forgive me—will you? I'm so sorry.

But God *had* forgiven her. She drew in a breath of the flower-scented air and moved from the tree onto the path toward the house. Hope and trust in God would help her through the moments when she'd ask Kane's forgiveness.

The silvery moth sailed by on its own journey. Gabi padded over and nudged her hand. She looked up at the house, bathed in remnants of moonlight that vied with the dawn's light. So much more to learn and do and experience hand-in-hand with her Lord.

Breakfast smelled as good this morning as the day they'd left on the hike.

"Gracious Heavenly Father, thank you for this day and for the joy we feel simply being together around this table." Evan Roberts's blessing as they held each other's hands was balm to Ali's spirit. They'd come so close to never coming home again.

Across from Ali, Cay spread butter onto a muffin. The housekeeper, Cristina, leaned over to fill Ali's coffee cup. The scent of lemon oil and fresh-baked bread surrounding the housekeeper smelled familiar—like home. Ali poured syrup onto her waffle then watched her father's fork find its mark in his omelet.

Cristina left, closing the double doors behind her, which seemed to change the atmosphere. A sudden blanket of silence hovered in the large dining room.

The seconds passed as slowly as her waffle absorbed syrup before her father put down his fork and broke through the quiet. He looked at Cay then Ali, his words delivered slowly and profoundly thoughtful.

"I have never experienced more of what felt like such deliberate roadblocks during a single day in my entire life. It felt as if someone had conspired to stop us from finding you yesterday. And at the same time, after a lot of prayer from every direction, God countered each barrier with a solution."

He looked at Ali. His face had set in expressions like this before, when he'd tightly controlled emotions he wouldn't let overwhelm him. Ali sensed a touch of awe and wonder. Her heart skipped a beat as she listened to her dad, a father who'd allowed neither faith nor belief in God into his life in the past. He spoke so easily about them now.

Cay's father nodded. "And it didn't only begin with things here. With no commercial flights leaving São Paulo until late yesterday, the Lord intervened. My friend Max's compassion, his pilot, and his jet put me on the ground here close to five yesterday morning."

Ali's father moved his plate out of the way and leaned on his forearms. "Deadlines were paramount. The flash drive had to be at the Port at seven o'clock. In the meantime, Evan and I had to decide whether or not to open all this up to the authorities." He glanced at Ali. "With your lives in the balance, Evan kept the appointment I had made, and tentatively intended to keep, with a detective soon after you called with the ransom demands, Ali."

Answering her question before she could ask, her father smiled and pulled a small cell phone from his pocket, holding up the phone. "An untraceable, unbuggable, handy little unit." He looked at Cay. "Your dad's suggestion." He paused.

Evan Roberts picked up his napkin and wiped his fingers, nodding. "As soon as the plane landed, we took some time to make plans. We ended up going in two directions. I went directly to the Manaus PD, Matt took a taxi to the Port, and then we met back here. We were very careful, and I have doubts we were followed, either one of us."

"And the decision to split up was a good one. I gave Evan a copy of my notes from one of the men"—her father glanced at Ali—"Cardozo, wasn't it?"

Ali nodded. "Cardozo and Velez."

"Yes, I gave him the details of their demands."

Ali smiled as Cay's father pushed his glasses back up on his nose and picked up the subject. "The detective I spoke with in Manaus understood the need to keep you safe. Abduction isn't a crime foreign to them. They're well versed in … but you'll hear more about that this afternoon."

Ali turned to her father. "What about the phone call you were supposed to get to tell you how to find us? How did you deal with that?"

"We felt to stay and wait for the call would have been useless. We covered all the bases. Manaus DPF, the *Departamento de Polícia Federal,* and stationed a detective with past experience in kidnappings at the house with instructions. Mrs. Roberts was by the phone in São Paulo, and we stayed in contact by radio. There wasn't anything or anyone we'd let stop us from leaving the Port and heading for Maria's to start searching as soon as possible. So, we'd made the right decisions. That phone call never materialized. Now we know why."

Her father shook his head. "We would have made Maria's sooner had we not had engine failure with the first boat we rented. More than two hours out of port, the inboard engine died, and we had to have the boat towed back and find another. We lost precious hours."

Cristina came bustling into the dining room and handed a note to Mr. Roberts. He looked at her father and stood. "Inspector Vega is on the line wanting to speak to you, and I need to call Pam in São Paulo.

Breakfast ended abruptly. The meeting with everyone to debrief this afternoon couldn't come fast enough for Ali.

CHAPTER THIRTY-THREE

Ali sat immersed in an atmosphere of peace in the elegant living room where they were about to meet with Inspector Vega. She saw through heightened senses, a new perspective, and an appreciation of what was real, yet temporal.

Content to stay at her feet, Gabi curled up on the area rug in front of the sofa where she and Cay sat flanked by their fathers. Jo claimed one of three blue side chairs opposite them. In animated conversation with her father, Jo looked relaxed and rested—laid back with a boot-clad foot across one knee. Almost everyone except Ali was engaged in quiet conversation.

Police inspectors from both Manaus's unit of DPF and Interpol entered the room escorted by the uniformed housekeeper. Her father stood and made brief introductions, and at her father's invitation, everyone made themselves comfortable. Inspector Vega immediately made use of an antique writing desk positioned between two of the windows, shuffling papers and making notes.

Cristina swept in and out of the room with plates of sandwiches, miniature cookies, sugar-dipped orange peel, and pitchers of iced tea. She set them on the low table in front of the sofa along with a tray of tiny white cups filled with steaming thick, sweet *cafezinho*.

Ali watched Rico Mendes, inspector from the DPF, activate a small pocket tape recorder. He picked up his notebook and pen and squeezed his ample girth into an armchair beside Jo.

Vega rose from the desk and took charge of the meeting. Small talk ceased as the roomful of people settled in to listen. The tall man, wearing an imposing blue suit, impeccable white shirt, and bright red tie fixed his solemn brown eyes on Ali, then Cay.

Ali shifted her gaze from the man's expressive face to the vivid tie, the crimson color no longer triggering emotions as before.

"You are very fortunate young women to have escaped your abductors and to have returned here safely. Many times, that is not the outcome." The inspector turned to Cay. "You inadvertently and unfortunately became a second victim when you and Miss Lamarque became friends—an additional money-maker for your abductors." Vega continued in his precise, clipped accent, looking at her father then Cay's. "Thank you, Doctor Lamarque, Mr. Roberts, for your hospitality."

Her father nodded. "We appreciate your agreement to meet here for our convenience and to fill us in on what you can."

From beside Cay, Evan Roberts spoke. "Yes, thank you, Inspector."

"I'll review the case in as much detail as possible, which will bring you up to date on what we have learned so far. Then we will conduct some individual interviews with each of you. I apologize this will all take considerable time, but it is necessary."

"Take whatever time you need, Inspector." Her father settled against the sofa cushions.

"Feel free to interrupt me if you have questions or comments." Vega picked up a small white cup and took a sip of the sweet Brazilian coffee. Ali had to smile at the sight of such a big man wielding a dainty porcelain cup.

Vega returned the cup to the table and paged through a small notebook before he continued. "Over the last few hours, we've interrogated Cardozo and Velez. Both men talked to us without reservation, probably hoping things would go easier for them. There is quite a bit I can tell you, and I believe you will find the information interesting."

He lowered his head, peering at her father as if looking over the top of eyeglasses. "Almost immediately, both men informed us of the plot to kidnap your daughter. And this may come as a surprise, Dr. Lamarque, but just as quickly, they implicated your associate, Dr. Madison Kaarding,"

Madison Kaarding was behind this? Shocked and suddenly light-headed, Ali gripped the edge of the pillow she held in her lap. She turned in time to see her father's dark eyebrows rise in a fleeting expression of surprise then change to a grim look as he nodded. Had Vega just confirmed suspicions he already felt?

A kaleidoscope of memories cascaded through Ali's mind, dovetailing with events, and things became clearer. Of course. Madison Kaarding was the only one besides her father who could verify the formula. And the words she'd spoken during the phone call she and Kane had overheard suddenly made perfect sense. Praying for serenity and calm, she took a deep breath, listening as the inspector continued.

Vega fixed his eyes on Cay. "Miss Roberts, your friendship with Miss Lamarque threw in an extra problem for your abductors but most certainly ended up saving your lives."

Ali smiled at his last few words.

"We've had Kaarding under surveillance for some time now." Vega placed his hand on the desk chair and continued. "The evidence against her continues to build. Interpol has been cooperating with the US Federal Bureau of Investigation in this." He looked at Ali's father, then at his watch. "In fact, she should be in their custody within the hour, and we aren't expecting any delays. A pity to lose such an excellent, scientific mind to crime."

Ali stared at her father. "Why would she *do* something like this, Dad?"

"Money, I suppose." Her father looked chagrined and shook his head. "I don't think I'll ever really understand why. She's been a tremendous asset to me and to Zoran—so much talent. I'm finding this very hard to believe."

Vega laid the notebook on the table and picked up his cup, pacing the tile floor with an occasional glance at Ali. "You asked why, Miss Lamarque?

I can tell you this much—and you may already be aware of many of these things. Some of our early investigation turned up the fact Dr. Kaarding lived considerably beyond her means. Owning an upscale condominium in Solvang, the costly habit of collecting rare art and sculpture, particularly South American works, and recently experiencing the dark side of margin trading in the US stock market, only touches a portion of her expenditures."

The inspector paused and pinched at his nose, looking down at his notes. "She also has a penchant for buying expensive shoes, clothing, and pets.

Ali recalled Dr. Kaarding often talking about her "babies," a Cavalier King Charles spaniel and two Himalayan cats and their delicate health. No wonder. The combination of these things could have easily created a mountain of debt for her.

Thoughtful, Vega contemplated his fingernails for a moment before proceeding. "In interviews with persons who know her, she's been referred to as svelte, coldly beautiful, self-centered, brilliant, and well-spoken. She's fluent in several languages, including Portuguese."

The description fit the doctor like the glass slipper on Cinderella's foot, and Ali came close to adding her verbal agreement.

"Of course, Doctor Lamarque, you were not interviewed due to your close professional relationship with her." The inspector reached for the carafe of cafezinho and refilled his cup.

"The overwhelming pressure of debt apparently set this little caper of hers in motion." He looked expectantly at her father. "I'm sure you were aware she traveled widely and often."

"Yes." Her father nodded.

"Lately, much of her travel had taken her to São Paulo." Vega shifted his gaze to Ali. "And that brings me to a renowned Brazilian businessman, Vicente Cassara."

Another jolt. The name had Ali's full attention. Somewhere she'd heard that one, or a similar name, before. The image of a sleek white helicopter invaded her thoughts. Vincent Castle, Mr. Batista's client? With Carlos Batista's accent, she might have misunderstood the name. Could his client have been Vicente Cassara, the wealthy horse breeder? And if so, was *Mr. Batista* possibly involved in some shady business dealings—maybe even their kidnapping?

As if to answer her unspoken questions, Vega looked her way. "Though Cassara and Batista have done business together, all our preliminary investigations do not implicate Batista or his family."

Ali looked over at Cay, but Cay focused on something else.

"Cardozo—" Cay stopped as if she realized she'd interrupted. But Vega nodded, encouraging her to continue.

"Cardozo used Cassara's name. I overheard him and Velez talking about someone by the name of Cassara. And I don't know if this is relevant, but it might be. He said Cassara would be meeting someone in Beijing on August 27th, and he said something about a drop."

The Manaus Federal Police inspector snatched up his cell phone from the end table, heaved himself up out of the chair and immediately left the room.

"Duly noted, Miss Roberts." Vega pinched at his aquiline nose again. "Thank you. Any dates or places might be crucial to the investigation. We've been building a case against Cassara for money laundering for about six months. He owns an exclusive gallery in São Paulo where he buys and sells both Chinese and native Brazilian Indian art."

Ali exchanged a glance with Cay. Coincidence? Or could this be the same gallery where Cay had spoken to the Chinese woman?

Thoughtful, the lanky man continued. "Cassara and Kaarding met on one of her trips to purchase artwork. Apparently knowing what she did for a living, Cassara escorted her to dinner several times, then—and this is pure conjecture so far—he lured her into a tempting situation. We believe he offered her an easy, one-time job, in exchange for freedom from debt and more. In any case, we know they entered into some kind of an agreement."

Ali leaned forward, fascinated with the inspector's monologue, still wondering at the strange Asian-South American art mix in Cassara's gallery. Was it significant?

"We know the following day, Cassara erased half Kaarding's debt, probably as a down payment for what he wanted her to do."

How did Vega know that? Were there bugs everywhere? Ali's spine straightened against the back of the sofa, her mind filled with silent questions.

Vega stopped speaking and looked at Ali. She was acutely uncomfortable beneath his piercing gaze. As sharp as he was, had he noticed her body language? He cocked his head and smiled. He knew, and she wasn't about to be privy to his exclusive loop of information. His eyes didn't leave her.

"Cassara also told Kaarding about Cardozo and Velez, who would be willing to do her dirty work—kidnapping Miss Lamarque. Money in excess of several million dollars would have been placed in an overseas account had they succeeded with the plan."

Gazing down at the ceramic tiles beneath his feet, the inspector seemed lost in the details of his description.

Millions of dollars! Ali's thoughts tumbled. If Madison Kaarding knew the formula could generate that amount of money, she also had to have known of someone who could easily pay that much, someone who didn't care who they hurt getting the formula. Ali felt this man, Cassara, had simply acted as an intermediary, mainly a go-between and money-handler.

"I have a question." Ali interjected, her words terse. Gabi stirred as Ali uncrossed her legs and slid forward. "Inspector, I understand Dr. Kaarding knew how valuable Dad's formula was, and I can understand how Cassara got to her. I even understand how they arranged for Cardozo and Velez to kidnap us, and why. But wouldn't there have to be someone who knew they could make that much money from the formula and had enough upfront money to finance our kidnapping? Someone who could both manufacture and market a medication using the formula and believe they could get away with it? And did Cassara's dealings in Asian art have any connection? A cover maybe?"

Vega moved two tiles closer to the carpet beneath Ali's feet. "Ah. An astute observation, Miss Lamarque. And, yes, you've sensed a large piece of the puzzle." The man stepped onto the area rug, towering over the coffee table between them.

"Cassara has contacts in China, and while Kaarding was in São Paulo to buy art, she also had several clandestine meetings with two Chinese research scientists. The group had everything necessary to profit handsomely from your father's remarkable formula." Vega took out a handkerchief and dabbed at his nose.

Cay took the opportunity to ask another question. "Have you known about the Chinese for very long?"

The inspector gave her one of his rare smiles. "Interpol has been keeping tabs on this Chinese duo for quite some time. We tracked them to Brazil mainly because they'd been keeping some questionable company—namely, Cassara. The Chinese government has been most cooperative in this case."

The Federal Police Inspector strode back into the room with a satisfied look on his face. He handed Vega a note, smiled, nodded at Cay and sat down. Vega frowned, brows meeting as he read the note then resumed speaking.

"When Dr. Kaarding abruptly appeared on the scene, we began including her activities in our investigation, continuing to cooperate with the FBI. Since she was a research scientist with Zoran Labs, she, of course, had detailed knowledge about what went on there. At first we assumed the Chinese were simply interested in buying rights to manufacture the formula, an innocent and perfectly legal thing to do.

"Cardozo, usually involved in petty offenses, increased our suspicions when we discovered he'd received some lengthy phone calls from Dr. Kaarding. At that point, we suspected something much larger might be afoot, which was why I was in Manaus in the first place. Then, when Cardozo and Velez made the trip to California, we were certain. However, they were able to stay one step ahead of us."

Ali gazed at him, both impressed and appalled. "Then you *knew* Cardozo and Velez were on the same flight to Brazil we were?"

Solemnly, he nodded. "We did know but at the time did not consider it of any particular significance. I am sorry for that." He hesitated as if he might say more on the subject but reconsidered. Still holding the note, he picked up his notebook and continued.

"This morning, there were a number of things Cardozo and Velez admitted to us, things giving them all the information necessary to plan and execute your kidnapping."

Vega looked up directly at Ali. "They followed you, stalked you, and they listened to you. The São Paulo and Manaus authorities located eavesdropping devices when we swept the Galante's house and this one late yesterday. They listened and learned all they needed to know."

Cay's father's voice filled the pause. "Yes, Dr. Lamarque and I reached the same conclusion but too late to avoid trouble."

Vega nodded. "We also found a parabolic microphone in their rented vehicle in São Paulo. More than likely they used the mic to pick up live personal conversations while you stayed with the Galantes."

Ali cringed remembering one particular night and the uneasy feelings that had gripped her. Gabi *had* been trying to warn her.

"A few other things your abductors disclosed. First, after the young women made their escape, Cardozo did not believe they would return to Manaus through the jungle alone."

Vega twisted in place, looking toward Ali and Cay. "With one of the three canoes gone, he correctly assumed you would go upriver because you were closer to Mauro de Mello's residence, about which they had full information, than you were to Manaus."

Thoughtful, he added, "But he couldn't have pulled off the kidnapping at all, or located the de Mello house, without the help of the Juma guide."

Ali held up a hand to interrupt.

"I think I know your question, but yes, please ask it."

"Are you going to try to capture the guide?"

Vega shook his head. "No. Juma natives know the territory better than any one of us ever could. We have put out notices he's wanted, but the chances are slim we will ever see him again. The few Jumas left in the

Amazon blend into the jungle as if it were a second skin. We simply do not have the manpower to chase him down."

Ali nodded, understanding. "You need to know something else. If it hadn't been for a woman who loosened my ropes, we might never have escaped. We believe she was the guide's mother."

"Mm, perhaps another reason for us not to pursue him. Again, you were very fortunate." The inspector pursed his lips and picked up where he'd left off.

"Cardozo then made a number of incorrect assumptions. He didn't think your father would be in a position to locate you. He apparently had no idea Mr. Roberts knew this area so well or that he could get here from São Paulo so quickly. Then, he neither anticipated Mr. dos Santos would be able to walk anywhere following the attack on him, nor did he realize he had a satellite phone. He obviously did not make a very thorough search of Mr. dos Santos's backpack."

Thank God, he hadn't. Ali closed her eyes. What might have happened if they'd found the phone? Such a small detail made all the difference.

"And then, of course," Inspector Vega paused and sat in a cream-colored armchair, "Cardozo didn't anticipate you'd be able to escape." He looked from Ali to Cay and back. "I'd like to hear exactly how you managed that." He planted his forearms on his thighs as if waiting for a long story.

Ali laughed. "Well, that could take us awhile." And for the next fifteen minutes, she and Cay related nearly everything that happened, while the inspectors listened and took notes.

They had nearly finished when Ali turned to Cay. "I never completely understood why they held us in two different places." She didn't expect a reply, but Cay glanced at Ali, her blue-green eyes intense, her expression thoughtful, and abruptly stood.

"So much happened so fast, I completely forgot to tell you. Do you remember when they put our blindfolds on for the second time, right before we took the turn into the first inlet—the time when Cardozo talked a blue-streak in Portuguese?"

Ali nodded, the memory vivid. Cay paced as she recalled the scene.

"He was talking about wanting to do something before it got too late. I couldn't hear all of it, but what I did hear indicated they had deliberately planned to stop there. It was sort of a halfway point. I heard things about a phone call, a house, and having to get somewhere before dark."

"That makes sense." Ali nodded. "It *was* getting dark when we got to the last place. They needed the time and the daylight to have me rehearse what to say to Dad, to make the call and then get us to a spot that would be more of a shelter than the first one was."

Cay picked up her glass of iced tea and sat back beside Ali, trembling. Ali laid her hand on Cay's arm. This interview had them reliving the terror they'd experienced, not easy for either of them.

"You know, the timing of all this borders on the miraculous." Ali's father shook his head, his expression one of awe.

"It does indeed." Vega held up the Inspector's note. "More so than perhaps we all realize. To be brief, be advised Cardozo is facing added charges. Evidence has pointed to him being ..." The Inspector hesitated, seeming to measure his words. "... involved in a double homicide in São Paulo shortly before their arrival in Manaus." He folded the note and tucked it into his notebook.

Beside her, Ali heard Cay's gasp, or had it been her own? Then Cardozo *had* intended to— Ali couldn't even form the words in her thoughts. She couldn't move as her face burned and her hand reached for her father's hand. Her father gave her hand a gentle squeeze.

Vega moved to the edge of his chair as her father looked directly at Jo, choosing to leave the terrifying subject behind, and spoke. "The fact you weren't seriously injured, and you immediately called me, set off a series of events on this end and helped move things along rapidly."

"And your presence of mind, Doctor, to contact the authorities in Manaus, helped your situation." Vega interjected as her father hesitated. "The moment the DPF unit provided Interpol with the facts about the kidnapping for ransom, we became deeply involved. Kidnapping and extortion were added to our investigation of money laundering and illicit trafficking in works of art."

Ali turned to her father. "Dad, what made you and Mr. Roberts decide to go to the police after what Cardozo said he'd do to us if you did?"

"It was too risky not to. I followed Cardozo's instructions to the letter, except about notifying the police. I called them as soon as I bought the disposable phone. That was when I learned they'd been watching Cardozo and Velez and were keeping a low profile at that point. Interpol was already on the scene with the investigation, so they were immediately involved. You two were in serious trouble, no matter what we did. We took as much care as we could, but it was vital for us to involve the authorities to help search. They ended up being instrumental in getting us to Maria's as fast as possible.

"After I placed the flash drive on the yacht and returned home as Cardozo had instructed, we made certain we were clear of being seen and followed, then returned to the Port. We picked up the first rental boat on our own, which died on us a little over two hours out."

Her father shot her a grin. "Then, after we rented a replacement boat, we found ourselves with an escort. The DPF had decided to help us out with the river search. As we left the Port, their yacht cleared the river traffic right and left, and they remained with us."

He shifted his attention to Evan Roberts. "Good decision to switch our communication to encrypted email, since we figured we were infested with "bugs." And your friend getting you to Manaus from São Paulo, and us ending up with the DPF's help—all pretty amazing."

He turned to the Federal police inspector, then to Vega. "I'm grateful you were able to get to the flash drive before the wrong people could pass on the formula."

Vega nodded. "Yes, and you're right about the timing. It proved crucial. We had a team in place that apprehended Vicente Cassara as soon as he disembarked the *O Marineiro* with the USB drive in his hands. The man made a strategic error in judgment when he decided to retrieve the drive himself, but now we have one less criminal mind on the streets."

Cristina brought in another pitcher of tea and carafe of cafezinho as their discussion moved to center on crime in Brazil. Ali broke a sweet biscuit in half, studying Jo's face. He'd been sitting quietly, listening as the talk swirled around him. A large white bandage covered his head wound. Earlier a doctor had checked and dressed Jo's injury, insisting he needed to rest, but Jo had ignored the advice with no intention of being left out of the meeting.

Ali drew in a breath. Finally, a break in an exchange of statistics between officials. She caught Jo's eye. "Jo, do you feel up to telling us what happened to you? After you went to find Gabi, the last thing I remember before we were taken is seeing you lying on the trail with blood everywhere and Gabi beside you with a dart in her side."

Recorders clicked on as Jo glanced at the man from Interpol as if waiting for his approval to speak.

"Yes, please, Mr. dos Santos. Tell us what happened to you." Unbuttoning his jacket, the inspector rose and went to the center of the room. He stood beneath the slowly rotating Casablanca fan. "How did you know where to find the girls, and how did you decide to go to your sister, Ms. de Mello—Maria's home?"

Her father leaned forward. "I think we'd all like to hear, Jo."

Jo seemed encouraged. He straightened in his chair and folded his arms over his round belly, his mustache lifting with the grin he sent her father.

"Ah … I draw you pictures. Right away, when I wake up, still down on my face in that place, I pray." He winked at Ali and touched his silver crucifix. "No better thing to do when trouble comes."

Ali's heart warmed at his words, and the inspector actually cracked his cool demeanor with another smile.

"Men come from behind. Only got short look at them before"—he touched his bandaged head—"thank God, no fire ants there! When head quit spinning and I see straight, my watch say two-thirty. Long time out. A lot of blood, some pain, but I am okay. I got up and checked trail. No sign of Cay or Ali anywhere. Leaves and dirt scuffed up everywhere. No dog.

Found dart on trail. Two men leave many deep boot prints near riverbank. Must be they carried girls and dog."

Ali shivered at the thought of Cardozo touching her unconscious form.

Jo paused, staring into space, his expression one of being in the midst of remembering a terrifying experience. He took out his bandana and rubbed perspiration from his face and eyes then continued his descriptive staccato monologue. Ali sat close to the edge of the couch, imagining what he must have gone through.

"Third man had sandals, no boots. His prints not so deep. Juma native, I think. Figure three men drug girls and dog to keep them quiet … easy to move. Trail ahead clear. River only other way, and thugs had big head start.

"Could tell three canoes beached there, and I decide they head out, upriver. Too far and too risky to go to Manaus with two 'out-like-lights' girls. More places to hide upriver." Jo sat back, emotions surfacing.

Vega returned to his seat as her father leaned forward. "So that's when you tried to call Evan, couldn't reach him, then called me?"

"Yes. Good thing men didn't find satellite phone at bottom of my pack. Called you then"—he grinned at her father—"mighty glad for that phone. Helped save our necks."

His grin faded. "I need to get help fast. My sister closest. She has radio. On way there, trail bend near river and clearing. I see empty canoes, men in jungle, alone. They eat, drink, talk, and sleep. I keep walking—slow in dark. Have to get to Maria's before them. Not know if girls dead or alive until I get to Maria's, but pray and hope they go to Maria's for safety."

He paused, breathless from the recanted memories. "Also figure if men alone, girls might be free and men follow them to Maria's." Jo shook his head. "Men seemed to know many things."

"And then you got to your sister's a few hours after the girls did?" Cay's father interjected the question with a look of amazement. "And in time to put together a pretty great offensive."

Jo nodded. "End of story. Good one too." He sat back, looking satisfied.

Inspector Vega stood and resumed his pacing, stroking his chin. "Not quite, my friend. I am led to making a point about the appreciation I have for you. An excellent strategy, your idea of using bows and arrows. Risky, but with the element of surprise, the plan worked well. Congratulations. You have my—our—admiration," he added with a sweep of his hand toward the others.

Jo, fiddling with his mustache, mumbled a slightly embarrassed, "Thank you."

The heavy rumble of distant thunder went ignored by everyone but Ali. Distracted and no longer listening to the conversation, she looked at the now-empty briefcase on the floor near the desk. The flash drive holding the completed formula was in a bank safety deposit box, in Manaus. People would be helped and healed because of the work her father had completed.

Unusual during the dry season, a storm approached. More thunder resounded, rattling the windows and reverberating inside the house. For a few moments, no one spoke as rain set up a rhythmic cadence, drumming on the metal roof of the portico before passing as quickly as arriving.

Ali thought of Kane, of how much she loved and missed him, of how thankful she was for him, and then looked at Cay. How deeply she appreciated her friend.

Our Father which art in heaven.

The words she'd prayed as a child, following after her mother's voice, formed in her thoughts as sweet tears formed in her eyes.

Thy kingdom come.

In the depths of the rain forest, she'd been pulled from the brink of death and found eternal life. She'd found peace of mind and body and spirit.

Forgive us.

No longer lonely, the guilt she'd harbored close to her heart for so long had vanished into the Amazonian mists. She could let her mother go, knowing where she was and understanding there would be no lasting separation.

For thine is the kingdom, and the power, and the glory, forever.

Ali's father leaned close and put his arm around her, giving her a hug. And as he did, the love and comfort of another hugged her as well, One whose presence was closer than breath.

EPILOGUE

Barely Friday morning, the waning moon drifted light through the second-story windows of Ali's bedroom, casting shadows against the walls. Thin mosquito netting draped over her bed gave the scene a melted, gauzy appearance. She and Cay went to bed Thursday night long after midnight … well, Cay went to bed and to sleep. Sleeplessness kept Ali twisted in the sheets, tossing and turning, restless, hearing sounds that reminded her of the not-so-distant jungle as she gazed out at the sky.

She watched Cay's quiet form on the other bed, listened to her slow, even breathing for a moment before rolling over. Ali straightened the sheets and put her arm beneath her head, thinking of Kane—so far away. Hot tears streamed into her hair. She pressed her palms against her temples and willed the tears to stop. Surely, the time would pass quickly, and she'd see him. They'd texted, emailed, talked, but she needed to see him.

Ali sighed and slid out from under the netting, pulled on her robe, and stood in front of the open window, drinking in the beauty of this small corner of Brazil—thinking and remembering.

The dynamics of all her plans were changing. Several more weeks would be spent here with her father. She'd return to São Paulo to meet Cay, and they would fly back to California together. Both men in her life were thrilled she'd be finishing her senior year without time away. Cay had a scholarship to UCLA and would be living with her Aunt Julie in Los Angeles, but she was already researching the possibility of transferring to the Santa Barbara campus. There would be plenty of room for Cay to bunk with Ali and Stefanie in their off-campus apartment.

And there was Jo. She smiled and snugged the sash of her robe around her. He would soon be on the river on his way to Maria's for two weeks. The funny man was crazy over the moon about his trip.

Yesterday she and Cay'd spent the morning in Manaus wandering through shops and near noon, claimed a table in the shade at a sidewalk café. They ordered and ate lunch, then sat talking. Ali couldn't recall a time when she experienced such a profound feeling of well-being. She listened as Cay told her of how the move her family had made from Manaus to São Paulo had deeply affected her. And Cay listened with compassion as Ali told her more about the accident and about Greg Steele—what she saw before the deadly crash. Her heart filled, the pain easing as she shared memories that hurt so much and Cay had pulled out a couple of tissues they both needed.

Ali yawned. She really needed to get some sleep. Another busy day ahead. She pulled in a breath of night air and glanced at a rumpled bed that looked better by the second.

The sinking sun turned the treetops gold as Kane McKenzie paid the taxi driver and paused at the wrought iron gates. He punched in the seven-digit entrance code Ali's dad emailed to him the Saturday before Ali and Cay's hike on Monday.

He looked up at the impressive home and grounds, his heartbeat competing with his breathing. The gates opened then closed as he passed through, piercing the wall between him and this other world where Ali was. A gated wall of protection, a place that harbored her from the jungle that nearly claimed her life. He could be thankful for that gated wall.

He fisted his hands to rid his arms of tension and stopped on the walk to take in the scents and sounds—all Ali heard and sensed every day. He shook his head. He was here. He just needed to meet whatever would be, head-on, trusting God and in how well he knew Ali's heart. He raked his fingers through his hair and straightened, boots clacking against the smooth flat stones of the walkway as he strode toward the *varanda*.

Anger gripped his gut at the men who'd stalked Ali, hounded her, kidnapped her ... hurt her. She'd been through so much. He smiled. She hadn't known he was on his way to her during the few brief texts and emails they exchanged. She'd told him her life had changed, that she had much to share with him, but hadn't given him a clue what she meant.

Had the experience changed her? He'd prayed hard for her safety, but he hadn't been there, hadn't protected her. He swallowed his frustration. There was no way he could have stayed in California and waited. He'd been crazy with concern about her and what he'd planned to say. But could he?

Lord, please get me through this. You've brought us this far—

Trust, breathe, think.

He pressed his hand against the box in his pocket holding his grandmother's diamond and platinum engagement ring. Ali had seen the ring. She'd been at the Bar-M ranch with him the day UPS delivered a box his grandfather had sent from Arizona after his grandmother died. Kane hadn't missed a trace of Ali's expression of appreciation when his mother opened the ring box to show them.

Then, the day he left for Brazil, smiling, her eyes brimming, his mother had pressed the ring into his hand. He was secure enough in the love he and Ali had to hope—to know—she'd say yes. But until she did ...

At least Dr. Lamarque knew who came through the gates. Kane stepped onto the porch, knuckles poised to knock.

In the living room after dinner, the sun low behind summer clouds, Ali sat in an armchair idly watching shadows grow.

With her mind filled with thoughts of Kane and memories of the hike, a simple decision—wasn't. Should she interrupt Cay upstairs emailing friends or take a walk? Cristina was still busy in the kitchen, and her father worked in his office adjacent to the living room. On the floor nearby, Gabi didn't have any such problem. Eyes closed, she yipped in her sleep.

Ali hugged her knees to her chest and laid her head against them reliving the moments when she and Kane had walked to the edge of the plateau. They'd left the sweet love of lifetime best friends and walked into a new dimension of love.

She wanted to smooth her fingers through his dark hair, to tell him of this breath-holding love she had for him now.

"Ali, honey, can you get the door? I just buzzed someone through the front gate."

The decision for a walk won by default. She unfolded her legs and slid into her sandals.

"Sure, Dad. Who is it?"

"You'll see."

"Kane!" She knew. She sensed his presence with such strength, there was no question. She jumped from the chair and went down the hall breathing his name. She reached the foyer and stopped, staring at the shadow through the etched glass panel beside the door, fire rising in her cheeks.

He'd come. Right here to Manaus, right to her front door. She couldn't take her eyes from the tall familiar shadow. She couldn't move.

He hadn't told her. No one had said he was coming. Her insides clenched with sudden apprehension. Was he angry she'd come here after he'd wanted so much for her to stay? Texts, emails, even their phone calls had been good, but a little strained. So much uncertainty.

Lord, I give all this to you too. I love him and I love You. I'll accept what is.

She had to open the door ...

Kane took a few steps back and waited. Maybe no one heard his knock … A rattle and the door burst open.

Ali.

His mind and heart flamed with relief to see her whole and beautiful before him, her face, her amber eyes shone in the light of early evening. All he could ever desire—everything that was Ali filled him with love and tenderness.

"Kane!" She pressed the door shut behind her and turned to him.

Then she was a blur of pink, blue jeans, and honey-gold hair that held the faint scent of strawberries as she spoke his name and raced into his arms.

Lost in the light of Kane's eyes, in the joy of his smile, Ali ran into his open arms. His jaw firm and his cheek warm against hers, his breath moved through her hair with his whisper near her ear. "Ali, Ali … how I love you."

The pulsing of his heart matched her own as he held her close against his chest, nestled in his embrace. He held her as if he'd never let her go. Her heart surged, her breathing, little gasps.

She caught herself and pressed away from him, her heart warmed at the sight of his silver cross, the soft luster gleaming from the V-neck of his shirt.

She touched his face, but as if beckoning her, a vision of the garden bench had her sliding her hand down his arm, her hand into his. "Come with me."

Her fingers tingled as he laced his fingers through hers and without a word, followed her down the veranda steps. She led him across the grass, down the stone path and into the tree shaded, flower-filled garden. She could have remained on the porch in his arms forever, but here in the garden, in the midst of God's natural beauty, in the midst of Brazil, all was as it should be.

Near the wrought iron bench, he stopped her. He pulled her out of the shadows, into his arms and kissed his way over her cheek to her forehead. He paused to look at her, his dark eyes gazing into hers before he held her face between his hands.

She didn't breathe as his fingers moved beneath her chin to lift it closer and as he lowered his lips to cover hers in a crushing, passionate kiss. Her arms around him, she closed her eyes and returned his kiss with all her heart.

Kane allowed a whisper of space between them, and she opened her eyes to look up at him. His cheeks were damp, his gentle eyes, tender and full of love.

"Ali, I couldn't have kept on living if anything had happened to you. I had to come—to hold you, to tell you things I'd left unsaid. Words God gave me a second chance to say. I love you. I will love you forever."

Her arms slipped from around him, her hands moving flat against his chest. Standing on tiptoe, she touched his lips then kissed him. "I adore you, Kanen McKenzie. I will love you always."

He sat on the bench and pulled her down to sit close beside him claiming her lips once more. Pulling away, he put a hand up for her to wait a moment.

Wait? What was he ...

Kane gave her no chance to wonder. He cocked his head and grinned at her, reached into his pocket and pulled out a small familiar box. "Ali, sweet love of my life, my dearest and best friend, I promise I'll always cherish you ... will you marry me?"

As she breathed "Yes!" his hands closed around her left hand. Lifting her hand to his lips, he kissed her palm and slid his grandmother's exquisite ring onto her third finger—the promise of forever.

The Beginning

Dear Reader, I hope you loved reading *Out of the Shadows* as much as I loved writing Ali's story for you. If you did, will you consider writing a review to recommend the book to others and post on Amazon or your social media? Reviews are a big encouragement to authors. Thank you!

Sally

ABOUT THE AUTHOR

Sally Chambers and her husband, Jerry, live in sunny Florida happy to have their two married children living nearby. After retiring from a career in insurance, she focused on her love of writing. An author of Christian fiction, she enjoys writing for women—creating suspenseful, faith-filled stories with a thread of romance. A finalist in the American Christian Fiction Writer's First Impressions contest for her first novel, *The Stonekeepers*, Sally has also won awards for her short stories and poetry. She loves being with family, reading, walking on the beach and trails, reading to children, reviewing and editing for writer friends, and taking photos with her iPhone camera.